Praise for *Sic...*

'A gripping debut from a unique new...
Bridges writes with a stinging auth...
that upends clichés of the passive...
character who will stay with you for a long time – and have
you looking over your shoulder.'
Erin Kelly, *Sunday Times* bestselling author of *The Skeleton Key*

'A slick and exciting debut that had me devouring each page. In
Emma Chris Bridges has created a character who is simultaneously
totally chilling yet totally believable, obsessive and malleable
yet driven by love for her child. A twist to rival *Gone Girl*
left me gasping.'
Katy Brent, author of *How to Kill Men and Get Away With It*

'This beautifully crafted thriller had my heart in my mouth. With the
kinds of twists and turns that make you gasp, and a protagonist to die
for (excuse the pun!) *Sick to Death* is hard to put down.'
**Jennie Godfrey, *Sunday Times* bestselling author of
*The List of Suspicious Things***

'A dazzling debut, skilfully crafted and full of surprises. Beautifully
written, utterly original and shockingly dark.'
Lesley Kara, *Sunday Times* bestselling author of *The Rumour*

'Thrilling, moving and thought-provoking, with a brilliant central
character. A skilful suspense novel.'
B.P. Walter, *Sunday Times* bestselling author of *The Dinner Guest*

'*Sick to Death* is an urgent and compelling thriller from a
much-needed new voice in crime fiction.'
Anna Bailey, Sunday Times bestselling author of *Tall Bones*

'More layers than a multi-story car park, and more twists than
a roller coaster... a murderously good thriller about anger,
illness and revenge.'
**Carole Hailey, author of Kindle Number One bestseller
*The Silence Project***

'A stunning debut... Emma is a deliciously complex woman (who
should be underestimated at your own peril)... the definition of a
propulsive and unforgettable psychological thriller.'
**Ashley Tate, international bestselling author of
*Twenty-Seven Minutes***

'It smoulders, until the very, very end. A tale of love, of betrayal, of dead ends, of twists, of turns, of hope, of despair, assembled in a way that is totally addictive.'
G. D. Wright, author of *After the Storm*

'Such a brilliant debut. So sharply written, with a frenetic pace and nothing you expect. Clever and twisty with such a kick… so refreshing.'
Louise Swanson, author of *End of Story*

'A unique and compelling debut that is impossible to put down… slick and riveting.'
Ruth Irons, author of *The Perfect Guest*

'*Sick to Death* is a sizzling saucepot of a domestic thriller. A plot that begins with soft bubbles of tension, suddenly erupts into a glorious volcano of original twists and unexpected turns. I flew through it!'
Mira V Shah, author of *Her*

'Twisty, dark, and full of heart. A gripping psychological debut that had me completely hooked with no idea what to expect next. I didn't want it to end!'
Natalie Simmonds, author of *Good Girls Die Last*

'*Sick to Death* is a taut slice of neo-noir that cleverly upturns tropes about disability, class and feminism!'
Rebecca DeWinter, author of *Best Friends*

'Crime fiction at its most intimate and honest as well as brutal in its execution of its final twist.'
Marie Tierney, author of *Deadly Animals*

'A twisty, sneaky little crime thriller… I found myself absolutely swept up into the life and mind of its disabled, furious and devious protagonist.'
Laura Elliott, author of *Guilty*

'I tore through this fresh and inventive debut that delivers a cracking plot, strong characters and a distinctive, witty voice.'
Jo Leevers, author of *Tell Me How This Ends*

'A super intense reading experience, much like reading a Daphne du Maurier and watching a Hitchcock film… at the same time. Like a thumbscrew, the tension never lets up until the inevitable yet surprising ending.'
Tania Tay, author of *The Other Woman*

Chris Bridges is an alumni of the 2022 London Writers Award.

He previously wrote a weekly column for an LGBTQ+ lifestyle website and was a theatre reviewer for various sites.

As a former NHS nurse with a hidden disability, he likes to feature the untold stories of sick, dying, and disabled people in his work and smash the trope of the passive disabled character with a background role.

Chris lives in South London. He is fanatical about crime fiction. When not writing, he can be found reading compulsively or walking his uptight poodle, Frida Kahlo.

SICK TO DEATH

CHRIS BRIDGES

avon.

Published by AVON
A division of HarperCollins*Publishers* Ltd
1 London Bridge Street
London SE1 9GF

www.harpercollins.co.uk

HarperCollins*Publishers*
Macken House
39/40 Mayor Street Upper
Dublin 1
D01 C9W8

A Paperback Original 2025
1
First published in Great Britain by HarperCollins*Publishers* 2025

A catalogue copy of this book is available from the British Library.

ISBN: 978-0-00-869814-0

Typeset in Sabon Lt Pro by HarperCollins*Publishers* India

Printed and bound in the UK using 100%
Renewable Electricity at CPI Group (UK) Ltd

This book contains FSC™ certified paper and other controlled sources to ensure responsible forest management.

For more information visit: www.harpercollins.co.uk/green

*To Paul, for being more than this sick
person could ever have hoped for.*

Prologue

We're like birds. You may not see us but pay attention. We're everywhere. Working alongside you. Walking down your street. Even hiding in your social circle.

The thing is, I'm almost exactly like you. I'm discreet, keeping my issues concealed, whenever I can. I'm not one of the people whose wheelchairs or prosthetics you try to ignore or, worse still, try frantically to demonstrate that you're not ignoring. I'm camouflaged and secreted away, caged by illness. Trapped in a life that I didn't choose.

There's something that you might not know about birds. They're not benign creatures. They can be frenzied and violent. Doing whatever it takes to survive, to make a space and claim their territory. Killing if they have to.

Which brings us to tonight. This night after a boneless day when fatigue pinned me down. The therapists tell me to manage this malaise through gradual exercise. To alternate between rest and action. Monitor my activities and dole my energy out evenly, like sharing a bag of seed between pigeons. I've followed their advice. I've preserved my strength and here I am, alert and awake, even at this time of the evening. Shut in this tiny dressing room in the cloying darkness, nestled within his clothes, the citrus scent of him overwhelming me.

Gripping the knife in my right hand, tensing my arm over and over, practising. I have to wait it out. Pause here, until the right moment. Then I'll demonstrate how powerful I can be. How I can fight for what I need. A bird killing for her territory.

Part One

Chapter One

Summer 2022

There was a point when I stopped really hearing the screaming in here. Like the nurses, I often don't notice it at all.

My favourite cleaner is on today and she's smiling to herself, humming as she works. One hand resting in her apron pocket whilst the other slides a mop across the worn floor.

'You're back again. I haven't seen you in a while.' She winks at me and smiles.

I manage not to shudder, remembering that time in the spring when I was here most weeks. I smile back as I lift my feet up onto the trolley so she can reach the floor underneath. She blows me a kiss as she leaves.

I sit back and take in the emergency department. The screaming has stopped now, but it's still the usual cacophony. A woman is shouting in a South London accent, demanding morphine. There's a repetitive moaning coming from some-where distant, harmonising with the sound of nurses at the desk laughing about something, or maybe some*one*. Overlaying all this is the constant beeping of machines. I breathe in deeply through my nose and out through my mouth like they've told me to, ignoring the sour tang that invades my nostrils.

It's rotation week, so some of the doctors will be new. Unfamiliarity carries threat, but someone different might be good. I've been here so often that the faces of some of the staff are beginning to look strained, disapproving even.

The nurse has taken my vital signs and an ECG. Vials of blood have been coaxed from my veins, my arm is a mess of cotton wool balls and tape, my chest sticky with electrode pads. She looks at me over her mask.

'I've just realised. It's Emma, isn't it? Jesus. It's been how long?'

I pretend not to know who she is. Looking away, I concentrate on a smear of dried blood on the wall. It's in the shape of a crow.

'It's Marie. Do you remember me? I didn't recognise you at first with short hair. It suits you.' My hair has been cropped into something more manageable, whilst I'm ill. 'What are you up to? I remember, when we were training, you used to hang out with that other girl—'

'I've been ill for quite a while. I've not been able to do much really.' She starts to say something back, but I speak over her. 'It's nice to see you, but do you mind if I rest? I'm not feeling great.'

I close my eyes and listen as she leaves. I wait for a while, as I'm expected to, and the doctor walks in. He's not part of the new intake of medical staff but is one of the ones I've seen before, a craggy older doctor in the public schoolboy uniform of striped shirt and chinos. He's brisk with words that feel scripted, firing sentences from behind his mask, like he's a doctor from a TV drama.

'Emma Miller? Date of birth twelfth of June 1992?'

'That's me.' I hug my knees to my chest, bracing myself for the unfamiliar pressure of hands on my skin. This intrusive physical contact from strangers that's become a routine. We go through the usual ritual and I tell him that my left arm and leg don't work properly, that I fall, faint even, sometimes. About the numb patches that plague parts of my body.

As he's finishing off the neurological examination a cardiac arrest bell sounds – a klaxon marking someone's likely death. He dashes out of the cubicle, barking at a passing nurse that I'm free to go home now.

* * *

The hospital entrance is flanked by smokers. A pale woman in her twenties smiles at me as I walk by her wheelchair. Her mother is standing behind her, resting a hand on her bony shoulder, like she's guarding her. I'm about to cross over the road when a wave of vertigo floors me and I lurch forwards. My bag falls from my shoulder, spewing books and pills onto the tarmac.

'Hey. Are you OK?'

There's a waft of citrus as a tall man in his mid-thirties rushes over to me. He's dressed in a soft blue shirt with the sleeves rolled up to the elbows. They all do that for infection control. He's not a doctor I've ever met. He must be part of the new intake. I'd have remembered this man if I'd seen him before. His hair is an artful mess of dark waves over deep-set eyes, eyelashes like spiders' legs. His features are film-star handsome.

'I . . . I'm fine. I just felt dizzy. It happens to me sometimes.'

'Do you need to sit down?'

I shake my head. I'm not sure I can say anything else yet. The pavement before me is only just righting itself.

'Here. Let me pick these up for you.' He squats at my feet and starts putting my books back into my bag.

I reach forward to take the bag and my hand accidentally skims his. It feels like an electric shock through my skin.

'Are you sure you're OK? You don't need to go back in and see someone?'

'No. I'm fine. Honestly. I'll let you get back to your work.' I walk away, hoping that he isn't watching my awkward gait as I make my way towards the hospital gates.

It's an effort to walk up the hill to the station. People push by me on the pavement, and I cower in towards the rust-addled railings of the hospital. My head spins with the constant motion of traffic, the searing noise of sirens. Once on the train, I pull out my medication bag and swallow a handful of pills dry, ignoring the stares of the man in a suit sitting next to me. There's a woman around my age sitting across from me with a young girl, both well dressed, shining hair falling beside glowing skin. The girl is reading, pausing to point out sections of her book to her mother. They smile and nod together, the mother pulling the girl into the curve of her body. She curls there, as if designed to fit. I try not to look at them, but my gaze keeps returning.

* * *

My stepfather isn't there when I arrive home. I can always tell when he's here from the moment I open the door. He emanates this musky smell, from his aftershave. He's a Nineties relic, red cheeks doused in designer fragrance.

Mum and Becky will still be at work, and Ava at the school holiday club that she goes to. The settee welcomes me. My cat, Sparrow, jumps up and curls up against my legs, purring, and my hand touches the silk of her fur.

I'm still half asleep when he comes in, but I sense him. His breath, the change in atmosphere. I feel the cat jump off my legs and hear her feet as she runs from the room. She avoids Peter and Winston, the wheezy bulldog who follows at his heels, drooling onto the carpet.

'Productive day again, then?' His mouth forms a sneer. 'I know you're awake. There's no one else here but us, Emma.'

I turn my face to the wall, hoping he'll go away. Knowing that he won't.

'Don't ignore me in my own house. We all bend over backwards for you, don't we? Tiptoeing round you and this bloody illness. It's not like it's even—'

I sit up, the blood rushing from my face, the room receding.

'But it's not though, is it? It's not your house, Peter. It's my mum's, isn't it?'

Staring straight ahead, I concentrate on the gaps where my father's things should be. The books, his clocks, the pictures of him. The negative spaces that scrape at me. They were all packed away within weeks of Peter moving in. He didn't do it all in one go but moved them bit by bit, my father gradually eroded. The one remaining photo of me and my parents now pushed back, outranked by a larger one of Peter and Mum grinning on the registrar's office steps.

I walk away, my eyes averted, making a steady exit. I resist the urge to run at him and make his skull ricochet off the wall. To hear the exquisite crumpling of bones and flesh as he falls to the floor, and watch him flail around helplessly before me. I don't think that I'm alone in having these thoughts – the fantasies that inhabit our subconscious. The daydream of punching an obnoxious colleague in the face. That idle thought of how satisfying it would be to push a troublesome family member to the ground, to sink a knife into the ribs of a tyrannical politician.

There's no refuge. He saw to that. Along with my father, all traces of me have been eradicated from this place too. My bedroom has been picked bare, scrubbed, painted, and recarpeted to DIY shop blandness. The few belongings I have are all hidden in the garage, where I won't go. My clothes now crammed in a wardrobe that I share with Ava. For a bed, I have the faded settee once everyone has gone to sleep. My old bedroom is now his office with grey filing cabinets and a desk wedged in. It was a temporary arrangement, deemed essential during the first wave of the virus, that hideous and claustrophobic time. It didn't end, though.

I've given up asking Mum when I can have my room back. I should move out, but I have no money for a flat and I figure I'm way down on the housing priority lists, even with my neurological condition. After all, I have a safe space, with my family, don't I? There's nothing to harm me here.

Or at least that's what people would think.

*　*　*

I go and sit on the garden bench and watch the birds, the laurel bushes shielding me from the house. Sparrow sits beside me, transfixed by the avian life, her head darting from side to side. We don't have so many birds visiting now. Not since Peter stopped me from feeding them. Since he told me that I was attracting rats. I clutch my jacket around me. Peter hasn't managed to take over the garden quite yet, this last trace of Daddy. We laid out the beds and the borders together in a snaking design, built log piles for the insects, a wildlife pond. I'm sometimes tempted to poke at the logs to see what comes out, but I never do. The beetles need their home. Peter is constantly threatening to rip it all out and pave it, to save on the upkeep. My mum has resisted so far but it's only a matter of time.

Sparrow walks away, her bell tinkling to warn off the wildlife. The only bird that remains is a solitary wren. People are often surprised when you tell them that they're one of the most common garden birds. They're so small and drab, flitting about in the undergrowth, hidden from sight. I stay behind the bushes until Mum and my stepsister Becky are back.

Chapter Two

London is a mixed town. I don't just mean culturally. I mean in terms of wealth. Provincial towns have clear demarcations. Rich and poor, everyone segregated in their own distinct zones. London isn't like that. You can be in the most expensive neighbourhood and then turn the corner, only to be confronted by a run-down estate. Streets of multi-million-pound houses with jarring blocks of modern local authority flats, sitting like cuckoos in the nest.

Our house is one of these interlopers. A row of buildings lurking on a grand Edwardian street in South East London. Only, even this dowdy section is no longer that. This is the only one left that is still owned by the council, untouched and shabby. We're in a row of six, built after the war, in the gap left by a German bomb that annihilated two or three families. Rising from a place of massacre. They're three storeys high, with a garage on the bottom floor. All of the others have been modernised. The ground floors turned into additional rooms with shiny new picture windows, lofts converted, paint freshened. Ours still has the warped garage door that I can't stand to look at.

It's cramped with so many of us here. Four adults, a child, a dog, and a cat. Though it seemed fine when Daddy was alive. Me, Mum, and Daddy danced around each other. Now, my stepsister Becky is crammed in one room with my eleven-year-old daughter, whilst I'm shunted out, in limbo.

* * *

I emerge from the usual long run of stuporous days that follow an episode of relapse. Peter is in his office, Becky is off work, Ava is home, sitting at the bottom of the stairs, reading. She looks up at me as I pass and I squeeze her shoulder. I'm glad to leave. I try to walk every day, although I can't always manage it. I wish Ava could come with me but my mum and Becky say that it wouldn't be safe. That I'm too ill for a child to be around on her own. I'm not sure that I agree with them. She's eleven now, after all. She would cope if I was unwell while we were out but I'm not in a position to argue my case. They're providing childcare for me when I can't manage so my bargaining powers are limited.

The next-door neighbours are on their drive, packing for a holiday, cramming pristine leather bags into the back of their car. She looks across at me, her gaze tinged with pity. She raises her hand in a weak gesture and offers a glazed-eyed greeting. He looks through me, his head held aloft with businessman arrogance. I spot their gleaming children, sitting high in the vehicle, poised like minor royalty. They both hold iPads inches from their noses. I manage to force an appropriate noise from my lips, to be polite to these people who've barely made any effort to get to know us. I see them congregate in each other's gardens, holding glasses of gin aloft over their plates of Mediterranean snacks, whilst we remain mercifully uninvited. Their voices different in tone and accent from ours – their casual clothes costing more than I get in a month's worth of benefits.

I skulk away and opt for the next side street, a broad avenue. Tree-lined and spaced out with towering white houses, each inhabiting their own plot. A flock of parakeets flies over, squawking as they go. Their feathers a flash of improbable green on a greyscale summer's day.

I stand still to watch them go over and before I know it, I'm under attack, pushed across the pavement in a rush of air and whirling dimensions. An improbable fizz of sound and a flash of pink Lycra and I stagger forward. I cower, anticipating the next blow, barely hearing the shouted apology of the jogger as she ploughs forward. Oblivious to the fact that this thoughtless collision of flesh has sent me lunging forward. She runs on, carefree. I steady myself using a garden wall and catch my breath. As I look up, I see the doctor from outside the hospital the other day approaching me. For a moment I think that he's a product of my imagination. A vision born of a mind that replays scenes over and over, as I lie unable to move, eyes closed.

It's not. He's real. He's jogging towards me, wearing a tight T-shirt and black shorts, showing off his muscular torso and tanned legs. He stops dead when he sees me.

'Hi! It's you again. You were outside the hospital the other day?' His dark eyes glitter in the sunlight. 'Do you live round here?'

I nod, attempting a carefree smile, though I'm sure it comes out more like a grimace.

'Me too.' He gestures at a vast house further down the road. 'Looks like we're neighbours. This is my street, actually.' I don't think I'm reading into it – he sounds happy to learn that we live so close.

14

'I don't think I said thank you the other day. It was kind of you to help.'

'Ah, no problem. I was happy to assist.'

In spite of his running clothes, he's pristine. His cheeks have a glow but he's barely sweating. I scrabble for something to say.

'I was just going for a walk. I'd stopped here to look at some parakeets. Do you know about them?' I realise as I'm saying it that it's a bizarre conversation opener. I don't talk to people often. I'm forgetting the rules. It's too late to stop now, though.

'Er, no. I don't think so.' He looks puzzled but I carry on.

'They're improbable, aren't they? Some people say that they originate from a pair owned by Jimi Hendrix or that they escaped from an old Humphrey Bogart film. Or from a pet shop damaged during a storm.'

As if on cue, they sweep over again, flashes of neon, chattering.

'Where did they really come from, then?' He seems genuinely curious. Not just going through the motions of polite conversation.

'That's the thing. No one knows. They probably escaped from an aviary, which is a less exciting story.' I stop before I tell him how they attack jackdaws and other birds, even viciously assault sleeping bats in tree hollows. I've learned to temper my dialogue.

'So are you a bird expert? An academic, maybe. I couldn't help but notice the ornithology books that you'd dropped the other day.'

My cheeks flush. 'No . . . I just like them.'

'Oh! Me too. They're fascinating aren't they? I have a woodpecker at home that comes and pecks at the tree outside my window.'

'We have one that comes to us as well. Maybe it's the same one. Did you know that woodpeckers have built-in shock absorbers in their skulls so that they can absorb the trauma of all that hammering?'

'Seriously? I love that. I wish some of the clientele in the ED had shock absorbers. Maybe then I wouldn't be spending my Saturday nights patching them up when they fall down drunk and smack their heads on the pavements.' His mouth broadens into a smile. I can't help but smile back, stretching unfamiliar muscles. This time there's nothing forced or effortful about the reshaping of my lips.

'I'm Adam, by the way.'

'Emma.'

'Are you off somewhere nice?' He looks around as if he's only just noticed how sunny the day is.

'Oh. Nowhere. I'm just walking.' My response feels purposeless, pathetic even. We both start walking forward, him to his house and me on my inconsequential walk. He continues talking, telling me it's his day off and he's been trying to exercise more. He already looks fit to me.

When we reach his house he pauses for a second or two.

'Well, it was fun talking to you.'

'I don't think that I'm ever fun.' I regret these abrupt words the moment they leave my mouth but can't think of anything to say to rescue the situation.

There's a moment of silence between us, broken by him looking down at his trainers. He goes to say something else but then stops himself.

'Goodbye, Adam.'

I walk away. As I reach the corner, I turn to look but he's gone inside.

*   *   *

16

I'm hemmed in by my treacherous body. This lack of stamina. I spend three days lying on the sofa, closing my eyes when Peter is nearby, enduring family meals with their brittle barbs, cowering from the achingly familiar waves of hostility. My hatred has no release. It's like a crazed bird in an aviary, flapping around with nowhere to go. I have nowhere to hide, no release or escape.

My only distraction is Adam. I think about how pleased he seemed to see me, ruminate on what it was he was about to say before he stopped himself. His face recurs in my brain like a shameful teenage obsession. I chastise myself for my foolishness, for the thought that he was doing anything other than showing sympathy for a poor sick woman who was walking by.

Still, I hope to see him again – and I do. I don't have to wait long before he reappears. I walk to the parade of shops by the main road, away from the big houses. It's like any area of London: chicken shops, an off-licence, a dated launderette. I'm standing in the chemist, filling in the boxes on the back of the prescription form, when I smell the citrus cologne that Adam was wearing. I turn to see him in the queue behind me. He's wearing a pair of rolled-up jeans, trainers and a clean white shirt. Fresh in spite of the warmth of the day. He looks up and smiles when he sees me.

'I'm starting to look like a stalker.' He holds up a box of Lemsip. 'My alibi. Stocking up for a cold I can feel coming on.' I try not to stare too hard at that flawless face. 'Will you wait for me? We can walk back together.'

I nod in response and walk outside, breathing hard as I leave behind the dusty racks of scented soaps and overpriced vitamins that no one seems to buy.

We walk side by side along the street of grand houses set in sprawling gardens that owe more to designers than to

17

nature. There's barely any noise, not even birdsong, in the midday hush. He softly questions me about my health, asks about what birds I've seen this week. There's something genteel and accommodating about his style of talking that lets me speak, haltingly at first but then with more confidence. I barely notice the pain in my leg.

We walk up his street. It's shaded by towering plane trees lining the road, rows of Edwardian villas, sitting in their own grounds, untroubled by traffic and pollution, other than the regular deliveries from Waitrose or John Lewis. Houses with doors and windows that shine with new paint. Where it's an effortless task to call in tradespeople when there's any sign of imperfection.

The area is peppered with occasional outcasts. Dilapidated villas with blackened net curtains, occupied by elderly recluses. Once they're found dead there'll be construction signs, loft conversions, decorators. And another identikit middle-class family will appear in their top-of-the-range car. Cushioned by their nannies, cleaners and gardeners who ensure that nothing sullies their middle-class idyll. Mothers of around my age but ones who rarely have to worry about NHS waiting times or how they're going to find the energy to clean their houses or care for their well-groomed children. Women who have the luxury of space and comfort. Of money.

We're almost at his house when my left side starts to give way. My body betrays me with a sickening reliability. I feel my left leg beginning to buckle and shame grips me.

'I'm sorry, I just need to stop for a minute.'

'Here. You're fine. Let me help you.' He puts out his arm to support me. The hot skin under my hand feels reassuring and safe. 'You do look a bit pale. Do you need to rest?'

'I . . . think I'll be OK.' The world feels like it's receding around me.

'Look, I think you need to sit down. My house is just there. Do you want to stop off and sit down in the garden? I can get you some water.'

I don't say anything. My mind is whirring.

'It's OK. I shouldn't have offered that. It probably sounded weird.' He looks down at the pavement and I think he might be blushing but I daren't look too closely. 'I can walk you back to your own house. It's not far, is it?'

I ignore the blood pounding in my ears. What else does today offer for me? 'No, I'd like that. I mean, I could do with sitting down for a few minutes?'

I know he's just being kind but I imagine all the romantic impossibilities spooling out in front of me. I have a vision of his hands touching my skin, flesh that only feels the caress of gloved hands on a hospital trolley. Thoughts of things that don't happen to people like me.

* * *

We walk straight round the side of his house and into the garden. The building is double-fronted, a chequer-tiled path leading through shrubs to a porch made of wrought iron. It must be six bedrooms, at least. The sun has finally appeared, and light reflects off the white of the paintwork and bounces from the sash windows. I've never been in one of these homes, even though I've spent my whole life walking along these streets. The garden is huge, five times the size of ours, the back wall a towering block of clean brick and bright windows.

He guides me to a chair on a patio lined with pots of lavender before heading inside to get me a drink. A vast expanse of landscaping stretches off towards distant trees. I sit back and close my eyes, waiting to regain my equilibrium.

He walks back out with a tray with coffee, glasses of iced water and a plate of biscuits. He passes me the water and sits facing me on a wooden chair, letting his body yield to the shape of it. He pulls some sunglasses from his shirt pocket and opens a few buttons at the neck of his shirt, discarding his trainers to one side, his feet bare. He looks like a model in a perfume advert.

'Your colour is returning.'

I nod, sipping the water, still embarrassed at my weakness.

'Do you want coffee, too?'

He passes the cup and saucer over and we sit for a minute, making small talk about the weather, the area. I scramble for things to talk about, my brain like clawed feet clutching for a perch. I see movement from the side of his seat, a mass of wiry fair hair. It's a dog, weasel-thin with large amber eyes that open and stare up at me with suspicion. It turns to Adam and he pats its head before it settles back down onto the warm flagstones with a dramatic sigh.

'This is Ripley. He's a poor old thing now. He's fourteen, unbelievably. I rescued him from Battersea Dogs' Home.' Adam reaches down and runs his hand along the dog's knobbly spine. The dog looks up at him with pure adoration.

I don't *dislike* dogs. I've just never known many. I'm sensible around them, wary and respectful.

'Shall I go now? You must be busy.'

'No, honestly. You're fine. I'm not doing anything much today other than recovering from a run of night shifts.'

I flail for something else to say. 'This house. This garden. It's amazing.'

'Not mine, I'm afraid. I live here with my soon-to-be ex-wife. Can't claim much credit for any of this. We have

20

a gardener. It's just the two of us in this ridiculous place. Which isn't at all harmonious if I'm honest.' He frowns momentarily. His fist is clenched.

A flush of embarrassment marks my cheeks when he mentions the word 'wife', regardless of the 'soon-to-be ex' part. The noun lodges in my throat. Foolish of me to think for even a second that this invitation was anything other than an act of charity to a sick woman. Wary that I've paused for a little too long, I fumble for something to say.

'At least you have space to avoid each other.'

'Well . . . yes. It's a difficult situation, but you don't need to hear about that yet.' I like the word 'yet' and its implications of future conversations but I'm still reeling from the fact that he's said that he's married.

'Do you still live with your family?'

I try not to let my tone sound too deadened when I respond, to hide the emotions that sit so brazenly near the surface of my flesh.

'My mum. My dad died when I was five.'

'Oh, I'm sorry to hear that. So, it's a house of women.'

'No, sadly not. My mum met a man not long after my father died. He was doing building work on the nursing home where she works. They were married within three months, and him and his daughter moved in. Now it's like I'm an unwelcome house guest.' I don't mention Ava. I keep that as my 'yet to be discussed'.

'Happy families are a pervasive myth. It's a shame, though. You need a strong family around you when you're unwell.' He smiles again. 'Let's avoid the subject of families for now. It doesn't sound like either of us are in a great place. Maybe we can just talk about ourselves.'

I decide to get it out of the way quickly and tell him about my illness. I'm so used to the language of doctors that

21

I can recite it as a concise monologue. I keep my tone light but my voice sounds scratchy and weak. He listens carefully and nods in the right places, asking occasional questions. He's not one of those doctors who just goes through the motions. His face looks like he's actually feeling some of the pain of my tedious illness.

'That must be rough. I met a young woman with the same condition when I was a medical student and her story was pretty harrowing. It sounds like you've been through a lot for someone as young as you are.'

'I'm not that young. I'm thirty.' My thirtieth birthday was an unremarkable event with a token effort by my family. Only Ava made a fuss of the occasion, making me cards and posters.

'Similar. I'm thirty-four.' He gestures at the biscuits, arranged on a ceramic plate that looks like it was handmade in some warm foreign country. The bounteous host offering food and drink to the impoverished visitor. I shake my head and resist the urge to fold myself inwards, to clasp my legs up to my chest.

'So, what did you do before you were a doctor? You must be older than the other trainees.'

'Well spotted – I was an actor, briefly. I studied drama at university, but it didn't really pan out. Like it doesn't for a lot of people. I was lucky to get in really, someone from my background. After I finished college I had a few theatre roles, but it fizzled out. It's a tough career path unless you know the right people. I reconsidered and went into medicine on a graduate entry scheme.'

'Couldn't you do both? Like, act and also be a doctor?'

'If I only had the energy. Honestly, I'm glad to leave that world behind. You traipse around auditions and feel subhuman. Like you're a non-person who's there to be discarded if you don't look right or have the right voice tone. I wouldn't go back.'

'My stepsister is like you. She was an actor, I mean. Becky was a child actor. In a soap opera. She was in it from the age of thirteen. She's older than me, though. She's thirty-seven.'

'Seriously? Her teenage years must have been weird. Did she just abandon it when she got older?'

'No. She still did it. She studied for a drama degree at Brunel. Now she's like you. In healthcare, I mean. She's a bit lower on the scale. She's a care assistant in a nursing home. My mum works there too, in the kitchens.'

He pauses for a minute, sits back, tilting the chair. I'm looking down the garden but I see him from the corner of my eye, sneaking a look at my face. I struggle to meet his gaze. It's been a long time since anyone has looked at me as anything other than a specimen to be examined.

'There's no lower or higher. Just the value that society throws at jobs. Every job has worth. My mother had two jobs: cleaning in the day and working in the local pub in the evening.'

We talk some more, him more than me initially. He enthuses about the vintage thriller he's reading, offering to let me have it when he's done. Talks about a TV show that we both watched. I manage to think up suitable responses. The heat of the sun, the inviting tones of his conversation and his warm laugh lull me.

I tell him a bit more about my father, about life with Peter in the house. Not too much, though. I don't want to sound churlish and hateful. I still don't mention Ava. He doesn't talk about the wife he lives with or the impending divorce that he alluded to.

'Where did the afternoon go?' Adam looks down at his fitness tracker.

I thank him for the coffee and tell him that I have to get back now, determined this time to show that I have good manners and not overstay my welcome. As I'm about to leave he pauses and does this bashful, boyish thing again where he looks down at his feet.

'It's been great talking to you. I don't really have any friends around here. Everyone is so up themselves. I think they see through my accent and get that I'm a working-class imposter.' He blushes as he asks if I'd mind exchanging numbers. 'Maybe if you're having a good day we could go for a coffee or a drive somewhere. You could show me a good birdwatching spot.'

I hesitate, wondering if this is a sympathy move. The benevolent doctor helping a pitiful ailing neighbour. Or if this is sexual. If I'm putting myself in danger.

I banish the dark thoughts and we swap numbers. He waves me off from the garden, the dog at his side, both of them staring after me.

Chapter Three

When I get home Peter is out and Mum is cooking, singing along to the radio. Peter won't buy this house. He says it's his right to have cheap rent and why would he buy and have to pay for repairs when he can get the council to do it for him? He repeatedly pestered them till they fitted these ugly kitchen units. I heard him on the phone, telling them that his poor daughter was seriously ill and that we needed a new kitchen and double glazing. I'm his daughter when it suits his purpose. The council must have become so sick of him in the end that they bumped him up the list for a full set of plastic windows and new units.

This end of the open-plan room is an expanse of beige cupboards and discount laminate worktops, already showing signs of wear, before it gives way to the over-furnished lounge. From how Mum went on about it, you'd think he'd obtained a room full of priceless antiques. Like the rest of the house, it's a symphony of bland.

I go up and lie down in Becky's room, succumbing to the familiar fantasy of the flat that exists solely in my head. My own flat. A place for Ava and me. Somewhere with light reflecting from glass-fronted bookcases, a rug, a candle burning. Where there's a soft bed just for me and a bedroom for Ava. Food that I have chosen for us, no incessant cascade of noise. I know every molecule of this place. Only today there's something new in my fantasy. Someone. Adam is sitting reading on the couch while Ava sits drawing at the table. They both look up and smile as I walk in. I indulge myself for a short time, but the house drags me back to reality.

Ava comes up to me and she tells me about her day. When we finally go downstairs together Becky is watching a quiz show with the volume up too loud while Mum bangs pans and plates in the kitchen area. I stretch back on one end of the sofa and try to ignore the noise. Ava sits next to me, holding a book.

'Ann, will you look after Ava tonight? I know Dad's out too but some of the women from work are going to the pub and I could do with a night off.' I've never met Becky's friends. She doesn't bring them back here, but who would? Like me, she wouldn't want this place, or these people, to define her.

Mum's lips tighten. 'I was thinking of going with Pete but if you need me to—'

I sit forward. 'You can both go out. I'll be here with Ava. We'll be fine.'

Becky and Mum both stare at me for a few seconds too long before Becky speaks.

'I don't think that's a good idea yet. Not after what happened before.'

'I could do with a rest anyway.' Mum makes a show of rubbing the back of her legs to demonstrate her weariness. 'I'll stay in. It'll do me good. Pete won't mind.'

I don't argue with them.

* * *

When Becky leaves, we stay sitting on the sofa. We watch mindless programs that my mum chooses, Ava tucked into my side. I spend more time looking at Ava than at the TV. She makes silly comments about the people on TV and we laugh together, pulling faces at each other until Mum shushes us. By nine o'clock we're both fighting sleep. We go up to the bedroom that Ava shares with Becky.

'Mummy, why do I have to share this room with Becky? Why can't we share a room?'

'Well, I haven't got a room but as soon as I do we can share it. Maybe one day we'll have a room each but we could still share sometimes if we wanted.'

'Does that mean you're getting better? That we can go out together?' She hasn't asked me this for a while. I consider lying for a moment but decide against it. I take the coward's option and respond with vagueness.

'I'm trying my best to get better for us both.'

We fall asleep, lying on Ava's bed, my arm draped across her. I don't wake till Becky gets back. Ava has curled against me and I have to slide myself out. I surrender the room and stagger back downstairs, taking my place on the sofa. Peter is still not back. He's with one of his friends from the building trade, probably holed up in the corner of some sticky-floored pub, making inane remarks about politics and women. I watch a repeat of a nature programme, with Mum dozing off in the chair as she waits for him, like a dog waiting for its master. I enjoy the feminine softness of the house before he appears again, beery-breathed and staggering.

I try to stop my thoughts sticking in that Adam-shaped groove again but fail. I suspect that he's lonely, like me. He isn't the answer to my situation, merely a temporary distraction. He's a phantom in my head, diverting me from my real purpose. The only way I'll ever find peace is if I can resolve the situation here. The situation with Peter.

There was never anything catastrophic or dramatic about Peter's arrival in our house. He's subtle and quick, sly in his actions. He latched on to Mum. Inserted himself into our lives, spreading like a soft poison. Insidiously overlaying everything with his noxious character. His presence a subtle change to the atmosphere, like a creeping odour that you don't notice till you re-enter the room. He layers every situation with snide remarks, and veiled threats that make me feel unsteady when I most need to be stable. It's like living with the school bully.

I tried with him. Truly. I skirted around him like a dog waiting to be kicked. Offering smiles, compliments and obsequious assistance. But he barely concealed his burgeoning contempt for me from the outset. A confidence-destroying disdain that he nurtured and grew.

He's taken my mum and drained her to a hard-edged, monochrome version of herself and he's robbed me of my space. My refuge, my territory is gone. That was all I had left. He chose to oust me from my place and it's just the start. He wants me gone from here.

I have thoughts about Peter. Not the usual fantasies that I amuse myself with but other, more cunning ideas. A slow drip of poisonous asides to feed to Mum and Becky, ploys to make his business fail, ways to upend his psyche. And violence. Violence that is beyond my physical strength.

I think about the violence the most.

Chapter Four

There is joy to be found in illness. Firstly, nostalgia. Think back to when you were a child and you fell ill. Unless you were unlucky, neglected perhaps, then your family's world halted when you were sick. All their attention became focused onto you. You were tucked up under a blanket on the settee with the illicit pleasure of TV in the daytime. Your favourite snacks and drinks were presented, to tempt your flagging appetite. The world shrank to a room and a few people but was filled with love. Love that was solely yours. That you could sink back into.

Then there's camaraderie. Illness is isolating but in this era we're never really alone. There's always a community at the end of a touchscreen or a keyboard. People only too willing to overshare their every physical symptom. To listen to yours – or at least pretend to, before reeling off more lines about their own current troubles. The moment I was diagnosed with this illness I joined forums and message boards, subscribed to blogs, followed Instagram accounts. My fingers scrolled and typed at random hours. I basked in the warmth and strength in numbers, reassuring myself that I wasn't alone. That there is nothing odd or deviant about this condition that I have. That it can affect anyone.

Illness also has a release. A relinquishing of all responsibility. If you're ill, then what does the world expect of you? You're not obliged to earn money, to achieve, strive, fight to earn your place, to impress. The world accepts that you do nothing but be ill, quietly and with as little fuss as possible. Your family supports you in this. Helps you financially, practically, emotionally. Your caring hub of health professionals guides and nurtures you. Your friends stick by you and admire your fortitude. There's a freedom in this. This withdrawal from life. This absolving of all responsibility.

This is fantasy, of course.

The few friends that I had fell away. Partly my fault – I didn't have the energy and they didn't have the persistence, or the loyalty, to keep asking me to meet up. My continual refusals drove them away. My friend from college, Jasminder, was the one who tried the hardest but even she demurred in time, as I knew and hoped she would. Power imbalances aren't conducive to lasting friendships. It's hard to have friends when you don't have the necessary energy. It's better to let them go.

I followed an account for a long time called NeuroNadeen. She blogged, posted, shared each moment of her photogenic life. Her concerned husband and her well-behaved daughter. Her doting parents who posed for anxious-faced selfies by her bed as they visited her during her many hospital stays. Nadeen has the same neurological illness that I have. Only Nadeen has so much more. Nadeen has what a sick person should have. The nostalgia, the release, the camaraderie. The space to live and breathe.

I removed her from my feeds a long time ago.

*　*　*

Today is entirely dedicated to illness. Thursdays are my day at the hospital. My weekly appointment with the specialist across town. It's not the best way to spend a day, but it's preferable to some of the stuff that I've been through. I could rank medical procedures in order of how hideous they are. Compile a top ten, write a guidebook, start an Instagram account even. The problem is, it's too gruesome for public consumption.

These appointments are worse than any test. At least with those it was part of a process. A search for answers on the road to restoration. Now, it's hard to think that recovery is even possible. I need a way to function *around* the illness, but we're not making much progress. I still come. I don't see much else that I can do, other than what I'm told to . . . and hope. I have to keep hoping.

'I don't feel better.'

Dr Bronson sits back. He's wearing a short-sleeved shirt today and I realise that I've never seen his arms before. They're bare, hairless, which I hadn't considered that they might be.

'No, no. You misunderstand me, Emma. I'm not diminishing how you feel. I just said that you look better. Your colour perhaps. I agree that you're still ill. That's not up for debate.'

'I'm still getting the pain in my legs. The numbness too.'

'Do you think that the pregbalin is helping?'

We go round and round. New drugs, new exercises to do. The usual dance where, at the end of it, I stay exactly the same.

'How are you getting on with your future goals?' Dr

31

Bronson flips back a few pages in his notebook. 'You were looking at—'

'I changed my goals. They're going all right, thank you.'

'OK. What are you planning?'

I tell him that I'll talk about them later, that they're not fully formed yet, which is a lie. They're bright, lit up vividly with rage. Peter's face filling my thoughts.

'Let me know and we can think of what kind of strategies we can use to achieve your goals.'

I'm not sure that he can help me with this. Confidentiality has a limit if the patient divulges that there's a crime involved. If he knew the thoughts that I have, he'd call the police or have me sectioned. I'm not mad, though. I'm desperate.

* * *

After the appointment, the train back home is empty. I see a single magpie by the side of the line. He's sitting, looking straight at me. His shiny plumage reflecting an array of colours in the sunlight. If you look closely, they're not just black and white but iridescent blues and greens. A single magpie is considered bad luck. They're perceived to be evil, dangerous somehow – which is nonsense. It's just a bird, like any other. Though they didn't help their own cause when they visited battlefields and picked at the corpses of the soldiers.

Maybe they need a rebrand.

* * *

I walk back via Adam's street. I've changed my route so that I pass the end of his road. I haven't seen him again since the afternoon in his garden five days ago. I think it was on the fourth time that I passed by the house that I saw the woman. A flash of colour as she bowled out of the front garden. An older woman with a determined stride. I dodged back behind an overhanging buddleia, so that I was shielded from view.

Peter is home. I smell him as soon as I open the front door. It's a relief to hear Becky and Ava in the bedroom. I manage to shoot upstairs without seeing him, although Winston barked when I walked in, almost giving me away.

I had a thought yesterday. I fetched my binoculars and checked. My guess was right. If I stand, wobbling on the closed toilet seat in the bathroom and look out of the window, then I can just make out a portion of their patio. I hid the binoculars behind some folded towels. I retrieve them now and climb up but Adam isn't there today. Nor is the woman. There's just a yawning expanse of flagstones, made glaring by the sun. The effort exhausts me and I steady myself as I stumble back down, only just managing to right myself.

I stagger to the bedroom. Becky helps me onto the bed and unties my trainers, easing my legs up, tucking the blanket around me. Sparrow lies down and purrs next to me.

'Now, Ava. You have to be quiet for a while. Mummy isn't feeling well and needs a rest.'

'I know. I always try to be quiet.' Ava glares at Becky.

I don't know what I'd have done without Becky being around to help me raise my daughter. There are faded photographs of a sulky teenage Becky, a quasi-adult from the early days of her acting career at the age of fourteen, holding my seven-year-old hand as I stare at the camera. The soap opera set is in the background, Becky plastered with make-up as she beams and puffs out her teenage chest.

Like me, Becky hasn't had an easy time of it. She ruefully celebrated her thirty-seventh birthday this year, complaining bitterly about being almost forty. Facing it like someone who's arrived at a buffet only to find that the best food has already been taken and she's been left with the scraps. She was always a pretty child, the smiling one, the one willing to entertain and charm people. She's still beautiful but with frayed edges.

Peter idolises Becky. His phone screensaver isn't a photo of my mum. It's Becky, beaming in a photoshoot from an early 2000s soap magazine. It was Mum and Peter who pushed teenage Becky forward with her ambitions for fame – or should I say, *their* ambitions. It started out as Becky's dream, but I think they pushed it too far. You'd think it would have been the happiest of times for Becky, but I'm not convinced that it was. She doesn't talk about it much, but from what she has said it sounds awful. Hours of acting combined with schoolwork. The adult actors treating her either like a doll or as a teen nuisance. Instead of hanging out with other teenagers, her life was just sweaty television sets, caked in make-up under hot lights. Sitting alone with a tutor in a windowless room. It's not a life that I'd choose for my child.

And she's different now that she's no longer acting. Much calmer, less impulsive.

* * *

Becky stays behind after Ava leaves to go and watch TV.

'How are you doing, little sister?' She's always called me that. When she first arrived to live here she was as truculent as you'd expect a girl to be when her mother had died a year before and she was being transplanted to a new family. My mum didn't have an easy time with her for the first couple of years, but she always treated me with kindness. Regaling me with stories of her amateur dramatics and, later, of her time working on the soap. I was like her acolyte, trailing after her, trying on the clothes and make-up that she'd been given for swanky parties and award ceremonies.

'I'm good.'

'Let me know if there's anything I can do to help. I know your mum and my dad aren't exactly easy for you to be around. You're not getting much fun out of life at the moment.'

I keep my eyes closed. 'I've met someone, actually.'

I feel her hand on mine. I can tell from her voice that she's smiling.

'Tell me more. And quickly.' Her tone is gleeful and I regret the stupidity of my comment. That I've raised her hopes for me over nothing.

'It's not anything really. He's a doctor. I met him outside the hospital, and it turned out that he lives around the corner. He invited me for a drink in his garden the other day. But he probably just wants to be friends.'

'Not enough. I have questions, questions, and then more questions. Are you seeing him again? Is he hot? Does he have a cute, rich older brother?' She gently prods me in the side with her finger and I try not to laugh.

'He's handsome. Too handsome for me, really. Like, stunningly handsome. More your league really. I'm not even sure that it's anything. We were just talking and stuff. We've been messaging and he's offered to take me out next week. For a drive up to the nature reserve at Nunhead Cemetery.'

'You're not so naïve that you think men generally just want to be friends with attractive young women, are you? It sounds like a date to me.' She wrinkles her perfectly formed nose. 'A creepy cemetery date but still a date. He must be interested in you if he's willing to trail along to one of your dismal nature resorts.'

'He's in a complicated situation,' I say, in spite of my ignorance of Adam's life.

'Married you mean?'

'Divorcing. But he's still living with his ex-wife.'

Maybe Becky can offer me some wisdom. I've already reached out for help to people I 'know' – the three friends who I still message. Twenty-first-century friends: other ill people who I've never met, and who I probably never will meet. It's not like the majority of us get out much. We talk online, sometimes repeatedly, sometimes with gaps, which we all accept and understand. I asked one of them about Adam. Told her about the way he looks at me, how he listens and responds. How he looks. Marcia's older than me and has three grown-up children, raising them alone after her husband left her for another woman. Her disapproval rang out through the angry replies that she sent back.

'*A married man is always trouble, whether or not he's "leaving his wife". Honestly, I think you should back away.*' Marcia hasn't met Adam, though. She can't comment. I deleted her messages and didn't reply. It's only fair to suspend judgement until he's explained himself. I won't ask her for more advice.

Becky squeezes my arm. 'Well, what else are you doing with your days at the moment, anyway? Go and meet him! But . . . be careful.'

I'm thinking about Adam so much that I can almost smell him in the room. That light citrusy scent. It's so strong in my thoughts that I almost ask Becky if she can smell it too, but I stop myself.

I'm interrupted by the sound of Peter laughing downstairs.

His intrusive braying filling the air. I hear him asking Mum where 'The Burden' is. Mum doesn't bother to scold him for using the nickname that he's bestowed on me. A ripple of hatred courses through me. Becky does what she usually does and pretends not to hear him.

The thing that I didn't tell Doctor Bronson today is that getting rid of Peter is my new rehab goal. It's time he's gone, whatever it takes. However devious or violent the methods need to be. That's what I hope to be well enough to do.

Chapter Five

The old cemeteries like this one at Nunhead fill me with joy. There's a ring of them around London. Built to accommodate the corpses of the Victorian era, when the churchyards became full, and the bodies were piling up, tainting the air. They're mostly now defunct, or parts of them are, clawed back by nature and the birds. Chapels with no roofs, angels with missing heads. Crumbling mausoleums with rotting doors and perilously leaning gravestones swathed in ivy. There are shrubs and flowers growing everywhere, housing hundreds of birds by day, bats by night. The sound of the birdsong is spectacular if you come at the right time.

Adam was wearing a pristine pale pink shirt and chinos when he picked me up. We drove here in his old MG sportscar – a rare gift from his wife, apparently, for getting into medical school. She didn't approve of the acting but welcomed this career. He looks embarrassed, smaller somehow, when he mentions her, as if he regrets allowing her into our day. It's endearing how this handsome and confident man has such boyish traits. He's left Ripley at home, which pleases me. I don't like the idea of his dog trampling through the nature reserve and disturbing the birds.

It's good to be driven by someone other than Peter in his battered white van with 'Whitehouse Building Services' on the side. Mum has taken his name, abandoning the 'Miller', another thing of Daddy's that was obliterated when Peter came along.

When we pull into the car park, he asks, 'How far can you walk? Is this OK for you?'

'I can manage. I use a stick sometimes but not today. Today's better.'

I've had a few better days of late. Days where I can stay awake in the day and not be pacing the lounge all night. Days where my leg and arm are stronger. Where I haven't fallen. It does happen sometimes and I embrace it because it never lasts long.

'Well, let's walk up to the top, then. I think that you get a view over London. I looked it up on my phone.' He's youthful in his enthusiasm. 'We'll take it slow though, and let me know if you get tired.'

We walk through the gravestones and past the towering tombs, stopping to read names, commenting on the hideously short life spans of the Victorians. Whole families dead by thirty in some cases. The benches at the top are taken, but we find a patch of dry yellowing grass with a view. I lay out the rug for us to sit on and arrange the food that I brought. The Shard is slate grey today, reflecting the sky. The buildings of the city hustle for our attention. They're an ugly intrusion on the skyline. It's as if someone in the 1980s imagined the future and got it all wrong.

I point across in the direction of where Saint Paul's is. 'I went to the Museum of London once and there's a stuffed bird there. A falcon who came from St Paul's.'

'Taxidermy is weird, isn't it? It freaks me out, actually. I don't understand this recent hipster fashion for it. A dead body in the home. I just don't get it.'

'Agreed. Apparently, this bird was shot in the leg in Victorian times, but they kept him alive. Thousands of people came to see him in his cage in the corner of some pub.'

'Poor thing. I wonder why he was at St Paul's in the first place. Was he a holy bird?' He smiles at me, and our eyes lock. The dark pupils of his eyes reflect the foliage.

'He probably liked the pigeons. Falcons can swoop down and rip them apart. A pigeon is a good dinner for them.' Adam doesn't flinch when I talk about the realities of bird life. Instead, his eyes widen and he leans forward intently.

'I hope you don't think any less of me for this, what with you being a bird lover, but I don't like pigeons. Really don't like them at all. I had a bad experience as a child. When I was a little boy, we went to Trafalgar Square and my mother brought some seed. It all started off fine. Throwing a bit of seed here and there and they came scuttling around, making me laugh. But before long they were climbing on my head, my shoulders, mobbing me. All those scratchy little claws ripping into my skin. I absolutely freaked out.'

'They're an acquired taste. Let's allocate you as "Team Peregrine". You can root for the falcons.'

He reaches across for a piece of quiche and something small and black falls from his pocket. It's a phone, made of flimsy plastic. It's a burner phone, like drug dealers and gangsters have. Anonymous and untraceable to the owner. There's a tightening in my chest. I pretend not to see it and I'm glad when he notices it there and tucks it back in his pocket.

'This place suits you.' He grins at my raised eyebrows.

'I don't mean the death stuff, obviously. I mean the nature. You're more relaxed here.'

'I've always loved nature. We used to go out a lot as children. My dad had a car and he'd drive us down to the countryside in Kent. I loved it.'

'Is that when you became interested in birds?' He's leaning on one elbow, looking up at me.

'Yes. I used to love the patterns made by the swallows or seeing the birds of prey hovering over the road. It was often just me and Dad on the trips. Mum didn't really like being out of London. She says that the countryside makes her nervous.'

'Sounds like you were close to your dad?'

'He was a lovely man. Soft and kind. Really clever too. He was always reading. The house was full of books. He knew stuff about everything, almost.' I pick up a bread roll from the picnic rug, picking at the crust to give my fingers something to do as tears prick my eyes.

'He sounds great. What was his job?'

'He repaired clocks. He had a shop. But he only opened it a few hours a day. Most of the time he'd be at home doing repairs. I used to think of it as a magical kingdom. All that ticking and the chimes.'

'Sounds lovely. There is something soothing about the noise of a clock.'

'Not according to my stepfather. He persuaded my mum to sell all the clocks from the house. Said that they drove him mad.'

'Yeesh. Well he sounds like a prize arsehole if you don't mind me saying so.'

'I really don't mind you saying so. He is. I know that I shouldn't say this but my life would be better without him in it.'

We both sit and watch a flock of starlings pass by, filling the air with raucous sound.

'Do you ever wish you could just escape it all? I'd love to get away but I can't. A new life would cost money that I just don't have.' Adam's soft demeanour makes this shameful admission slip from me with ease.

'I'm actually more similar to you than you'd think. Stuck in a shitty situation that I'm struggling to escape. This accent, my clothes – it's all acquired. I didn't grow up with money. I was brought up on an estate in Tower Hamlets. My mum was a cleaner. She raised me on her own, helped me through uni after my dad pissed off to Norfolk with another woman.'

'Do you have family who could help with your "situation"?'

'Nah. It's just me. Only child and my mum moved to Spain a couple of years back. She has a habit of moving on from one man to another and the latest one wanted to live on the Costa del Sol.'

He doesn't mention his wife. The one he referred to as his 'soon-to-be ex-wife'. I don't have the words, the courage, to bring her up but the questions bubble inside me. The concept of her sits in my mouth, stuck to my tongue.

We finish the picnic and Adam is lying on his back, looking up at the grey sky. I'm sitting up with my knees to my chest, sneaking sideways glances at him. My eyes are constantly drawn to him, to his profile, his hair, his upper body tone. He beckons me, pats the rug for me to lie down too. It's the natural thing to go to him, entirely right. We both lie there and I sense the narrow space between us, his chest rising and falling. For once, there are no thoughts of my illness in my head, just Adam and me and the sound of the birds.

Eventually he sits up and stretches and as I move forward my balance goes and I keel sideways. The leftover picnic is displaced by my fall, squashed into the rug or scattered on the grass. Pressed into my clothes and face. Adam darts to my side, telling me that things are all right. My shoulders fall down from around my neck and I feel my limbs loosen. For a moment I think that I'm here with Daddy. Adam: a reassuring presence beside me. But then humiliation grips me and the tension returns.

* * *

I don't speak much on the drive back. I'm preoccupied, keeping quiet as we pass railway lines, rows of houses, parades of shops with faded awnings and less-than-fresh fruit stacked outside, collecting traffic fumes. The occasional chain coffee shop or homewares store is creeping in, cleansing the area of character like drops of bleach in water. Adam fills the void of silence by talking about inconsequential things. I wait until we reach the house before I speak about what happened.

'I'm so sorry.'

'For what?'

'For falling. For messing up the picnic.'

'You're apologising for being ill?'

I nod.

'Emma, I'm a doctor. If illness bothered me then I wouldn't do my job.'

'But it makes me so much *less*.' Tears well up in my eyes.

'You're not less. You're really not.' He reaches over and kisses me softly, on the forehead.

The urge to take the back of his head and press his mouth against mine is overwhelming.

'I almost forgot. I bought you something. I hope this is OK.' He reaches across into the back seat of the car and pulls out a parcel. The cuff of his shirt rides up as he stretches back and I see that his forearm has a bruise on it. Finger marks circling the lean muscle. I look away.

He gives me the gift, wrapped in plain blood-red paper. I unwrap it and reveal the most beautiful book I've ever seen. It's an old hardback, yellowed at the edges. On each page is a painted Victorian illustration of flocks of birds. An unkindness of ravens, a quarrel of sparrows, a parliament of rooks. I flick through the stiff pages, running my finger over the paintings, unable to speak for a moment.

'Adam, I can't take this. It's too much.'

'You deserve nice things. I saw this in the window of an antique shop and it made me think of you.'

I do take it. It's perfect.

I look up as I enter the house and Becky is waving to me from the lounge window. I go straight up to Ava who's reading on the bed. I show her the book but don't tell her who it came from. We talk through the collective nouns for the birds and she's soon laughing at the most absurd ones. We make up some new ones of our own. I half-heartedly tell her off when she blurts out the occasional crude word.

Chapter Six

Mealtimes are the most desperate times of all. Today, my body is begging me to sleep but my settee is taken. Peter's watching sport on the TV, the cheering feral and raucous. His thick legs draped open across the cushions. He's wearing shorts, which he does all year round, his fat white legs on display. Ava is in the corner of the sofa, drawing. She looks across at me and we lock eyes. I long to go and look at what she's creating but I'm too tired. I can't imagine words having the impetus to come from my mouth.

I start to walk upstairs to go and lie on Becky's bed, but Mum catches me. 'Emma. Please stay down here. I'm about to dish up the food.'

I slump into a chair at the dining table and get out my *Observer Book of Birds*. It's a vintage edition from 1960 that Daddy gave to me. I'm learning the Latin names. Ava is first to join me at the table. Words form on my tongue but stay imprisoned behind my teeth. I don't have a way to make this better. No solutions or explanations that are good enough to offer to this child who I can't look after. No truth about the future that might be palatable. My daughter whose care I've deferred to my stepsister and mother.

She has my physique and colouring – thin for an eleven-year-old. She's a girl who people barely notice. Until she speaks and then they see the sharp-edged energy that she has.

The food is the usual stodgy stuff. The only thing that Peter will eat. Things with added fat or butter, nothing green or wholesome. Tonight, it's sausages and mash, swimming in thin gravy.

'So, how are we all?' Mum adopts a relentlessly cheery tone that rarely wavers but always seems artificial. She kept it up even after Daddy died. Her response to my persistent sadness was a blank wall of forced jolliness. As if she could chivvy me out of it. I'd sit crying in my room and I'd hear her footsteps as she lingered outside my door for a few seconds before she moved across to her own room and closed the door. As if ignoring me would make my sorrow resolve.

Becky is quick to answer. 'Pretty good. I'm still training up those two new women, so that's eating into my time but it's going OK.' Becky and Mum both work at The Meadows Nursing Home. It's off the South Circular. There isn't so much as a blade of grass there, so the name is preposterous. Mum has worked there for years doing the meals and some cleaning, whilst Becky works full-time as a senior care assistant. After her acting career stalled, she tried various jobs: something in events, then working at a high-end shop in the West End. Nothing worked out for her, and she reluctantly ended up working with Mum as a last resort. Becky accepted this fall from grace with an air of reluctant resignation. Now she seems to go through the motions of life. Like she's acting at being OK. She's not the stepsister I once knew.

'Is there a job for this one?' Peter points at me. I look at his thumb and think about how satisfying it would be to snap it back until the bone cracked.

'I'm not ready to work yet.'

'Bloody hell. It's just time you need, is it? Well, we're all here waiting. Three years' training down the pan. Maybe you could put it to use somehow and make some of your own money instead of spending ours.' I look across at Mum for help, but she's staring down at the table.

'I'm. Not. Well.' I spit out the words, whilst looking down at the mess on my plate. I'm not hungry now. I imagine the knife fitting into his eye socket. I suspect it's not sharp enough. It would have to happen on a night when we have steak.

The thought of him being out of my life is delicious. It would be a liberation, a renewal. Like washing a soiled garment and having it fresh again.

'Leave me alone.'

He pushes across the table and grabs my wrist, his stubby fingers clasping me. Sending the ketchup bottle skittering across, banging into Becky's plate.

'Don't speak to me like that in my house! All right? You're nothing here. You don't even look after your own bloody child. We have to do that for you too.'

Becky rests her hand on his arm and he lets go of me. 'Dad! Let her be. Let's just eat, shall we?'

He slumps back, scowling, not looking at me or Mum. I flop back, the chair legs scraping the floor. Mum rights the ketchup bottle and then looks at me. As if she's scrutinising an item of furniture for marks or scratches. My arm has a red welt where he snatched my wrist. The imprint of his fingers visible. I catch Ava looking across at me, her eyes wide, brow furrowed.

'Why don't we all just talk about something else?

How's the holiday club going, Ava?' Mum's forced tone grates at me.

Ava glances at Peter before answering. Her voice is thin and reedy. 'It's OK but the other kids want to play stupid outdoor games all the time. I stay inside and read on my own when the teachers let me.'

'You should join in. Get some sun on your skin. How about the teachers? Are they nice?' Mum persists, in spite of it being obvious that Ava doesn't want to talk.

'They're OK, I suppose.'

'Knock us out with the enthusiasm, Ava, why don't you?' Becky looks across at her with a smile that isn't really a smile.

'Well, it's boring, isn't it? And unfair.'

'What do you mean by that?' Peter looks at her sharply.

'It's the holidays. Other kids round here get to go on holidays.' Her voice becomes louder, more petulant. 'I want to stay at home. I hate it there.'

'Seriously? You know how hard me and your grandparents work to keep you in a home and give you everything you need. A little gratitude wouldn't go astray.'

'He's not my grandfather.' Ava sounds flat. Resigned to having to tolerate this.

There's a moment of silence. Becky looks nervously across at Ava. Then Mum and Peter start shouting. Ava just continues to eat, as if she can't hear them. Peter's voice fades out and he sits shaking his head in disapproval while Mum launches into a lecture about why she believes that Ava is being selfish, rude and thoughtless.

I want to take Ava and hug her to me. Tell her that she can be exactly where she wants to be. That she can stay at home with me. I don't because I know that danger lies ahead if I do that. That I'll be making promises that I'm not well enough to keep. The moment I start to comment on Mum and Becky's child-rearing methods then an argument that I can't win will start. I'll be shamed again for my inability to care for my own child. For being a terrible mother. I try to think of the words Dr Bronson has said to me when we talk about this. That this isn't my fault. That I tried. Tried more than once before I had to admit defeat. That this is about illness. Not weakness. I repeat the last part as a mantra and remember that I haven't chosen this. It chose me.

Mum finally stops lecturing my daughter. Ava finishes her meal and asks to be excused. I slip away from the table, before I say something that will make things worse, and dash down into the garden. I don't have a jacket and it's cold. There's not much bird activity. Just the sound of a solitary blackbird.

*　*　*

When I go back in at dusk, Peter and Mum are watching TV and Becky is in her room with Ava. Ava is already asleep. I try not to be angry with myself for not coming in sooner, so that I could reassure my child. I'll talk to her about what happened tonight when we're alone tomorrow. Becky looks up from her phone briefly but doesn't speak. Her expression blank.

I take refuge in the bathroom. I've taken my binoculars from under the towels in the airing cupboard.

Adam's wife is in the garden, pacing the patio, a mobile phone pressed to her ear. She's frowning. I can't hear her but I imagine that her voice is braying, a flawless accent that echoes across their garden.

She looks like someone I'd dislike. Someone entitled and

rich who has no idea what it's like to live the way I have to. Someone who's always been protected by the armour of money. A person who couldn't conceive of what it is to have to find the energy to scratch a life for herself and her child. She'd look down on me and Ava as working-class scum.

Dislike is the wrong word. I could grow to hate this woman.

Chapter Seven

Technology is double-edged. The portals available to us can lead us to places we shouldn't go. I decided to look up Adam. And his wife. To see if there are photos from when he was an actor. It's just research. And I needed to see his face again. To have something to focus on. We've become friends. We've seen each other every few days for the last couple of weeks. Sat together in his garden in the afternoon, walked in the park, driven round Greenwich. But he's working again and it's been three days. I miss talking to him.

He has no social media presence but there is a photo from a performance of a play in a pub theatre in North London. There's a headshot, him smiling with his hair swept back from his face. I save the picture, printing it out on Peter's computer when no one's around. I lay it between the pages of *The Folklore of Birds*. There are a couple more photos, but I only allow myself to print one more. I resist going through them all. I don't want to be obsessive.

Adam didn't tell me that his wife is semi-famous. One of the photographs that came up on my search was of them both at an event together a few years ago. I fall down a rabbit hole of clicking from site to site, researching her. Reading magazine articles she's written about food, her life, her personal experiences. She's not hugely well-known, but she has a media presence. She's a chef and cookbook writer in her late forties called Celeste Dupont. She even has a weekly food column in the evening paper, makes occasional appearances on television shows. Her Instagram page has the occasional picture of Adam. Photographs where he's been posed in her kitchen like a mannequin, used and manipulated. A prop for Celeste to make her life look more beautiful.

Her voice and tone in the YouTube videos I watch are as arch as I'd expected – all clipped tones that sound condescending, sarcastic, verging on sardonic. She's one of those people who crops up on those weekend morning programs where middle-class people sit on settees and witter endlessly about food. Piled-up red hair with subtle highlights and high cheekbones. Skin plumped up with facial creams that, doubtless, have an eye-watering cost. A slash of crimson lipstick, the colour of a goldfinch's cheek. Her posture suggests that she had lessons in deportment at one of those exclusive girls' schools that poor people never breach. Her appearance is that of someone who has the luxury of having ample time and energy to devote to her own selfish needs.

I've spotted her twice more now from the bathroom window, lying back on a lounger, stretching out her long legs in the afternoon sun. I see her in the street too when I'm walking past their house. She's purposeful, always dressed in cotton dresses and wide-brimmed hats. She walks at a pace that someone like me couldn't match.

A bubble of dislike is rising up within me.

The sort of dislike that drives me to think about her. Again and again.

That makes me taunt myself with her existence and give myself over to my irritation.

Compelling me to follow and watch her.

* * *

She's emerging from the house. My left foot is numb today and I'm walking like a ship at sea, lilting from side to side. I guess where she's going. A steady stream of locals leave their houses on a warm Sunday morning, all toting baskets or reusable jute bags. Making their way up the hill to the farmers' market in Blackheath Village. She must be headed there, destined to come back with a basket full of fresh herbs and artisan loaves of bread.

I get the bus to the market. The disabled seats are taken so I have to make my way to the back of the bus, clinging on to the poles as it lurches up the hill past the ornate villas that tower up on each side of the route.

A line of starlings waits on the fence of the railway car park near the market, poised to swoop for any crumbs. The stalls are loaded up with things that I neither want nor can afford. There's a sickening smell of roasted pork, a line of people walking away with hot rolls, grease rolling down their chins, which they dab at daintily with cloth handkerchiefs. I ignore the nausea that's nudging at me. I buy a bunch of sunflowers for Ava, denting my meagre budget for the week.

I spot her standing by the herbs, holding up a sage plant. Her fingers long and manicured with scarlet-painted nails. She slides a debit card towards the stallholder and slips the pot into her basket, next to some fresh scallops and one of the ubiquitous sourdough loaves. I glance round at the people milling around, with their dachshunds and poodle-mix dogs on loose leads. My black trousers and shirt look out of place among their shorts and pastel casual wear. A spot of oil in a glass of milk.

I move closer. There's a rich vanilla fragrance coming from Celeste's skin. She's immaculate and groomed to perfection in her chic vintage dress. I move back and pretend to look at jars of local honey whilst she strides over to the fresh pasta and olives, sold at eye-watering prices. I imagine that the people here think that people of my class wouldn't want to eat like this, that we're happy with our pre-sliced white loaves, our frozen food from Iceland and McDonald's Happy Meals for our children as a special treat. That we wouldn't relish imported morsels and freshly grown organic produce. That it wouldn't suit our untutored palates.

That's if they think about people like me at all. Which I don't suspect that Celeste Dupont ever does.

I reach to put the honey back and misjudge the distance, overestimating the grip in my left hand. I stretch forward in a futile attempt to stop it falling but come short, slipping forward onto my knees. Sticky globules of the stuff pour down the gingham cloth and onto the tarmac, forming clots on the ground, like spilled blood. There are glass shards by my knees as I try in vain to raise myself back up. The sunflowers are crushed at my side.

'It's OK, love. Don't worry. There's plenty more. Let's help you up. Doesn't look like there's any damage to you.' His accent sounds rural, soft rolled R's. I offer to pay for the broken jar, but he refuses, waving my cash away, refusing my hopeless offer of help to clean up the mess. The woman from the flower stall sees me and passes over a fresh bunch of sunflowers and my eyes prick with tears at her kindness. None of the well-groomed people in Sunday casuals speak. It's only the stallholders who show me compassion.

As I pull myself up from the tarmac, I see Celeste on the periphery of my vision. Her lip slightly curled, as if there's something rotten in her vicinity. Looking at me as if I'm litter on the tarmac. Her eyes blank and cold as she appraises me. She pushes past me, almost knocking me sideways. I'm invisible, now I'm no longer a spectacle. I often am to people like her. Her hand clutches two twenty-pound notes, which she thrusts at the stallholder.

My face flushes as a knot of pure rage forms in my stomach. I understand why Adam needs to leave her. Why he must hate her. She embodies everything that I loathe. This rude and entitled woman who has everything that I will never have. This self-satisfied woman who still has a hold over Adam.

The image of me slapping her smug face is so strong in my head that I almost feel the sting in my palms. Hear the sound of my hand colliding with her flesh.

Chapter Eight

Romance is harder when you have space to ruminate, to scrutinise each interaction. To pick over every word spoken. To examine messages, to contemplate why there was no kiss at the end of a message. Or why there's no text at all that day.

Adam's messages are warm and friendly enough but at night when I lie awake, it twists around in my mind. The burner phone. The fact that he's married. That's he's barely mentioned his wife or the divorce. The finger-mark bruises on his arm. I think about his beauty, his house, his job – about why someone like him would be interested in me. Someone with so little to offer.

Most of all I think about Celeste Dupont and her self-satisfied face. I hate-scroll through her newspaper columns, mentally noting every slight. Every sneering phrase that she's written.

Birdwatching has taught me patience – but I've not seen her in the street since the farmers' market, and every time I've stood at the bathroom window, the garden has been empty. I spotted her letting Ripley out twice. She recoils when he passes her.

I thought that all my hatred was channelled solely into Peter, but I was wrong. It's limitless.

* * *

Adam has been working nights and catching up on sleep in the day. I've spent time thinking about him in the hospital, hoping that his days haven't been too frantic. Hoping that he stayed safe – at work and at home. The days have loitered and stifled. I had a visit to the doctor's surgery, the pharmacy – but other than that, I've mostly drifted in and out of sleep. Peter was working from home and Becky and Mum were out at work in the day, so I curled up on Becky's bed and listened to the radio. When Ava was at home we watched TV together with Sparrow beside us. Until the others came back, when I'd sneak down into the garden and hide behind the shrubs. At night, I lay on the settee, sleeping fitfully. My dreams were vivid and brash. Filled with fist meeting bone. Hands gripping hair. Nails scratching.

I've been checking my phone constantly. No one but Adam has called or messaged. I always had friends at school, or at least a friend or two. I didn't fit in well in groups but would gravitate to the reserved, softer girls. It was the same at college. I was never exactly part of a large circle of friends but always part of small allegiances of quieter girls who populated the fringes. But my friends all fell away when I had to leave school. The same thing happened with my friends from work. I'd met some people who I liked, and we were becoming friends, but it all ended when I left abruptly.

My phone beeps and there's a message from Adam, suggesting that we meet by the Thames later today. My mouth widens into a smile. The sensation no longer feeling unfamiliar. I push the worrying thoughts away for now. Once we know each other better, then I'll ask him about my concerns. And I'll ask him more about his impending divorce. About why he's still in that house. With that horrible woman. About what he wants from me.

* * *

The South Bank is as busy as you'd expect on a stark summer day. My leg is better at the moment, and I haven't fallen for days. The Thames is noisy at high tide with waves slapping against the concrete defences. There's little between me and nature. The water could engulf me at any moment. All the little beaches are obliterated. There's a group of cormorants on a buoy, stretching out their wings in the sunshine.

A steady stream of people walk by, the occasional bike swerving round me. I spot Marie, the nurse from the hospital, walking past with a tall man, but I could be mistaken. I've been dreaming a lot lately and a whole cast of nurses populates my nightmares.

Whilst I'm waiting, I stand by the stone barriers watching the gulls soar overhead, They swoop down and skim the surfaces of the rust-rotted barges that chug by, screeching as they circle the air. I read somewhere that they find a body in the Thames most weeks. They're mostly people who have killed themselves. I tell Adam this when he arrives, which isn't the best conversational opener. But he seems to like it.

He doesn't kiss me on the cheek when he appears. We don't even embrace. He just touches me on the arm, in a companiable way. There's something restless and uncontained about him today. My stomach contracts and I try to stop looking for signals, to not obsessively analyse his motives.

He has Ripley with him. The dog glances at me and then looks away, staring at the pavement. Adam unclips his lead and hangs it around his neck. The dog trots beside him, his body rubbing against Adam's leg.

It's disconcerting being out in central London but with Adam beside me I'm free and safe. Even with the strange energy he has today, his presence emboldens me. I'm launched back into the world, released from those same few streets that I haunt. Adam is helping me to open the door of my cage. The air feels different as I breathe deeply to slow my racing heartbeat.

The day is frenetic with heat and tourism. I distract myself from the press of the crowds of people by picturing a familiar body floating past. Peter's face, blue and swollen, grazed as the water smashes it against the walls of the Thames embankment. I smile up at Adam. He asks about my health and listens intently, making pertinent remarks in return. There's nothing oppressive about his queries, no hint that he'd be displeased if I was to answer that I felt terrible. But I do feel better today. The distraction helps. Not because I'm imagining that something could develop between me and Adam but more that I have something external. My head becomes an echo chamber, my world just a cell of illness when I have nothing else to concentrate on.

A family of tourists walks by, resolutely middle class in Boden casuals, the mother swinging tote bags printed with book cover designs from the crook of her toned arm. Two children link her and her impossibly wholesome-looking partner as they walk in a line, holding hands.

Oblivious to the people having to move out of their way. An older woman walks behind, patiently coaxing a toddler to walk.

'I envy those people with big warm families around them, don't you? All supportive and caring. It must be comforting.' He smiles at me, displaying rows of perfectly straight teeth.

'Be careful what you wish for. You could have one like mine. Four adults crammed together with a child, a cat and a dog and never a moment of privacy.'

'Or two adults who hate each other rattling round a big house and trying desperately to avoid each other before they put their hands around each other's necks.' He swallows hard again. The cartilage of his throat rising and falling. 'You mentioned a child? You haven't mentioned a child before.'

I don't answer immediately. But it's inevitable. I've always known that. 'She's mine. My daughter, Ava. Short for Avis. It's Latin for bird. But Becky and Mum said she'd get teased if we actually called her that. So it's Ava.'

He's silent for a beat. 'How old is she?'

'She's eleven. She'll be going to high school next year.' I can't help but smile when I think about her. The way she clutches on to something and becomes obsessive: a type of animal, a historical figure, a particular book. These things absorb and animate her to the exclusion of everything else. Bent over a book, scribbling notes, compiling scrapbooks – leaving her oblivious to her surroundings. She can live in her imagination. But when she emerges from her thoughts, she's diverting and amusing. She's perfect.

'Is Ava like you?'

'Yes. She's a lot like me. She lives up to her name. She's like a little bird. But a feisty one. There was always something intense about her, even when she was a baby. She always looked like she was thinking everything through.'

'And you're not . . . with her father still?' There's a note of anxiety in his voice, which makes my pulse quicken with excitement.

'God, no. He's long gone.' I feel like I owe him more so I continue. 'I met her dad, Tommy, at school when I was twelve. He was two years older. We were planning to get married. Got engaged at seventeen, which was madness. We were just children. Tommy planned to get us a little flat. He'd left school and was working as an apprentice electrician. I was doing my exams and it was all mapped out. Tiny flat, dull jobs. Work our way up to a two-bed starter home in Kent. The pub on a Saturday night the highlight of the week. Then a drive out somewhere on a Sunday if I was lucky. Maybe an annual holiday in Margate.'

'What went wrong?'

'Just stuff. Things happened. We grew apart after Ava was born. The usual stuff, I was too young.' I feel the usual lurch in the pit of my stomach when I remember the shame of my late-teenage pregnancy, my broken education. The abandoned A levels. The dream of a university place lost. Tommy walking away from me and Ava. 'Then we grew up and we didn't want the same things anymore. I'll tell you about it all another time. It's a bit of a downer of a story, I'm afraid. I don't want to spoil the day.'

'A sad story but also a joyful one. Fractured relationships are rough but there's Ava. Children are amazing. I'm sure that you're an incredible mother.'

I don't know how to respond to this. I'm less of a mother than I'd hoped to be. I've failed her. But I like Adam's sentiments. I can imagine him with Ava. Us three together.

How he'd enrich our lives. How much she'd enjoy his presence.

A torrent of thoughts overwhelms me and I make do with saying 'Thank you.'

We carry on walking towards Westminster. There's a sense of life in the throngs of tourists, the repetitive buskers, the smash of the waves. I'm emboldened by it, anonymised in this crowd. Finally able to edge towards the subject we've both been avoiding.

'How about you? You said you were divorcing?'

'I am. I'll have to move out soon but it's a wrench. A total ball-ache. Not leaving her,' he's quick to add. 'Leaving her will be an ecstatic moment for me. I'll feel safe again. I mean leaving the house behind.'

I note his odd choice of words. 'Safe'. I don't comment on it, yet. 'Isn't it half yours?'

'A doctor in training gets paid less than you think. I couldn't afford that place. The house belongs to my wife. Celeste.' He says her name like it's a bitter pill stuck in his mouth. I don't mention that I know who she is. That I've seen her. Followed her.

'I'm stuck there for now. I can't afford to leave, so I'm sticking it out for a short time. I can't rent anywhere decent on my own and I couldn't face a grotty flat-share with strangers nicking my yogurts out of the fridge and leaving their pubic hair in the bath. I've worked hard to have a good life. It's not easy for people like us to get on, is it?'

'Well, you have potential, don't you? It might only be a temporary thing. A few more years and you'll be past being an F2 and be a registrar, then eventually a consultant. You'll be earning a good wage and free, in time, won't you?'

'Maybe, maybe not.' He turns and looks at me.

Scrutinising my face. 'How do you know about medical ranks?'

Another tale of failure: 'I completed my nurse training, but I didn't stick at it for long after I qualified.'

He glances at me, his eyes crinkling with warmth. As if the fact that I was a nurse, however briefly, has increased my standing. My fists clench, waiting for him to start asking difficult questions. He doesn't.

'The problem is, Emma, that I'm trapped at the moment. London does that to you, doesn't it? Leaves you trapped. The only people with any freedom are the rich.'

'But you can't just stay there for somewhere to live. Doesn't she want you to go? Now that you're getting divorced?'

'The opposite. She desperately wants me to stay. Even with us brawling and throwing insults at each other. Sleeping in separate rooms. Me being there is enough for her. It's not pretty at the moment but I'm stuck.' He stands still and takes a deep breath. 'I . . . I'll tell you the grisly details another time. It's not easy for me to talk about.'

I don't push him any further. We're slowly learning about each other's desperation. Appreciating how caged we both are. I know he hasn't told me everything yet but it surprises me that Adam feels confined. That the world isn't his to take. But even seemingly perfect people have problems, I suppose. Misery and hopelessness isn't exclusive to people like me.

We walk further along the Thames. Adam calls Ripley back and clips his lead on. Ripley stands staring, salivating over the food of two women eating lunch on the grass. We reach the London Eye. It's like a Disney version of London. Fake smiles and manufactured atmosphere, a version based on commerce. You can't even use the toilets here unless you have money to spare. Couples are sprawled on the grass of Jubilee Gardens, eating expensive sandwiches from Pret a Manger, ignoring the scaly-footed pigeons that walk between them in endless circles, begging for dropped crumbs. The carousel turns in spite of there only being one bored-looking woman and sticky-faced child on board. A lank-haired busker is butchering a Taylor Swift song.

Adam steers me aside, out of the path of a cyclist, and I spot a man and woman weaving through the crowds, skimming their bodies against the tourists as their hands try to reach for unattended wallets. They're lithe and quick. A contrast to my waning energy. I huddle closer to Adam, and we walk back towards the concrete block of the National Theatre, making it as far as Foyle's bookshop where we stop to look at a window display.

For a moment, the crowds thin and there's no one about. He looks around and then he leans over and kisses me on the mouth, his hand cupping the back of my head. The rush of joy is immediate as I savour the uncontained urgency of his kiss, but it is quickly followed by the familiar wave of self-doubt. The rush of sensations in my stomach feels like nausea.

Why is he here with me when I have so little to offer him? There must be plenty of other women who he could choose to spend time with. I think of all those doctors and nurses who I've met in the past few years with their shiny hair and vibrant health. Women who'd look appropriate next to him. I look at our reflection in the shop window. I'm not ugly but I'm no model. The imbalance is clear.

Adam steps back. 'Was that OK? Did you mind me doing that?'

I nod, trying to ignore my whirring thoughts.

'I . . . I maybe shouldn't have kissed you.' His cheeks fill with blood and he starts scuffing his feet on the ground. 'I don't know what I was thinking.'

I try to make eye contact but he's looking down. 'I wanted you to kiss me.'

'I'm just a bit worried about getting you involved in my mess. What with me still being married at the moment and everything. It's not fair on you.'

I hesitate for a moment before answering. The noise of the South Bank filling the pause. 'I'm trying not to think about it. I do want to be with you, so . . .'

He kisses me again and this time my mind quietens and I give myself over to the sensation.

The heat is escalating. I can feel the sun scorching my face. The imprint of where his lips met mine. Adam rolls up the sleeves of his shirt. There are red welts. Deep, angry marks that travel up his forearm.

'Adam, what have you done to your arm?'

'Just a few scratches from a patient. A woman with dementia who didn't know where she was. It's nothing.' My questions freeze on my lips as he reaches down and takes my hand and puts it to his lips. My chest feels ready to explode.

I recognise the emotion that crossed Adam's face before he lied about the scratches. Adam is full of rage too. When he talks about Celeste his body language changes and he morphs into something else. The clench of his fists. The tension in his muscles. If you study him closely you can detect the faint flashes of darkness beneath his flawless face. It's beautiful.

I know that those scratches weren't from a patient. That they're more likely to be an injury from those long red nails of that hateful woman. He'll tell me what's going on when he's ready. I suspect his life is bleaker than he'd want me to know. And I want to make it better for him.

I like what I see in Adam. People should be angry. People should fight back.

Chapter Nine

The next day, Becky is at work so I make use of her bed and hide out. When I emerge at teatime Ava is engrossed in her project work. I walk over and stroke the back of her head and she lets me. Her long hair obscures half her face. I have an urge to tie it back for her, to show off her beautiful features. I don't, though.

I make my way through to the kitchen, take some carrots from the fridge and start to chop them. Mum smiles at the unexpected help and reaches over to hug me. It takes me by surprise. Her affection is so rare these days. I unintentionally stiffen against her embrace.

I can hear Peter in the background. His voice carries. I turn up the radio to drown out the noise. When he walks into the room he comes up behind Mum. Smothering her with his body, gripping her from behind and pressing himself against her. His pelvis pushes into her back, and she turns her head around and kisses him. I grip the knife.

The usual attack starts over dinner. 'I sometimes think that you belong somewhere. Some kind of institution.'

'Please don't start that, Dad.' Becky looks exhausted

today. Worn away by the soul-destroying job she does and by caring for my daughter.

'Well, fucking look at her.' Peter's eyes are unfocused, his movements too deliberate. It's a sure sign that he's been drinking. 'She's like a cat on hot bricks. Pacing round the house at all hours of the day and night. She should be getting herself right. Not sleeping all the time and coming out with all that crap about fucking birds. It's not *normal* for someone her age. She should be more like you, Becky. Going out, working. Normal stuff.'

He takes a violent gulp of water and slams his glass down.

'What are you doing to help yourself, Emma? Fuck all, that's what. You need to get some exercise. Eat better. How do you think you're going to get well? I'm not asking you to enter the fucking Paralympics. Just to make an effort.'

I feel my muscles tense. 'Fine. But I want my room back, for a start. And you off my back. Maybe that's what would help me "make an effort". I need space to rest properly.'

'Rest? You've spent how many years resting? It's not exactly working, is it? You're still a lump of useless flesh, leeching off the rest of us. Tell you what. Get yourself a job and then you can have your own room. In the meantime, it's my office. I'm running a business that keeps this family afloat. Don't forget that.' He loads mashed potato onto his fork and wedges it into his mouth. He hasn't swallowed it all before he continues.

'If you beg him, then maybe old Tommy boy would have you back? Have you still got his number?'

'Don't talk about my life. You know nothing.' We lock eyes.

Ava's stare bores into Peter. She pushes her chair back and walks over to the sofa, where she picks up a book. Her chair scrapes on the floor as she sits back down, eating with one hand and flicking the pages of the book with the other. My chest constricts and I look at Peter to see what his reaction will be. Ready to leap to Ava's defence. He can attack me all he wants, but if he crosses the line with Ava then I'll attack back. I'm waiting for it to happen.

'What the fuck do you think you're doing? Did you ask permission to leave the table?' I didn't think Peter's face could get any redder but it has. I'm about to run to Ava's side but Mum intervenes first.

'Can we not just have a normal meal for once? I'm so fucking sick of you two arguing. Stop it, both of you.' She slams her cutlery down on the table. 'Put the book down, Ava. Have some bloody manners. Now. Shall we all just carry on eating? Like a normal family.'

Mum peers over at Ava's book. 'What's that, Ava? Is it for your project?'

Typical Mum: pretending that this is all normal again. Her usual ploy. Like we're in some TV advert enjoying oven chips together. Not this dysfunctional tumour of people.

Ava looks as startled as if Mum's asked her to recite a poem during a car crash. She answers anyway. Her voice is strong and defiant. 'No, I'm just reading it because I want to.'

Peter continues stuffing food into his mouth. Becky gives me a half-smile and mouths 'Sorry.' I shake my head. It's not her fault.

Ava finishes her meal and picks the book up again.

'Are you thick? What have you just been told? Put the book down now.' Peter snatches the book from her hand and throws it to the floor.

Ava's chair falls to the floor with a crash and she runs from the room. I hear her crying as she runs up the stairs.

I don't even bother to speak. I rush out of the room and follow her.

I hear Peter behind me as I'm dashing up the stairs. His hand circles my ankle and I fall forwards, my wrists jarring.

'If you talk to me like that again then you'll be sorry. I'll pull you right down these stairs next time.' He gives a tug on my leg and it's all that I can do to maintain my grip on the step. The nylon carpet burning my palms. 'Remember who's in charge here, you stupid little bitch. All right?'

'Let go of me!'

'Scream for help if you like. I'm faster and tougher than you. Do you think anyone would be surprised if a cripple like you fell down the stairs? Do you think they'd even care? Go on, fuck off out of my way.'

I feel his hand relax and release my leg, but the stain of his touch remains. I walk back up the bedroom. I don't look around but he's still there. Standing at the bottom of the staircase with his hands on his hips, his eyes ripping into me.

* * *

When I've calmed Ava, I make my escape from the house, leaving her with Becky. She's safe. I've managed to hide how rattled I feel from Ava but I need to get out now, before I explode. I walk for a while, till my left foot is burning too much to go any further. Turning into the main road, my father's shop confronts me. It's still vacant, shuttered up and unused. The sign still reads, 'Tim Miller: Clock Repairs and Sales'. I turn my face away from the litter-choked doorway and the dusty window.

Adam is walking towards me. He's wearing a pair of top-of-the-range headphones. I'm almost upon him before he sees me. He instinctively knows that something is wrong.

He takes my hand and leads me to a side street, pulling me into an alleyway that leads to a Thirties mansion block. He wraps me in his arms and holds me and I eventually stop trembling. I tell him about Peter. About the hatred and threat of violence. I show him my red palms, kissed with carpet grazes.

'Fuck it, Emma. You don't deserve this.' He takes my hand and looks at the specks of blood coming through my skin. 'Something should be done about that bastard.' I agree with him.

The scratches on his arm still look angry, the skin puckered around them. A reminder of our mutual distress. I run my finger along the skin by the side of them.

'*We* don't deserve this. These people shouldn't be allowed to treat us this way.'

* * *

As I lie on the settee, long after midnight, restless and uncomfortable, my fantasies darken. I list possibilities in order of how feasible they are, feverish scrawls in my notebook. When you're ill you really have to plan ahead, or things don't work out.

The abstract thoughts of violence gather, solidify and become tangible. No longer just Peter tumbling against the wall and smacking his skull against plaster. Now the visions are of my hands propelling his repugnant flesh, causing him to stumble and fall. My hands pushing him from the top of a flight of stairs and watching him crumple into a broken heap at the bottom. My hands holding the knife that slices across his throat.

Only it isn't just Peter's throat that I see. I see Celeste. The two now interchangeable.

71

Chapter Ten

A few days later Adam picks me up from the main road again and we drive to Dulwich Park. Dulwich Village is a compound for the rich. Immense properties, shops that sell overpriced organic produce and baby clothes that are destined to be expensive receptacles for food stains.

I sit in the car, my eyes straying to the glove compartment. Wondering what evidence of his wife might be in there. A pair of gloves, designer sunglasses, a bottle of perfume, perhaps. I keep my hands in my lap to prevent me carrying out my desire to rip open the compartment and throw anything of hers onto the pavement.

* * *

The grass is dry and rough under our feet as we walk to the lake. The sun is becoming uncomfortable and harsh. We walk in silence until he asks me if I want to talk about the time when I was a nurse. I'm surprised he's asked but find that I do want to unload. I see him looking at my face as I talk, and I remember what it's like to feel attractive again.

'After I left school I looked after Ava, with Mum helping, which I loved doing – and then I worked in the care home with Mum and Becky. Doing my nurse training seemed the logical next step.' The afternoon is hefty with heat. I'm nauseated again but I remind myself that this doesn't mean that I'll actually be sick. I just have to breathe through it.

'And did you like it?' He sounds like an elderly uncle at Christmas, asking after my wellbeing. I suppress a nervous laugh.

'Not entirely. It was like a series of jolts. Every day a new shock of some sort. Seeing people in pain, dying even. People shouting at me. Even stupid things like the hospital smells. Everything had this taint of sweat and bodily fluids.' I recall the awkwardness that I felt, hovering on wards in a shantytown of a hospital in South East London. Wearing a scratchy uniform that made me feel like I was a child who was dressing up in adult clothes. The certainty that I'd be rumbled at any moment, always feeling like an imposter. The worst of it was the realisation. The shock that bodies falter and malfunction to such levels.

I wonder if I would have looked at those people and their decimated lives differently, had I known that my own life would soon echo theirs?

'It wasn't all bad. There was joy to be found in it, like there is in most things. Some of the patients were pretty vile, but some of them weren't.' I shoot him a smirk. 'Same goes for the staff.'

Now it's Adam who laughs. 'I've met people like that and I try not to be them.'

'Oh, I can't imagine you would be like that.'

'But you graduated, though?' Adam squeezes my hand and points to a vacant bench by the lake. Two swans are chasing a duck across the water, hisses filling the air. Wings

73

churning the water. The park feels like an expanse of nothing around us, one of the wide-open spaces that pepper London.

'I did and then I went to work on an elderly care ward.'

'Tough speciality.' He pulls me into him and I lean against his side. I'm glad that I don't have to look at him for the next part.

'I was enjoying it. Finding my feet. But then it all changed.'

'What went wrong?' he asks.

'Well, there was this older woman, who I liked. She was recovering from a heart attack. And something awful happened.'

It started innocuously enough on a drizzly Monday morning. I was in the ward sister's office, asking if I could swap a shift, and a bird hit the window. There was a hideous bang on the pane of glass and we both started, her coffee slopping onto the desk. A greasy-greyish stain remained on the glass.

It was a usual shift. Racing up and down the ward with drug trolleys and armfuls of clean sheets. Towards lunchtime I was accompanying the doctors on the ward round, recounting observations, outlining progress. They'd left one woman till the end of the round, passing over her room deliberately, to return later. I remember that her name was Ann, like my mum, and I'd thought to myself just how unalike they were.

She had this dressing gown that I liked. It was patterned with tiny swallows, flying over a navy-blue fabric. She'd seen me running my fingers down the material and smiled when she told me the story of how she'd bought it in Thailand, alluding to her life before illness had sucked her under. Of travel, study and the man who she'd been desperately in love with for a time.

74

In the rare spare minutes I had during shifts I'd pop into her room and we'd talk. I fell into a routine of going to sit with her for half an hour or so at the end of my shift. Like all patients, she had a previous life – hers had been as a lecturer in zoology at a London university. She appreciated the company and I enjoyed her knowledge and offbeat energy.

The consultant sat on her bed, which was a cardinal sin but none of us commented. He gently told her that her lungs had now failed to such a degree that this was as well as they could make her. The pills that were helping were also destroying her kidneys. Her new baseline was to be dependent on paid carers and barely able to walk a few steps unaided. To always be breathless, fighting to oxygenate herself.

She looked at the doctors apologetically, as if she was some terrible burden to them. 'So how long have I got?' She scanned all of our faces, resting finally on mine.

She was told by the doctor that it was likely to be a few months at best, a few weeks at worst and she nodded sagely, not bothering to hide the moistening of her eyes. I was pathetically glad of the tear rolling down her cheek so I could grab a tissue and at least do something to help. We all left the room, me grasping her hand and promising to return in five minutes and talk. Nursing is never predictable and I ended up stuck with an insufferable man who was having a meltdown about the quality of his lunch.

It was about thirty minutes before I went back. She wasn't in the room and the door to her toilet was closed. So, I knocked gently, then harder but there was no response. So, I just kind of pushed at the door but it wouldn't give. I pushed again and that's when I saw her. She'd hanged herself, from a hook on the back of the door, with the cord of that dressing gown. Her eyes were wide open and her face was swollen. This weird colour, like rain clouds. The whole scene a reproach to my failure to return.

The nurses on the ward were less than kind. They were all older; hardened by years of dealing with tragedy. I was getting changed when I overheard one of them muttering to another, saying, 'Have you seen the state she's in?' Commenting on nurse–patient relationships crossed the boundaries. One of the nurses was a harassed-looking part-timer, who was kinder, taking me into the sister's office for a coffee. Resting a hand on my arm. She listened to me as I rocked in the chair, clutching my knees to my chest, repeatedly blaming myself. I was walking out of the room when she said, 'But why didn't you go back, when you knew she needed you?' I didn't answer.

'I never returned,' I tell Adam. 'I was asked to come in to the hospital to talk to someone. I didn't go at first. Mum and Becky tried to talk to me about it but I just lay in bed, my face to the wall. I think that I stayed in bed for a week but it could have been longer. I kept hearing Peter shouting in the background: "When is she going to get up? This isn't normal." That kind of stuff. Being normal is one of his obsessions.'

'Seriously? What is wrong with that man?' Adam spits this comment out and I appreciate his anger on my behalf.

I didn't hear anything from any of the other nurses on the ward. The only messages were from Jasminder. She'd been my closest friend throughout college. We'd been inseparable, hanging out together in her chaotic but loving family home off the South Circular. But I couldn't think what to say in response.

'I'd lie there with Sparrow beside me and hear Mum, Peter and Becky in the kitchen, talking, and laughing. Like they were in another universe from me. Ava came and sat with me but I told her to go and play. I didn't want to infect her with my misery.'

'You needed someone to help you through it. Your family should have been more supportive. As should the hospital.' Adam holds on to my hand, the warmth of his palm passing into mine.

I don't tell Adam the final part. It feels too ethereal. I was lying in bed one day and I'd just been staring, staring without seeing anything, my vision not so much blurred as blank. My gaze fixed on the bookcase full of my childhood books. One of them caught my eye. There was no spiritual element to it. I don't believe it was a message from Daddy. Nothing as silly as that. I spotted an old book called *Owl Moon*. I stared at it for a few hours and finally got up and hugged it to my chest for a while, eventually opening the pages.

It's about a little girl and her father who go owl watching at night. She's cold and afraid but eventually they see an owl and she's energised by the experience. Her father tells her that to go 'owling' all you need is hope. Just hope. I think I reread that book thirty or forty times over the next few days, finally giving in to waves of weeping.

I'll tell Adam this part later. We have plenty of time. I know that he'll listen when I'm ready. That he'll understand. That he won't make facile remarks.

I resumed life, of course, and Becky came with me to the inquest where I had to give evidence. Mum was busy at work. I'd expected it to be a wood-panelled courtroom like something on TV but it wasn't. Just a drab, corporate little place, like a hotel function room. People glanced at Becky, like they always did, like she was some rarefied being. That always happened. The coroner was gentle with me and I managed not to cry and not to look across at the woman's daughters who sat, dabbing at their eyes, looking like younger versions of her.

I took up the counselling that they'd offered me in the end and it helped. I found a job in a bookshop in Lewisham. Rubbish pay but it was calm. The biggest emergency was if a delivery was late and we couldn't put the latest bestseller on the shelves quickly enough.

But in time they grew tired of me. People do. I was also starting to get ill for the first time. The creeping numbness and vacant episodes had begun and their tolerance for sickness and disability, whilst good on paper and in HR policies, didn't translate to reality. Understandable when I was absent so frequently. They'll only pay you for so long when you keep failing to turn up for work. Once my illness peaked I was more of a decorative addition to a rota than a functional employee. It didn't take long before the manager took me into her office and said they'd have to let me go. I didn't blame her. But it's such a strange turn of phrase, as if they were restraining me and were finally setting me free.

I wasn't set free at all. I was consigned to being on benefits. Endless form-filling, each box feeling designed to trip me up. Not exaggerating my situation but making sure I was obviously sick enough for them to understand that I was unfit for work. Then an assessment with a man with a clenched jaw and ineptly shaved beard who made me stutter with anxiety. Months of no money coming in and then I was finally rewarded with a pitiful state disability income, half of which I have to give up to Peter, for my 'expenses'.

Now Adam knows. Enough for him to understand why I'm not a nurse anymore, at least. Why I won't ever be one again, regardless of my health.

He holds my face between his hands and kisses my eyelids, then my lips and I feel renewed.

'Were your family understanding?'

'Mum and Becky were but Peter viewed it as a personal failing on my part. It gave him a whole new repertoire of insults to throw at me. Snide remarks to make.'

'What a fucker.' He squeezes my arm. 'You did nothing wrong, but you know that, don't you? It sounds like you would have been a great nurse.'

'It's not just the fact that she died, though, Adam. She was dying anyway. It's that she had to do it on her own, in a bathroom. I should have been there for her, and I wasn't.'

* * *

As we go to leave I notice that the swans have stepped out of the water onto the bank. A couple are posing with a toddler between them, to take a photograph. The swans look ready to strike.

Chapter Eleven

We walk back towards the edge of the lake. The swans are flapping their wings now. A violent combination of water and feathers drowning out ambient noise. Adam takes my hand.

'You look tired. Let's go back.' He pulls back the roof and we ease ourselves into the car. The leather of the seat is hot against my back.

We have no choice but to sit in silence as he drives. Impossible to speak in this open-top car with the air beating our faces. Each time we stop in traffic, I see people look across at Adam and stare at his striking profile. He remains oblivious. As we near my street he takes the wrong turn. A finger of alarm prods my stomach as we veer the wrong way, up the hill towards Blackheath. He steers us past the shops and restaurants, parks the car on the edge of the common and turns to me.

'I was thinking about things whilst I was driving. I wanted to talk more. I hope that's OK.' I nod my assent. He turns in his seat to face me full on. 'Emma, I don't mean to pry . . . but are you safe at home? Has Peter hurt you again?'

'I'm safe.'

'It's just that the things that you've said worry me.'

I feel his muscles contract and he goes to speak but stops himself. Pausing and staring back towards the vast expanse of grass that makes up the common. Two men with a greyhound walk by, nodding to us as they pass. A quarrel of sparrows fly up from one of the gorse bushes, startled by the dog. The sight of them makes me smile. Their numbers have declined in recent decades, causing concern for their survival. But they're resurging, growing stronger.

I take a breath and force the words out that I've been holding in. 'I'm coping. It's OK. But can I ask a question too? Why do you use a burner phone? I saw it when you dropped it in the cemetery.'

There's a pause. The only sound is me swallowing.

'It's ironic really. My wife's the one who cheats repeatedly but she's paranoid that I'm being unfaithful. She checks my phone.'

'Right. I'm guessing that I'm not the first, then? If you already had the phone to make secret calls.'

'No, Emma – that's not true. There hasn't been anyone else. I got the other phone a while back to message friends without all the interrogations. I had a text one time from a friend called Sam. She spotted the name when I was typing and demanded to know if Sam was a man or a woman. It was constant.' I don't look at him. Knowing if someone is lying takes thought. You need to tune in to their tones and patterns of speech. I listen hard.

'So, tell me about your marriage. I should have asked this before. It's not fair that I don't know. Not when . . . not when we've kissed.'

'OK. I should have talked about it more. I'm sorry. She's fifteen years older than me but it didn't seem to matter when we got married. It was all so quick. Romantic seeming.'

'A whirlwind thing?'

'You could call it that. We were married within six months of meeting. Big fancy wedding at this country estate that one of her friend's families owned. Magazine spread. Then moving in to that big house. It was like a weird dream. Something that a twenty-one-year-old boy from a North London council estate could have only dreamed of. I mean, I was definitely in love with her.' My stomach lurches with envy.

'But I was also in love with the lifestyle.' He looks down at his lap, his face turning towards me, like a child who wants to admit that he's broken a vase or eaten something that he wasn't meant to. 'Now I just fantasise about being free.'

'How long were you happy for? With Celeste, I mean.' I glance at myself in the wing mirror. I'm hunched up on the car seat like a roosting bird. Adam is sitting with his thighs apart, leaning back in his seat.

'Things aren't always linear in life. I'm sure you know that. It was gradual. She started getting meaner, harder. An insidious thing. Constantly criticising me. Imbalances aren't good in relationships, whether it's age or experience. And the most destructive thing for a couple is money.'

He turns to face me fully. 'Then Celeste had her first affair. When I was younger, I always said to myself that if a partner was unfaithful then that'd be it. It'd have to be the end. It was just something I couldn't imagine tolerating. But I did put up with it. It hurt but I did it. Then it happened again, and I tolerated it again and it still hurt – but less each time.' He reaches over and touches my hand.

'I think I'd have had to end it after the first time.'

'You say that – but then it happens, and you just get on with life. I also said that if someone ever hit me then that would be it. There's never a place for violence in a relationship. If someone does that then there's something rotten in them. But then she did and I just got on with it, each time. I never go. Pathetic, isn't it? I'd rather be cheated on and slapped around than have to support myself.' He lifts his hand up and holds it to his cheek, as if he's remembering an old injury.

'Is that how you really got the scratches on your arm?' I feel my muscles tense, as if ready to fight off an attacker.

He doesn't answer. He stares across at Blackheath Common, his eyes unfocused. He drops his head down and closes his eyes. I sit back, giving him space. I want to help him but I'm not sure how. I've spent so long now feeling helpless and trapped. I'm barely managing to scratch a life for myself.

What I can do, though, is try to understand and listen. I sense him looking up again. I slide closer to him and reach my hand to his cheek. He leans in and buries his face in my shoulder and I feel him crying. I put my arm around him and my lips graze the top of his head. He stops and we sit like that for a while.

'Can I give you this? It'll make things safer for you.' He passes me a burner phone.

'Safer?'

'If Celeste found my phone, then I don't want her having your real number and finding you. This will be better. Just until all this is sorted.' He swallows hard. 'I'm so sorry that you're being dragged into this. I wish I'd met you in a few months' time.' I reach across and squeeze his hand.

Adam opens the door and steps out onto the grass, facing the church in the distance. His hands on his hips like he's posing for a catalogue photo. A woman with a toddler passes by, smiling at Adam but ignoring me. I stand beside him, the warm wind blowing across the common tugging at my clothes.

'Wouldn't life just be better if we didn't have to put up with these people? If I didn't have a bitch of a wife and you didn't have that moron of a stepfather?' His tone is tentative.

'I agree. But I don't think that Peter's going anywhere anytime soon.' I know I shouldn't tell him what I say next, but I do anyway. 'Sometimes I have these dark thoughts. I shouldn't admit to them, really.'

'No. You can tell me, Emma. We all have dark thoughts.' His hand rests on mine and he looks directly at me.

'I think about Peter being dead.'

'I think that's understandable.' He doesn't seem alarmed by what I've said.

'No, it's not just that. I think about killing him. I think about it a lot.'

A couple walk by, in the throes of a heated argument. She gets into the car and slams the door whilst he stays at the side of the car, lighting a cigarette, scowling into space.

He pauses for a second. As if debating whether to say what he's thinking. 'Well, if that's an abnormal thing then I don't think I'm normal either. I mean – whatever normal is. I think about it too. I imagine Celeste dead.'

He leans in nearer to me, his voice hushed. 'Did you ever see that old black and white film where two men meet up by chance and they both need people in their lives removed?' His eyes shine in the sunlight.

'Removed? I don't think I've seen that film. Sorry.'

He continues. 'They meet on a train and when they start to talk, they realise that they both have something that they can offer each other. One of them needs his bully of a father to die and the other wants his unfaithful wife dead. So they . . . they decide to swap murders. Neither of them will be suspected of the murder they do commit, because they don't have a motive for it. And they both have cast-iron alibis. The perfect murders.'

I like his choice of words. Like the death of a bullying parent or a tyrannical wife is a necessity rather than a desire. Adam understands.

'You mean like they become assassins for each other? I love that. Can we watch it sometime?'

'We'll do it. I can find it online.'

'The thing is, Adam, that's just fantasy, isn't it? No one would do those things in real life.' I test him out.

'God, no. Of course not. I'm not about to commit murder. Nor would I expect anyone to do that for me. It's twisted. But sometimes the brain finds escape routes, doesn't it? However dark. It's a coping mechanism.'

* * *

When everyone has gone to bed I indulge my thoughts. I lie on the settee and I think about being rid of Peter. I stay awake, my body tight and contorted, running through the catalogue of cruel remarks and intended sleights. Thinking about how much lighter life for the rest of us would be without his unwelcome presence.

I think about Celeste too. How much she's hurting Adam. Only, I don't wish a painless, merciful death on either Peter or Celeste. My fantasies are soaked in blood.

Chapter Twelve

I've been trusted to look after Ava for a few hours. It only happens when it suits Mum. When there's a gap in childcare my illness becomes conveniently irrelevant. Before we left Mum gave Ava a talking-to about what to do if I collapse. As if Ava is five, not eleven.

We're low on food and I'm having a better day so we've walked to the supermarket. Like we're a normal mother and daughter.

'Watch out.'

Ava's reading the back of cereal boxes with such rapt concentration that she almost steps back into a woman who's passing by with a trolley.

'You always get this one, don't you?' I point at the usual cereal box and smile at her.

She looks back at me. 'I was trying to find one that's healthier. I was reading about how eating sugar is like smoking now.'

She picks up another box and steps backwards again, this time bumping directly into another passing woman, knocking a loaf of fresh bread from her basket onto the floor.

'Be careful!' The shocked reproach is from a voice that I recognise from online. I look back towards the voice. It's Celeste. She's iridescent, clad in an old-fashioned dress in pale yellow. That idiotic wicker basket hooked over her elbow.

As if my circling thoughts have been made flesh.

Ava grabs the loaf from the floor and hands it to her. 'I'm sorry.'

I'm already about three metres further down the aisle. I step forward to rush to Ava's side. To tell this ridiculous woman to stop being so reactionary. That Ava's a child and it was an accident. But my leg freezes. My limbs are heavy and tired from the walk here. This treacherous left leg numb in places, a lifeless dead thing. My illness reminding me again of how limited my parenting skills are.

Celeste barely looks at Ava, just snatches the bread from her and paces towards the checkout. As she walks her phone rings and she scrabbles at her bag.

'Mummy, are you OK? Do you know that lady? She looks rich.' Ava is looking at me as I stand in the middle of the aisle, staring after Celeste. 'Why are posh people so rude?'

I try to think what bird Celeste would be but I come up with nothing. She's too chic and glamorous. Female birds are generally the drab ones of their species. Celeste isn't like a bird at all. She's more feline than avian.

* * *

When I get home, I look Celeste up online again. I need something solid to channel my hatred into. Sometimes resentment needs feeding. There are articles about her restaurant in the City of London. Probably filled with braying bankers and their put-upon wives or rented companions.

There's stuff about how she decided to launch a cookbook of her favourite anglicised versions of Northern French cuisine. There's a couple of photos from book launches, a few stills from those TV cookery shows.

I find a new photograph from last week of her and Adam. It's from the society events page of a lifestyle magazine. A shot of them both at an event in Bloomsbury, on a night when Adam told me he was working in the ED. She's dressed in a high-necked, emerald-green dress. She's laughing, her head thrown back slightly. A familiar hand is resting against her waist as he leans in to her, his face pressed to hers as he plants a kiss on her cheek. His face is joyful and light. His eye is seeking out the camera. They look perfect together – happy and in love.

I close the screen down.

He was always too good to be true. He told me that he hates her. This is not a depiction of hatred as I know it. He lied. Whatever game he's playing – it isn't one I'm going to be part of.

* * *

There's nowhere for me to hide in the house. Peter is watching football again and Ava is playing on Becky's phone in their room. Peter takes advantage of the fact that we're alone together.

'Are you going to help your mum? You could make the dinner instead of mooning about the house like some fucking ghost. She's been busting a gut at work whilst you've been doing fuck all.' I ignore him and walk to the fridge and get myself a drink of juice. 'Oh, so you can eat and drink the things I buy but you can't be bothered to even talk to me. You're one fucking piece of work, you really are. The fruit doesn't fall far from the tree, either. That daughter of yours has a chip on her shoulder too.'

'I don't care what you think.' I resent this role that he's pushed me into. That I'm a sulky teenager at my age, venting my rage at the 'grown-ups'. 'And don't talk about my daughter. I'm watching you, so don't start on her.'

Peter continues shouting after me as I walk out. I go and sit in the garden and send a WhatsApp to Adam with the link to the picture of him and Celeste. A robin sits on the arm of the bench, and I flap him away, hissing at him.

I loathe robins. They're not the cosy little birds that you might think that they are. Some people believe that they're a representation of the dead, coming back to comfort us. I don't believe that. The dead are gone. But robins are vicious bullies, attacking other birds, hating their own species. They're solitary creatures and if they see another robin, they'll try to kill them. They're skilled murderers. Pure malice. They go straight for the neck, severing the spinal column, slaughtering their rivals.

Chapter Thirteen

Mum wakes me at nine. I'd gone back to sleep after Peter left for work and Ava was dispatched to summer school. Apart from Ava, they've all stopped trying to be quiet around my sleeping form now. Disturbing my torturous dreams with laughing and shouting. Peter, making snide remarks about what the point of me is. I think again about ways I could kill him. About the press of my hand as I rush at him and knock him from the kerbside. The smack of a lorry as it reduces him to pulp. The thoughts distract me from thinking about Adam and Celeste. But not for long. The weight in my stomach remains. He answered my message saying he could explain. But isn't that what cheating married men always say? He messaged again and I deleted them unread. My finger jabbing at the screen.

Last night I sat, hunched into a ball till midnight, numb, waiting for Peter to vacate the sofa when he tired of watching reality TV shows about repairing old cars. He eventually stumbled out of the room, leaving a mess of empty beer bottles and Pringles crumbs around the chair. I dragged myself to the sink with the bottles and picked up as many of the crumbs as I could manage to, steadying myself against the chair with my stronger hand. I eventually slept at around three, my muscles tired and aching, the phantom sensations creeping over my lower legs. Spidery fingers brushing my face. Bugs crawling along my limbs.

'Come on, Emma. You said you'd help me with my new outfit, remember?' She doesn't need my help. Becky would be a better choice of companion when it comes to choosing clothes. There were endless attempts to find ways to rehabilitate me when I first became unwell. The cajoling and the demands that verged on bullying have stopped. There's still the odd day when she tries to pretend that life remains normal but it's thankfully rare. I'm the flaw in the home that can't be fixed by ringing the council. The unpalatable reminder that we're all likely to wither away and become dysfunctional one day.

I reluctantly dress, slicking my hair down with water and spraying myself with some of Becky's perfume, slipping into my usual black clothes. My face glares back at me. I widen my eyes, try and fail to smile, before giving up.

The bus transports us from our rows of Edwardian houses into the grime of the main road. We pass barbers' shops with men smoking outside, grimy cafés with tired counter staff and random shops that look like no one ever enters them. The common theme is a pervasive grey dust from the road that clings to the buildings. The market is loaded with plastic bowls full of cheap fruit and vegetables, destined to rot within days once bought. The smell of the fish stall slaps a wave of nausea into my guts.

'Do you need to sit down? You look pale.' We stop in the middle of the pavement and people weave around us. Mum sighs and ushers me to the side of the street and I lean for a moment against the glass of a window. A shoeless woman with dirt-rimmed feet is sitting on the pavement to my left.

She looks up at me and then nods at Mum. Mum pretends she can't see her.

'I'm OK.' She offers the crook of her elbow and I take it, her skin sticky in the burgeoning heat of the morning.

I find a stool to sit on at the end of the shoe section whilst she flits around between aisles in TK Maxx. People walk past, either trying not to look at me or trying not to be seen to be trying not to be looking at me. I sit here like a sickly art installation, leaning forward and resting my head on my hands, zoning out from the noise around me. There's a choice to be made here. Try to look well. Sit up. Smile and keep my eyes focused, ignoring the zoning in and out of my brain. Or I can give in to this and embrace my shame, look like what I am. The poor little sick girl.

I'm engrossed in thoughts about Adam and Celeste when a thin man in a worn suit sidles across to me. His fingers and teeth are stained by tar from a million cigarettes even though he's probably only in his thirties.

'All right, love? You want a hand up?' I ignore him but he's persistent. His hand reaches down as if to assist me, purposely skimming my breast through my T-shirt. I recoil, slapping his hand away and letting out a shout. An elderly woman looks across and then quickly looks away.

'You can't help some people these days, can you?' He hisses the words, his face an inch from mine before he retreats. I curl into myself more, closing my eyes, imagining I'm somewhere else.

I feel a hand touch my shoulder and I jolt upright on the stool, ready to fight him off again.

'Emma. Bloody hell. I can't believe it.' I sit up and the air rushes around my face like the slap of a hot hand. Jasminder is standing there, a baby in a papoose on her chest. 'Is it OK to talk to you?'

'Jasminder. Hi.' That's all I can manage. My words are seized up.

Jasminder is one of the softest, most benign people who I've ever met. Her optimism is boundless. She gravitated to me during our nurse training even though we're nothing alike. We worked together. My reality checks keeping her grounded and her joie de vivre buoying me along.

I understand her tentative stance today. I'm the one who hasn't answered any of her WhatsApp messages. I ignored the steady stream that came at first when I was taken ill, relieved when they petered out. I didn't want a reminder of the old me.

'I've missed you, Emma. I thought maybe I'd done something wrong. I was anxious that—'

'You didn't do anything wrong. I was just ill. I've been . . . I am really ill . . . I kind of hid away.' I see her eyes flick down to my arm, lying useless by my side and the way my leg is twisted. She quickly looks away again.

'Shit. I'm sorry to hear that. You look different. I mean – it's the hair. It looks great.' Typical Jasminder to find a positive spin on my withered state. I catch a glimpse of myself in the shop mirror. Jasminder isn't telling the truth. I look worn and fragile, my skin ashy and translucent.

'My mum and dad will be so pleased that I've seen you. They still ask about you.'

I smile in spite of myself. Her parents were always accommodating. They lived in a chaotic house just north of the South Circular, where everyone laughed a lot. Her mum used to have this running joke that I should marry one of Jasminder's feckless brothers. Become her new daughter. There were moments when I was tempted.

'Oh look!' Mum appears, grappling Jasminder into an awkward hug, almost squashing the baby. She stands back, cooing over him. 'I always knew you'd be a great mum one day. Some women are just suited to it.'

Mum shoots a look my way and I know that her comment to Jasminder is a reproach aimed at me. How easily she's forgotten those early years when I was well and I doted on Ava.

It's only when the baby starts to wail – a thin, piercing noise – that Jasminder rushes away to change him. As she leaves I see it: the tiny flash of pity in her eyes. It always happens. And if it's not pity from people it's a strained empathy, effortful and laboured. Or worst of all, a vague sense of disgust, contempt sometimes. She leaves in a hail of shouted pleas across the aisles that I must message her, that we absolutely have to meet up. I won't.

*   *   *

The café is crowded and humid. Mum helps me into a plastic bucket seat and weaves through to fetch me a latte.

'Here you go! A little treat for helping me do the shopping.' Mum places a coffee and a dried-up Danish pastry in front of me. She stares at me for a moment. 'What's wrong with you now?'

'I'm tired. I'm just so tired of it all, Mum.'

'Well what do you want me to do?' Her tone doesn't imply helpfulness. More exasperation.

I take a piece of the pastry and swallow it down with effort.

'I mean Peter. I'm tired of Peter. The way he treats me. And you *can* help me. You just choose not to. You could tell him to give me my bedroom back. Let me have somewhere to actually rest.' My throat constricts and I feel my heartbeat in my chest as I wait for her reply. Hoping that for once she'll see how much I need her.

'Emma, can we not just have a normal day out? I just wanted to come and buy clothes like a normal mum and daughter. You know that Pete needs somewhere to work from. His business isn't doing as well as it ought to and he can't afford office rental.' Mum carries on eating, unperturbed. Subject closed.

I bang my coffee cup down on the table. 'So, as usual you've decided to choose that revolting man over me – your daughter. Like you have since the moment you met him. Like you have all the times when you stand by and watch him bully and attack me. It's cruel. He's cruel and the rest of you are cruel too, for just standing by.'

She doesn't look up, just carries on eating, until the plate is cleared, her eyes fixed on the sticky table.

'He'll hurt me one day. He looks at me like he wants to punch me in the face. And there's no one. No one who'll help me.'

A tired-looking waitress starts clearing the table, a damp cloth in one hand. Mum looks at her and her face colours. What other people think of us has always been Mum's primary concern.

'Emma! He does not. He cares about you. I know he doesn't always show it but he's trying. Things aren't easy for him either. We're all doing our best for you, you know? Me and Becky are busting a gut helping with Ava till you get better and Pete is paying the bills—'

'But that's it – I won't get better. That's not an option. I'm trapped here with you all and this amazing man who pays the bills for you. Stuck in this fucking place with all this nothing. It's all just nothing. Less than nothing.'

I ease myself out from the chair, my thighs damp with

sweat from the heat and the plastic. As I walk towards the door I hear my mother apologising to the waitress for the swearing from her 'rude' daughter, telling her that she's tried with me but that I don't want to be helped. The waitress makes sympathetic sounds.

Mum doesn't follow me as I limp past the watching crowd of customers, orphaned by her indifference.

* * *

I'm blinded by rage as I push my way up the high street, my leg dragging behind me. An elderly woman clocks me and eases herself up when I get on the bus, waving me into the disabled seat. I flop back, my eyes drooping with fatigue. It's like a toxin that seeps through my body, running me down and leaving me as flaccid as a deflated balloon.

I don't go home. Peter is there today, working from his office – my bedroom. I can't stand to see his face. The weight of each slight, each act of aggression is in me like muscle memory. Years of minor insults about every aspect of my persona, my clothes, my looks. The relentless regime of petty rows, of escalating acts designed to make me uncomfortable. Of him erasing every trace of my father. The barely concealed hatred. The prospect of sitting, knowing that he'll be in and out of the room to make repetitive mugs of brown tea, is unappealing. Even my violent fantasies won't ease me today.

The park is shady, the chestnut trees with heat-singed leaves providing a canopy. Dog walkers slope by with their tired-looking animals. The birds are quiet. I pull out my phone. There's a WhatsApp message from Jasminder, which I ignore. Three more messages from Adam, which I delete.

What I have decided today is that I'm going to have to step this up. I don't have to rely on people like my mother or Adam. I can be in control. Why shouldn't I be the hero of this story? My illness doesn't mean that I have to be relegated to a supporting role, the background character who dies at the end or fades away.

I can even be the villain if I want to.

Chapter Fourteen

It's been two weeks since I saw the photo. Adam has stopped messaging. I'd been deleting his texts unread. But when I lie awake at night my mind is an echo chamber with just my voice in it. Doubts begin to fester and rot away my certainty. I run through scenarios in my head. I ask my friend from the illness forum what she thinks. Not the one whose husband left her. I know what her answer will be. I go for Charlie, a single woman in Edinburgh who's around my age. She isn't a big help.

'Keep away from him. He sounds like a liar and a cheat. It's enough trying to get through life while ill. He might even have a weird fetish for sick people. How's your leg doing?'

I've changed my route to avoid his house and if I have to, I'll go to a different emergency department in another hospital. I don't want to have to see his face. I do what I always do when I feel like this: sleep.

Becky finds me on her bed. The afternoon has morphed to evening as I slept. She eases off her shoes and curls up next to me on the bed, groaning as she lets herself sink into the mattress.

'What's going on, honey? You seem out of sorts.'

'Nothing. I'm OK.'

'You're not, though. I can see that something's wrong.' She reaches her arm across my chest.

Words start to leak out. I keep it brief. There isn't much to say after all. 'I know it's stupid. He's a married man trying to get laid on the side, isn't he? I've just been duped.'

Becky puffs out a sigh. 'I'm not exactly the one to ask for advice on picking men. I'm the woman whose husband turned out to be gay.'

'Wow, thanks for the wise sisterly support. Maybe we're better single, anyway.' I prod her. My next words sound pathetic. 'I thought there *was* something there.'

'Sometimes there isn't a quick answer. You just have to wait things out.'

'Thanks, Confucius.' I prod her again and she laughs.

She blows a kiss at me as she leaves the room. 'Right, I'm off to fetch your daughter. See you later.'

I ignore her final choice of words. The subtle dig about Ava doesn't rankle today. Family relationships are like fields after war; acres of grass with unexploded bombs to dodge, and the occasional fresh nettle to graze your bare skin.

When I wake up there's another message from Adam. I thought there wouldn't be any more. I hesitate for a moment but decide to read this one.

'*I miss you.*'

I feel a lurch in my stomach and wish I didn't.

* * *

I've watched them both from the bathroom window for a while. My view is limited but I saw that they were both lying back on loungers, not talking, their seats as far apart as they can be on the patio. Him, just in shorts, reading a book, his lotion-greased legs crossed at the ankles, naked torso reflecting the sun. She's just lying back with her eyes closed, face barely visible under a straw hat.

I'm sick of the endless thoughts in my head, evolving like erratic flight patterns. Twisting round and round like a murmuration of starlings. Solidity giving way when I examine it and becoming something more fragile.

It's not just my emotions about Adam. I can put feelings aside, with effort. I've learned to school myself in lowering my expectations. It's also about what Adam represents. He could be an escape route for me and Ava. But the question is whether he's a genuine lifeline or just another in one of the hordes of men looking for extramarital sex. There's only one way to gather these random doubts. I need to speak to him but to be detached and analytical. To hear him out but not be beguiled.

I message him that I need to see him. That I'm willing to listen to what he has to say. I watch him look at the phone and smile at the message. This is a test, to see how willing he is to see me. Will he just walk away from his wife and make an excuse to come to me now? Choose me above her? Or will he stay by her side?

He jumps up as soon as he's read the message and walks towards the house. A message comes back telling me to wait in the local park in fifteen minutes.

* * *

The park is quiet. There are few people but it's crowded with pigeons, picking at rice that a woman in a sari is depositing for them in great handfuls. A group of teenagers in a cloud of cannabis smoke that sticks in my throat. Adam looks

100

fresh from the sun, pink-cheeked, in a clean blue shirt. He's put on fresh clothes for me and sprayed himself with that citrus cologne.

'Did you think that I wouldn't find out that you and Celeste aren't estranged? You posed for press photos!'

His face is unreadable as I speak. 'I'm so glad that you messaged me. I've been beside myself. Wondering how I could explain and whether you'd ever believe me. I messaged you but I'm guessing you didn't read them.' I don't respond. 'Do you know what I was doing when you called? Sitting beside Celeste and imagining that it was you. That the house was ours. That *we* owned it.'

I don't tell him yet that this is exactly my fantasy. I hadn't been thinking of that fictitious flat for the three of us anymore. My ambitions were higher. I'd imagined Adam and I lounging on that terrace, drinks in hand, watching the swallows swoop over at sunset. In that house, laughing over board games with Ava, going for walks as a family on my better days. But the photo wrecked all that.

'That photo. It was just a set-up for the cameras, you know? Like an acting job. She'd badgered me all week to go with her. To keep up the pretence of our perfect marriage.' He spits the words. 'Apparently, I'm good PR for her.'

'It looked . . . intimate.' My mouth feels barren and I want to sit, to steady my trembling limbs.

'Emma, I promise you it was anything but. It was just a pose that the photographer asked for, and me playing the part. Like a gigolo. Touching her makes me feel physically sick.' A beat. 'I can't even bring myself to tell you about some of the things that she's done over the years.'

I try to think quickly. I'm wary of being too naïve, too trusting. But then I think about the bruises and scratches on his arms and I know that there's so much that he isn't telling me, yet.

He steers me towards a bench. There's a plaque on the back for someone who died aged thirty. Every year flowers appear on her birthday and at Christmas. Sad bouquets wrapped in plastic that die within a day or two.

'It's just so . . . humiliating.' I can see the rage surging in him again, his posture reacting. He takes a breath and deflates back onto the bench. 'Those things I've attended with her are grim. You've no idea. So many of them over the years. I'm there as window dressing. I'm a brainless decoration to make the photos look good. It's hateful. All those privileged twats with their public-school laughs.'

He pouts and narrows his eyes. Then he switches to a shy smile, followed by a fake laugh with his head raised and slightly thrown back. It's uncanny. 'They're some of the faces I put on when the photographers are shouting at me. I can do more. It's like being an actor again and being back in that phony world.'

I surprise myself by laughing. I make the move this time, reaching across and taking him in my arms. Whispering in his ear: 'You deserve better than Celeste.'

I push it further, thinking about the things that I know she's doing to him. 'She deserves to suffer for what she's doing to you.'

Adam pulls back and looks at me. I hold my breath, waiting to see if he disapproves of what I whispered. His face creases into a smile and then we kiss.

We sit and talk until the sky darkens. Adam is real. I didn't imagine how he feels. We're going to find a way to be together.

Chapter Fifteen

The following day is sweat-rimed and filled with malaise. Adam isn't free until the evening, and I wait, impatiently. The remnants of the day's warmth rise from the pavements. The drying leaves rustle as I walk around the corner to see him.

I blanch when he invites me to see inside the house. Their house. Hers. Territory matters and this isn't my space.

It's almost night and the swallows are circling, diminishing in number as autumn is in the air. He answers the door looking flustered, damp-haired. He doesn't turn the light on until I'm in the hall, shielding me from view, hiding me from prurient neighbours.

The hallway is wide, Minton-tiled and painted in some shade of grey that's bound to have a preposterous name. Wherever I turn, reflections of him tempt me. I long for his touch, a hand on my breast, the casual meeting of mouths. My skin feels alive.

He kisses me quickly and waves me through to the kitchen, bouncing up the stairs to fetch a jumper. Shouting a flustered apology over his shoulder, for not being quite ready.

I walk through a panelled door and the kitchen stretches out in front of me. The footprint of our entire house would fit in this one room. It's clean enough to perform surgery here. I suspect that Celeste will have cleaners, of course. The temple-like atmosphere is only broken by the low murmur of Radio Four from an artfully battered Roberts Radio. Ripley doesn't look up from his basket, just carries on sleeping. I walk over and pause for a second before stroking his head. He looks up at me with soft amber eyes ringed with black.

I step gingerly back, like a child. Pools of low light radiate from antique glass pendants. I move towards the seating area. A comfortable couch, a shelf of cookbooks and a few volumes of poetry. A coffee table with carefully arranged books on modern art. I want to lie down on the settee and never have to get up again. There's a bird feeder filled with Nyjer seed, looped over a branch by the window. A goldfinch hops down in a fluster of red and yellow plumage. I stand and watch as a pair of them take it in turns divebombing the feeder.

'You like the house?' Adam appears behind me. He sweeps his arm up, pointing out some of the more obvious features: the marble island, the skylights, the bifold doors.

'I do.' I love it, actually. It sickens me that someone as cruel and entitled as Celeste has all of this when Ava and I have so little. We could be happy here.

I take the glass of wine that he's offered me.

'Shall I put some music on? What do you like?' That hateful question. The moment anyone asks me what music I like, which books, which films, my mind is a blank. As if I have no personal tastes or preferences beyond birds.

'You pick something.' He floods the room with

something ambient and soft. He tidies away the art books, slipping a postcard into the pages of the top one before closing it.

He's dressed in smart trousers and a jumper, standing awkwardly in the centre of room, like he's not sure what to do next. There's something vulnerable about him. Like he's still a council estate boy playing at being rich. He takes my hand and leads me through to the lounge, beckoning me to sit on the settee with him, facing a mantelpiece covered in embossed invitation cards. I'm waiting for his arm to snake round my shoulders, fingers to creep down towards my breast. For him to reveal exactly what this has been all along. Just a married man looking to have casual sex with someone who's available and easy to charm.

But he doesn't lean in. He just sits a respectable couple of feet away and we both sink back into the couch, holding hands.

'You're so lucky to live here. To have all this space and privacy.' I gesture at the high ceiling, the vast door, the soft drape of the long curtains.

'Yeah . . . it's a weird place for someone like me to be. Me and my mum were crammed in a tiny council flat. Then I went to uni and it was shared halls of residence, which was torture. A sleepless year of listening to drunk drama students staggering around at night reciting lines or doing songs from the musicals. Then a flat-share with a couple of total morons who put a huge amount of energy into writing passive-aggressive notes.'

I flop back into the settee. It's enveloping and cool, unlike the battered one that I sleep on at home. Adam gestures for me to lie back and pull up my legs, so I do. He guides them onto his lap. The warmth of his body enervates me. We stay like this. Me, wanting him so much and him so restrained and gentlemanly.

* * *

The slow but effortful walk back home gives me no time at all to think. I get in and they're all watching something on TV. It's an action film with continual car chases that all blend into one. I sit between Mum and Becky and let it wash over me. There's something hypnotic about the screech of tyres coming from the TV. Mum gets up occasionally to fetch fresh beer bottles for Peter. Eventually Mum and Peter go up to bed and it's just Becky and me.

'I'm so tired.' Becky slumps down the couch.

'Go up then. You need to sleep if you're working tomorrow.'

She takes my hand and looks at me. 'I don't mean that. I mean tired of all this. I don't know how much longer I can do this. It's too much. Work and home. I feel like I'm slaving my guts out just to get by every week. It's just so endless.'

'I wish I could help. With childcare, with money.'

She reaches across and kisses me on the forehead. 'That's OK. You focus on getting better.'

'I could help with Ava. She's older now and she'd be OK if—'

'Not yet. Rest. That's all you need to do.'

I don't sleep much. I lie on the sofa thinking about Adam. I picture us walking around that spectacular house and garden. This time, Ava is there too, eating good quality food, having somewhere to sit and do her homework, comfortable perches to rest on and read her books. The three of us living a peaceful life around each other. The house now the territory of Adam, Ava and me. A calm place.

My fantasies are morphing again.

They're so vivid that they impinge on my reality.

I think about Celeste and Peter both dead. Adam and I both free and avenged.

Chapter Sixteen

'You look amazing. You should wear colours more, instead of dressing like a Victorian waif.'

I'm draped in a dusky pink satin dress that belongs to Becky. She pulled it from the back of her wardrobe. She has a couple of expensive dresses left that she wore during her acting days. Becky has applied layers of make-up to my face that make it look like I'm not wearing any make-up. An exercise that took an interminable amount of time. My reflection is a surprise in its imitation of normality.

Peter is putting his key in the door as I reach the bottom of the stairs, a nerve-jangling scrape of metal on metal as he fumbles with the lock. He looks up at me and doesn't speak. His eyes travel from my face down to the flat pumps that I've squeezed my feet into. I wait but he doesn't say a word. He raises his head back up and smirks, slowly shaking his head, as if in disbelief. He pushes himself against the doorframe and folds his arms, so that I have to squeeze myself past him. I force myself to keep my shoulders up, to not let his scorn shred my poise.

I imagine snatching the keys from his fist and ramming

them into his cheek, tearing the flesh of his sagging jowls. Issuing forth torrents of blood.

Adam is waiting for me at the corner of the street, at exactly the time he said he'd be there. He's leaning against the wall, looking down at his phone. It's not the burner phone that's twin to the one in my pocket. It's an expensive smartphone. His hair is sticking up at the back, a single endearing tuft that makes him look boyish and wholesome. His handsome face beams at me, and he touches my arm.

'You look stunning.'

'Thanks.' Compliments feel unfamiliar and I fight my reaction to field it with a disparaging remark about myself.

'Two minutes. The god of Uber is smiling down on us.'

I'm glad we're being driven. My leg is sluggish and without this paint smothering my face, I suspect that my face would be sallow and sickly. I've been fretting for days about whether I'd have the energy for this. My recent past is a string of let-downs. Failures by me; all the times I've had to retreat to the sofa leaving a wake of embarrassing refusals. Parents' evenings missed, family weddings that I've slept through, meals out where my place has sat empty.

When our ride arrives, he holds open the door of the car and guides me in. South London gives way and we cross into Central London, the pace of life quickening as we near the centre of the city. The heat of the day is dissipating. Soft lights illuminate London to a children's-book-illustration splendour. Adam reaches over and kisses me on the cheek.

The car drops us around the corner from the theatre. There's a smell of drains that taints the air. A reminder that even the most affluent area is built on a network of sewers, carrying away the filth and waste. When we arrive at the theatre I see that I've made a mistake. No one else has bothered to dress up. I'm an anomaly. The working-class girl who got the dress code wrong. No one else is primped and squeezed into unforgiving satin. People are in crumpled linen, or loosened work clothes. They confront this thing that for me is a big event with a casualness that I don't possess.

We walk through the Art Deco foyer and mount the stairs. I mange not to trip, my leg behaving in an unusual act of bodily solidarity. I hesitate in the door of the bar, wishing I could turn back around. Go back to the house, to be anywhere but here in this place where shame waits so eagerly to ambush me. Adam senses my discomfort and takes my hand, guiding me to a table in the corner of the bar.

I scan the women in the bar as we pass them, leaning casually on one hip, holding glasses of eight-pounds-a-glass wine as they talk to their companions. Throwing their heads back and laughing, taking their bodies for granted. I look across at Adam. He could easily slot into any one of these couples, replace the male companions and be comfortable with these well-groomed middle-class people. Be part of a matching pair.

No. I refuse to allow my thoughts to spiral. Remind myself that he's here with me now. My harsh inner voice scolds me, the acid-toned thoughts that Dr Bronson warns me to challenge. I'm starting to guess why he's chosen me. There's something about Adam that is exactly like me. Something dark. He hasn't called me morbid like people always do. There's something in me that Adam sees that other people don't. He must like it.

'Do you mind if we have one of these seats? My girlfriend needs to sit down.' An overweight older man jumps up and waves us towards the table.

'I hope that didn't embarrass you there. I just don't want you to wear yourself out.'

I shake my head. Still reeling from him using the word 'girlfriend'. It lodges in my stomach, filling me with a gentle warmth. Adam offers to buy me a drink but I demur. The prices are too alarming. I ask for tap water from the jug on the bar. I watch him as he fetches it, enjoying the masculine grace of his movements.

The theatre is imposing with vast chandeliers and ornate mouldings, seats that force me close to the neighbouring woman. I find that I'm holding my breath. Adam's hand slips across and he takes mine in his, enveloping my fingers. My shoulders relax downwards and I'm relieved when the lights dim.

The story thrills me. It's a modernised version of *Macbeth* where they're all in Eighties wedding outfits. The men in narrow-legged suits in shiny metallic fabrics and the women in garish dresses with shoulder pads and big hair. There's a corvid theme. Crows perch from the edges of the set, glaring with malevolence. Each time the lights come back up after a scene change there are more and more birds there. I don't understand the language at first but it becomes rhythmic and a shift occurs in me. There's a Greek chorus of women in bird masks chanting things at Lady Macbeth. They follow her around yelling verses of hissed warnings at her back.

We stay in our seats at the interval. Adam pretends that he's happy here and doesn't need to get another drink, so that I don't have to leave my seat and exert myself too much. He talks me through the play but doesn't patronise me, points things out in the programme that he bought for me.

'I hope you don't mind all this bloodshed. I've brought you to the grisliest play possible.' He has a mischievous look in his eyes, like he knows I won't be offended by violence.

'I'm loving it. I haven't seen this play before. On TV or anywhere, I mean. I love how powerful they are.'

'Well, she's the one with the power. He just does what he's told.'

'Collusion is collusion. They both have to want to kill to be able to do it.'

* * *

I watch him during the rest of the play, darting glances across and scrutinising his face. His eyes are wide with glee as he watches the carnage ensue on the stage. He's unflinching in the face of the violence and the spurting stage blood that soaks through Lady Macbeth's wedding dress.

We step out into the night, Adam watching me discreetly as I walk, ensuring that I'm not going to stumble. As we move away from the theatre, he takes my wrist and drapes my arms around his waist, kissing me hard on the mouth.

'Thank you,' he says.

'Don't thank me. You bought the tickets and paid for everything. I should be thanking you.'

'The tickets were free, actually. I know the set designer. Do you think you could walk for a while?'

I'm not sure how far that I can walk. I never am. My body ambushes me at the worst possible moments. I agree to it, anyway, knowing that Adam won't be impatient or annoyed if I have to stop.

We walk through Soho, past stumbling, enervated drunks. I see men and women look at Adam. Hungry furtive glances, sometimes unabashed appreciation and lingering stares, taking in his face and body, his thighs, his crotch. He suits this place. The clubs and bars look slick and inviting but unavailable. I couldn't stand for long, squeezed into that muggy atmosphere, dank with sweat. I start to apologise that we can't go anywhere because of my fatigue but he

112

cuts me off and waves my apologies away with his hand, pulling me closer. He continues to watch me as I walk. He's subtle, tempering his observation and gently supervising me. Caring as opposed to oppressive.

There's a man walking towards us in head-to-toe Boden clothes. Casual trousers compressing his midriff and a shirt that look freshly ironed. Jumper slung over his shoulders and a pair of shiny brogues. He has a look of Adam. Like they could both play the same role in a play. His toothsome female companion looks like she could tame a wild horse with a single word. I think they're going to walk past us but I realise that the man is making straight for Adam.

'Hey. Did you get the part?'

Adam's expression changes, tension contorting his face.

'I'm sorry, mate, but I've got no idea who you are.'

'We were talking before the audition for *Miss Julie* in Dalston last week? It's Adam, isn't it?'

'Sorry. I think you've mistaken me for someone else. I have one of those faces.'

The man goes to speak again but Adam steers me away, lifting his hand up to signify to the man that the conversation is over.

'Did you really not know him?' I ask as we stand waiting for the Uber to arrive.

'Did he look like someone I'd know? He's just some generic actor who's been drinking too much.' The man didn't look drunk. But he did look like someone who Adam would know. 'I haven't been to an audition in years.'

'But he knew your name? And that you were an actor.'

'The joys of coincidence. It's hardly the most uncommon name, is it? It happens to me a lot. I think I have the dual combination of an everyman kind of face and name. And I'm

113

an ex-actor now. I escaped. Maybe he saw me in something once and is mixing things up.'

He checks his phone. 'The Uber is saying three minutes away. Not long till we can get you sitting down again.'

It feels like he's closed the conversation down. I don't mention the man again.

* * *

I don't sleep when I get home. My body feels at its limits, flesh heavy like it's falling through space. My mind is reeling and it keeps me alert. I lie with Sparrow by my side and look at the ceiling, thinking about Adam. About my suspicions that he lied tonight about the audition and why he would do that. About whether I should even care if he is lying to me. If he had been to an audition, then is that a big deal? Maybe he's trying to relaunch his acting career as a side hustle and he's embarrassed in case he fails. We all have small secrets, don't we? Or is this something bigger and darker?

My thoughts swarm again. I try harder and manage to home in on the play we saw. I think about Lady Macbeth in her blood-soaked gown. About how two people can become so much more than one.

These thoughts soothe me into sleep.

Chapter Seventeen

There's a dying bird in the garden today. For a moment, I think that she's resting, perching on the path. She doesn't fly away when I approach. I crouch down, touching the soft brown breast of the blackbird. She's glassy-eyed, her little beak opened. There are no marks on her, not a speck of blood. I'm about to lift her corpse up when she twitches, some final shreds of life remaining in this tiny body. I twist her neck to speed her along as an act of mercy. I'm exhausted by the time I've buried her, too tired to even put the trowel away. I feel like I should cry for the poor broken body lying there. I don't though. I'm exhausted and shaking by the time I finish so I sit back on a bench. My eyes keep moving back to the patch of bare earth with the trowel beside it. I eventually give in to the fatigue and let myself fall asleep in the shade.

* * *

The banister on the stairs is loose. Peter is refusing to fix it, despite being more than capable of doing so. He's on one of his campaigns again where he's ringing the council daily, using my illness as leverage. I notice an unfamiliar smell as I walk up the stairs, a sickly sweet perfume, and the sound of coughing. That can only mean one thing – Peter's mother is here.

His mother, Doreen, is enthroned upon a dining chair, dominant in her position of height. She had her seventy-fifth birthday recently but looks ten years older. Her face has deep creases from a lifetime of package tours to Majorca and endless cigarettes. She's stopped smoking and is vaping now, surrounded by a perpetual cloud of cherry-scented steam.

I evade the questions that Doreen fires at me and dash for the stairs, passing Peter on his way down from the bathroom. He doesn't speak and I have to give way, flattening myself against the wall, holding my breath. I close my eyes as he passes, waiting for the remark, the grip of his hand. He carries on past.

'Are you coming back down? My mum will want to see you.' He looks up at me, a smarmy smile disfiguring his face.

'What? So that you can pretend we're some big happy family? Maybe I will come down – and tell your mother what a horrendous bully you are. How you push me around. How you don't even let me have anywhere to sleep. Maybe your mum would like to hear about how you nearly dragged me down the stairs by my ankle?'

'Fuck off and hide then. Be a pathetic loser.'

I raise my ankle. 'Here you go. Want to drag me down the stairs now, with Doreen in earshot?'

He ignores me, turning around and calling out to his mum in welcome, suddenly infantile. It would be endearing if it wasn't him.

* * *

116

I go to my usual spot in the bathroom and look for Celeste. There's no one in the garden. I'm about to climb back down from my spot when I see her, a flash of emerald green clothing. Celeste walks across the lawn with something in her hand. She reaches up and starts to fill the bird feeder. Ripley is snaffling round her feet, trying to catch any dropped peanuts. She says something to him. As she turns and walks back to the house a flock of blue tits flies down. Celeste turns back and sees them. I see her mouth opening and closing. She's talking to the birds. Her face breaks out into an uncharacteristic smile.

There's a softening within me but I remind myself of her sneering face at Blackheath Market. Of what she's done and is doing to Adam. I won't be fooled by this. She's monstrous. Even villains have occasional redeeming features.

When Celeste has gone in I lurk in Becky's room till Doreen leaves. I can't rest tonight because Becky has hurt her right hand at work, a burn from scalding tea that a confused old man had knocked onto her. She came home from work just before Doreen left, wearing a neatly herringboned bandage to cushion the burgeoning blisters. Still furious about the carelessness of the new care assistant who'd left the hot drink too near to the man. She winces when she moves it. She's asked me to help Ava to wash her hair. There are children with head lice at the school holiday club, yet again, and she needs conditioner applying.

'Why can't I do this on my own? I'm eleven. I'm old enough now.' Ava is sitting, staring into the bathwater, head down. 'I've washed my hair before, you know?'

'It's easier if I do it, because I can run the comb through with the conditioner and check for nits for you.' I try to hold on to this moment. She'll be at high school before long and everything will start to change as she hurtles towards adolescence.

'Gross!' She contorts her face and crosses her eyes, making me laugh. I shampoo her hair and sluice water over her head. 'Other kids are disgusting, aren't they? Imagine having hair that's crawling with things. Eurgh.'

She relaxes back and lets me finish. There's something meditative about this task.

'Can we go somewhere together, Mummy, before I start at high school? Like a day out.'

'I'll try. Becky and your granny are worried about me still being ill and having an accident again.'

'Becky is . . . less fun than you. You're still my mum.'

'Fun? I'm not fun. I just sleep all the time.'

'I don't mind you sleeping. I read a thing about nocturnal animals in one of my library books and it made me think of you. I think there might be some night people too. Maybe you're nocturnal because you sleep in the day. You're like a fox.'

'I'd rather be like an owl.'

'OK, you can be the Owl Mum.'

I twit twoo, and we both fall into fits of giggles.

Owls are driven. They stalk their prey, carrying them away with their talons plunged into their flesh, before swallowing them whole. I like their energy.

*   *   *

When I see Adam the next evening, I recoil. There are bruises all over the left side of his face, his eye swollen and smoky grey, yellow bruises blooming across his cheek. His lip is split, an angry parting of flesh.

'What happened? What did she do?'

118

His hand reaches up as if he'd forgotten that his face was disfigured and a flash of crimson rises in his cheeks. He mumbles something and starts to tell me some story about being mugged but I know he's lying. He peters out when I put my hand to his forehead, my fingers tracing the outline of the damage. We don't speak as I kiss the edges of the lesions.

'Celeste.' He doesn't contradict me. He tells me in his own time, a shameful account of being attacked, Celeste launching into him with her fists and feet. A minor dispute about the divorce that he wants and she doesn't. It's the usual tale. Another onslaught from a violent partner, followed by contrition and lies that it won't happen again.

'Have you called the police?'

'I . . . I couldn't. No one would believe me anyway. She looks so much weaker. And people know her off the TV. She's untouchable. They'd be sneering at me.'

I understand what he's saying. I thought about reporting Peter's escalating violence to the police but I can't imagine there'd be much of a response. There's no evidence I could show them. I don't have bruising or broken bones. Yet. No one in my house would back me up, either.

Adam has evidence imprinted on his face but he must feel too belittled by what's happened. I don't push him. It's not for me to tell him what I think the police might say or do. He's an adult who can make choices. The only thing I can do is support him in those choices. And urge him to stay safe.

'We need to do *something* and quickly, Adam. Before she really hurts you. She deserves to suffer for this.'

I kiss the unmarked side of his face and he yields to me, taking my hand. We walk upstairs to their bedroom and lie silently next to each other for a while.

'Why do we both have to put up with all this shit? We're not bad people. We don't deserve this.' He sits up as he speaks and I feel him looking at me. 'This could be you. Peter could hurt you. Maybe you should go to the police about the times he's attacked and threatened you.'

I shake my head.

There's something chaste about us, his hand avoiding my breast as it runs down my side. His kisses tinged by his underserved humiliation, rather than lust.

I hold my breath for a second before speaking. 'Do you ever think you could actually kill Celeste? I sometimes think that I could kill Peter. I'm certain I could. But then I think that maybe I'm being childish. Playing silly games in my head. Looking for a solution. A way to have space and peace for me and Ava.'

I look away from him, even though he can't see my eyes in the dark.

'What if I were to kill Peter for you? If I found a time when you had an alibi.' There's a note of glee in his voice. Like he's about to laugh.

'I like that. Then I could kill Celeste for you. Like in the film you told me about. How would you kill him?' My breaths rasp between words as I speak. The urge to laugh bubbles in my chest.

'Let's think. How about a random stabbing in the street?' His voice sounds urgent. Excited even.

'What? And pass it off as a mugging? Or maybe a head injury? How easy is it to crack someone's skull open?'

'I imagine you just need enough force and the element of surprise. What about pushing him under a car? Or a lorry?' He raises both hands and pretends to push at my shoulders. The laugh escapes from me and I raise my hand to cover my mouth.

'Satisfying but too risky. You might be seen.' I'm thinking hard as I speak.

'Not if I was dressed in dark enough clothes. Although, CCTV is everywhere now, isn't it? You're probably right.' He frowns like he's thinking hard but I know he thinks this is just a game.

'It would be tough on the driver. Don't you have any way of doing it via your job? You must have access to some pretty lethal drugs.'

'Like an insulin injection? That's an old cliché. Too risky on post-mortem. They'd look between the toes for injection marks.'

We turn to face each other, and this time we both start to laugh.

'Shall I kill Celeste in return? I'd do it but I'm not sure I'd be capable.'

'Why not? You have good days. Maybe you'd be lying in wait in the house and could give her a sneaky push down the stairs?'

'Or stabbing. I could stab her with my good arm, as long as she wasn't expecting it. I'd have to sneak up on her.'

He nods enthusiastically.

'I could definitely do it if we planned it properly.' Everything in life needs planning when you're chronically ill.

'Emma, this is fun. Twisted but fun. But we need a real plan. Maybe, we could leave here together. Find somewhere for us both to live.' He sits up and clicks on the lamp. His face is drawn and tired.

I'm about to answer him when he speaks again. His words faster now. 'I'm sorry. That was stupid of me. We barely know each other. It's too soon. Pretend that I didn't say that.'

'Don't be sorry. You've just said what I was thinking. I'd like nothing more than to escape with you. We could have a new beginning together.' He responds to my answer by pulling me in, against his body, and I push my back into him, feeling the shudders of his body as he starts to cry.

Chapter Eighteen

The following day, we have sex for the first time. It felt awkward at first and I was self-conscious, my mind racing, unable to be in the moment. It's been a long time since I was touched like this. But he was patient and gentle. I thought that sleeping with a doctor might feel like I was being examined. Like he'd pull out a tendon hammer midway through and start tapping my knee. It wasn't like that at all. It was soft and romantic but urgent and passionate too. It didn't feel like he was a doctor, just like he was Adam. That he cares about me.

We're at their house. She's off sourcing food somewhere. Some ridiculous overnight trip to the Cotswolds to find a particular cheese or pâté to sell to the ludicrously well-off diners. This may be an excuse, a cover for her infidelity. Adam says she has a lover who lives nearby but he thinks there may be more scattered around. She's probably in a hotel room or bedroom somewhere right now with someone.

The vanilla taint of her perfume on the sheets doesn't deter me. I don't care that it's her territory. I'm starting to belong here now. I'm wearing her perfume too. I sprayed a generous mist of it onto myself in the bathroom and rubbed one of her lotions into my hands. This house could almost be mine. I've imagined this for so long. A place for me and Ava.

* * *

We've carried on planning how can we kill Peter and Celeste. Whatever we do, wherever we go, our talk turns to killing and we come up with violent solutions. Sometimes it's fantastical, absurd methods, like faking Peter's suicide by luring him to the top of St Paul's or poisoning Celeste in front of all the diners in her stuck-up restaurant. Watching her through the glass of the window as she clutches at her throat, clawing for air. More often we're realistic and practical. We're gleeful in our inventiveness. In playing our game. We're good at this.

Only all the time I'm playing these games I'm watching Adam's reaction and gauging when he'll be ready to push this further. When I can make him see that this is an achievable solution and not just a sick game. I'm scheming and thinking hard. The logistics of murder aren't easy.

I'm just like everyone else: working on achieving something that I need. But instead of the usual dull goals – eat less, move more, less screen time – I'm contemplating murder. Revenge with fringe benefits.

My dreams are ordinary, modest even. I need space to live and breathe. Safety and peace for Ava. I want a home for the three of us, maybe for us to be able to pay for a wedding one day. Although, we haven't discussed that part yet. Imagine if we could afford to travel. I think about the birds that I could see in Asia, the Caribbean, America.

We just have some obstacles to clear first. People in our way.

*　*　*

Adam has become my constant support. He messages when he says he will. Texts pinging between these flimsy burner phones. We visit places that I've never been, crossing the Thames into North London, visiting the Natural History Museum, having lunch in Chelsea. He's even bought me a scarf from Liberty. It's a beautiful orange and green silk. I chastised him for spending the money that he doesn't have. Yet. We're together now. I'm part of a couple, both of us stronger with support.

He's at the hospital today. He messages me on his break, telling me that it's the usual mayhem. I tuck the flimsy phone into my pocket, enjoying the press of it against my body. Becky finds me in the garden, watching a thrush smash a snail shell apart and gobble down the victim's slimy body. Sparrow is under the bench, ignoring everything, sleeping in a shaft of sunlight that's snaked through the slats.

'It's too hot for working. I'm done for.' She kicks off her shoes and they land at the foot of some lupins. 'Some bloody woman stopped me in the street on my way back and told me that I looked like Tania from *Castle Street*.'

'What did you say?'

'I said, "Well, that's not great. She was a right dog." She was red as a beetroot when she walked away.' We both laugh. It still happens all the time. Often people confuse Becky with the character she played, unable to distance reality and fiction. She was once screamed at in the street by a man who was angry about the way she was treating her 'mum'. I remember standing wide-eyed in my plastic sandals as seventeen-year-old Becky told him to piss off.

'What are you up to, anyway?'

'Just sitting.' I wait for a snide comment that doesn't

come. I've endured years of little digs. She looks after my daughter, my cuckoo, but she makes sure that I know how much of a burden it is.

'How's it going with the new man?'

'Really good. Yes. Good.'

'Don't take offence at this, but I worry about you. Being ill makes you a bit more . . . vulnerable.'

'It's fine.'

'It's just that you don't have much experience with men. I wondered if you wanted advice from an older woman who's been around the block a bit.'

Becky's dating history is chequered. Her public shame after the fairy-tale show-business marriage that turned into a horror story. All paid for by a glossy magazine in exchange for exclusive rights on the photographs. Mum and I were given expensive clothes to wear so that we didn't look out of place, but we still jarred. Our postures were wrong as we slouched in the corner, looking exactly as uncomfortable as we felt with her husband's wealthy family and her actor friends. There were no photographs of me or Mum in the magazine spread.

'I feel different. Like I'm becoming more the person I was,' I tell her.

'That sounds great. Any news on his divorce?'

'It's complicated.'

'You sound like an old-school Facebook relationship status.' She stops and spins herself around, stretching herself out like a cat on the bench, her legs resting over mine.

'No. Not like that. Just that there are some things to sort out but it's early days. He's working on it. We'll work it all out.'

'Well, on the plus side, you look better than you have done in a while.'

126

Being told I look better usually smarts. Invisible illness is a fine balance. I don't want people to bestow sympathy. I want my independence, to be seen as capable and not a charity case. Conversely, I want them to know that they have to reduce their expectations. To expect me to be flaky, unreliable, unable at times. Not to think that I'm cured when I'm not.

'If he's making you happy, then go for it. You only live once.' She reaches across and kisses me on the cheek. 'I'm happy that things are going well for you. But please be careful.'

She grabs my hand and interlaces her fingers in mine.

'Emma, don't get mad when I tell you this. There's something that you need to know. There's something going on with my dad. He wants to turn your old bedroom into a room for Ava.'

'OK. Well that's better than it being a room for his crappy desk and filing cabinets.' I shrug.

'That's not all, though. I've heard him on the phone to the council again and to your doctor's secretary. Making a fuss, like he always does. He's been asked to send medical reports and letters through to the council and he's getting on to the hospital to try to get them. He was yelling at them about us all being in crisis due to your illness and the lack of space. Telling them how it's affecting your health.' She eases herself up so that she's facing me.

'He's after accommodation for you. Any accommodation, anywhere. A bedsit even, somewhere with shared facilities. Maybe not even in this area. I heard him talking and they might be offering you somewhere out of London because the housing stock is so limited here.'

'What?' I lean forward.

'I heard him again today. Ann knows too. I thought I

should warn you. He wants you gone,' she says. 'I heard him talking about you being moved somewhere like Luton or Kettering. I don't know if they would do that with you having Ava, though. Although I suppose with you not being able to look after her . . .' She bites her lip. 'Don't tell them I told you. I'm trying to keep the peace, but I couldn't not warn you.'

I wait for the panic to set in, for rage to blossom in my chest but it doesn't. I don't care now. Peter can do exactly what he wants to and it won't touch me. He won't separate me from my daughter.

My future with Adam is almost sorted.

Whatever happens, we'll escape here and my home will be with him.

Chapter Nineteen

Two days later we go to look at the first property. A step towards a realistic solution to both of our housing issues. I relayed to Adam about Peter's plans and he was horrified at the thought of me being shunted out of London. I knew that he would be. The flat is in a stained butterscotch-coloured house, just off the South Circular. Adam drives us past the takeaways and unkempt houses with their front gardens full of weeds, discarded shopping trolleys and stained mattresses. Windows with built-up layers of exhaust fumes. The estate agent doesn't make eye contact when she tells us the rental price, which is well over half of Adam's monthly salary. The day doesn't get any better and by the fourth flat, an ex-council flat with an air of neglect and an antique-looking gas cooker, Adam looks despondent. He climbs into the car and doesn't put his seat belt on straight away.

'We'll find somewhere. I'm sure we will. Maybe we just need to look somewhere further out,' I reassure him.

I squeeze his hand but he continues looking down at his knees. The flats, although not strictly pleasant, look tempting to me. Somewhere I could sleep when I wanted to, have my own space, a bedroom for Ava. 'Won't you get money from the divorce?'

'I signed a prenup agreement. It felt like that was the right thing to do at the time. Given that she had so much and I had so little. I get nothing if we divorce.' He sits quietly for a moment. 'The only way I'd get a penny from Celeste is if she died and I inherited the house and had the life insurance pay out. But that's not going to happen. She's in perfect health.'

He turns to face me but his eyes shift downwards, avoiding my full gaze. 'I haven't told you everything. I'm ashamed to say this, but I'm in a lot of debt. I was an idiot. A total fucking idiot. I'm even still paying off my student loans. It's my life with Celeste. I couldn't stand her paying for everything and I felt like I needed to keep up. I ended up splashing out on expensive meals and holidays. Buying the right clothes to fit in with her circle. By the time I've made all my repayments every month there's barely enough to feed me, never mind rent a flat. I don't know what I was thinking, believing that I could escape.'

He starts to drive and I say nothing. Now isn't the time to remind Adam of the plans we laughed over. He's not ready to cement them into reality. I don't want to show my hand too soon and scare Adam away. I want this twisted plan to feel like a joint decision.

But I can and will kill Celeste.

The term for it would be *'folie à deux'*. It's where two people are gripped by a delusion or psychosis and commit a criminal act. In this case a joint murder.

But neither myself nor Adam is delusional. No one would say that. We've just been pushed too far. We need to find a way out.

130

When I get back I hide out in Becky's room. Avoiding dinner, eating a sandwich before Mum and Peter arrive back and telling them I need to lie down. When it's dark, I go round to see Adam. Celeste is working in her restaurant. Charming the people who don't see through her. Who don't know what a despicable woman she is. The information that Becky told me and the fruitless flat search spur me on and I blurt it out.

'I think we should kill them, Adam. In real life, I mean.'

He leans on the bed on one elbow, hair messed up. His skin is glowing. I run my hand across the soft hair on his lower torso.

'I think that we should do whatever has to be done.' He puts his hands on my upper arms. There's an urgency to his grip. He runs his hands up my body. Cupping my face between his hands, he moves his lips to mine and we kiss. When he pulls away he's smiling. The passion we have has evolved into something solid, something that's hard to contain. I no longer doubt him. The urgency of his body with mine is all I need as proof.

After sex we talk more. We have the best conversations after sex.

'Maybe we need to revise our plans, if you want us to do this for real?' I hear his breath catch as he speaks. Like he's been running.

'How?' I lie back, my limbs soft against the cotton sheets.

'Maybe we don't need to kill them both now.' I knew this moment would come. That Adam would decide that this had gone too far. I wait for the crush of disappointment to hit me.

'It was only a game, wasn't it?' I try not to sound too despondent.

'No. That's not what I meant. I meant that if we can get you away from Peter then why kill him? We're just doubling the risk of us being caught. You could just leave him behind like the garbage he is.'

'OK.' Though I can't imagine ever not wanting to harm Peter. My rage isn't likely to abate.

'If Celeste were dead, then we'd be rich. She has life insurance, this house, the royalties from her books. There's a lot to gain from her dying. We'd both have enough money to be free.' He nudges me. 'And I won't make you sign a prenup. If we get married one day then whatever is mine is yours too.'

The idea of being Adam's wife is a recurring motif in my fantasies, but to hear him say that is spectacular. I push myself up and stroke his face tenderly. 'So you think that we could kill Celeste?'

'I like the idea but we have to be realistic too. We'd need a foolproof method because the police will have me as the prime suspect straight away. Husbands always are. I don't see how—'

'That's the beauty of my idea. I'll kill Celeste. Like I said I would when we talked about it. I'm the real-life foolproof method.' I don't bother to hide my smile.

* * *

I have to wait up when I get back. There's a film on and Mum is asleep on the settee, curled up into Peter's side. The TV is loud, the mid-point of some crime drama involving drug gangs. My limbs are jittery and alive.

When Mum finally wakes and they stumble to bed, I lie back on the settee and think about murder. Picture Celeste's face as my hands meet around her neck. I will get strong

132

enough to do this for me and Adam. I think that's what he wants me to do.

Thoughts of death lull me to sleep around dawn.

I wake up in hospital.

Chapter Twenty

I've slept through the ambulance journey and the emergency department admission. I'm lying in a bed, in a stiff hospital gown. My feet are tucked in, tight bedclothes pressing my feet down and hurting the tips of my toes. I close my eyes again, trying to rest for as long as possible. The thing about being in hospital is that no one lets you sleep. You're woken up by harassed nurses for blood pressure recordings, by bored-looking catering staff to ask what microwaved slop you want to eat later, by groups of doctors who invade your privacy.

There are no messages from anyone on my phone. I try to message Adam but there's no reception from my bed. Anxiety gnaws at me like rodents' teeth. What will Adam think when he doesn't hear from me? That I've bailed on him because of what we talked about? I want to tell him what's happened. Only I don't remember anyway. I suspect I collapsed at home and Mum or Becky called an ambulance and sent me here alone.

I lie in the tunnel through yet another MRI scan, the road drill throb of the machine a familiar friend that lulls me to sleep. I keep my eyes closed as the porter brings me back to my bed, ignoring the mayhem of the hospital corridor, keeping my eyes averted as staff and visitors squeeze past the trolley. After being decanted back into the bed, I try not to look at the other woman in the two-bed ward with me. There's now a bar of reception on the burner phone, so I message Adam, telling him I'm in the hospital but that I'm fine, that he's not to worry about me.

My body is electric with panic as I feel our plans – our future – slipping away. I'm useless. I'll never escape this life. I force myself to sleep by reciting the Latin names of birds. The hospital recedes into blackness around me.

I'm woken by the voice of a junior doctor with a heart-shaped face and a soft Northern inflection. She's crouching down, talking evenly to the young woman in the bed opposite. She approaches my bedside next, not leaning in close, as she was with my neighbour, but standing upright at the bedside. I hear the soft click of the thick paper curtains as they're pulled around me.

'How are you feeling now?' Her tone is weary, a monotone, and I anticipate that this won't go well. Experience has taught me how to gauge these people.

'I don't know. I'm sleepy. Can you come back later?'

'You don't need to do anything, do you? Just lie back and I'll have a look at you.' Her tone is brusque. She pulls back the sheets in one sharp manoeuvre and begins another neurological examination. I could answer these questions in my sleep. We establish that my left-hand side is numb and I'm able to answer a few questions about the blackout, which doesn't take long as I can't recall a thing.

'Are you still seeing Dr Bronson?' She's standing with her arms folded, as if she's waiting for the moment when she can leave and do some real work.

'Yes. I am. I go weekly at the moment.'

135

'We've had a quick look at the MRI results and much like the others that you've had, we can't see anything wrong.'

'Fine. I know.' My tone is more defensive than I intend it to be.

'You know that there's nothing *actually* wrong with you, Emma? Not physically anyway. Dr Bronson is a good psychiatrist. Try to stay away from here if you can. It's not a healthy place to be. Do you understand me?'

I nod at her, keeping my eyes averted.

Of course I understand – but she's wrong. This is the kind of thing that doctors often say to me. Sometimes they choose their words kindly; sometimes it's laden with scorn. Health professionals operate on a continuum between empathy and disgust. Most often, for someone like me, someone with my condition, it's disdain. After a day of dealing with 'genuine' emergencies they haven't got the energy to sympathise with me and 'my issues'.

As far as some of them are concerned, I'm not even ill. I know that in Victorian times, I'd have been labelled as a hysteric or a malingerer. At worst, confined to an institution. At best, hidden away in a back bedroom by an embarrassed family. I'd have been turned away with contempt. I sometimes still am.

I have some of the symptoms of neurological disorders like multiple sclerosis and epilepsy but none of the 'organic factors' that would back up that diagnosis. I have a disease without concrete evidence, without affirmative scans or validated cause. There are no lesions or tumours on my brain or spine, no areas of damage or growth. No matter how many times I sit with slimy pads applied to my scalp, my electrical impulses don't demonstrate seizure activity.

And yet, I am still ill. This *is* an illness and it has a name.

Sometimes there are flashes of kindness, like the third neurologist out of the multitude who I've seen.

'We can see no structural damage that explains your symptoms but for some reason messages aren't getting through. In simple terms, whilst there's nothing wrong with your brain's "hardware", there is a fault with the "software".' He was older, handsome in a careworn way.

'But why? Why has this happened?'

'There could be numerous causes for this. And we need to get some expert help to see if there's anything we can resolve. The problem, however, is that no one knows an easy fix for this. There isn't just one medicine or an exercise programme that's going to sort it out straight away. We need a combined approach of treatments.'

He told me some of the names for it: functional neurological disorder, medically unexplained symptoms, persistent physical symptoms. Whether people choose to believe that this is real or not, my brain isn't functioning as it should. I'm not faking this. I'm not manifesting it either. I may stay like this forever. Prone to occasional blackouts. Numb and tired. More than tired – crushed by fatigue that pins me down and sucks life from me for days on end.

* * *

It started with a dragging of my leg when I walked. Then the areas of numbness. Sometimes uncanny illusions: non-existent fingers that brushed against my arm late at night. The gentle tickle of spiders' legs that would creep across my eyelids, down my face. Spells of fatigue that floored me, with even restful days and nights leaving me itchy-eyed and heavy-limbed.

Mum sat with me through anxious hospital

appointments as they searched my brain and body for something sinister: for multiple sclerosis scarring, tumours, or nerve damage. I'd lie listening to the chorus of knocking from the MRI scanner. Pins were poked in my feet. Needles pushed into my spinal column to extract fluid.

Then the blackouts started. Yanking me from reality and leaving me dazed and bewildered when I'd wake up. My family all responded with concern, but their compassion soon dwindled as confusion grew into exasperation. As doctor after doctor told them that there was nothing organically wrong. My hospital attendances are now something that I do alone, which I'm glad about. The final one that Mum and Peter attended was an exercise in humiliation, as I avoided the contempt of the consultant and his new ally: Peter, on hand to add a scornful commentary.

My illness didn't crush me straight away. I was proactive and determined. I researched. Months spent skimming over pages of medical websites, Instagram accounts of fellow sufferers, information from functional neurological disorder support groups. I tried exercise regimens, pacing. I tolerated harsh elimination diets, took handfuls of supplements, meditated.

But whatever I did, I stayed exactly the same. My enthusiasm sloughed away like dead skin and I fell into this. Into what people have pushed me to become.

* * *

The doctor with the Northern accent leaves, with a deadpan encouragement for me to 'keep at it' with the psychiatry appointments. She gives me this cloying look as she leaves, as if she's remembered at the last minute that she's paid to be empathetic.

I don't hate seeing Doctor Bronson. The third neurologist, the kind one, said that it might be helpful to see a psychiatrist to look at whether there were any unresolved traumas in my past that may have triggered this. Not caused. Triggered. But we all have traumas, don't we? The death of my father hit me hard, as did the loss of my career, but I worked my way through it as best as I could.

He doesn't see me as a fake or a hysteric. Because I'm not. He thinks it's more complicated than that. We're working now on how I can accept and live with my symptoms. How I can live around this illness. That's been the most difficult part so far. Acceptance.

For now, I'm stuck in the hospital, the inevitable wait for a discharge letter to be typed up. I message Adam again and he responds with the kindness and concern that I'd hoped for. The desperate thoughts of aborted plans, of him feeling disappointed in me and deserting me, start to fall away.

I hear the noise of wheels on lino and sense someone by my bedside.

'How are you feeling?' It's a younger female voice with a South London accent like mine.

I quickly mop my eyes. 'I'm OK, thanks. I'm going home soon.' My voice is scratchy and underused.

'Me too. Though I sometimes hate going home when I still feel like shit, don't you? I like at least a bit of resolution before I'm turfed out.'

She's pretty, make-up carefully applied, although the eyeliner is slightly off kilter.

'I'm Lauren, by the way. Hope you don't mind but I saw that you'd been crying and didn't want to leave you on your own like that.'

'I don't mind being on my own, I'm OK, but thanks.'

Her right leg is jarringly lifeless, propped up on the

footplate at an unusual angle. She wheels herself nearer and lays her hand on mine. Her tremor is barely perceptible but it's there. I look away.

'Well, I mind. So, you're stuck with me, for the moment. Sorry for my wobbly granny hand, by the way.' She holds up a fake-tanned arm, a tiny watch sliding up and down on her wrist. 'I'm not usually this bad. I've only been in the wheelchair for three weeks. I can usually hobble about. This relapse has been a bit of a shitstorm. Knocked me senseless. Nasty urine infection sparked up my MS again.'

I already know this. I couldn't help but hear the Northern doctor talking to her in a soft, compassionate hum, the curtains not being soundproof, like they always seem to think that they are. She has a *real* illness. Multiple sclerosis, a quantifiable disease for the doctors to look at on scans or in drops of spinal fluid.

'It's lonely being in hospital.' Her voice is surprisingly soft. 'All these people surrounding us but no one with any time to ask us anything much other than whether we've had a crap or whether we can feel it when they poke our feet with a pin. My boyfriend always suddenly has more shifts at work whenever I get a flare-up.'

I look at her again. She's tiny. The wheelchair looks like it's come from an adolescent ward. Her hand is pleasantly warm on my arm.

'There's nothing wrong with me, actually.' I speak again before she can respond to my challenge. I'm bold in the face of my humiliation. 'I'm not ill like you. I'm just someone with a fake illness. There's nothing to see, on my scans. Just a mad girl whose body has decided not to work.'

'Is that what you really believe?'

I don't answer her straight away. I'm not sure what to say. She moves her hand to scratch her thigh. 'Sorry. I haven't got scabies or anything. It's a nerve thing. Feels like insects on my legs. Do you get that too? It usually comes with me after the numbness. I can't decide if it's worse than being numb.'

'Yes. I get that, too. I've got functional neurological disorder.'

'Ah yes, my old friend, FND. They thought I had that for a while, till they found a lesion on a scan. Then they suddenly started to be nice to me. I'm not judging you. I've seen you dragging your leg to the bathroom.' She starts scratching again, this time at her cheek. 'It isn't all in your head. Ignore the idiots and do what you can to get by.'

She starts to roll the chair backwards. 'Anyway, let's not descend to swapping symptoms or point scoring on who's had the most scans or has the best deformity. We need a diversion. I've watched a ridiculous amount of TV for the last few weeks and I need someone to talk to about some of the crap I've seen. You watch TV, don't you?'

'Er . . . not much. Just nature programs mostly.'

She rummages in her dressing gown pocket and pulls out a pack of cigarettes. 'I've also not had a ciggie for three days now. If I don't smoke a Marlboro in the next ten minutes I might have a psychotic break. I've got my eye on the tall nurse with the greasy hair. She looks enough of a pushover that she might be convinced to take me outside, don't you think? Give her a shout, will you?'

Chapter Twenty-One

I walked to the park today and looked at the abandoned herons' nests on the park, tattered after the efforts of breeding season. There were no herons in sight but the swans on the lake were circling. Hissing at any other birds who approached their growing signets.

Swans mate for life. It may sound romantic but it's just practicality. Birds need stamina and expertise for raising chicks. They don't want to waste their precious energy on searching for a new mate each season, instead preferring to stay with the same one, increasing their chances of species survival. I pity them. Some of them must strive to escape. Being with the wrong partner is surely a living death.

Which is why Adam needs me to help him. And I can. The stay in hospital wasn't the disaster that I first thought it was. It gave me time to think. To consolidate.

Since I was discharged a week ago, I've been walking daily. It helps me to solidify our plans. Strengthen my own resolve. My leg has improved and there haven't been any more blackouts. I've been strong enough to start following Celeste again. There's nothing to see from the bathroom window – the weather is turning cooler and she's barely been in the garden. So I've taken to the streets.

Celeste walks faster than me, but she's a creature of habit. If it's late afternoon or evening then she takes a train into Central London to her restaurant. I follow her and sit watching her from further down the carriage. She hasn't noticed me yet. I get to London Bridge and come straight back. In the daytime it's always Blackheath, a café on the parade of shops or to a house a couple of streets away. That must be where her lover lives. The more I see her, the more I can see the bitterness and venom in her. It's writ large on her hateful face.

She has a way of walking. It's haughty: straight back, head high and small steps. As if she went to one of those Swiss schools that you read about in stories where they make the girls walk round with books on their heads. Her shoes cost more than my entire ensemble of clothes. I poked through her wardrobe whilst Adam was in the shower one evening and then looked at the prices on Google when I got home.

I've been researching her further. The copies of her cookbooks arrived in the post from Amazon, second-hand and grease-spotted. She has a standard way of posing in the glossy photos between the ludicrous recipes with obscure ingredients. Pages of pretentious nonsense where she purports to be some kind of domestic goddess. If only people knew the truth about her.

I'm standing on the corner of the street, just down from our house. If I stand back, I'm masked from view by a sprawling buddleia that overflows from someone's front garden, an anomaly among the well-trimmed hedges and immaculate walls. I can see her house but she wouldn't be able to see me. I pretend to look at my phone, as if I'm waiting for someone. I rarely see the same people and dogs passing by. But it wouldn't matter if I did. My status makes me invisible to them.

Today she's veering either towards the parade of shops or the house that she visits. That wicker basket is on her arm, hooked over the crook of her elbow, a red and white gingham cloth covering the top. She's business-like, never once looking back. She's the same on the train when I follow her to the restaurant. Celeste takes a seat and doesn't look up from whatever Booker-Prize-nominated novel she's reading. Ignores the view of the monoliths of the City of London on the horizon as if they're beneath her. Her aura of aloofness keeps people from sitting next to her.

I'm so close today that I can see goose-pimpled skin on the back of her neck. She's wearing ridiculous cotton gloves, alternating the basket between her elbow and her hand. The hands that beat Adam. Toxic people like her don't deserve what they have. They prosper on abuse and bullying, spilling their caustic nature and harming the people around them. Celeste doesn't deserve her life. She doesn't deserve to live full stop.

The kerb opposite the parade is steep. She hovers there, looking both ways as a bus passes by, then a lorry that hurtles down the street, ignoring the speed restriction. Maybe I don't need to wait. The small of her back is arched, exactly the right shape for my hand to fit in. I could push her and send her into the path of a vehicle. A satisfying smash of metal and bone. I pause to take a breath. My phone rings as Celeste strides into the road and swerves around a teenager on an electric scooter.

It's Lauren on the phone. She's walking again, albeit unsteadily, and wonders if I want to meet her in the café near my house. I hadn't expected her to call. In the time it

144

takes me to agree, Celeste has jetted down the side street and I can't catch up. She must be going to that house again. I've seen her let herself in with a key, although, one time a man opened the door for her, kissing her on the cheek.

I wait for Lauren in the café, making a latte last me half an hour. It has one of those twee names: 'The Cake Box'. It used to have bolted-down plastic chairs and served breakfast all day for construction workers and ragged-looking pensioners. Now it's all artfully angled leather settees and the cake slices are four pounds each. I don't usually come here anymore. When she finally arrives, Lauren looks better, her health much improved. I watch her step off the bus in impractical shoes, unclipping the TFL Hidden Disability badge, as she limps into the café.

'I fucking hate that badge but it works. Only when I point at it, mind you. I have to guilt-trip them with an exaggerated withered arm and puppy-dog eyes.'

She twists her arm up in an unnatural position. Her make-up is immaculate today and she looks like she has false eyelashes on. If you didn't know, you might think she was perfectly well, just limping from a running injury perhaps.

Lauren expects nothing from me and I reciprocate. We talk in shorthand, not having to painstakingly explain our maladies. Not offering excuses or feigning bravado. I feel no shame around her, no need for laboured pretence. We're both dysfunctional, just in different ways. The budding friendship with her is effortless.

There are bird prints in the café, blocky pictures in primary colours. I point out that the one above my head is a pelican and am about to regale Lauren with one of my grisliest stories, a particular favourite. It's the one about when a pelican devoured a live pigeon in front of a crowd of screaming tourists in St James' Park. I notice that she's squirming.

'Eurgh. I'm trying to ignore that thing. I can't stand birds. I've got a phobia. I walked towards a bunch of crows when I was a kid. Expected them to fly away, like they usually do. Turned out that they were protecting an injured bird, so they tried to peck the face off me. Put me off birds for life.'

I'm glad I didn't tell her about the pelican.

And I don't correct her about the crows; it's a murder, not a bunch.

Lauren lives ten minutes away on the bus, on a big council estate. She's a beautician, on minimum wage but currently off work sick, with a moderately understanding boss.

'So, have you got a boyfriend? Full disclosure: I'm asking this so that I can then slide into a rant about how shit men are and moan about the feckless bastard who I've been seeing.'

'It's complex.'

'I understand complex.' She props her face on a hand and leans forward with a hungry look. I can't help but laugh.

'I'm seeing someone – but it's a bit . . . messy. I'm not sure how to describe it . . . He can't get out of something.'

'You mean he's married and he's shagging you on the side? Fair play if you're OK with that but they don't often leave their wives. You do know that, don't you?' A look of concern crosses her face.

'No, he's different. Like I said, it's complicated. That's all I can say.' I sit back and try to smile.

'No problem. As long as you don't get hurt. What do I know anyway? Your married man might be the exception.' I am pleased when she changes the subject. 'I was going to order a cake but have you seen these fucking prices? Jesus

146

Christ. Let's set up a café. We could call it the Crip Café. I reckon we could look pitiful and rustle up a sponge cake for a couple of quid. We'd get the worthy sympathy crowd all coming in virtue signalling. Anyway, fuck their cake. Next time I'll bring some from Greggs in my bag and we can eat them under the table. Now, let me tell you about my hopeless lump of a boyfriend and you can tell me whether I should boot him out.'

I'm exhausted by the time that I get home but my step is lighter today. I can see an end to this. Once I'm in, I try to rest but there's nowhere to go. I'm wedged next to Mum, Ava slouching on the floor, too close to the TV. Becky in the bedroom. Peter walks in, scratching himself, and glares at me.

'Productive day, Emma? Found a job yet or are you going to carry on leeching off all of us forever?'

I don't bother to respond. I just stare at him and start to laugh as I walk away.

Chapter Twenty-Two

When I see Adam the next day, he looks drawn, his usual confidence diminished. He ushers me into the house and straight to the kitchen. He's distracted, forgetting to put sugar in my coffee.

'Did she hit you again?' We're standing facing each other by the kitchen island.

'No. Not yet anyway.' I feel the fury surge through me in waves. 'But she came back from the restaurant in the afternoon in a foul mood. She was impossible. It's the usual pattern. This will just get worse and worse over the coming weeks till she explodes again.'

I saw crows on the way here so I distract Adam by telling him about them. The tale fits: crows don't forgive. They remember and take glorious revenge. They circle around a wrongdoer, an invader, forming a court in which to pass judgement, eyes sharp and cold. They hunch over, like mourners, their black feathers shining. They let their hatred take form. Their court does one of two things. They either release the transgressor, allowing them to live, or they kill them. Death, if and when it finally comes, is in a frenzy of violent pecking, blood spilled amongst dislodged plumage, a corpse discarded.

I understand birds more than people, sometimes. They follow their instincts. Sometimes criminals need to be punished. What Celeste has done – is doing . . . The acts she's perpetrating are criminal. The law wouldn't touch her. Who would believe Adam against her? She'd use her money to wriggle out of anything. Fancy lawyers would rip Adam to shreds, leaving him penniless and homeless. Deepening the emotional damage that he already needs my help to get through. He'd walk away from this mess with nothing.

'I've got something else to tell you.' Adam reaches across and takes my hands in his. I breathe again when he smiles. 'It's not bad news. It just changes things. Makes them more urgent.'

'Tell me.' My words are quick and firm.

'Celeste is going away in four weeks' time. She's off to film a cookery show in Rome.' I've always wanted to go to Rome. The city is inundated in autumn by starlings who overwinter there. Sinister black shapes twist over the city as they perform their intricate aerial displays.

'So we have a deadline?' I stifle a laugh at my choice of word.

Adam laughs too. 'I've been thinking of some exercises you could do to make your arm stronger. And I could show you where to aim the knife to avoid hitting her ribs.'

Finally. I have a rehabilitation goal that I can commit to. Dr Bronson would be proud.

* * *

We go to the bedroom. We don't have sex but sit and talk, propped up on the vast bed. Adam is drinking wine and his lips are stained crimson. I like the taste of it in his mouth.

149

'I'm rethinking this. I don't want you to do anything, Emma . . .' He doesn't look at me as he speaks. Propped on one elbow on the bed, his hand toying with my hair. 'I should do it. I'll have to do it myself. It's not fair on you.'

I wriggle up the bed, leaning onto my elbow.

He looks at me like I haven't understood him. 'I'll kill Celeste, I mean. I'm going to do it.'

'But we talked about this. You'll be caught. Straight away. The police always suspect the partner if someone gets murdered. It's the obvious choice. If you don't have a cast-iron alibi then you'll be charged in no time.' The hours on the sofa with my family, forced to watch crime dramas, have taught me this basic fact. 'How would *you* do it anyway? Without there being a trace?'

'I could fake an attack in the street and—'

'And be seen by someone or recorded on CCTV. Then you'd be serving a life sentence. We already have our answer. I'll kill her. Like we've planned. The plan is good.'

He lies back on the bed and I kiss him hard on the lips. He yields to me.

* * *

The next few days pass by like I'm dreaming. Lauren wants to meet for coffee again but I tell her that there's too much stuff happening.

I spend an afternoon with Adam in a hotel near the Thames. I can't go to the house again yet. Not till afterwards. It feels wrong to be there now that we're definitely going to kill Celeste. Like a line has been drawn.

Adam dozes and I watch birds swooping past the window. It's in bed that Adam talks the most. I've learned so much about him. About how inferior he feels amongst

150

his contemporaries. How hard it has been for him to shake his North London working-class childhood and become part of the medical profession. Surrounded by public-school boys or middle-class women with offensively good bone structure who know nothing of real suffering. His parents sound horrendous – a drunk of a father and an absent mother. It's no wonder he fell straight into a relationship with an unfaithful and abusive woman. I watch him wake up and stretch his back.

'I've got them. There's enough now.' Adam places a strip of sleeping tablets on the bed. Patients often bring their pills into hospital, tied up in plastic bags, and they give them to the doctor so that he can read the labels and prescribe them. The pills frequently get lost or misplaced. When the patient goes home, they get a new selection of drugs from the hospital, anyway, so no one loses out. And right now, we need them more than the hospital does.

We're not staging an overdose. We just need Celeste to be drowsy enough for it be easy for me to kill her. As much as I'd love to fight her, it'd be an uneven battle. She'd overpower me and all would be lost.

Adam will poison her bedtime drink, to make her sleepy.

Then I'll kill her with one of own kitchen knives, just to add a splash of irony.

Chapter Twenty-Three

My mood in the night is turbulent. My body is electric with anticipation. Wakefulness leaves me restless and pensive. Three-a.m. thinking is corrosive and my mood turns. My mind slips into well-worn grooves. A parade of hurt and shame: the year that school went wrong for me, the end of my nurse training, Daddy dying so suddenly. A heart attack while he was down in the garage mending a clock. Mum sent me down to tell him his dinner was ready and I found him there. Lifeless and grey. It was another ten minutes before Mum came down and found us. Five-year-old me, sitting holding his ice-cold hand. I try to push the thoughts down, but they bob back up like ducks resurfacing on a lake.

And I think about Ava. About rescuing her from this place. About what my freedom will mean for us both. About how much has been stolen from us by my illness.

It's hard to think of happy thoughts but I have some that come to me. Dr Bronson and I set up a strategy of things to do when I slip into one of these cycles. Places I can go in my head, things I can do to distract myself. The best thoughts and memories are usually about Daddy.

There's one that I return to most. I must have been five.

It was the year that Daddy died. I opened my bedroom door to him waving the car keys at me. The binoculars bounced against my chest as I ran down to the garage. The car smelt of hot plastic, the seats sticky on my legs, and I was lulled by the slow rhythm of old music from the radio.

After a time, we reached a nature reserve, somewhere in Kent. We saw the usual suspects: water birds on a reed-choked lake and finches in the bushes. In my memory the sun was shining – but memory can do that can't it? Overlay the reality with a rose tint. But I know that the picnic was far from idyllic. Some squashed bread with a thick layer of meat paste and bags of broken Quavers. He'd forgotten to bring anything to drink but I didn't mind. We had Polos.

I was cross-legged, staring at a greenfinch who was hopping about on a branch when I felt Daddy's hand on my arm. He had a finger over his lips and gestured with his hand for me to listen. It's the one and only time that I've heard a cuckoo. The noise hypnotised me.

'Do you know how the cuckoo survives?' Daddy asked. 'Well, it's a bit of a naughty bird. It's sneaky and sly. They're parasites. A bit like nits.'

I pulled a face and started scratching my head, like you do when someone mentions nits.

'The female lays an egg in another bird's nest, usually a dunnock or a reed warbler. Poor little unsuspecting birds. Then when the egg hatches, the chick pushes the unsuspecting host parents' eggs out and kills the genuine chicks, posing as their baby. Do you see? That way the cuckoo gets to raise a baby without having to feed it or care for it. Sneaky, hey?'

'Don't the mummy and daddy birds realise that that's not their baby?'

'That's the awful part. They think it's their chick and work hard to feed it and look after it. Whilst the lazy cuckoo is off flying around, the chick gets bigger and bigger until it's even bigger than the parents. Then when it's grown, the baby cuckoo flies away and they never see it again.'

* * *

I'm surrounded by human cuckoos. Adam, transplanted from his working-class life into this realm of wealth. Peter replacing my father and ousting his memory. Becky with her brief show-business career and her marriage into an upper middle-class family.

But the worst of the cuckoos is me. I've abandoned my child. Placed my cuckoo chick in someone else's nest, letting her grow without me. It's hard to forgive myself for not being there for my daughter. My own justifications feel like excuses. Being pregnant when I was still at school was hard, but we managed. We dealt with the fallout as best as we could. Mum helped me to look after her. I went to nursing college when she was a bit older, sitting silently at the back, doing my work and passing exams, working my way through the course with neither distinction nor disgrace. We survived until this illness knocked me out of life.

I was looking after Ava one day and I had a seizure. Coming round there was a pan burning dry on the stove, the shrill reproach of the smoke alarm. My blurred vision made out the kitchen floor where I was lying, clouds of smoke above me. Her desperate face looking at me as she stood frozen like a startled animal. That was the day I stepped back. What use is a mother who can't look after her own child? What about one who can't earn money, can't provide shelter or food? Can't offer a safe home.

I withdrew from my own daughter. I erected an emotional

154

shield between me and Ava to keep her safe. It hurt me but it felt like it would be better for her if she had no mother, rather than me. I shrank away, to save us both. I had no choice but to protect her and to protect myself.

And yes, I admit that there was a delicious retreat from the relentlessness of childcare as I yielded to the state of sickness that left me without choice. The constant noise, the moving of objects from one place to another, the perpetual state of unrest. Illness claimed me as its own, exempting me from the chaos.

There's no way to entirely stop longing. To stop yourself yearning for the dead, the lost. I yearn for Daddy. I long for Ava constantly. Ava is one of my primary reasons for this plan. She's why I need to escape. Why I'd do anything. She's old enough to be able to cope with my illness now. We can finally be together, whatever Mum and Becky say.

My family hasn't always been supportive. I'm grateful for their help with childcare, but they've also assigned new labels for me. I've became the unreliable mother. Too unpredictable, too dangerous. Even on the better days when I feel capable of being alone with Ava, Mum and Becky are there, reminding me of how unsafe I am and how I'd nearly 'burnt the house down that time'.

I can't erase my past actions but I can make a future for us. We just need territory, space to grow together.

*　　*　　*

Peter is working away somewhere in Kent and Mum and Becky have gone shopping. Ava balked at the last minute and asked if she could stay at home with me. They reluctantly agreed but warned me not to use the stove or oven while they were out. Apparently I'm only allowed to operate the microwave. Ava has instructions to call them if anything goes wrong, like she's the adult and I'm the child.

The house is comforting without them all. Ava perches at the other end of the settee whilst we watch a programme about zoos on the iPlayer.

Ava is sitting hunched over and staring at the television, carefully taking Haribo from a packet and slipping them into her mouth, savouring each one. She's dressed in clothes that I didn't choose. Clothes that look too adult – shorts and a crop top that shows her midriff.

'Mum, do you mind me being here with you today?'

'No. Of course not. It's the best thing ever.'

She reaches across and puts her hand in mine.

There are so many words trapped in my chest. Apologies and justifications that I can't expect Ava to comprehend. They sit caged in shame. The twisted rationale of why I couldn't be the 'perfect mother' that I thought I had to be. The motivations that made me withdraw entirely, that seemed so sensible when I was younger but now look so naïve and binary. How in the haze of illness I couldn't see that I could be a part-mother. I succumbed to the myth that a mother is the one who does *everything* for the child. Is the protector, the carer, the educator. The roles that were beyond me. That it had to be all or nothing. So I chose nothing.

I see Ava staring at me and realise that I've been muttering to myself. That my eyes are unfocused. Ava is sneaking sideways glances at me.

We sit for a while longer. There are some parrots in the zoo on TV and I softly tell her about how a macaw has a strong beak to break through the shells of nuts. How they can break through the skin of a person's finger, even shearing through bone, shattering joints. She looks at me, transfixed, and smiles back. We watch in silence whilst the birds fly around the keeper.

'Do you like living here, Ava?'

She looks off to one side, as if she's seen something flying past the window. 'It's OK. I like Granny but I don't always like Becky and Peter.'

'I'm trying really hard. I'm going to get somewhere to live when I can.'

'On your own?' Her head flicks round so she's facing me.

'No. For us. Where there's no one bothering us.' I reach across and beckon to her. She looks startled but slides across and her body fits into my side. She's rigid at first but she yields and softens. 'I haven't been . . . able. I've tried but I just haven't been able. But when I can, I'll make things better for us, Ava.'

She doesn't speak for a while. We work our way through the microwaved meal that Mum left for us. I'm following their rules and avoiding the cooker. When the programme ends, Ava helps me to clear the plates away, encouraging me to sit down and rest while she does it. But I insist that we work together.

'I'd like it.'

'Like what?'

'If you could be my mummy again.'

I hide my damp eyes as I bend down to wedge the pans into the overcrowded cupboard.

Chapter Twenty-Four

Adam drives me to the nature reserve at Nunhead Cemetery. Ripley sits in the back of the car, staring silently at the streets of towering Edwardian houses passing by. We park the car near to two young women who are getting out of a battered Ford. I see them looking at Adam, taking in his face and body, his car. One of them whispers something to the other one and they giggle like coy schoolgirls. It happens a lot. People's heads veer towards him like there's a magnetic pull. I like it.

We walk through the gates, past the Victorian carvings of flaming torches, held upside down to signify death.

'Come on, boy.' He lets Ripley off the lead but the dog stays at his side, like he too is hypnotised by Adam's persona.

The grass by the ruined chapel is scorched and crunchy. We stop on a bench, at Adam's insistence, and drink coffee from a flask. He's always conscious of pacing me, not stripping me of my strength with too much walking. Ripley lies at his feet, ignoring the other dogs on the grass whilst we load up on caffeine.

'I love it here.' I tune in to the birdsong, lifting my face towards the sun. I feel normal. Not like an ill person today, regardless of the numbness and the creeping exhaustion in the background. I can place that to one side for a moment, not worry about how my body will react to this exercise. My thoughts focus on the birds, on Adam and on killing Celeste.

We stop at the bench overlooking the expanse of London. It looks like a toy before us. Like we're children and we have it all to play with as we wish.

'I've got a bit of a bombshell, Emma.'

I feel my stomach clench. He's going to back out of this. Tell me that he's come to his senses. That we can't kill her. That we just have to remain stuck in this claustrophobic cycle of living. If you can call it living.

'Celeste's brought her work trip to Italy forward. There's been a change in the production schedule. She's planning to go in two days' time now. And she's going to stay away for a week or two.'

'So what do we do?' I hold my breath, wishing like a child that he won't say that we'll abort the plans.

'We should do it tomorrow.'

I reach across and put my arms around him. My heart is racing. I hope Adam can't feel it against his chest or detect the way my hands are trembling. The word 'tomorrow' is stuck in my head like an impassable barrier. I can't begin to think this through so quickly.

'Just concentrate on all of the places we can go soon. Maybe by the end of the year we'll be in a forest in Asia. We'll have to celebrate.' His voice is filled with naïve enthusiasm. It's hard to resist.

'Space of our own. That's all I want.' I feel my panic starting to subside.

He answers without hesitation. 'Well, we'd have to think about the Ava issue too.'

'What's the issue?' A rush of nausea starts to build at my naivety. We should have talked about this more before we made *'the plan'*. Discussed me definitely wanting Ava to be with us. Maybe I wasn't resolute enough. I made a stupid assumption that he'd accept Ava as part of our new family, based on a few casual comments.

'We need to think hard about whether we'd want a state or a private secondary school. We could afford a public school with the life insurance. There's a good one at Catford that's co-ed.'

I exhale deeply and concentrate on the wide trunks of the trees.

'Thank you.' I force the words out. I feel winded. Overjoyed that Adam cares enough about a girl he hasn't met yet that he's thought about schools for her.

'Do you know what the worst part is?' My breath catches as I wait in expectation for Adam to express some doubt about murdering Celeste. 'It's us having to be apart for so long after she dies.'

His hand reaches for mine. We've debated the time period. That gap when Adam plays the part of the startled widower that people will expect to see. I have no doubt that he'll do it well.

We've agreed on three months of secret meetings in hotels outside of London before we start our 'unexpected romance'; six months minimum before I move in. We'll have to cope with the waiting. It's the only choice.

We walk deeper into the dark canopy of the ancient trees, past the ivy-choked graves that tumble forwards, twisted branches snaking out over our heads. Nature's barely contained, carpets of ferns encroaching on the narrow paths. Ripley darts past us. A streak of yellow fur diving into the undergrowth between two chipped monuments. Adam shouts after him. He's intent on something. His body twists round and he heads back to us, his mouth a mess of red.

He deposits the corpse at our feet and for a moment I can't make out what it is. Then I see the feathers and the beak. The glassy eye staring up at me, sightless and blank now.

'Oh fuck.' Adam grapples with the dog, trying to get the blood from his muzzle with a handkerchief, and kicks the body of the bird into the undergrowth.

I fall to my knees, pushing aside brambles to find the body. The thick drift of greenery envelops me, the corpse warm in my fist. There's a fallen stick and I use it to scrape at the ground, trying to dig a makeshift grave. Bits of dry earth scratch away but it's useless. Adam appears at my side.

'Sorry, Emma. He hasn't done that before. I wonder if the bird was already wounded or . . . Here, let me do that for you.' He drops to his knees and scratches at the earth with the stick, managing to fashion a barely adequate hole. I lower the blackbird in, and we cover him with dry earth and leaves, leaving him to return to nature. For his body to putrefy. For the maggots to take over.

We walk back to the car in silence. The blood is still under my nails. The dog sits staring in the back of the car with his face tinged with red.

'Let's get you home.' Adam kisses me. 'You're not squeamish. It's a good job really, isn't it? It's one of the many things that I love about you.'

The horror of Ripley killing the bird is expunged. Bad thoughts shouldered out by what Adam has just said. He's never used the word 'love' before. I knew that's what this is. Of course I did. Given what we're planning to do to be together.

It's love that's driving our plans.

Chapter Twenty-Five

'Here.' Adam lowers his hand onto his lower abdomen. 'Start here.'

I lift the knife and push the tip down towards him so that it rests against his shirt.

'Try again. You'll need more swing. We need to have momentum.'

I bite my bottom lip and focus my vision in, pulling my arm further back. The handle of the knife is comforting in my hands. Adam talks me through each blow. How to balance my body. How to retract and slice. Where to aim for. I stop each time when the point of the knife hits his flesh. Not piercing his perfect skin. He guides the knife for me, showing me the place between the ribs on the left side where the blade will puncture her heart. My hand shook when we first tried, but now it's steady, focused.

'Now, go back in the dressing room and run out again. I want to check how much noise there is.' We've oiled the hinges. My footsteps are light and purposeful.

I do as he tells me. I'm becoming sleek and fast. Unexpectedly capable. Adam is right – stabbing is the best way to do this. Wielding a knife only needs one hand.

'Again, Emma. You need to try to walk more softly. Like this.' He shows me the gait he thinks will work. I copy him and he nods.

'Beautiful. You're so beautiful.' The kiss is firm and reassuring. We can do this.

I'm exhausted when I get home. Later, I stagger into sleep. My dreams are mechanical and blood-soaked. When I close my eyes I see red. Rivulets of fluid that congeal and clot as they pool under the bed.

* * *

I'm resting today but it's difficult. Adam's on a night shift later, which is the perfect alibi for him. There's no way that he could be suspected of killing Celeste tonight and he'll have a whole emergency department full of staff and patients to corroborate his story. I'm ready. I've told Mum that I'm seeing Lauren and that we plan to go to the cinema to a late showing. I don't really need an alibi. Why would I? There's nothing to link me to Adam or Celeste. No evidence but a few texts on a burner phone. Adam has destroyed his phone already and mine will be deposited in the park lake tomorrow.

I go out for a short walk to distract myself. I should have guessed that I'd encounter Celeste. Should have avoided her street. She enters her house and glances back at me. Our eyes lock for a fraction of a second but it's meaningless. She doesn't know what a pivotal day this is for us both.

When I get back, I go and hide out in the garden, but it's not long before I hear Peter and one of his men from the building firm.

The employee, little more than a boy, is carrying a clipboard, and Peter is barking commands of what to write. The boy drops the pencil twice. Winston runs up and barks at me and I stare coldly at him. It's obvious what's happening. Peter's planning to rip out the garden. The last remnants of Daddy.

'What are you doing?' I struggle to keep my voice level.

'I'm not sure what business of yours it is what I'm doing in *my* house.' Peter flashes an aggressive smile. 'If you really need to know I'm planning what we're doing with all this mess.' He waves dismissively at the garden.

'What's wrong with it?'

'Like I said. It's my business. It doesn't involve you.' He turns his back on me and kicks at the log pile with his boot.

The broad expanse of his flesh screams for a knife to rip between the shoulder blades. I can't imagine that I'm the first person to have these fantasies about him. Only it doesn't matter now. Peter is a pointless target. I wish that he could know how close he came to death. To know that there was a target daubed upon his back.

What does any of it matter anyway? This garden, this house. They're nothing. I just have to get through tonight and then, in a few months' time, I'll be living with Adam. We can have a beautiful garden of our own with a wildlife pond for Ava and me. Somewhere that the birds can visit, eat, and drink. Somewhere that they can find shelter.

I hear the upstairs window of the house bang shut as I walk back in. Becky hates having her sleep disturbed after a shift in the nursing home. I go back inside and wait out the morning on the sofa.

* * *

'OK, I'm going to say this but don't be offended. I mean it kindly. What the fuck is going on with you today? You're all twitchy.' Lauren leans back, looking me up and down.

Pulls her cup across the café table. I should have guessed that Lauren would be perceptive enough to notice my nervous exhilaration. I had to get away from the house, and she was free. I stupidly thought that this would be a good distraction. That I could mask my emotions.

'It's nothing.'

'Is it something at home? Do you need to come and stay at mine? I've got a spare bedroom – and I've finally booted out the dead weight. It's just me there.'

'That's kind, but no thank you. Good stuff is happening for us. We've got a big plan.' I push my hands under my thighs to stop them from shaking. 'I'm sorry about your boyfriend.'

'Nothing to be sorry about. He's no loss. I'm guessing that the plan is to do with your man?' She waits for me to reply but I don't. 'Do you want another overpriced latte, or will it make you pee too much?'

'I'm OK.'

'Seriously, though. I am a bit worried about you. You really are jittery. You keep zoning out too.' I don't answer her. My focus returns and the dripping red stains fall from my surroundings.

'If you need some breathing space, then just come to me for a while. I'm not much trouble to be around. I wouldn't give you a massive list of chores. Well, maybe a short list.' She winks at me. Her enormous lash hypnotises me as her lid moves.

'Everything is good.' I force myself to smile at her, to focus. I appreciate her offer but I'm fine. More than fine.

Chapter Twenty-Six

The night is approaching. I can do this. I haven't blacked out in weeks. My right arm is strong. Adam thinks I'm capable of this and I agree.

The worst scenario would be that I faint in the dressing room. We've talked it through, though. Celeste is going to be so out of it that she wouldn't hear me fall and I'd wake up and leave before she came round. Then we'd try again another night. Keep trying until the job is done.

The knife feels good in my hand. I've been practising, exercising. I've sized up the items that I'll take. Electrical goods mainly, her purse. I'll stash them in our garden shed tonight, then tomorrow they'll go in the Thames, on my way to my usual appointment at the psychiatrist's office. There's a brand-new holdall that Adam has left ready under the settee in his lounge.

The back door will be left open. Adam will find her in a pool of blood tomorrow morning when he gets in from the hospital. The residual drug-laced cocoa powder in the cannister will be discarded, replaced with a new pack that I have in my bag.

* * *

In preparation, I sleep most of the afternoon. I go out at ten and walk through the streets to Celeste's house. Mum and Peter are watching TV, Ava is sleeping and Becky is at work. No one notices me leave. The streets are noiseless, no sounds of children or birdsong. No people around. Only the staccato rhythm of a dog barking in the distance.

I need to let myself in and find my way through the house in the dark. It wouldn't pay to draw attention by putting on the lights. Not that the house is overlooked. Like most rich people Celeste has the luxury of privacy with a deep front garden and trees to provide a shady enclave. Not like my house that is only metres away from the bustling street.

Two teenagers pass by as I let myself into the front garden. They're laughing about something or someone and they don't register my presence. I close the front door softly. I'm in. My shoes make no noise on the Minton tiles as I walk through the hall. Something brushes against my leg. I look down and see that it's Ripley, looking up at me with a docile expression on his face. I ignore him and walk through to the kitchen. He follows, his claws clicking on the tiles, and sinks into his bed with a heavy sigh.

Moonlight illuminates the dimensions of the kitchen but the furniture is hard to make out. The sofa and chair crouch in the corner like waiting beasts. Celeste will come in here first. She's a creature of habit, apparently, making an expensive drinking chocolate with high-percentage cocoa every night. Using the same mug with its orange Penguin book cover. We've tasted the tiniest dab of the sedative-laced powder. The acrid taste of the pills that Adam crushed is masked perfectly by the bitterness of the drink.

There's a hefty dose of sedation crushed up and mixed in with the few centimetres of cocoa powder that were left in the cannister. More than enough to ensure that Celeste helps herself to a dose large enough to render her defenceless. We worked out the maths of it together. If required, then it's easily explained on post-mortem by the pills we've also put in the drawer of her bedside table. Adam will insist that she was taking them habitually. That he thinks she might have obtained them from a private doctor in Harley Street. That he'd discouraged her from taking them.

I scan my eyes round the room. Nothing looks out of place. It's like a stage set waiting for the actors to come out and air their violent grievances. There's a faint smell of lavender in the air as if the place has been scrubbed and polished. I suspect she pays someone to do the jobs that ordinary women have to do themselves.

The stairs creak under my feet. I lift my feet carefully, mindful of tripping with my mutinous leg. This feels like a pivotal journey. When I come back down these stairs I'll be a different person with a knowledge that few possess. The sensations of murder pulsing through my hands.

I sit in her bedroom, on the side of her bed, careful not to lie back in case I fall asleep. I can smell her. The taint of her perfume stains the air and makes me want to retch. My mind blanks out and I'm nothing but purpose. I no longer feel human; my brain is devoid of all thoughts but killing. The knife awaits me in the dressing room.

I hear her arrive back at eleven or thereabouts. Their ridiculously sized bedroom has a bathroom and a dressing room. I've already slipped into the dressing room to wait for her to come up. I stand on the side that contains Adam's clothes and breathe in the rich citrus scent of his cologne. Her dresses on the opposite rack hang accusingly. I run my hands down the soft fabric of Adam's shirts and jackets.

She won't come in here. Adam says that she only comes in here in the morning. At night she drapes her clothes over the chair by the wall or throws them into the laundry basket, before changing into pyjamas laid out on the bed.

The door of the bathroom clicks shut and I listen to the distant sounds of running water. I crouch down and peer through the keyhole of the door and watch and wait, keeping my breaths shallow and quiet. Flexing my arm, shifting my position when my legs start to cramp.

Then I hear the door open and she walks over to the bed. The room is bathed in a soft glow from a bedside lamp and the cloying scent of her shower gel seeps out of the bathroom. I look away as she drops her dressing gown and stands naked for a second before putting on the pyjamas that were where Adam said they'd be.

The light catches her face. She looks older and more pathetic without her customary layer of make-up. She rubs hand cream on and smooths down the sleeves of her silk pyjamas, lifting her Pilates-toned legs into the bed with enviable ease. Her hand reaches for the mug but it isn't the orange mug tonight. She has an earthenware cup and saucer in a liverish red. She lifts her drink to her lips, propped up in bed, a hardback book on her lap.

A flutter of panic courses through me. Adam said she'd definitely use the orange mug. The plan can't deviate. But then I allow myself to kneel back for a moment, soundlessly shifting my torso. It's only a mug. This is nothing. Maybe her usual mug is in the dishwasher. Or it got broken.

Celeste Dupont will soon be dead. And this bed, this room, this house will be mine and Adam's. We'll be together. We'll have enough money to make a decent life for the three of us. Money equals freedom. Liberty to have our own territory. To have space.

Celeste Dupont will be a footnote in celebrity history.

The famous chef who was murdered in a burglary that went horribly wrong. I'm wearing gloves so there'll be no fingerprints from tonight. Adam has been cleaning the house and has obliterated any traces of me being in this house before. It will be as though I never existed.

I'll wake her, of course. Give her a shake, flash the knife. She needs to be startled, afraid and desperately trying to move her drugged and sluggish body away. She needs to pay for her behaviour. She'll be too weak from the pills to fight as I sink the knife into her back. I like the idea that she'll suffer.

Does Celeste guess that there's a reckoning coming? Has she sensed it? Maybe the evil within her has already sniffed out the evil in me.

In Welsh folklore there's a bird who arrives to announce an impending death. The 'corpse bird' flies to a person's door and when it's time, it makes a spectral sound. The screech sounds like a word in Welsh: '*Dewch*'.

'*Come.*' Beckoning the person out of the earthly world into the afterlife. '*Come.*'

I wonder if she hears them. The waiting corpse birds. The scratch of talons, the faint buzz of a wing moving as they circle. The fierce beaks poised, ready to pierce flesh. I hear them. I can feel their feathers brushing against me. They crowd me and I am one of them. The central figure in a frenzy of flapping, their screams echoing.

This knife is my claw. A sharpened beak. A tool of evisceration.

I open my eyes and centre myself, focusing on my surroundings.

And I wait for her to fall into her final sleep.

Part Two

Chapter Twenty-Seven

Celeste

August 2022 – Earlier that day

I woke up today with a feeling of doom. Nothing specific, just that general thing that hits me in the guts every now and then. It doesn't help that I have an appointment with Clive – or Creepy Clive as my stepbrother, Bobby, calls him.

I arrive at the damp-smelling office. It's an incongruously dull room. This place should have drama, an atmosphere that befits the situation that has brought me here. Some mournful Debussy in the background.

My draft divorce papers and my new will are laid out in front of me. The documents that will end this terrifying marriage and leave all my belongings to a charity supporting fertility research. The typed font is a stark reminder of my position as the latest in a parade of wronged women. The end of a long line who made contemptible choices in men.

'We'll need to get you back in a week to have the finalised papers signed off.' Clive stuffs the papers into the scuffed briefcase that he always carries. He makes eye contact for the first time as I stand and leave his office, moistening his lower lip with his pale pink tongue, the usual crimson flush staining his cheeks and neck. He hovers near me by the doorway.

'I'm in Italy for a few weeks, filming. I'll get on to them as soon as I get back.'

I burst out of the office and gasp for breath.

'I've done it, Bobby.' The phone is hot against my ear as I walk down the street towards Holborn tube station.

'Hurray to divorce. I'm proud of you. Now tell me, did you leave me all of your money? Or have you gone all tragic spinster with a sudden passion for donkey sanctuaries?' My stepbrother's voice is gravelly on the other end of the phone and I have to strain to hear him against the hubbub of traffic and the shouts of a group of street drinkers huddled in a doorway.

'I don't think that "spinster" is PC now. Let's go for glamorous divorcee.' I try to summon a carefree laugh but nothing comes.

'A second marriage on the brink of ending. That calls for a hat and a veil. We can crack open the good champagne and raise a toast to the end of this foolish era when you come round later.'

I don't feel like celebrating. Bobby's campery doesn't do its usual trick in lightening my mood. I suspect that by the time I get there he'll have forgotten about the champagne, anyway.

* * *

The streets are oppressively hot, the air dusty and fume-laden. My poorly chosen wool suit presses in on me, my scalp damp and face reddened. The journey home is interminable. I rehearse in my head how I'm going to tell Adam that I want him out of my life. That this time it really is over. I fail to find the right phrases, producing nothing but a sensation of nausea. A creeping dread of what he'll do. Of whether I'll need to involve the police this time.

I see that young woman again as I'm walking down the path to my house. The one who I saw before with that woman from the soap opera. She's walking languidly down the street, limping slightly. Furtively glancing at me as I fumble in my bag for my keys. It's the third time that I've seen her staring at me since that time she dropped that jar of honey in Blackheath market. She walks on down the street and doesn't look back.

The house is a still life. Adam has barely been around of late. We live like strangers. Since the last fight, the monstrous fight, I've avoided him for the past month. When I do see him he tries the lost little boy act that he does so well, but it stops abruptly when he sees I'm not buying it. His face falls back to the look of contempt that seems to be his default around me. The image of him with his hands around my throat is imprinted on my retinas. His features were light with joy, relishing the violence.

He's scared me before, but never like that. He's never really hurt me badly before. Nothing that left marks, anyway. This is a deviation from the shouted words through gritted teeth that started a year or so after we married. The progression in the last year to grabbing my shoulders and shaking me like a rag doll when he runs out of spiteful words. These small acts of violence that have become a feature of our marriage. It's the first time that I've had to cover bruises, tying that lurid Liberty scarf that he bought for me around my neck to hide the yellowing marks. I wish

I'd gone to the police straight away but shame stopped me. Shame at being a middle-aged fool. Well, I'm doing something now.

In the past few weeks he's touched me only once, a gentle brush of his hand on my arm as I passed. A platonic touch that – despite his betrayals, his violence, despite everything – still set my skin alive.

He's away most evenings, staggering in late and making his way to the spare room. He always says he's been visiting friends. He's a liar, of course. He knows that I know that. This marriage is decomposing. The thing about a bad marriage is that life continues to happen around its crumbling walls. So much is changing in my life. I'm unmoored and I haven't got the energy for cowering, for listening to lies, for tolerating treachery. I'm struggling to cope with the situation with my stepbrother. I don't need this albatross of a marriage around my neck.

Bobby is getting worse, moving towards the end of his life. I'm facing the prospect of losing the person I love most in the world and I need to focus my attention. It's startling how the prospect of death changes your perspective.

I now have the perfect motivation to escape this marriage. It turns out that my future doesn't involve Adam and his serial adultery. I'll be free soon.

No longer afraid.

Chapter Twenty-Eight

Celeste

Autumn feels like a good season for divorce. The ending of things. The weather is about to turn cooler. The streets will empty out, children will evacuate their back gardens and the air will be mercifully free of their shouts again.

I walk round to Bobby's, toting my wicker basket, gloves on, navy raincoat slung over the other arm, head to toe in vintage clothes. This whole 1950s style is so absurd, but it's what I do now. It started with a photoshoot for one of my books and developed into a habit, a persona. They were desperate for a hook of some kind. A woman with a penchant for French cuisine wasn't quite enough on its own. They'd drafted in this loud-voiced stylist, draped me in these old clothes and hats and pushed my startled fingers into gloves. My lips smeared with that orangey-red Fifties lipstick that you don't see much of now.

'Celeste, stop smiling. It's much better when you do that bitch face that you have. Look at me like I'm a rotting carcass.' The photographer was terrifying and by this point I'd have stood naked if she'd asked me to.

My image was quickly sealed, along with my public persona. I was marketed as the new Nigella Lawson. Only rather than welcoming and suggestive, I was stark and reserved. Whereas Nigella's sultry gaze said, 'Come to bed,' my expression was saying, 'Get up now and buy better quality bed linen.' If you look, that book is probably still on the bookcases of some of your middle-class friends' homes, gathering dust. Unused, I imagine.

I know how that feels. I've hit that time of life when women start to become invisible. Unused and unwanted like my book.

* * *

I'm wearing that same lipstick today. I always keep up the façade. I've grown to like it. It's become a cloak that I can hide behind. An elaborate act of misdirection away from whatever I'm feeling inside. Bobby's house is silent when I arrive. For a moment, I wonder if he's dead. If instead of the usual greeting, I'll be faced by a yellowing corpse. I push the harrowing thought aside and climb the stairs.

I've never spent time with the dying before and I'm surprised how much fun it is. Of course, Bobby was always exuberant. I should have guessed that he'd stay true to himself right to the end. Bobby has been my one constant. The person who has seen me through so much. The trauma that I endured with David, my first husband, the IVF, the ups and downs of the restaurant, my turbulent marriage to Adam. I would never have predicted that the skinny little boy in the Clarks sandals, who my mother introduced as my new stepbrother, would become my lifelong friend. We're like survivors of a terrible tragedy, clinging to each other for support, even decades later. In our case the tragedy we endured was being around my mother.

'Celeste!' He's groggy from one of his many naps of the day. They're starting to morph into one long sleep – the periods of alertness evaporating.

'I'm here.' I plant a chaste kiss on his clammy forehead. Shocked at how gaunt he is.

'Are you ready for Italy?'

'I'm . . . I think so.' I hesitate to say it but looking at Bobby today, I don't think that I'm going to go. Katrina, my agent, will be incensed but Bobby looks like he's deteriorating, and I don't want to be so far away.

'So, how's life with the vapid Underwear Model?' Bobby's nickname for Adam.

'Much the same – but let's talk about something else. Not darken the afternoon.'

'How about a jolly chat about my terminal cancer then?' He hasn't lost the glint in his eye that he had when we met as children.

We follow the well-practised routine. He orders me about, as usual, instructing me where to put things. He even manages to feign an appetite to appease me, picking at and disassembling food but not actually eating any. I quell my own nausea and eat too to maintain a semblance of normality. We lie back on the brass bed, watching old films from our childhood until it gets dark and he's asleep again beside me. I've decided I'm definitely going to cancel Rome. I need to be near.

His carer passes as I'm going out of the front door, nods a greeting and presses herself back, hard against the wall, to let me past. As if I'm someone to be feared.

My house is in darkness when I return. Adam has told me he won't be back for a few days. Some lame excuse about a friend in North London. It's oppressively noiseless until Ripley starts to bark, startling me. He pads across to the bottom of the stairs and stands there. His hackles raise on his back and he lets out a long howling bark. I've never been good with animals. We don't seem to understand each other. I can't do those high-octave pet voices that people do. I prefer birds. Adam scolds me for feeding them as he says they're vermin, but I love to watch them. Especially the crows who strut across the lawn with comical pomposity. Their rolling gait reminds me of the fat little priests from my childhood in Paris. They're clever – birds. They have social structures and hierarchies, apparently. They even gang up and judge each other. Which is like being around some of my 'friends'.

I usher Ripley back through to his basket and give him a couple of the overpriced treats that Adam buys for him with my money. I force myself to stroke his head and he lies down and goes back to sleep. I wash my hands in antibacterial wash after touching him.

There's something wrong in the kitchen. A cool ripple runs down my arms as I quickly catalogue the items in the room. I can't see what it is yet but I know something is amiss. I check that the doors are locked and look again. I see it now.

I let out a sigh. It's nothing, other than some uncharacteristic carelessness from Adam. My nervous system is on high alert. I need to breathe. I'm safe here.

It's nothing. The cannisters are all in the wrong places. They've been pushed along the worktop by a few inches, left in an untidy cluster. The one with the Fortnum's cocoa is foremost and there's a smear of spilled cocoa on the work surface, leaving a stain like dried blood. Odd as Adam never drinks it and he's always so tidy. I put them back.

I ignore the creaks and sighs of the house. This building is of an age where it's unquiet, announcing its presence day and night. The sounds of occupation would carry easily. I hear nothing. It's become my habit to listen out in case Adam has decided to come back unexpectedly. The rush of relief that I feel from the silence reassures me that the divorce is the right thing. The defensiveness I've had to adopt when my husband is around is exhausting. My exhalation sounds deafening in this dead room.

The stairs creak as I climb up, carrying my cup of Earl Grey. I feel too full for my usual cocoa after eating so many cakes in my gung-ho attempt to chivvy Bobby along. I don't turn on the light. I don't want to look at these stairs and remember what happened. Remember how Adam launched himself at me at the top. The climax of bitter words he'd been spewing all evening when he grabbed at my throat. That bubbling threat of violence that led to what I thought might be my death. Until his face shifted, like a cloud breaking into rain, and he released me, leaving me gasping on the landing. Fighting off images of myself lying at the bottom of the stairs, my neck twisted to an impossible angle.

I push my mind back to the present, which is just as unappealing and laden with issues. I force myself to unclench my hands and start problem-solving. Think about where the safest place would be to tell Adam about the divorce. What Katrina will say when I cancel the Italian jaunt and how to handle her disappointment in me. Her reminders of my plummeting book sales and the publisher's threats to drop me if I don't make more effort with the promotional work.

The bedroom is a collage of shadows from the lamps. Silk shades cast pleated light into the room, leaving patches of intrigue where there's no visibility. The interior designer spoke a lot about creating an atmosphere of drama. I now long for a complete absence of drama. The shower relaxes my tense muscles and by the time I leave the Neal's Yard-scented bathroom I feel less troubled. Exhaustion hits me like a blanket. My bed welcomes me. I've just set myself up in bed with my tea and book when I hear the noise. A strange thump, coming from the dressing room. Like a bag of laundry has fallen against the door, only it sounds too substantial for that. I'm not alarmed, initially. I just assume it's something that I'd left at a precarious angle. I get up and check.

I don't recognise the young woman lying there at first but I do recognise the knife by her side. Chefs know their own knives.

Then I realise who she is. She's the one who I see limping around the streets.

The one who fell over at the market.

Chapter Twenty-Nine

Celeste

It's strange how the human mind works. How hard it is to correlate things at speed. There's a woman lying on my dressing room floor with a deadly weapon by her side, and all I can think of is her audacity at choosing my own knife to arm herself with.

Then my anger kicks in. A searing outrage that this woman has invaded my home. I have enough to cope with. My jaw clenches shut with force.

She's dressed in a shapeless black top and some loose black trousers with dark canvas pumps. She's pretty. Less fragile than I first thought. I watch her breathing for a moment. It's regular and calm. She looks like a child sleeping. She's fainted, perhaps.

'What are you doing here? You shouldn't be here.' She doesn't open her eyes or respond to my raised voice. I nudge her side, hard with my toe, and still nothing.

I crouch down and shake her but she remains motionless. Her skin looks downy soft, a faint flush to her pallid cheeks. I pick up the knife and dash out. Depositing the sharp blade out of the way in the bedroom before I go to fetch a pillow and a soft blanket to cover her.

A rush of indignation passes through me as I reach for the bedding. There's an intruder in *my* house and I'm treating her like an unfortunate diner who's fainted in my restaurant. I don't know whether to be angry with her or myself for being so ridiculous. I should be running for my phone to call 999. Screaming and yelling. I yield to the urge to go back to her. I can't just leave her lying there, unwell.

When I enter the dressing room again there's no one there. My hands unfold and the blanket and pillow fall to the floor. I lurch back against the doorframe. I know that I wasn't hallucinating. She was definitely there.

My head spins around, scanning the bedroom behind me, but she's nowhere to be seen. A deep breath helps and I straighten my pyjamas, wishing I had my robe on. I feel exposed.

As I look up she springs out from behind the door. Her hands clawing at my face. I feel my legs begin to give and I keel backwards onto the countertop, bottles of skin cream skittling onto the floor. My hair falls out of place, grazing my forehead, and I push back at this flailing creature, my palm hitting her upper chest, knocking her onto the clothes rail. She stumbles back, clutching at Adam's clothes on the hangers, before falling to the floor with a yell.

'I have the knife. Don't move.' I don't know why I shout this. The knife is in the bedroom, well out of my reach. And knife wielding wasn't something we learned at boarding school. Even if I had, I don't think that I'd have it in me to use it on her.

She's breathing heavily now. Her left side is positioned oddly, as if she's a doll that a child has discarded. I clench my fists, wondering whether fight or flight is better.

184

But I can't leave her like this. She looks ghastly. I crouch down with my legs underneath me, kneeling by her side. The skirt of my silk dressing gown arranged carefully around me for modesty. I wait, sucking in air. Her eyes stay closed.

I don't know what to do. I'm not sure whether to call the police or call an ambulance – or to just do nothing. I choose the latter, or at least my body chooses for me; I kneel, frozen. Her eyes start to open again.

'Don't try to get up. I think you fainted again.' I stand up and step back, ready to run if she attacks me again. 'I've called the police. They'll be here any second.'

I'm hoping that she's too out of it to realise that I haven't had chance to call anyone.

'I'm sorry. I have these blackouts. I'll be OK in a minute.' She blinks and takes in her surroundings. As if she's remembering what just happened.

Her eyelids droop again but snap open a few seconds later. She stares at me with burning hatred. It makes me shiver.

'I know why you're here. Becky sent you, didn't she? I'm afraid you'll have to wait there while I call the police.' I imbue as much authority as I can muster into my tone, hoping she doesn't remember that I said I'd already called the police. I tap back into the swirl of anger.

She sits up, her colour returning. 'What do you mean about my stepsister? How do you know my stepsister?' She's attractive. More delicate, less obvious than her stepsister.

'I'm not here to answer your questions. Just go. Now. Or the police will take you away.' The quaking shock I'm feeling isn't showing yet. I'm using my restaurant personnel skills. As if I'm chiding a tardy waitress or a kitchen hand who's been caught stealing joints of meat. She gets up, unsteadily, and walks past me. I flatten myself against the wall. I don't try to stop her. Nor does the next attack that I was anticipating come. She's quickly out of the room and down the stairs. I let her go, following at a safe distance, grabbing the knife from the bedside table before I leave the bedroom. Following to make sure she leaves.

She doesn't go. She lingers in the kitchen. I stand by the door, waiting for her to leave, ready to bolt if she tries to attack me again.

'Just go. Now. How many times do I need to say this?' My voice is loud enough to make my temples throb.

She walks around the room. She knows her way around my house. Adam and his girlfriend must have brought her here. That tacky soap actor. Becky Whitehouse. The latest one in Adam's line of affairs. I have a file on Becky. Adam and Becky must have sent her here to rob me. The depths of his contempt for me are so ludicrous that I almost laugh. Or howl with rage. I'm not sure which one I want to do more. My hand rises to my throat and up to my dry mouth. My pulse resounds through my entire body.

My phone is on the other side of the kitchen and I need to summon help – I'm hardly capable of brawling if she tries to stop me reaching it. I'm suddenly absurdly self-conscious, embarrassed to be seen without any make-up. Preposterous and feeble, with this useless weapon that I could never use.

She still doesn't leave. She stands still, her face creasing up in puzzlement.

'What do you mean about my stepsister? I don't understand.' There's something childlike about her now, pathetic and harmless even.

'She's sleeping with my husband, isn't she? You know that.' I gesture at the door behind me, as if pointing will work any more than my shouting did. The dog looks up

186

from his basket, peers round at us both and then goes back to sleep. Of course the one time it would be useful for him to bark, he doesn't.

'That's not true. Adam is *my* boyfriend. He doesn't even know Becky.' She sits herself down at my kitchen worktop, visibly shrunk as she hunches over.

I rush to the worktop and snatch my phone, opening the folder with trembling fingers. It's not a struggle to find it. I've been drawn to it repeatedly, looking when I know I should stop, desperately trying to decipher my emotions. I let her hold my phone and she stares at the photographs, scrolling through them rapidly. Her face is unreadable as she looks at the evidence of them kissing on the South Bank, walking hand in hand in Nunhead Cemetery, checking in to a hotel together.

'I found a detective.' I can't help but blush at the silliness of it. I'm still holding the knife in my left hand, like I'm standing here about to chop a pile of shallots. 'So I could confront Adam again. There's a term that people use now for what he's been doing to me. Gaslighting. Making me feel like I'm the crazy wife, whilst he deceives me.'

She looks ghastly. Like a deflated balloon. It's a feeling that I know only too well. Then she starts rocking on the stool, her hands over her head, a low keening howl coming from her, piercing the air. She clamps her hands over her ears.

The truth hits me. It's not one of those moments when you suddenly understand something and feel no rush of relief or satisfaction. The answer to this is sickening.

'You didn't know, did you? Adam was sleeping with both of you! And he sent you here to do what? What did he want you to take?'

'I wasn't going to take anything.' She stands up and

walks away from me, runs herself a glass of tap water before walking towards my kitchen sofa.

She lies herself down and closes her eyes, as if this is her home. This woman thinks she can claim my place. She tried to steal from me and now she's daring to taunt me. To ignore my threats. To occupy my house.

'I was here to kill you.'

Chapter Thirty

Celeste

The human capacity for lying – and for accepting lies – is impressive but never more so than when it comes to lying to yourself.

There's the daily lies that people tell themselves: that they're not clever enough, pretty enough, capable of things. But the most heinous lies that people tell themselves surround relationships. That he wasn't looking at that woman in the bar, that the late-night text message was from his friend, like he told you. That he'd never be unfaithful, never leave you, wouldn't do anything to hurt you. We believe lies and in turn lie to ourselves.

I've been telling myself that I'm safe with my husband. Stupidly. Even after I'd seen the darkness that he has in him. Even after he had his hands around my throat. I didn't fear him enough. I didn't foresee attempted murder. I just blithely lied to myself that things would be better. And then when I knew that they wouldn't, I lied to myself that he'd make a graceful exit. I ignored my gut instincts.

I've feared for my sanity, my health, my marriage. The

worry of financial ruin kept me awake at night, mentally calculating imagined business losses. I've never been afraid for my life, though. I've never for a second dreamt that someone would try to kill me, in my own home, within my marriage. And until this evening, someone outside of it.

I met Adam when I was in my early forties, reeling from my divorce from David the year before. I'd just bought this house and the remodelling had begun. I was a wounded animal with a new cage to rattle around in alone. The weight of my defeat heavy on me. My sparse circle of friends made cursory efforts to haul me out of the trough that I was in, and I begrudgingly accepted an invite to a pub theatre in Chelsea.

I don't recall the play. I was too distracted by the lead actor, Adam Duke. Delighted when he gravitated towards me in the bar after the performance. This arresting man, fresh out of drama school and soon to be stepping into my bedroom, filling a David-shaped gap in my life with relative ease. I experienced a stirring of passion that I hadn't felt in some time. I thought that I was ready to unleash my emotions again.

I should have remembered that emotions can be dangerous things. Where they can lead. And that handsome men can have ugly desires and motivations under their charming exteriors.

* * *

She's shivering a little, so I fetch a cashmere pashmina and drape it over her. She sips at the coffee I've made for her. Looking up at me with doe-eyed innocence. This deadly woman who moments ago was prepared to kill me with my own knife. I've no idea what she is. Duped innocent or toxic psychopath. For now I stand between her and the knife block, calculating my moves with adrenaline-soaked precision.

I've teased it out of her and I see it. I see it all clearly. She's recounted her meeting with Adam, told me all about her stepsister. I see what Becky and Adam have in common. Much like misery, failure loves company. She blushes as she talks, skirting round anything that might hint at sex. I respect her for that. Adam is skilled at attraction. I was always drawn to him, my hands longing to be back in contact with his body. My desire only waned when the first signs of violence erupted.

I'm not surprised by his methods. I see parallels. The convenient times he bumped into her. The boyish charm. The romantic days out, artfully designed to appeal. The subtle but insistent wooing. The ludicrous stories that cast a shadow of oh-so-appealing hurt vulnerability around him.

The orchestrators of my would-be murder will both have unshakeable alibis for tonight. Adam's girlfriend is working a night shift in a nursing home. He'll be safely ensconced with a friend or his parents. This poor young woman just an improbable weapon in their hands. A remote-control killer.

I imagine that in the months following my death he'd have rapidly distanced himself from this sickly woman and then reappeared a suitable time later with her stepsister. Leaving her with no recourse to anything, nothing solid to go to the police about. Nothing she could recount that wouldn't implicate her.

That's if the police didn't get to her first.

The thing he hadn't counted on was that I'd take an impromptu day off work and spend the evening with my sick brother. I was nauseated with distress watching Bobby as he slept. Those sallow cheeks and the dreadful cleft that has appeared by his jutting collarbone. Adam couldn't have predicted that I'd leave my usual hot chocolate untouched for a change. Along with the crushed up sleeping pills she's told me about.

'When are the police coming?' She sits up on the sofa, awaiting her fate. 'I'll tell them everything.'

'I . . . I haven't called them yet.'

'I don't think that I would have done it.' She speaks after a couple of minutes of mutual silence that felt longer or shorter. I'm not entirely sure which.

'Well, you were in my bedroom with a knife. The drugs would have knocked me out. The intention was certainly there, wasn't it?' My tone is abrasive.

She looks like she wants to cry. This child-woman who's only a few years away from being the right age to be my own daughter. I can see that she's reeling with pain but I ignore my flawed instincts to soothe her, pushing them beneath my fury.

'Yes. I was.' She keeps her eyes down, staring at the rug. Avoiding me. She's shaking. Her skin goose-pimpled, in spite of the heat. Her fingers are splayed on her lap, long and elegant.

'But I don't think I could have *actually* done it. Not really. It was just a sick fantasy.' She would say that now, wouldn't she? 'I like your house, by the way. It's lovely.'

'Thank you.' A funny little laugh escapes from my mouth at the absurdity of our social niceties. I instantly look forward to telling Bobby about all of this. The now habitual pitching of my stomach preceding that thought as I recall that he won't be here for me for much longer.

'I don't mean to be cruel, Emma, but it seems you've been duped. That we've both been duped. By Adam and your stepsister.'

'Yes.' She stares down at her pale hands. 'My mind . . . I can't understand myself.'

'I shouldn't pity you, should I? I should be furious.' I swallow back the bile in my mouth. 'I've seen what Adam does to people, though. He's beautiful, you know that, but the thing you haven't discovered yet is that he's also incredibly ugly.'

There's a flash of something again and she stares directly at me. 'Do you think I need pity?'

I look away, taking her mug and putting it in the dishwasher. She's stopped shivering now. She's alert, her eyes wide. She's looking more robust by the minute. I watch her as she stands up and walks around the room, mindful of where she's going. Of what she might do. There's a slight drag to her leg as she walks. She sits again, sighing deeply. I face her across the kitchen island.

'Do you mind me asking what's wrong with you? That's not too impolite, is it?'

She's flat-voiced as she gives me a brief explanation. As if it's a script she's had to learn. Something that she perpetually has to expound upon. 'I saw you one time, you know? I slipped at the farmers' market and you were looking at me. You looked . . . disgusted by me. I think that's the right word.' She faces me full on.

'Why would I be disgusted? You're ill.' I try to make myself smile, to look at least a little empathetic. 'I just have the sort of face that suggests disdain or ennui. Boredom, that is.'

I reach across and touch her hand, briefly, before putting my hand back firmly on my lap.

'I know what ennui means,' she says, voice harsh again.

'So, you might get better from this?' I ignore her reproach.

'I might, but a lot of people don't. They give me physio

193

and I see a doctor at the Maudsley in case there's some underlying "trauma" that triggered this.' She looks down again, fidgeting in her chair. Correction: my chair.

'And is there one? A trauma?'

'That's none of your business. I don't know you.' She rocks forward again, gripping her knees, childlike. 'I'm sorry. That was rude of me. You're being nice, aren't you? Even after all this. After what I was going to do to you. I'm sorry.'

I supress a shudder. She sits back up and covers her eyes with her hand.

'Becky . . . Why did I fall for this? Why was I so stupid?'

I want to tell her that I understand. That in spite of being privately educated and having a glittering career, I was duped too. Adam sneaks into the cracks in a woman's confidence.

By the time she's finished telling me more about her stepfather, her family and her claustrophobic life she looks grey and drained. Her short, stuttering sentences start to trail off. She looks like a little girl, trying to stay awake past her bedtime.

A memory assaults me. I see myself sitting in a doctor's office as he gently tells me that my chances of having a child are dwindling. I imagined David and I adopting a child who was in a desperate situation. Someone who I could rescue and love. David vetoed that idea immediately, much as he vetoed our marriage. I was to remain as I was. Stuck with this feeling that I'd always be alone and unloved.

I want to reach out and take Emma in my arms and hold her, rock her. To tell her that everything will be all right. Absurd, really, because we're both far from being safe. And I'm not her mother. And she did just intend to stab me in my bed.

194

That's when the maddest thing of the evening happens. Even more insane than the story she's told me. I resolve to help her. That is, as long as she doesn't try to kill me again.

* * *

'Adam and Becky's plans are now foiled. We need to think what they might do next. We could both be in danger. They might try to kill me again. They might even harm you too.'

Her whole body is sagging, like she's a set of clothes left on a washing line in the rain. 'I know.'

'And what will you do?' I hate myself for sounding like a schoolmistress. Maybe I wouldn't have been a suitable mother after all.

'Nothing. Nothing at all. I'm trapped. Someone like me doesn't have options.'

'I can help. I can take you somewhere.'

I'm entirely still, waiting for her to answer. Waiting for a thank you or a small smile of gratitude.

Instead she lets out a whispered reply. 'I don't need charity.'

'It's hardly charity. You need protecting from Adam and Becky. Actually, scrap that. We *both* need protecting from them. We need a plan. You might hate me, but we have a lot in common.'

Her voice sounds weaker. Childlike, even. 'I don't hate you. I hate myself.' She turns to face me. Her eyelids are drooping and she's supporting herself on the countertop as if it's a crutch. She looks like she could crumple into a heap again at any moment. 'So, what will we do? Do we need to hide before he's back from the hospital?'

'What hospital?'

'He's on a night shift in ED, isn't he?'

I see it all as she says it. He's pretended to be a doctor to appeal to this poor, ill woman. What better confidant than an empathetic medic. He'd play that role well. In fact, I think he once did on a daytime soap. He only lasted two episodes.

I don't answer her. Her brow creases as she looks at me. 'He's not a doctor is he?' Her voice is a monotone.

Chapter Thirty-One

Becky

August 2022 – Two days before

I'm used to humiliation. This has been my life since I was a teenager, when the press reported on my every awkward movement with glee. Each drunken stumble, every cigarette smoked, man kissed – all documented. Then the shouting about my public sacking with relish, followed later by the jubilation over my failed marriage. I've been splashed over the front of the tabloids on a predictably regular basis. Or more latterly mentioned in passing in the mid-section, with the other items of waning interest.

I've even died in public. My on-screen demise quashing all hope of a return. I stopped existing and then faced the anti-climax of unemployment and wondering if I would ever work again. And I was right to be afraid. Nothing but a string of disastrous jobs, ever slipping down the rungs of the ladder. A Cinderella story in reverse. The odds for child soap actors like me working again aren't good. There wasn't even reality TV to turn to at that time. Behold my fate: little Tania from *Castle Street* is no more.

I'm now Becky Whitehouse, a thirty-seven-year-old care assistant in a South London depository for the elderly. Tumbled down the ranks. Ejected from my rightful position as a rising star. My budget not stretching to Chanel and Gucci anymore. No longer fawned over by the press and public.

There's something that only me and Adam know. I'm about to rise up again. To glitter and sparkle in a way you can only do when you've got money.

Some might call it greed. I call it restitution. I'm going to claw back what I deserve.

* * *

Working at the nursing home doesn't suit my temperament. The constant having to pretend to care. The menial work. The thankless conversations with the dreary women who work there. Colourless drones who mop up body fluids after others. Worst of all, they don't resent doing it. Women who wouldn't know Prada from Primark.

Thank fuck that I'm out of here soon.

One of the new residents keeps calling me Tania. I can still act, of course, so I smile sweetly and gently remind him of my name. Repeatedly. It goes on all night. He doesn't sleep, following me like a dog. It's easier when they can't walk. There's a limit to how much trouble they can be when they're lying in bed. If it was up to me I'd lock him in his room.

By the morning, I'm sweaty and aching, baked by the urine-scented warmth of this place. I pop into the staffroom to grab my bag.

198

Denise is holding a magazine, one of those cheap ones with stories about incest and ghosts. The other two are peering over at it and they go quiet, just for a second. They start up again, too quickly, with some nonsense about Carol's impending holiday. I take the magazine from her hands, not saying a word, guessing what's coming. They morph into a trio of naughty schoolchildren, Denise ashen, the others staring at their feet.

'It's nothing, Becks. Don't look.'

'Well, you all were, weren't you? Looking, I mean.' It's a strain to keep my tone light and sunny, when I'd quite like to smack the smug smiles off their faces.

It's one of those 'Where Are They Now?' features and it's about me and a couple of other has-been soap actors. I'm the star feature. The most unflattering photo of me walking down the street, hair scraped back and no make-up on. Dressed in the best that Primark can offer. Ava is with me, face blurred out, thankfully. They've put it next to the photos of me and my ex, Harry, soap-scrubbed and grinning on our wedding day, both in those matching white Chanel suits, bejewelled and styled. I was blissfully unaware that it was all temporary. Of the lengths I'd have to go to get back everything I once had.

Apparently, I'm washed up and desperate, working in a nursing home and full to the brim with bitterness, never quite recovered from the divorce. Naturally, they haven't actually asked me about any of this. Though they're partly right.

I try for an upset and tearful look until I'm round the corner, where I can shout 'Fuck!' without anyone I know hearing me. Like I said: humiliation. It never gets old.

Home isn't much of a refuge.

'Emma's in bed still. I think she said she's off out to

meet her friend later.' Ann's singing along with the radio, ramming a sandwich box into Ava's backpack. Her varicose veins straining out of too-white skin before she even starts the day. She rushes out of the door and I see that she's left her own sandwiches on the counter. I don't run after her. I'm starving. I eat the cheap white bread and Asda value tuna. I'll be having better food than this soon but it'll do for today. It'll be hand-made sourdough and artisan cheeses when all this is finished.

By the time I get to bed I'm too tired to sleep. I pull out my second phone from the back of my knicker drawer and send a message to Adam:

'How is the plan?'

'Emma will do it in two days' time.'

The game is on. Six weeks. That's all it's taken us.

I lull myself to sleep planning how me and Adam will live once the deed is done. The opulence and wealth that will cushion us from the dirt of reality.

If people thought my downfall was iconic, they better wait. My rise will be monumental.

* * *

There's something not right with my stepsister. I don't mean the disability. All that fainting that she used to do and the sleeping. Unlike Dad, I do believe it's real. What I mean is that there's something *lacking* about her. Just try spending a day in her company and listening to her grisly bird tales. Watch her face. You'd soon see it. That's why I think she can do this. She's ready to believe anything. So desperate to escape that she'd go to any lengths.

It's ambitious and far from perfect – but what plan ever is?

For the record, I don't hate Emma. She was my teenage accomplice, a willing spectator to my acts of mischief, an eager child listener to my twisted tales. Malice isn't why we're doing this. I just don't care about Emma enough, which is a different thing entirely. I'm not *overjoyed* by the risk of us sacrificing her, but I'm not overly worried either. If we can get her to do this, then the worst-case scenario is that she'll serve a few years in jail or maybe a psychiatric unit. It might even do her good. There's bound to be birds to look at out of the window of her cell. It's not like she ever does much with her time.

You might not believe me when I tell you this but the easiest way to commit a crime is to just do nothing. Stand back and watch as someone else perpetrates the deed for you. Don't get me wrong. You need to prepare well. It's got to be the right person. The right time. Observations and assessments beforehand.

And who better than your own family to do it all for you? You already know their strengths and weaknesses, what their limitations are.

In fact, Emma gave me the idea. She handed it to me like a gift. We were sitting together, watching a Netflix thing, some mindless romcom. The main character had a disabled sister who walked with a stick; the sickliest embodiment of humanity you've ever seen on screen. She died at the end of the drama, of course.

'Why do ill people in dramas have to always be so bland? They could make them more rounded. I'd like to see a drama where the sick character is bad for a change. Maybe even the villain.' She laughed as she said it.

Thank you, little sister. You're a true inspiration.

Chapter Thirty-Two

Becky

The next day I'm taking Annoying Ava to summer club. Dad waves bye and Ava stares coldly at him.

'You could show some bloody manners.'

She blanks me.

You've no idea how demeaning I find this. It's way beneath me. She's not even my child and if she was then Adam and I would hire a nanny.

I stay up after the school run and occupy myself with housework, wiping down the frayed furniture. Like I'm the servant here. Balancing endless tasks; the calendar scrawled with reminders about bills to pay, and to buy worming tablets for Emma's cat. There's a pile of accusatory Post-it notes bearing my own writing, stuck to the edge of the shelf over the cooker. Lists that I don't ever complete.

Maid, secretary, nanny. These menial roles don't suit someone like me. I'm an actor. At this stage of my career I should be walking a red carpet. Not be the woman vacuuming it. I had a cleaner when I lived with Harry. I shouldn't have to *be* one in this dump.

It's not like I haven't got other things to occupy me. Crimes don't just commit themselves, even when you have someone else doing the job for you. You have to line things up, ready for them to all to come toppling down in the right order. Luckily my accomplice is good. Much like my sister, Adam didn't take much convincing.

* * *

Adam wasn't single when we met. The best men are often taken but nothing is forever. Relationships can break down. Or be broken. He had an insipid girlfriend. One of the Chelsea set with a trust fund. He always aimed high.

Adam and I did a play together when I was on my descent to obscurity. A sticky pub theatre in Islington where you had to project to be heard above the football showing on the massive TV in the bar. I think we knew what would happen the first time we set greedy eyes on each other. The girlfriend clung to him but we found a way to meet. A couple of glorious afternoons in shabby hotel rooms. The play ended and I thought that was it. He was back pursuing the Poor Little Rich Girl. I understood. She had more currency than me. But he was one of those men who you think about. Popping up in my head occasionally. Not a crush or anything that inane. I just connected with him.

We met again by chance, at the local park, a year ago. The rest is history. Our beautiful and despicable history. The plan began inauspiciously in a cheap hotel room. We spend a lot of time in hotel rooms.

'If only you were single.' I trailed my hand down Adam's warm torso as he lounged back on the bed. The room was stifling from the radiator and from our afternoon's activity, the unseasonal cold of a sharp spring day held at bay. 'We could get out of here. Be together.'

Finding somewhere to live with Adam was always just a part of it for me. Having wealth. A cleaner again. The flashy clothes and jewellery that I need. Only this time, not just loaned to me to wear at the British Soap Awards but entirely mine.

'If only. Without my bitch of a wife I'd be single but penniless. That fucking prenup agreement.' He took my hand and moved it back down under the duvet and I didn't resist. I rarely could with him.

'I'm sure we'll work something out.' I surrendered to his insistent kisses, thoughts popping into my brain.

There was only one way in the end. Our conversations spiralled until we alighted on a twisted solution. It was always on my agenda. It just needed seeding into his. What if Celeste died and we had all her money to ourselves? If we were bolstered by the life insurance pay-out, owned that house, coined it in from the royalties on those cookbooks. *Imagine* the boost in sales if she was killed.

Naturally, we couldn't just do it ourselves. Adam would be the number-one suspect. The husband always is.

I wondered at first whether I should kill her. I'm more than capable. The thing is, there are traces of me. Adam and I are intricately linked and I'm too noticeable. You can't be lovers for this length of time and not leave remnants, a hint of a bond, a memory. There was bound to be some gleeful hotel receptionist who remembers me from *Castle Street* and dashes forward to tell the police that she saw us together.

So, I offered up Emma as the sacrificial lamb and he lapped it up, like I knew he would. Adam's part in this is immense, of course. He had to do most of the work, the wooing, even fuck her. Luckily, he was more than capable. There was no way she wouldn't have reciprocated. There aren't many people who can resist Adam.

I knew exactly what would appeal to Emma. She's a simple target, starved of affection. Her ambitions are pitiful. Laughable, even. Escape is enough for her. Simply to be free and have a room of her own for her and that wretched mini-me child. I'm aiming much higher than that.

I created a dossier about Emma's pathetic bird obsession, her childhood bereavement, and her medical condition. And then I created the persona of her perfect boyfriend, which Adam would bring to life.

'I like that bit.' He laughed out loud, reaching across the bed to point at the notes on my phone. 'The pitiful council estate upbringing. Genius. It's hilarious, considering my real background. I don't know where my nanny would have slept in a grotty council flat?'

That time, I didn't laugh back.

* * *

Luck was on our side and it began better than either of us could have imagined. Adam had been following Emma, waiting for the right moment to swoop, when she had one of her attacks. He'd been lingering outside the hospital, poised there because I'd relayed Emma's text message that she was leaving the ED. As if on cue, she dropped her bag and was pathetically stumbling around. She made an assumption that worked entirely in our favour. She thought that Adam was another public-schoolboy doctor. Making an assumption because of the rolled-up sleeves and the plummy accent. Thanks, Emma. I'm annoyed that I didn't think of that one myself.

Of course, it's not all been straightforward. I made my first mistake on the day when she 'accidentally' bumped into him in the street. I'd sent him another text, so he was in position to pounce, dressed as if he'd been running. So wholesome and appealing. I met him afterwards. Or should I say that I was having 'lunch with my friends'. The imaginary friends who I go out with every week. But it was the usual thing: an afternoon of fucking in a mid-price hotel.

I came back and went straight upstairs to sit with Emma. Thought that I'd stoke things up a bit, try and lead the conversation and encourage her where I could. Only I'd forgotten about Adam and that bloody aftershave. The cloying lemony smell that was clinging to me after a few hours pressed against him. I could see Emma's nose twitching as she lay there, half-dozing, and I waited for her to comment on the scent, for it all to unravel. But she didn't say a thing, just lay there inert, smiling. I warned Adam not to wear that aftershave on the days when we met.

Then there was the burner phone that Adam stupidly dropped. It's not like him to make mistakes. He's so slick. And him and Emma in Soho, bumping into that twat from the failed audition. Minor blips that we pushed through.

The worst thing was my hand. That one was really stupid. I'd gouged a few light scratches down his arm, which she lapped up. Then he slipped on the treadmill and she focused in on the bruises. So we ramped it up. I did a stage punch on Adam's face whilst he gripped a doorframe. I'd done it many times before. My soap character was a fiery child who was free with her fists. Only, we didn't anticipate quite how much it would hurt in real life, or the extent to which my knuckles would redden and swell. We lay wincing with pain in the hotel room. Pain that turned to laughter, to insistent touching. You can imagine where that led. I passed my swollen hand off as a burn from the nursing home and covered it with a bandage.

Emma didn't suspect a thing.

* * *

I meet Adam after work in our usual hotel room. We've upgraded from the pitiful holes we first used to meet in. I've insisted that we use five-star hotels only. It's not like he can't afford it. Adam isn't exactly poor, like he told Emma he was. He doesn't have a penny of debt, thanks to his mummy and daddy clearing up his messes. And he has the allowance from Celeste. We just need more money than he has right now. He doesn't have enough for the kind of lifestyle that we deserve.

'How was Emma last night? Did you have fun?' He knows exactly what I'm referring to. He sits up, the bed sheet falling away from that beautiful upper body, and reaches for my hand.

'You do know that I hate having to fuck your weird stepsister?' He lets out a sigh. His 'sorrowful' face is well rehearsed. I'd give him an eight out of ten for this performance.

'Aw, poor little rich boy. Having to have sex with three women. Your life must be unbearable.' I almost hide my smirk. My gaze lingers on his flat torso again.

'You know that I love you, don't you? That it's just you and no one else?' He makes those sad eyes that he does so well.

207

I reach across and kiss his lips, our mouths glued together. We both learned how to snog in acting classes. I'm always acting a little but I'm certain that he is too.

* * *

When I arrive home Dad is mindlessly flicking through the TV channels, Ann curled into his side like a tragic facsimile of a lovesick teenager. Ava is sitting on the floor, flicking through a book. Ignoring everyone, as usual.

There are a few key ways to manipulate Emma. Ava is top of the list. It's always good to have a back-up plan. I've been steadily drip-feeding things to Dad and Ann, too. About how I think Emma's not capable of safely caring for her daughter. They lap it up and of course it ripples back to Emma and makes her more desperate. The only hitch is that because Emma isn't looking after the little weirdo, I then have to do it. She's an odd child. Sometimes I catch her staring at me. It's unnerving, like she sees through to the real me. She reminds me of Emma.

'It's your show, Becky.' My dad grins at me as the familiar music of *Castle Street* sounds out. 'Do you think they'd ever have you back?'

I clench my fists and stare ahead. 'I died, didn't I? I can't go back.'

'Shame. You were bloody good.'

The room is too small for three adults, a child and two animals. The remnants of last night's fried food linger in the air. I don't speak; I just walk up to the bathroom and put on my make-up for work.

I adopt the appropriate face and stance, enter the 'Good Becky' role, and take a deep breath. Go to check on Emma before I leave for work.

'How are you?' I sit down next to her on the bed. The inevitable chaos of family life in the background. Ava seems to be singing 'Fuck You' by Lily Allen, which bothers me less than it probably should.

'I'm OK. Fine in fact. I've been a bit better lately, haven't I?' Her eyes are manic-wide.

'I think so. You're doing great, little sister. Just great.'

She's doing more than 'great'.

She'd better keep it up.

Chapter Thirty-Three

Emma

The sick girl finally finds her voice and channels her rage only to learn she's a puppet. I would laugh, gasp in gleeful horror maybe, if I heard this story. But it's a story about me.

There's a new image that's flying around my head, pecking at my consciousness. Every time I close my eyes I see Celeste again. I don't see the caricature villain that Adam created: the cruel abuser, the sneering monster, the faithless wife. Instead, I see Celeste bending over me, draping that shawl across my body. Her eyes soft as if she's tending to an ailing relative, or a much-loved child.

I want to kneel down and vomit until there's nothing but bile coming from my throat.

I've known for a long time about my stepsister. I've often thought of Becky as being a particular bird. A savage bird that's rooted in our urban landscape. She's a sparrowhawk. They swoop down and take what they want, piercing the body of smaller birds with their razor-sharp talons before ripping them apart and devouring their flesh. Sometimes not even waiting till their prey is dead before they take what they want. Eating a half-living victim. The female sparrowhawk is the worst of the species. Bigger and stronger than the male with more capacity to kill.

I lost my focus. Thought that my stepsister had changed. I was tricked by her act. Stupid, gullible me – not only fooled by love but also duped by my family.

I was tempted by something bright and sparkling. By fakery and artifice. Adam is like a bird too, one of those foppish, exotic male birds. In the bird world it's often the male who is more colourful than the female, designed to attract with their colourful plumage. They're the ones who are there to woo, going to elaborate lengths to court the females who are in short supply, too occupied with rearing the chicks. The males need to divert and beguile to get what they want. That's Adam: all surface pattern and beguiling colour. A creature who knows exactly what to home in on to breach a woman's defences. My weakness was my desperate desire for someone who cared and would understand my opaque illness, like no one else had. What better ploy to get me to lower my defences than to pretend to be a caring doctor?

Real fury is pervasive. It fills you and invades every muscle of your body, eating into your thoughts. It moves targets, slamming from one person to another. My hatred for Celeste was founded on untruths. I've been raging at a phantom, a construct of Adam's lies. My new focus for my rage flits between Adam and Becky.

But then it clings to another target. I hate myself for falling for this, for almost killing this poor woman next to me, as part of someone else's twisted plan. I almost wish that Celeste would take the knife and hurt me.

But she wouldn't do that.

People think that they know all about my stepsister, Becky. Go back ten years and her face was spread across their breakfast tables in tawdry newspapers. The sweet adolescent from the TV who morphed into the real-life troubled teenager, then disappeared. The wronged woman who vanished when her husband left her for a man in a blaze of headlines. That isn't her. None of those versions are.

Becky has always had a shine that hid her twisted interior. I see it in the old photographs. She loved to act at school. Then ITV announced a new soap opera called *Castle Street*, the second-rate *EastEnders* rival that grabbed the public imagination. Set in South East London, as opposed to the East End, it focused on the workers on an outdoor market and the estate that backed onto it. A sanitised version of the grubby stalls of a backstreet market but without the stolen TV sets, pickpockets and knock-off CDs for sale. Rough but polished enough for TV. A London estate without drug dealers and petty crime, a place where no one swore.

They'd put out an open call for local child actors, a cheap publicity stunt with pre-arranged tabloid cameras snapping the line of hopeful kids. Becky tells me that the production team took one look at her in her shabby skirt and blouse, heard her accent, and salivated with joy. She was exactly what they'd visualised for Tania Braithwaite. A feisty adolescent from a family of hard-working, 'salt of the earth' Londoners. A walking cliché.

I suspect that was when her ego started to inflate. My first memories of her are as a boisterous twelve-year-old, motherless and full of rage after she was transplanted into our home with her oafish father. She took her grief at her mother's premature death out on my mum and Peter for a while but it burned out and she learned to be nice. Or at least she learned to pretend to be nice. Here was a box-fresh sister. Not only that, but she also understood the pain of losing a parent, like I did. Only whereas I was sad, Becky seemed stuck in a state of perpetual rage. Which she talked about endlessly while I listened.

Teenagers seem impossibly sophisticated when you're a child. I was happy to be the one she talked to. Only when I look back with an adult perspective, I see that the whole 'confidante' thing she fostered in me was a ploy. She just wanted someone to show off to. Someone who'd be easily impressed.

I'd be sitting there aged six, wide-eyed, with thirteen-year-old Becky telling me about all the ways she had of enacting her hatred. Teaching me how to get ahead in life through lies and manipulation. The actors she dispatched through deceit and trickery. Spates of robberies where the stolen goods would be found in a washed-up thespian's locker. A trail of child porn sites on a discourteous actor's laptop. A brattish child star dispatched after a campaign of anonymous letters. She didn't believe in getting her hands dirty. It was all done remotely.

By the time I was nine, her character in the soap just got meaner and she became frenetic. High on success. The public loved the new nasty Tania that the scriptwriters came up with, complete with burgeoning sensuality. She was even booed once at a soap awards dinner, which made her preen like a cockerel. There was hate mail too, but it was outweighed by the fan mail (which occasionally comprised a few indecent snaps sent in by young men and some by not so young men, who should have known better).

Becky didn't tell me at the time that the actor she planted the child porn on killed himself. I found that out online a few years later.

I've sometimes wondered if she has a conscience at all.

Chapter Thirty-Four

Emma

'Have you called them yet?' I look across at Celeste, sitting on the other side of the kitchen island. She's alert and wide-eyed, like an angry cat ready to pounce on her prey.

'Called who?' She speaks sharply.

'The police. You do need to call the police. I've done something terrible, haven't I?'

'I'm . . . thinking hard about what to do. But I'm not calling the police. Yet.' She shakes her head and goes to say something else but stops herself. She closes her eyes for a second. As if she can't decide what words to use.

Then when she does start to speak she outlines her plan. This strange and wonderful idea.

Celeste is offering me something unexpected and bizarre: a chance to run. Escape routes are always tempting. Look at how I reacted to Adam's offers to flee from Peter's cruelty. Shame hits me in sickening waves. Here she is, wanting to protect me, to take me somewhere safe.

'You have to promise not to hurt me, Emma. One hint of

anything, and I mean anything, that suggests violence and I *will* call the police, OK?'

'Of course. I don't want to hurt you.' She nods, as if we've just shaken hands on a deal. 'But why are you doing this? I don't deserve your help.'

'It's a horrible, shameful word but I'm going to use it. We're victims. Both of us are. Victims in different ways but we're still both casualties of Adam.'

That's when I sense her fear. I don't know whether it's just Adam she's scared of. But still she stoops to nurture me in spite of that. Rather than running and thinking only of herself she's treating me like I'm a wounded bird she's found in the garden. Something she wants to mother back to health.

It's not even ten o'clock but my eyelids feel weighted, my limbs leaden. Like I've been boned and filleted. Celeste looks across at me. I'm more rag doll than human. She's different. Softer, the haughtiness diminished.

'You look like you're about to collapse. Adam won't come back till the morning and I need some time to think. Why don't you rest?' The fact that Adam would have come back to find her dead is unspoken between us.

I'm dependent, at her mercy. A loose sack of bones and flesh. My mutinous body deciding to seize up and betray me again. Maybe I should thank this illness. If I hadn't collapsed then I'd have killed Celeste and set in motion the next part of Adam and Becky's plan. The plan where I was a casualty too. I knew there had to be a positive to this one day. Celeste is alive and I'm escaping.

She guides me up to a spare bedroom and I sink onto a brass bed, engulfed by the soft mattress. I surrender. Too tired to even speak. The last sound I hear is her footsteps walking up and down the corridor.

When I wake up, Celeste is under the window of this room. Outside on the back patio talking to someone on her mobile phone. For a second I think that she's talking to the police. I jump up, preparing to accept my fate.

A loud voice sounds out into the night through the speaker of her phone and upwards. Posh people's voices carry. I move closer to the open window, hidden behind the curtain.

'Where's Lizzie Borden now?'

I wince.

'Don't be so mean. Anyway, Emma didn't have an axe. It was one of my kitchen knives. I'm letting her sleep.' She gulps in air. 'Bobby, I'm scared. What do I do?'

'Go to the police, obviously, but it sounds like you've made up your own mind already.'

'Adam will do something bad to her. She has nowhere to go and she's as much a victim—'

'Remind me again, which one of you was lying there whilst the other one hid in a cupboard with a knife? I still think you should call the police.'

'I don't think there's that much harm in her. She looks dazed. I suppose that you would be somewhat thrown if you'd just found out that the man who you'd become lovesick for was duping you. Even worse, duping you with the help of your own sister.'

I know that I should move away. The man's comments are deserved. I own that. It's the empathy from Celeste that smarts more, flooding me with nausea-tinged shame.

'Well, she must have been seriously lovesick to try to slaughter you whilst you slept.' I miss the next part as the sound is drowned out by a couple walking past, wrapped in a heated argument.

'I can't get over the thought that you were almost usurped by Tania from *Castle Street*.' A bark of laughter. 'Imagine.'

'I have to do something.'

'Go to Rome like you'd planned. Just get on the plane and leave all this behind. Do the filming and have a holiday. It'll all still be here when you get back.'

'Rome isn't going to happen. I've already emailed Katrina and I'm waiting for the fallout. It's too far, anyway. I want to be nearby in case you need me.'

There's a long gap before the man speaks. He sounds exasperated.

'I'm not going to argue because you always know best but it sounds like a plan that'll involve getting yourself killed. Although, you survived your mother and your resting bitch face could repel any attacker, I'm sure. Just . . . be careful.'

Chapter Thirty-Five

Emma

Celeste walks with me to my house and I sneak in, grabbing a few clothes, my medications, some books. I creep up the stairs, avoiding the creaking tread halfway up, so as not to wake Mum or Peter. Ava is curled on her side, stray strands of hair stuck to her face. She's beautiful. I resist the urge to kiss her cheek, forcing myself from the room like an addict trying to abandon their drug of choice.

Celeste has been talking to me in a gentle tone, like she's coaxing a frightened child, but her voice became harder when I argued with her about Ava. I wanted to bring her with us but Celeste quashed that idea. She's the bossy mother, with me in the role of naughty child. I accept the part and play it well. She told me that taking Ava from the house would raise too much suspicion. Mum's off work for a few days now, and Becky is working so it'll be Mum who cares for her. Celeste says she'll be safe. I really hope she's right.

We both have cover stories. Celeste was due to fly to Rome, of course, so she'll text Adam 'from the airport' to remind him about her trip. She'll tell him that she didn't come home last night but spent the evening with her stepbrother Bobby, leaving straight from there.

I've messaged Lauren and asked her if she could cover for me, no questions. She was quick to agree, thinking I'm holed up on some kind of sex marathon with my married man. She sends back a borderline obscene GIF. I've told my mum that I'm staying over at Lauren's. The last message I sent was to Adam.

'Celeste not there. We'll have to try again another time. So tired from the stress. I need a break. Staying at Lauren's. Will message tomorrow.'

I turned the phone off straight after sending that one. He'll think nothing of me not answering. He'll suspect that I've fallen into a stupor, which suits the plan.

Becky is working nights so I didn't have to face her, yet. The night shift was going to be her perfect alibi – whilst I killed for her. I shudder, suddenly cold as I glance at Celeste beside me. I see her in my peripheral vision, glancing down at my leg as I walk, checking that I'm OK. I can't help but keep looking around for movements in the shadows. Even though I know Adam and Becky won't be here.

We walk towards her stepbrother's house, the one Adam said was her lover's, with her periodically offering to take my holdall. I refuse her help, trying and failing to hide my awkward limp. My bag digs into my shoulder as we make our way down avenues that rustle with the sound of parched leaves. No other noise except the holdall hitting my hip, the occasional scraping of my foot on the pavement.

We've left her house in perfect condition. We worked together: the bed straightened, the cups washed and put in the cupboard. The drugged hot chocolate now in the dustbin and the canister refilled. The pills removed from the

220

drawer. It's pristine with no hint of what really happened. Adam will think I cleared up after Celeste failed to arrive home.

'My stepbrother Bobby lives a few streets away. He's terribly sick, I'm afraid. He has bowel cancer. He won't be put out by us arriving, though. His sense of day and night has all gone to pot.'

'Are you sure it's OK for me to be there?'

She shakes her hand in dismissal.

'I've watched you going there. I thought you were having an affair. Well, that's what Adam told me.'

'An affair?' She gasps. A shrill sound piercing the night.

'He told me that you have a lot of affairs. And that you beat him. He had scratches on his arm and bruises all over his face. He said it was you.'

Her frown gives way to grim understanding. 'He told *me* that he'd fallen in the gym. So, I'm a serial philanderer and a husband beater? Oh, to have the time and energy for all that. The passion even. I can barely keep afloat with running the restaurant.' Her laugh is strained.

We pass no one on the streets as we walk, the roads tinted orange by the streetlamps. Houses with empty eye sockets for windows and no signs of activity; a group of emboldened London rats pick at discarded food, ignoring us as we walk by.

The rhythm of night walking, of moving one leg and then another, is meditative. Celeste speaks and I jump slightly. I'd almost forgotten I wasn't alone.

'Do you think we'll be able to able to do this?' Her voice sounds weaker, more hesitant.

I'm confused for a moment and I answer with the thought that's been calming me. 'You mean to get revenge on Adam and Becky?'

221

She recoils slightly at my answer then composes herself. 'That's a tempting thought but I was thinking more of finding a way to clean up this mess and for us both to get out of it unscathed.'

'Yes. Of course I'm with you. I'm grateful to you for—'

She puts a hand up to stop me and just nods.

We carry on walking. A convertible car passes us. I can't make out the colour or make in the darkness. I freeze for a second and see a man lean forward to peer at us as he passes. It's not Adam.

'Are you OK?' She reaches out her arm to me as I stumble on a root-lifted paving slab. I right myself against a garden wall. Her skin is cool as she lays her fingers on my arm to steady me, like a mother with a toddler on a wobbly bicycle. 'We're nearly there. Let me help you.'

I take a sharp breath and loop my arm through hers and finally allow her to take the holdall. It's threadbare, worn away in places, and I wince at the thought of what she must think of it.

The house is in darkness. There's that smell in the air, the one that comes with sickness. She leads me straight up to the spare room. It's immaculate, one of those rooms that I suspect all rich people keep. A room sitting vacant, ready for someone to stumble in and slip beneath the covers after a missed train or a late meal. A house with enough space that whole rooms can just sit vacant, waiting for occasional inhabitants to disturb the air. Rather than our house where we jostle for space to breathe.

It's beautiful. I catch my reflection in the mirror of a pale wood dressing table. I'm wrong here. Too cheap, not cleansed and sophisticated. I'm like a smear on clean glass. I arrange my pitiful collection of things neatly. She watches over me like an overprotective parent. Something I know that she's never been. I read some of what she's written about that subject when I fell down a rabbit hole researching her.

I strip to my underwear, desperate for the cool release of the bed, tiredness making me feel like I'm trapped behind glass. I have no inhibitions about being unclothed in front of people these days. I've undressed in front of so many doctors and nurses that I'm beyond caring.

As she turns to go, I blurt out, 'Thank you.'

She turns back and frowns in puzzlement. 'There's no need to thank me.'

'But there is. For bringing me here. For not going to the police. For trying to keep me safe. For helping me to—'

'Like I said. There's really no need. This whole thing. It's not exactly . . . black and white. You're a victim here too.' She turns and leaves, telling me that we'll talk properly tomorrow. That I'll be safe here for now. The memory of Ava's sleeping face enters my mind. I reassure myself that she'll be safe with Mum. Becky wouldn't hurt her. She's been looking after her for long enough. At least that's what I tell myself.

Just before I sink into sleep, cutting off the storm of thoughts in my head, I hear the door across the landing. Classical music seeps through the darkness before the door shuts again. There's a male voice and I pull myself up, fighting the fatigue. I strain at the open door to hear what's happening.

'Is Rose West with you?'

I hear the click of a lock. I don't blame her for locking herself in.

Chapter Thirty- Six

Celeste

The doorbell is shrill. Like the scrape of knives being sharpened. I move to the top of the stairs and peer through the slats of the half-opened shutters at the quiet morning street. Adam's familiar mop of hair is below. His finger moves to the bell, jabbing at it again and again. I'm not answering. Hoping that he still thinks I've left for the airport. That he's just double-checking that I'm not here because Emma has gone AWOL.

I covered my tracks. I want him to think things are as usual. I quickly packed a small case with clothes and toiletries before we left, grabbing a book, my iPad and phone. The standard stuff I'd take on a trip. A robotic focus came over me. I thought I'd pulled it off but realised this morning that, in my haste, I've forgotten my laptop. The one I'd be using to draft articles on. Adam won't notice this, though. He sees my study as the pointless folly of an irrelevant woman.

'Who the hell is that?' Bobby's voice croaks across from the bedroom.

'It's Adam.'

'Of course it is. He'll be double-checking that you've gone. Ignore the arsehole. Call the police. Whatever makes him stop that noise.'

Bobby's mention of the police jolts me from this fog of exhaustion that I've woken with. I need to think harder. Adam is wily and quick. He'll know something is amiss when he talks to his girlfriend. Emma told me that she doesn't normally go to stay anywhere else. She's always holed up in that house. I suspect that they'll both quickly start to wonder where she is and what really happened. Which means that Adam will start to wonder where *I* really am too.

Adam turns and walks away and I dart back from the window, almost stumbling. There's no sound of movement from behind the spare room door. Emma must still be sleeping. Or hiding.

I push down my fear and try to think. My stomach clenching at the thought of Adam's proximity.

I run through my options again. Confronting Adam is too dangerous and doesn't promise any sort of resolution. The police aren't an option. I have no proof that Adam attacked me recently, or ever. I was always too ashamed to keep photographic evidence. There's no record of the finger marks on my arms, the ghost imprints of the slaps. No actual crime was committed yesterday and who'd believe Emma? She has no evidence against Adam other than some messages on a burner phone. The one he sent the messages on is probably already discarded somewhere. Given her illness, he'd have no trouble convincing the – most likely male – authorities that he was an innocent being hounded by a madwoman.

And running away without Emma, tempting as it is, feels wrong. Leaving her here at the mercy of my husband and her stepsister would feel like leaving an injured creature in a trap.

And then there's the thing that I'm hiding from both Emma and Bobby. The thing that I'm hiding because it makes me seem so needy and desperate. The fact that I don't want to be alone. I wouldn't have chosen a woman who was prepared to kill me as my accomplice, but my options are limited.

I'm about to lose Bobby, my lifelong companion. It's always been Bobby. My female friendships have been superficial and transient. It's hard to be open and honest when you're living a lie of a marriage. Friendships wither and die when people think that you're holding things back. They label you as aloof and unavailable.

Emma is here now and women need to help each other out where they can.

*　*　*

I'm hypervigilant when I shower and dress. Listening for the doorbell again. For him to be here. He'll be back to verify that I've gone to Rome. My perfect husband. The one who was always too good to be true.

When marriages disintegrate it's expected that you might find out unpalatable truths about your ex-partner. I just didn't expect to find out that I was married to an aspiring murderer.

My marriage to Adam was what everyone dreams of. Passionate and romantic. To begin with. We'd laugh a lot. Youth returned briefly for me with a lightening of my step. I was utterly bewitched by him. By his looks, initially, of course. But he was also refreshing to be around. Like Pimm's on the first warm day of summer. The polar opposite of David and his staid life plans. Adam knew about my infertility and was empathetic, stating from the outset that he didn't want children. In retrospect, I suppose that he'd already studied the column I wrote about my issues. He'd researched me well, knew exactly what to say. How to act the role of my perfect partner.

The unfamiliar desire of a man who wanted just me made me weaken, block out risible thoughts in a pathetic haze of lust. I became complacent, ignoring the red flags, the diametric opposite of the sensible woman I usually am.

We'd jet off at the last minute to Barcelona, Paris, Berlin. Spend hours walking through cities at night. Staying in hotels, visiting restaurants and galleries – which I paid for, naturally. He liked everything that I liked but had his own interests too. It took me a few years to see that his passions were carefully curated artifice. Indie rock music, modern art, a love of classic cars. They were all performative ways of rounding off his personality to mask the cruelty and cunning that lay beneath the surface. His elderly dog is just another accessory used to hint at compassion.

His appearances in the restaurant were major events that sent the staff into a frantic state of excitement. Then there was the social media. Adam had no accounts of his own but asked if he could appear on my Instagram feed, to see if it would help with his failing acting career. The photographs of us together lit up my account. The likes and followers racking up.

The wedding was in an acquaintance's country house. Me in a cream linen dress, decked in flowers, entirely age-appropriate. Adam beside me in a well-chosen suit. This thing of great beauty that had landed in my life like an exotic butterfly.

His acting career stalled, briefly resurrected, and then died for good. He had a few jobs when we first met. Nothing stellar. The odd bit of fringe theatre and bit parts playing long-suffering husbands in minor TV thrillers. The problem with Adam's career is that he thought that his talents were Oscar-worthy. The industry thought differently. They recognised the truth: that the height of his fame was likely to be daytime soaps.

It was around this time that I began to emerge from my fugue state. It was like waking from a long coma and wondering who the man sitting by my hospital bed was. Things started to catch at me. I started to see his narcissism, traits that were painfully familiar from living with my mother. Much like Adele, Adam held a fragile sense of self, bolstered by the belief that he was capable of anything. Not just capable: expert. Any person delivering slights to his ego was punished, ostracised and ignored. Cut Adam and he would bleed – but so would you when he was ready to wield the knife. And you'd bleed more.

It took me a long time to really see him. To see the extent of his artifice. Take for example his laugh. He only had one laugh. Not the usual repertoire of noises that we all have. He'd punctuate conversation with these timed explosions. Just this one noise, the same tone and timbre. It was RADA 101, a practised stage act. He could pretend to be funny, regurgitating jokes he'd heard other people say and talking about things that most people found humorous. But to genuinely laugh? Never.

He's kept up a beguiling front for this poor young woman too. Playing Adam, the good doctor. Preying on someone who's sick and unsupported. Presenting that same façade that he presented to me. I don't blame her. It's convincing. My passion for him was once so fierce and discombobulating that, like her, I might even have contemplated murder for him.

But my fake Adam didn't last. He only puts the work in when it has an end goal, and once we'd signed the marriage papers and he was unpacked in my house, the effort steeply declined.

The evidence of his transgressions was vague at first. The classic tropes: unfamiliar perfume smells, unexplained absences, frequent messaging on his phone. Then more substantial facts that were harder to explain away: reports from so-called 'friends' of sightings of him with other women, his growing inability to hide his contempt for me, his sexual disinterest – which matched my waning passion for him.

There was a predictable pattern of mood. The early period of euphoria when he briefly thought that this new conquest would complete him. Then the growing restlessness as he realised that she was never going to fulfil him. How could they? He's incapable of genuine emotion. This would be followed by the foul dejection when he ended it, where his mask would fall. Misery leaching out and staining everyone around him. The natural history of his affairs clear to see.

I'd wearily confront him, sit through the grovelling apologies and the projection of it all onto me. Why he felt unloved. Why he'd had to seek out solace elsewhere. How I had failed him and caused him to seek out other women. The love that I felt for him shrank to nothing but a hard knot in my stomach. The problem was that Adam's subtle digs and casual barbs had left me feeling aged and unattractive. His slow poison convincing me that I couldn't cope with life without him by my side. I couldn't imagine starting again. And so we continued.

Becky was a whole new phenomenon. The euphoria didn't give way. I charted his moods, waiting for the fall. But the fall didn't come this time. He stayed buoyant. This one was enduring.

If only I'd known that this wasn't a 'to-die-for' romance but a romance they wanted me to die from.

Chapter Thirty-Seven

Emma

Celeste lays her hand on my arm to wake me and I instinctively grasp her wrist. As my eyes snap open I relax, unfurling my fingers.

'Adam was outside. I saw him.' Her voice is a tremulous hiss. 'I didn't answer.'

For a moment, I want to drag myself from the bed and run down to find him. Then it all comes back to me, with a rush of adrenaline. The panicky feeling floods me as if I've almost stepped in front of a car and stepped back onto the pavement just in time.

'He's gone now but he'll be back. I think he's double-checking your story about me already being gone. Seeing if I'd come here.'

She has a plan that she says can keep us safe.

Bobby owns a holiday house in Whitstable. Apparently Adam knows nothing about this spare property.

'Adam didn't take an interest in my stepbrother. There was nothing in Bobby for him to use. If you'd had time to get know him better, then you'd have learned people need to have a value for Adam or he has no interest in them. He turns off that boyish charm.' She looks at me but it's more pitying than accusatory.

I can't think of anything to say in response so I just look at her. The idea of having a spare house that you don't use makes no sense to me. A flicker of envy rises up but I push it away.

'I've calculated that if we go to the coast, then we can be back in ninety minutes by train or taxi if Bobby needs me. I've spoken to his care assistant and called his palliative care nurse. They know where I am and how to contact me if Bobby deteriorates.' She takes a breath and I see her throat move as she swallows hard. The throat that I spent so long thinking about circling with my hands. 'Just in case Adam grills them, I've asked them not to tell him that they've seen me. I've hinted at some marital difficulty that seemed to strike a chord.'

At this point, I'm glad that someone else is being the parent and taking charge. That my carousel of a mind is being given instructions.

* * *

It's one of those hot early autumn days: an unexpected sunny afternoon. The shingled beaches are crowded with families, grasping at the remainder of the season. There are children running about. Celeste looks across at them but turns her head away sharply. The waves smack against stone and wood. I've never liked the sea. I see hidden horrors, danger, drowning even. Every news story about the destruction it wreaks lodges in my brain. Mothers lie back on towels as their children hurtle around screaming. It's akin to bringing them to play at the side of a dual carriageway.

I stumble again as we walk up the path to the house. The building shines in the sunlight. The white boards freshly painted, the garden of driftwood and salty-leaved plants stark and beautiful. I try to take it in, but my head is spinning and I'm still checking for Becky or Adam in my peripheral vision. I jolt when I see someone of his build, with her posture, before I realise it's just a facsimile. That Adam and Becky are present everywhere. Their kind of beauty is commonplace. Their ugly interiors the truly unique thing about them.

'Welcome to the beach house. We're just far enough back to avoid the tourists and drunks but near enough so that you can hear the sea.'

'I don't like it,' I say.

'What don't you like? The house? Wait till you see the inside. It's very chic.' She waves her arm towards the house, like an estate agent with a client. 'The birds are different here too. I've seen some—'

'No, not the house. It looks nice. I like the house. I mean the sound of the sea. I don't like the sea. It's dangerous.'

'How peculiar. I'm exactly the same. I can't even swim. I hate even seeing people swimming, actually. The thought of them drowning makes me feel physically sick. I find myself tracking them to make sure that they come back to shore.'

'I . . . yes. Me too. Swimming is lunacy.'

The house smells of expensive floor polish. Gleaming elegance. Coloured antique glass and clashing fabrics blend in harmony, like something straight from the pages of a magazine.

'So, what do we do now?' I put down my bag and look, wide-eyed, at the sitting room. I can't help myself. My head moves slowly to take in the room, scanning each area, hands clenched in front of me. Scared to touch anything in yet another place where I feel that I don't belong.

'Well, how about you don't try to kill me again? Then I don't have to hide the knives and sleep with one eye open, do I?' There's a lightness to her eyes as she says this and she's smiling. It's faint but it's still a smile.

'No. You don't. You really don't.' I stare down at the floor. Words feel inadequate to justify what I almost did.

'Sorry, it was a joke. An inappropriate one.' She tries to force a laugh but it's shrill and discordant. 'We'll just rest and hide out for now. Then we can plan what we both do next.'

I need this. Rest and time to think. Then Celeste and I will make our next move.

Chapter Thirty-Eight

Becky

Something has gone horribly wrong. When Adam got home last night, where there should have been a corpse marked by stab wounds was a neatly made bed. No iron scent of blood in the air. The house immaculately tidy with no sign of Emma or Celeste. Celeste isn't picking up her phone when Adam calls. She's messaged him to say that she's sorry if she missed saying goodbye, but she was needed at Bobby's. She says that she didn't come home from the restaurant last night. That she'd picked up her luggage earlier and went to the airport this morning straight from staying over at her stepbrother's house.

Emma is claiming she's gone to stay with her new friend. I don't believe it for a minute. She replied to my WhatsApp with the sort of bland message you'd see written on an old-time postcard. She doesn't go anywhere. She hasn't stayed overnight with someone since she became ill. This is too much of a coincidence.

Her communication with Adam is no more illuminating. A stark message telling him that Celeste was a no-show and that she's not feeling well and needs to recuperate.

We were so close. I've resisted smashing my phone against the wall.

*　*　*

I've arranged to meet Adam in a hotel. The bar feels like it's trying too hard, like one of those women on Instagram with the contoured faces. It's all stripped oak refectory tables with industrial lighting. The waiting staff must have stage skills equal to mine and Adam's because they're managing to look superior to the customers, despite their paltry salaries and crappy working conditions.

I have this feeling that someone is watching me. Like Emma or Celeste might be nearby. My peripheral vision picks out threats that don't exist. It's familiar. There were times in my life when I was frequently followed, scrutinised. When there was always some moron who couldn't tell me apart from the character I was playing. Then there were the supposed fans, sending me perverted letters or worst of all, a tabloid photographer lurking on the sidelines. They were always there to catch me with my skirt riding up or my hair stuck across my forehead, eyeliner smudged.

In reality, there are no eyes on me now. No more than usual, anyway. I've kept my looks. It's just a hostile place for a woman to be alone. A couple at the end of the bar catch my eye. At first glance they're just like all the other people who are forking out for ten-pound Martinis. Rumpled workwear and jaded glances, nothing special in the sea of off-duty bankers and lawyers released from their strip-lit prisons. Maybe it's her posture that made me look twice. She's completely still, like a cornered animal waiting for the predator to either attack or move on. He's leaning towards her, talking slowly, deliberately. His lips barely moving, words hissing out of clenched teeth. There's no expression on his face.

It's none of my business. People make their own choices. Good luck to them. I wouldn't end up like her. Adam and I are equals.

Adam eyes the empty glass I'm clenching on the bar in front of me. His words are soft and even, but his posture is tight.

He whispers in my ear: 'Shall we just go on up to the room? I'm still fucking exhausted from having been three different people for the last few months. I need time just being alone with you.' He winks and grins. I look away from the couple, not caring anymore. Let his hot hand touch my thigh and melt away the rage.

*   *   *

An hour later and Adam's lying back on the bed, in just his underwear, hands behind his head. I want to laugh at how pleased with himself he looks. The way he's deliberately posed himself to show off his chest, the light catching his face at the right angle.

I finish putting my clothes back on. The hotel room is pristine. Decorated in the kind of bland neutrals that you can only live with if you're above dirt. The crappy life I'm clawing to escape involves me clearing up after Ava, after Emma, Dad and Ann or the residents at work. All wrong. This is more how it should be. A spotless place where someone attends to me.

I turn to Adam. 'You've done well, by the way. Regardless of the outcome. Shame you can't get a BAFTA for it. I can see the critics now, commenting on your "naïve ingénue". The raw vulnerability of your "abused husband" act. The wholesomeness of your "young doctor".'

'Not to mention my method acting with the raw cheekbone where you smacked me senseless. You're quite something.' He rubs the memory of the bruise on his face. 'If this comes to nothing after all our fucking work . . .'

He leans over and cups my face in his hands, kissing me on the forehead. He's placid but I sense the fear in him. 'What will we do next? Do you have another plan?'

'We don't have a choice, do we? We have to find Emma. Get her to try again when Celeste is back from her trip.'

'About that trip. I have something to show you, but I wanted to do it in person.' He reaches for his phone. 'She's left her laptop behind and it's still logged in to her email account.'

It's a picture of her email account, showing a message sent to a woman called Katrina, telling her that she can't go to Rome because her brother is too sick.

'And you didn't find this when you searched the house last night because . . . ?' He ignores my sarcasm, which irritates me more. 'For fuck's sake, Adam. We need to be thorough.'

'I am being thorough. Give me a break, Becky. This is a lot.'

'Oh, a lot is it? And are you sure you didn't see anything suspicious yesterday?' My nails grip into my palms. Adam has been superb so far at playing his part but things are fragmenting. I'm worried he won't be up to whatever comes next. All this thinking and planning. It's draining but also strangely fun. Or it would be if the stakes weren't so high.

I sent him to Bobby's house. The first time he called, no one answered. The second time, a frazzled-looking woman spoke to him at the door and told him that she hadn't seen Celeste since yesterday.

But it doesn't matter how many people she has covering for her. The emails will give her away.

* * *

'So she's too bloody sick to look after her own kid but she can swan off and stay with a friend.' Dad is filling the crowded kitchen with his voice, slamming about. I see Ava turning to listen, her brow furrowed. I don't comfort her. She's not my child, so why should I?

I move closer to Dad. 'She's on the brink of something, if you ask me.'

'The brink of what?'

'Some kind of breakdown. She's been saying weird stuff. Going on and on about a man who lives round the corner. I caught her peering out of the window with her binoculars. She's escalating.'

'Fuck me. Is she safe around the kid?' He drops his voice to a stage whisper.

'What do you think? That's why I've told her that I'll do all the childcare. In case she has one of those fits again. And now I'm worried about her mental health. I think we might have to speak to Ann.'

Another seed sown. It's called insurance. Emma is somewhere and unlike Adam, I'm not gullible enough to think that she's just ambled away from this. She'll be back and it'll be carnage.

My brain is working overtime. I have this troubling thought that Celeste and Emma may have joined forces but I bat it away. They don't exactly inhabit the same worlds and I can't see that combination ever being a thing. A fleeting image of Celeste capturing Emma after a failed murder attempt enters my head. The concept of an enraged Celeste holding Emma hostage is too absurd and improbable. Celeste is feeble under her frosty exterior. If I was in the mood for amusement then it'd be laughable.

There aren't many places that Emma can be. That's the sadness of her diminished life. I take myself upstairs, glad of the fresher air coming in from the open windows in my room. First, I need to find this Lauren. I spend a fruitless hour looking through Laurens on Facebook and Instagram. There's nothing that fits, and Emma's profiles are set to private. I slam the laptop shut.

I search the meagre belongings that Emma has stashed in mine and Ava's room. There's nothing amiss, no hidden diaries or notes. Her canvas tote bag is missing but that doesn't mean anything. She carts that bag around with her.

I hear Dad outside as he lumbers to the toilet, a thin little whistle of a tune coming from his lips before the crashing sound of urine hitting water. I close the door. That's when I notice it. There's a picture missing from the frames on my window ledge. It's Emma's favourite. Her and her speccy dad, both scowling at the camera in some woods somewhere. So like Emma to make sure she grabbed that photograph of him. She's not coming back any time soon. She probably risked sneaking back here just to take it.

I try to calm myself, breathing deeply and focusing on one image. It's of me smashing Emma's skull hard into a brick wall until the blood pours down her face.

* * *

Adam looks tired today. His hair messy, dark rings under his eyes. Nothing like the fresh-faced man I first met when I was in that play. Adam was seen by the rest of the cast as the handsome actor, on his way up. I was viewed as being the washed-up trainwreck who'd descended from prime-time television. The subject of cast gossip about my career in reverse. Everyone was whispering about Adam for different reasons. Namely his tight buttocks, piercing eyes and toned torso.

The rising star, who didn't rise any further, met the falling star. But we recognised something entirely different in each other. Something darker that no one else saw. We were inevitable.

The noise of the café is grating. A bunch of police officers are just leaving as they pay for their greasy breakfasts and head back to their vehicles. Groups of builders are scattered around, fuelling up for a day of labour.

'I bought you a gift.' He pulls out a green and orange Liberty print scarf from his pocket.

'Where am I supposed to wear this? On the school run? The other mums would think it was a fake, which defeats the object.'

Adam ignores my ingratitude, his face glowing with self-satisfaction. He reaches down and pulls Celeste's laptop from his bag. I scan the café to make sure no one is watching or listening. 'Celeste still doesn't seem to be at her brother's house, but I've found a way to track her along with the emails. Her electronic calendar. She has invites to restaurant events. If she's still in London she might go to one of them. I can be there to check.'

Well, he's got the time. Although I think it'll be futile. I lean forward and take the laptop from him to look for myself, hopeful of some fleck of information that we can work on. 'Well, that's supposing that she's actually even in London. She could be anywhere. Has she emailed anyone else yet?'

'Not yet. But she will.' He lounges back on the chair.

'So, we'll just sit back and wait, shall we?'

'I said I'm checking her diary, for fuck's sake. I don't know what to think. Other than that I'm leaning towards thinking that she *had* already gone when Emma arrived there.' He tries to smile at me but it doesn't quite work. His acting wouldn't convince anyone today.

That's when it dawns on me. Adam might be wrong.

Maybe we've both got this upside down.

Why would Celeste have left the house before Emma arrived if she wasn't rushing off to Rome? Celeste is a creature of habit. She'd have gone home that night. Me and Adam have monitored her enough to know her routines. I meticulously timed Emma's positioning. And I'm sure that Emma would have gone to the house and waited, like she was told to. Adam had her hooked on this 'plan'. She was determined to kill for him.

Yet Celeste isn't dead. She could have fought Emma off and then gone to the police. But she didn't do that or Adam and Emma would be in police cells now.

There's another answer. Especially given Emma's implausible story of staying with a friend.

The improbable thought comes back again. Only this time I don't bat it away. They're not in different places. They're together.

'Emma's with Celeste. I just know it.'

'Becky, that makes no sense at all.'

I push my chair back.

'You find the answers then. I'm tired, Adam. I'm tired of thinking. I know one thing, though. If she knows about us, then we're in trouble,' I say. 'She's my family after all. I know what she's like.'

He smiles at me again and reaches across for my hand on the Formica table. 'Emma's just a sheep.'

242

Granules of sugar scratch into my skin as my hand pushes down onto the surface of the plastic table.

'Don't underestimate her. Emma *is* sweet and thoughtful but there's a part of her that she keeps hidden. There's rage there. You should see her face when she's around my dad. There's a part of Emma that's like us.'

Chapter Thirty-Nine

Emma

I wasn't always angry. I was a placid schoolchild, quiet and contained. Even my career was gentle. Like most newly qualified nurses, I was idealistic and forgiving, spending my days eagerly dispensing empathy. The embodiment of calm and soothing care. I was patient and compassionate. Helping people is a surprising thing. It makes you feel good too.

I was a working mother. Juggling having Ava with my intense job, balancing childcare around my shifts and the hospital nursery. It was rewarding, delightful even at times. But like most parents I felt stretched and tested too.

It was illness that changed me, but not for the reasons people might think. I'm not a 'bitter invalid' railing against the world because my life has become something unpalatable. Someone who takes their pain out on the world. That's a tired cliché. I did what I could to be well but I also accepted what was happening, in time. I had no choice.

What I couldn't accept was the way people changed around me. How rapidly they revealed that their sympathy for me was time-limited and sparse. How people avoided me. Valuing me only for my ability to contribute and not for my thoughts or feelings. I retreated into survival mode. Trying to keep myself safe. Trying to shield my daughter from the effects of this condition.

The thing that roused this fury within me was having to find the energy to constantly justify myself to my family. Needing to shield myself from their loaded words, their blatant insults, their obvious lack of care. Over time it chipped away at me.

Everyone has limits of what they can tolerate. It turns out that they couldn't take me being ill. I can't stand their lack of care. Why wouldn't I become angry?

The thing about anger is that it's like being kind. But whereas being kind to people fills you with dopamine, anger erodes you.

* * *

I'm not at all angry now as I watch from the stairs as Celeste takes my bag from the back of one of the dining chairs. Invading my undeserved privacy with a deft hand. The house is painfully quiet, none of the sounds of a London suburb, not even a distant symphony of foxes screaming. Just the constant threatening rush of the sea in the distance. I'd need time to learn the rhythms here. For it to gain my trust. London is all that I've ever known.

My Samsung is locked. I see Celeste staring at the screensaver. The picture of Ava looks back at her. She pauses and I see her long fingers trying to pick out a code. Soft well-tended skin tapping out 1234 before giving in. Then she takes the burner phone. It looks like a cheap plastic toy from a Christmas cracker in her manicured hands. There's only one number on there that I've dialled or messaged. Adam's burner. She won't find anything – no calls for days, not a single recent text. Just the string of seemingly innocuous sent messages going back weeks. They're innocent enough unless you know the subtext with our talk of 'the plan'. The plan for her murder.

The pull of the phone, of Adam, has been there. I won't deny that. There's still an imprint of his skin on mine. The fingers that lingered on my flesh, the soft mouth on my lips. Adam breached my defences with his clever act. It's been hard to resist the draw of him, until the image of Becky's face fills my mind, making my muscles tense, my fists clench. Becky, who is undoubtably the person behind that clever act.

The new knowledge of the monster Adam really is, and the saviour Celeste has been, floods into me. I'm returning to myself, sloughing away whatever it was I became. Like a bird moulting. Picking away dead things to allow something new and wholesome to grow. Leaving behind that twisted fever dream.

'I came down to tell you about the owl. I could hear an owl. I thought that since you like birds too you might be interested.' She jumps at the sound of my voice. In spite of the stillness of this place, she didn't hear me coming. I feel like a ghost. Slowly moving towards her. The white of the cotton nightgown she lent to me reflecting in the windows, shining in the light from the streetlamp that is filtering in.

'You have to try to trust me now, Celeste.' I take the two phones from the table, unlocking the Samsung and passing it to her. 'We need each other, remember?'

She doesn't speak straight away. Her face looks paler. She's taken off her make-up and her features look less distinct.

'I'm trying. But it's not easy.' She holds the phone in her hand, not looking at it yet. 'Are the messages bad? Explicit, I mean.'

'No! We didn't send anything—'

'I mean violent. Explicitly violent. I don't know if I can read things that you both said about killing me. It's too much.' Her hand moves to her chest. As if anticipating a knife blow.

She feels smaller tonight, although we're a similar height. I see that her face is reddening like Ava's does when she's on the verge of tears. My instinct is to hold her, to take her hand in mine at least, but I resist this. We're not at that stage yet.

'There's nothing terrible. Adam told me to be careful in case anything went wrong and the police saw the phones.'

'I'm sorry, Emma. I'm being silly. It's just that I'm scared. I'm not very good at being scared.'

'No, me neither. But there's nothing to be afraid of. We're stronger together.'

Chapter Forty

Celeste

There's a list of missed calls on the burner phone, all from Adam. I scroll through them with a shaking hand. A couple of innocuous texts that say exactly what she said they would. Vague texts about a plan. Arrangements for when and where they'd meet. There's a few on her Samsung from Becky, asking after her health. Sickly sweet. There are no calls or messages from her mother.

The sent message folder on her Samsung phone is empty. She shows the phone to me, promising that she didn't delete them.

'I've been thinking about it. I think Becky has been doing stuff with my phone to set me up. I think that she took these.' The muscles in her face are set. Her expression unreadable. Dark circles under her puffy eyes, like she's been crying.

She navigates to a folder in her photo gallery. There's about ten pictures in there, all of Adam. All taken from a distance. Adam entering my house. Adam walking down the street. Adam getting into his car. She tells me that she didn't take these. That she thinks the folder must have appeared on the last day she was at home. That Becky must have put it there as insurance, in case things went wrong.

'I don't understand.' I walk across to the window. Her reflection looks back at me. This practicality and focus on detail calms me.

'It's obvious, isn't it? I've been set up. Assigned a role. I'm the lovesick neighbour. The obsessive. There's a narrative here. Look at me: poor little sick girl.' She stares at me, her expression chilling and unreadable. 'Handsome man gets pursued by a twisted, sick woman. She goes insane, stalks him and then kills his wife. I wonder who thought it all up? Which one of them?'

'Adam's pretty good at persuading people. He should have done better in his acting career. Maybe they both should.'

She looks at me face on and studies me for a moment. 'You can keep my phones if it helps. I want you to know that you're safe from me. You do know that *I'm* not the danger, though?'

She starts to pace the room.

'They tried to sacrifice me, too. Maybe even throw me to the police as an easy distraction. Do you think I would've gone to prison or a special hospital? Not that you'd have ever found out.' Her flow of words is rapid and increasing in volume. 'We have to do something soon.'

She stops pacing. Like a clockwork toy whose key has wound down. Her limbs sapped of energy. Her head too heavy to lift. She sinks down onto a chair and puts her head in her hands.

I do what feels like the right thing to do. The only thing. I walk across and take her into my arms, holding on to her, feeling her deflate against my chest. It's only when I stand again that I realise we're both crying.

'I'm sorry. I shouldn't have looked at your phones.' The only sounds are footsteps as someone passes the house on the coastal path. 'You can't exactly blame me for checking, though. And let's both dispense with the apologies from now on. I don't think it's helping either of us.'

'OK. But we need to think now.' Her voice is soft and I lean in to listen. 'We need to help each other. We're going to have to find some evidence against Adam for one of us to take to the police. I'll deal with Becky myself.'

* * *

Emma's been asleep for most of the morning and afternoon. I go up at lunchtime to offer her soup. That's about the extent of my knowledge of caring for an invalid. Let them rest and give them soup. When I walk in, she's lying there, totally still, face turned towards the wall. I stand for a moment, watching her breathing, looking at the contours of her face. I think about the things she said last night. The things that kept me awake as I rattled through scenarios in my head. Emma's right. Finding a foolproof and safe way of incriminating Adam is the only way we'll get out of this mess. Then we'll both be safe.

She refuses the soup, which is fine with me. Given my job, I always feel the weight of expectation. People think that I'll rustle up some rustic French broth in half an hour, with a side order of home-made crusty bread. The reality is a tin of Heinz: tomato or chicken with a slice of sourdough from the deli on the High Street. It's my dirty secret that I love processed food. Such a treat. It harks back to my childhood when Adele wouldn't have anything like that in the house, insisting on high-quality produce. Meals always freshly made but made by someone other than her. My rare outings to friend's houses where they had golden items like sugary tinned spaghetti, sweet biscuits, and crisps, were sheer bliss. I've eaten beans on toast for lunch today, not even good-quality ones but a cheap tin from the corner shop, laden with sugar, butter clotting into the lurid orange sauce.

I leave her lying there and sit alone, alert for noises. Listening for anyone near the doors or windows. I try to read for a while, but end up scrolling through Instagram and Twitter, to see what my competitors are churning out. My PR person pops stuff on my profiles on my behalf. We take batches of pictures of me and she posts them over a period of time. Usually I'm standing behind a kitchen counter, with a faint, strained smile, holding some pretentious display of overpriced food. Mostly just me, placed primly in the kitchen at home or work. They like Adam to appear occasionally too, either at my side or in the background, a handsome garnish. It's a compelling fantasy. Those beautifully shot photographs of the life that I'm purportedly living. Ironically, they've posted one today: Adam smiling as he drapes an arm over my shoulder, the light from the kitchen window creating a halo around us both.

* * *

Adam was my second mistake. The first was David. He wasn't handsome, like Adam, or anywhere near as charming – but he was solid and wholesome. He did something in banking. Like many partners of bankers, I tried and failed to have enough interest in what he did at work to ever comprehend it.

It's easy to become embroiled in someone else's ambition. We worked through the timeline of what we ought to do.

The dinners and the routine sexual activity after the first few dates. The first holidays together. The engagement with a predictably tasteful diamond ring. The compact flat in Bayswater. When added together we both equalled an unobjectionable pairing.

The first home. The second home. The cars. It was all going to plan. To David's plan, anyway. Then my womb decided that it wasn't going to co-operate. I broke the timeline, disrupted the narrative. My body declared that no amount of unimaginative sex was going to produce a child. His valiant attempts to impregnate me became even more of a chore. David grunting away with determination, planting his seed into the poisoned ground of my body as I filled in charts, took temperatures, booked appointments.

The house grew bigger around the two of us. Two solitary people, the expansive lawns untrampled by childish games of cricket or rounders. The walls pristine, not child-scuffed. I'd ricochet around the empty house while he was at work, wander aimlessly around the commuter village where we'd settled. Distanced from the other women my age and their hordes of sticky-fingered toddlers.

The predictable thing happened. I'd like to be able to give you a different ending, a less tawdry one, where women are not pitted against each other like cows at an auction. I can't though. I was released from our marriage by the intern whose fruitful organs started to grow a mini-David for him. I staggered, battered, into a void of freedom.

But freedom is dangerous and choices can be disastrous. You might just take the wrong path and end up in a pool of blood.

* * *

Emma and I are almost there. We're capable of entrapping Adam, somehow. We both need to think. I've been the driver for our plans so far, taking control of the narrative. I'm the one with the resources after all. The spare house, the money to travel. She doesn't have those things. But I'm running out of ideas.

Emma's emerged from her sleep. I make her coffee and we sit, watching the light fade. We don't speak for a while, just sit in companiable silence.

'I haven't been asleep all the time. Sometimes I just lie there. My body feels weighted down.' She stretches her leg out, as if she's testing it. 'It's hard to describe.'

'It's fine. Honestly. I've been reading.' Almost the truth. The Women's Prize winning novel might as well be in a foreign language. My mind can't focus for long.

'I've been thinking while I was lying there. I've considered our options and I have some ideas. I want to contribute something.'

'Go on.' I feel myself start to relax when she tells me about her new plan. It's genius. I have a co-conspirator. I'm not in sole charge of escaping from this mess. The relief is overwhelming.

She's a clever young woman. Any mother should be proud of her.

Chapter Forty-One

Emma

I don't mind anymore when I catch her watching over me. It's comforting to have a new ally. One who is genuine and kind. I lie here cloaked in layers of fatigue that weigh my limbs to the bed. But my mind is active. My senses alert.

When I do sleep, I dream that I'm at home with Becky. Or trapped with Peter. Or worse: laughing in Celeste's bed with Adam. I wake up disconcerted. Confused as to where I am and who I should be hating today.

Being around Celeste is calming but guilt-laden. Her occasional maternal embraces both soothe and reproach me. Her fussing and care feels generous but undeserved.

I always sense her in the room. I detect the heady fragrance that follows her around. I savour the aroma. It's the soothing smell of wealth and privilege. But there's a faint odour underlying that. It's the smell of fear. I know it well.

I comfort her when I can and tell her my new plan again. She visibly relaxes.

It took me a while but I came up with this. Celeste laughed

254

and covered her mouth with her hand when I outlined it. Her glee validated me.

I've ordered some devices from Amazon. Celeste paid. Who knew that you could become a virtual spy in just a few clicks. The recording devices are arriving today. They're shiny black things, the size of credit cards. Voice-activated and easy to hide in a room and remain undetected.

Celeste and I will stay holed up here for a few more days before we plant the devices. That way we can both regain more strength. I'm actually enjoying her company. I feel a bit stronger every day.

When I'm awake, we play games of cards, or we talk. Haltingly at first, but it's begun to feel easier now. We go over the plan again and again but that's not all. She's told me about her first marriage, about the things Adam has done to her, the recent violence. I've told her about life at home, and a little bit about when I was a nurse. I talk about Ava, tentatively at first because I'm worried about being insensitive, given what she's told me about the trouble she had trying to conceive a child. I needn't have worried. She's animated when I show her pictures of Ava. Delighted for me that I have something so positive in my life. Waxing lyrical about how much she likes children.

There's a similarity between us, which I hadn't thought of before. We're women who some of the harsher people in society would see as failures. The woman who couldn't have a child and the one incapable of looking after one. A pair of deviations from the standard expectations.

Mostly, though, we talk about birds. I tell her my bird anecdotes and she laps them up. Like I'm the adult this time, reading bedtime stories, and she's the child.

I've messaged Mum and Adam to say that I'm staying with Lauren for a little longer. Celeste is still pretending to Adam that she's in Italy. Once we're back in London, Celeste will sneak in and plant the devices around her house and then she'll stay at Bobby's, where it's safer, telling Adam that she wants to be close to her stepbrother in his final days.

There'll be one device in Adam's room, one in her own bedroom and one in the sitting room. They're voice-activated. Perfect for recording one side of a phone conversation. The minute he starts to speak on the phone, the device will kick in and record him. Just him.

Once I have Adam on the burner, I'll get him talking. Coax him into saying what I need him to. That way we'll have him on record, planning Celeste's murder. Perfect leverage to make Adam leave me and Celeste alone for good. The things I say to entrap him won't be picked up. We can then retrieve the recordings and we'll have our proof. Celeste will pretend she has no idea who he was talking to. I don't think Adam will tell the police about me. What profit is there in that for him? If he does, then I can't think that there's evidence against me anyway.

I'm going to go back to my house. I'm stronger again now but when I'm back home I'm going to do something abhorrent and unthinkable, something that I've never done before. I'll fake an episode of my illness and stay in bed. I tell myself the ends justify the means.

I want both Becky and Adam to be at a disadvantage, not knowing just how strong I can be. From now on, let them underestimate me at their own peril.

I've reopened communication lines with Adam and I will start to form a revised plan with him, but by phone call, rather than in person. I started messaging him again this morning, and his speedy, desperate replies made me want to vomit.

I'll be too ill to meet him, too ill to even leave my bedroom. Becky will be hovering around but I'm not worried about her. I can retreat into myself and evade her. I'll think about what to do about Becky later. One step at a time.

There's a part of me that feels like this plan is too restrained. Part of me that wants to wreak havoc. To swoop in like a bird whose nest is under attack and rip the intruders apart with my claws.

But that time will come. This is just stage one.

Chapter Forty-Two

Celeste

I sit at the window and watch holidaymakers walk by. For a second, I almost feel like I'm on holiday myself. Being an intended murder victim has liberated me from my usual responsibilities. My mood shatters when my phone rings. It's my mother. Adele.

'Hello, Maman. How are you?' I cringe at how easily I fall into the role of scared, dutiful daughter.

'How am I? I'm festering in this hole of a place, am I not? Down here in the countryside with all these animals knocking at my door. These pig women.'

'Mummy, please don't be mean about them. They're the carers. They're there to help you.'

'Carers? What do they care? Do you know what one of them told me last week? To put out my cigarette whilst she was in the room. How do these people have the nerve?'

It goes on for a while. A one-woman diatribe against humankind. Old age hasn't softened Adele but instead has made her more hateful and less tolerant, her simmering fury reaching periodical boiling points.

'Your pretty little husband was here looking for you, by the way. Am I supposed to keep a record and report back to him?' There's the click of a cigarette lighter in the background and she inhales deeply. 'Where are you? And what are you hiding from, little Celeste? Has he been having affairs with your friends, spending your money? Men are no good. I always told you that, didn't I?'

I wince when she says my name. I've never liked it and the particular way she says it makes me shudder. Names are indelible parental stains. You can change them but there'll always be someone who still knows you by your original one. People who won't let you shake it off.

'I'm just away for a few days in Italy. Adam must have forgotten. I'll call him now, Maman.' My voice sounds almost convincing. Almost hides the quaking inside me.

'Ah, poor little Adam. At least he must realise that you don't have another man. Not at your age.' She chokes on the cigarette smoke and her own laughter.

* * *

Emma has appeared behind me in the kitchen. She's leaning on the wooden worktop, less indolent and firmer, more solid.

'Bad news. Adam's been there looking for me.' I put my phone back in my bag.

'So, he knows you're not in Rome.' She shrinks inwards.

I place my hand on her arm. 'Don't worry. We're almost done with all this. Thanks to your clever little plan.'

She looks blank, as if the effort of thinking is so much that her face can't form expressions at the same time.

'You look a bit better for sleeping. Do you have the energy to walk? Just a short walk to the seafront. It'll be quieter today with this weather.'

259

The house feels like it's closing in around me. Bobby's calming décor isn't enough to soothe me today. I need distraction. I'm not sure that it's wise or that there's much chance of curing Emma with old-fashioned British exercise but it's unlikely to harm her, as long as we're mindful of her limitations.

She reaches for her shoes from the rack by the door.

The seafront is less frenetic. It's just hardy people with rough-coated dogs today, throwing balls and sticks. A gay couple with matching lumberjack beards smile and say hello as they walk past holding hands, one of them hissing to the other about who I am once he thinks we're out of earshot. The hordes of children are gone, no primary-coloured plastic in sight. Emma walks beside me, she's limping a little, stumbling occasionally, but she's more purposeful than this morning.

I'm frequently publicly scrutinised, which is mostly painless. The two men noticing me is nothing unusual but today my muscles are tense, adrenaline bristling through me in preparation for fight or flight. Scanning for a glimpse of Adam in my peripheral vision. I start to re-evaluate how sensible it was to leave the house. I'm a wreck.

My hand grasps tightly around the strap of my bag. We pass the oyster restaurants and make it as far as the harbour. Places look shut up and blank. The boats are chipped and tatty, lacking in charm, and the shouts of the fishermen grate my nerves. The air is heavily scented with fish.

I feel a presence before I see it. I become acutely aware that there's nothing between me and the drop into the water of the harbour as the footsteps behind us get louder and more urgent. Emma tenses her muscles in sync with mine. I sense Adam behind me. I should have been more watchful, stuck to safer paths.

A hand clutches my arm and I jolt, turning, planting my feet wider apart to resist the push into the seawater.

'Celeste! I knew it was you. My husband said he wasn't sure, but I said it just had to be.' She's in her late thirties, decked out in nautical-themed casuals.

'I'm sorry. Do I know you?' There's something everywoman about her face.

'No. No. I'm sorry for being so forward. I wouldn't normally do this kind of thing, but I'm just such a fan. That article you wrote in *The Observer* about your decision to stop IVF . . . It affected me so deeply. You gave me so much comfort at a time of need. You've no idea.' Her eyes are damp.

I talk to her for a few minutes but I'm distracted. I can't summon anything more than a few soothing words and a polite thank you. Emma stays motionless by the side of the harbour, staring at a black bird that's stretching its wings on a buoy.

We walk to a little café that opens late. The owners have tried to make it jaunty and festive. Soft, pastel walls, carefully battered furniture, and a seashell theme. Entirely predictable. The tables are unexpectedly clean, and the menu isn't too dreadful – wholesome vegan food and a selection of teas. I order for us.

'Are you OK, Emma? You haven't said much for the last hour.' My breathing has resumed to normal. My shoulders are nearly back down from around my neck.

'I'm just thinking through things. You hired the private detective and found out about Becky a whole year ago. But you still didn't confront him?' She looks puzzled.

'I suppose part of it was that I was numb. I had the pictures and I kept looking at them. Testing myself to see if I could feel anything. But there was nothing.' I feel so stupid saying all this. It's like I'm discussing a stranger. 'I felt trapped too.

261

Adam had pecked away at my self-confidence. I'd started to believe so many things. That I was old and withered. That I was nothing without him. The kind of things men want you to think when they're asserting control. So, I just continued. Incomprehensible, really.'

'I don't think it is. I understand being trapped.' She sips at the coffee, ignoring the food. 'You're not ugly or old or stupid. You know that, don't you?'

'It was the violence in the end. He started to cross a line. Things felt too dangerous. I'd started the divorce process with my solicitor, but Adam didn't know yet. I was scared how he'd react.' She's barely touched the sandwiches or crisps. 'Are you going to eat your cake? It's surprisingly good.' I push the plate nearer to her, but she ignores it.

She doesn't fall for my ploy to end the conversation.

'Adam has hurt you so much.'

My hand instinctively goes to my neck where the bruises once were and I feel a prickle of tears in my eyes.

This time it's Emma who comforts me.

* * *

We pass a screaming child on the pavement outside; his dropped ice cream is being feasted upon by a mean-eyed gull. I'm not paying enough attention and I almost trip over the jutting-out legs of a man on the pavement. He's propped up against a doorway, surrounded by a precarious pile of crushed lager cans. His swollen eyelids closed against daylight, bare feet encrusted by dirt, oblivious to the light rain that's started to fall, soaking his trousers.

'At least there's one thing about this whole sorry saga. He's helped wake me up to the fact that I need to hurry up and get this divorce completed.'

'Yes.' She's quieter again. Her voice muffled.

The coastal path back to the house is busier. Day trippers trying to pretend that it's not a grey and drizzly day.

'We should try to get you out of that house, too. See if there's some way of getting you rehoused. You can't go back there with your stepsister after everything that's happened,' I say.

We move ourselves to the sides of the path, to allow a steely-faced couple to pass by, mid argument. Both matching each other's volume as they spit words at each other.

'They won't rehouse me and Ava. It's not that simple for someone like me. I'm trapped. I understand that you mean well but you've got no idea what it's like to not have money.' Her tone is more resigned than angry.

I'm spared answering by my phone ringing. It comes up as 'Private Number', so I let it ring out. It's not easy to hear the voicemail from the Macmillan nurse, against the roar of the waves and shifting of the stones on the beach, but I get the gist.

'We have to go back to London now. My stepbrother is deteriorating. I need to be there.' I feel an urge to run. To sprint back to the house and start to pack.

We're going back to London.

Back where Adam and Becky can find us.

The image of that knife on the carpet keeps coming back into my mind and squeezing at my chest.

But what choice do I have? My brother needs me.

Chapter Forty-Three

Becky

Emma will come back home at some point. She's like one of those animals bred in captivity who, when released, darts back into the cage. She's predictable – we might not be blood relatives but she's more like me than anyone would know, carrying hatred within her.

I have no shame about my hate. That's not why I keep it hidden.

I'd like to spew my resentment and rage. I'd have a Twitter feed devoted to Celeste, to my ex-husband Harry, to our affluent neighbours who glare at us with disdain disguised as sympathy for the burden of our poverty. To the journalists who've plagued my life. Denise from the care home with her gleeful face as she crows at my downfall. Pages and pages filled with my desire to wreak havoc.

But who'd read that? If anyone did notice, then I'd be labelled as bitter and psychotic. Like angry women always are.

You might think that my hatred would have focused on

Emma now. It's hasn't yet. I have a grudging admiration that she's escaped all this unscathed. So far.

I might be willing to threaten her, to sacrifice her to the police if needed, but I'm not going to physically harm her or her daughter. Not unless we have to.

My fury today isn't abstract. I'm angry with myself and Adam for our foolish incompetence. With Adam for leaving me to think this through. His solution is to sit and rant about how he much he hates them. To bemoan all the time he wasted with my sister. Time that he claims left him sick to the core. Who knows if he's telling the truth about that one? He fucked her enough times.

We need to find Celeste.

I'm thinking. Thinking what our next move will be. About how we can salvage this. Dispose of Celeste and quieten my sister, before all chance of an upturn in our finances is gone.

I sit on the bed and exhaustion hits me, dragging me under. I'm turning into my sister, passing out like some Victorian hysteric.

When I wake again there are five messages from Adam on my phone.

I can't help but smile when I read them.

Celeste has finally emailed her agent to say she's coming back to London today.

And I'm sure that if Celeste returns then so will Emma.

When I'm in the kitchen, bending down, pulling chicken nuggets from the freezer, my burner phone starts to vibrate. There's no one around so I answer.

'There's another new email. Celeste's made an appointment with her solicitor. If she changes the will then what's the fucking point? Why bother killing her? We won't ever have any fucking money.'

I really do find his defeatism pathetic.

I have a plan. Adam doesn't know it yet – but he's going to kill Celeste himself. And soon.

She won't make that solicitor's appointment.

Chapter Forty-Four

Celeste

'He's upstairs. I told him he wasn't allowed in, but he said you'd said it was OK, now. That you two had made things up.' The care assistant's accent is thick Bristolian, which I'd never noticed before.

'Who's upstairs?' I ask, already knowing the answer.

'Your husband.'

I throw down my bags, scattering them across the tiles, and make for the staircase. I gesture back towards Emma to go into the sitting room, away from Adam's view, and she nods back at me. I hear her whisper a hurried thank you, reassuring the care assistant that it's all OK, that she's done nothing wrong, asking her what her name is. I've never once asked this.

Bobby is asleep and Adam is by the far wall. He turns and I notice that the dresser drawer is open. He adopts his fake smile.

'Why are you going through Bobby's things?'

'Good to see you too, darling. Bobby asked me to get something for him.'

'He's not even awake, Adam.'

Bobby looks beyond ghastly today. There's a clammy sheen to his face. The hollows in his collarbone look deeper still, sharp bones straining against his skin. As if they might break through flesh at any moment. His face has a green hue, shiny with sweat, his top lip damp.

Adam, by contrast, looks sickeningly radiant, his skin glowing and his hair immaculately messy, a neatly ironed navy shirt open a few buttons at the neck. It's a shirt that I bought for him. The urge to grab something from the bedside table and smash it into his face is contrasted by my conditioned urge to kiss him.

He ignores the fact that I caught him rifling through the drawer.

'I thought I'd come and see how Bobby was doing while you were away. How are you, anyway, darling? How was Rome?' He leans forward towards me. His paltry acting talent is evident. He's all innocent concern, the blameless ingénue.

'Well, it's been a hell of a week.' I regret my comment the moment it leaves my lips. I don't want to let anything slip yet. If he doesn't already know that we're onto him then I don't want him to know what I've discovered. Not from me anyway. He can hear it from the police. 'Everything's fine, though.'

'You're back sooner than I thought that you would be. Did you manage to relax at all after the filming?' The urge to just sink into the corner of the room and put my hands over my ears is overwhelming.

I muster up a voice from somewhere. It's me speaking but I feel distanced from it. Like I'm listening to someone else's voice.

'It was tiring. I came back because Bobby's nurse called me. I . . . I just want to be alone with Bobby right now.'

A flash of irritation crosses Adam's face. It's a look I know too well. 'OK. Well, I'll see you at home later.'

'I think I'll stay with Bobby tonight, darling.' The 'darling' is like bitter fruit on my tongue.

'Fine.' He turns without saying goodbye.

I hear the front door slam as Adam leaves.

Bobby still hasn't woken, so I sit in the chair by his bed, trying not to disturb him, as I regain my composure. Taking shuddering breaths from the stale air of the room. He finally opens one eye. 'Aha, so she's not slit your throat yet, then? Why are you sitting there? Come on, Celie. Jump up.' He pats the bed, as if calling a small dog to his side. I climb up.

'Where's the psychopath?'

'I'm guessing you mean Emma. She's hiding in the sitting room. The real psychopath was here when I arrived. The care assistant had let Adam in.' He pushes himself up onto the pillows, with effort, waving my hand away when I move to help him.

'Don't blame poor Pauline. You know how charming Adam can be. He can make women do whatever he wants. And certain men.' He flops back against the headboard. 'Why are you here, anyway? I thought you were staying away for a week or two. Oh, don't tell me. I know the answer. That beastly Nurse Yvonne called to tell you that I'm about to peg it?'

'Yvonne's a good woman. She was just being a sensible nurse and doing what was needed.' I pass Bobby a glass of San Pellegrino from his bedside table and offer to fetch ice and lemon for him. He shakes his head and takes a cursory sip of the water.

'Always good to be in at the death, isn't it? Speaking of which, bring in Aileen Wuornos. She must be lonely downstairs. It's desperately unentertaining in here. I think that a potential murderer is just what this situation calls for.'

He ignores my reproach at the name-calling and my entreaties that he's not really up to meeting new people. 'Now is exactly the time, surely? It's not like I'll have to tolerate her for long if I can't stand her, will I?'

Emma is standing in the middle of the sitting room, staring at a particularly grisly Egon Schiele print over the fireplace. It's hideous: a woman with elongated fingers that stretch out towards us. I've never liked it. For a horrible second, I consider that I'll be able to remove the picture once Bobby dies. I shudder and turn back to Emma and recount the incident with Adam to her.

She's reluctant to come up to see Bobby at first but she yields, taking the stairs slowly in front of me, pausing at the threshold of his room. The smell of sickness is off-putting. It seeps out, under the fragrance of the Conran Shop oil diffusers and the Pears soap that Pauline has washed Bobby with.

Emma is first to speak.

'Thank you for letting me stay here. And for letting me stay in Whitstable. I feel much better for being there.'

'You're welcome. Do you like what I've done with the place?' His sunken eyes make an unguarded appraisal of her.

'Of course. Who wouldn't?'

'Bobby's a theatre designer.' I throw out a conversational opener. Bobby is staring hard at Emma, and she looks bewildered.

'I know. I saw a play you'd designed the sets for. It was beautiful.'

She's hit on a guaranteed way to draw Bobby in. He was never immune to praise, preening like a peacock under it.

His insecurity and imposter syndrome, never entirely left behind from his days as the bullied schoolchild in the Clarks sandals.

'I went to see *Macbeth* with . . . with someone. I loved the birds. I looked up your work online afterwards.'

I flash of indignation passes through me. Emma has tried to protect me by not mentioning Adam's name but I guess who she was with. I gave Adam those tickets and he said he was taking a work colleague. They were free tickets that Bobby had given to me, but I'd had to cancel due to a staffing crisis at my restaurant: Loisirs. Adam *would* choose to use them to take another woman.

'Ah, my swansong. The curtain call.' Bobby wriggles up the bed a little, stretching his thin flesh into a parody of his smile. 'I'm sorry to hear about your recent woes. What a crashing bore for you. It's awful to be duped. I could tell you some long and torturous tales about the ways men have duped me too. Painful, isn't it?'

'Yes.'

'And what are your plans now?' Bobby's tone changes and his eyes meet Emma's. I may need to head him off. I'm not sure Emma is up to one of his protective stepbrother interrogations. Beneath his lightness he has a steely core.

'I . . . we . . .' Emma looks across at me and I nod approval. 'We've come up with a plan to entrap Adam.'

'No, *you* devised the plan. She's been ever so clever, Bobby. Let her tell you.' I sit beside Bobby, and Emma perches on the side of the bed.

Emma tells him what we're going to do and Bobby manages to keep his eyes open and listen, laughing even at one point.

'Thank you, Emma. I worry about my big sister. She's not as strong as she likes to think she is.' I'm about to launch into a self-depreciating monologue but he speaks again.

'And don't be embarrassed about the Adam thing, Emma. Celeste couldn't resist him, either. She thought he was so pretty that she married him within six months of them meeting. Actually, Celeste, could you get Emma and me some coffee? Or would you prefer something stronger?' I scuttle down to the kitchen, part bemused, part slighted.

* * *

Later, I go and lie on the bed next to Bobby, with the door unlocked this time. I finally get to sleep near dawn but am woken by the screaming of foxes. The bedroom is illuminated by the security lights. I look out and several of them are chasing each other, snarling, whilst Bobby dozes on in a morphine haze. It's not mating season, so I suspect this is a dominance thing. A fight that will leave the mangey old beasts with further scars.

Chapter Forty-Five

Emma

The foxes keep me awake long into the night. Their screams echoing through the air. Wakefulness isn't kind tonight. Electric shocks are coursing through my sleep-eluded limbs. It's my last night here before I go back to face my family.

Adam's visit today shook me. I didn't see him, but I could smell him when I walked up the stairs to Bobby's room. That cloying citrus still staining the air. I wasn't fearful while he was here. I was waiting and listening. Ready to bolt up the stairs if needed and take him by surprise. Smash him over the head with something if he tried to hurt Celeste.

We need to hold on to our fury, though, and wait this out. Our plan is in motion.

* * *

By morning, abrasive thoughts are grating at me. My mind echoes with images from the past few days – the sound of Adam's voice. The memory of Celeste talking to her cruel mother on the phone. The sallow face of her soon-to-be-dead stepbrother. Most of all I think about Celeste's startling kindness towards me. Of her spreading out her angelic wings and taking a potential killer under them for shelter.

It's clear to me now. Celeste may be a different age, a higher class, but she's been as bullied and pushed down as I've been. She's just a woman trying to get through life as best as she can.

The big difference between us now is that Celeste thinks that she can halt Adam and Becky by entrapment. It might stop Adam, but Becky will be free to continue.

I know it'll take something more radical to stop Becky.

I'm enjoying thinking about this aspect of my plan. The part that I haven't told Celeste about.

* * *

Peter is there when I get back, sitting at the kitchen counter, reading *The Sun*, while Mum cleans the room around him.

'Nice holiday?' Sarcasm drips from him. I ignore it. Why do I care what he says or does? Peter is a threat, but I now know the real threat is his daughter. As if his own presence wasn't malignant enough, he brought a more poisonous force into our lives.

'Oh, you're back. Do you feel better for resting?' My mum is ignoring the undercurrents between Peter and me.

'I'm not feeling great. I might go upstairs to lie down.'

'Maybe you should have stayed at your friend's flat for good, hey? Have you asked her?'

I walk out of the room.

Pretending to be more ill than I actually am is much harder than I thought it would be. It's not something that I've ever done, despite what some of the crueller doctors implied. I think hard about what my gait would be like when

274

I'm going through a bad period. How my body droops with fatigue. How each step feels filled with effortful intention. I exaggerate each of these symptoms, hoping I can pull off this act. If Adam and Becky can perform, then so can I.

I may as well not have bothered. Peter didn't even look up from his paper to see my performance. But others will be watching me more closely.

I go up and lie on Becky's bed, preparing myself for the next act. There's one of Ava's battered teddies on the pillow of her bed. I bought her this one when she was a toddler. She still sleeps with it every night. I pick it up and hold it to my chest.

I can do this.

Be exactly what Becky expects me to be.

She and Adam underestimate me.

Such a dangerous thing for them to do.

Chapter Forty-Six

Celeste

Emma is stronger still today, looking less like she's trapped behind misted glass. Her family are all out so she's cast off the pretence that she's virtually bedbound and walked round to Bobby's house. I've stayed with Bobby. I couldn't be anywhere else. Adam has sent non-committal replies to the messages I've sent telling him that I'm here but that me and Bobby need time alone together.

It's strange to say, but I've genuinely missed her, my peculiar murderer-turned-confidante. She lets me embrace her and I kiss her on both cheeks.

We take a tray of food up to Bobby. A pointless exercise: he won't eat.

'No more invasions from the Calvin Klein model?' Bobby pauses for a moment, taking an effortful breath. He turns to speak to Emma but his eyes focus on me. Beneath the layers of sickness I see his impish grin. Like we're children again. 'Actually, Emma, maybe you could help me. I've been asking Celeste this for years, but she just won't tell me. Maybe you could answer the question. Just how big is Adam's—'

'Bobby! That's too much. I think that Emma's worked out that you're gay. There's no need to put on all this silly campery just to demonstrate. Now, be quiet and try to eat. People pay good money for my food and you're getting it for free.' I revert back to the older sister/younger brother dynamic that we always had. Mother/son, even, when Adele and his father were too busy fighting, or too involved in the inevitable post-row bedroom reconciliations, to notice us.

'Celeste, get over yourself. It's a croissant from Waitrose that you've warmed in the oven.' He says this with a wink at Emma.

I send Emma downstairs to fetch Bobby's medication and he reaches across and takes my hand. 'I'm sorry for my silliness. I'm glad that you can see through the act. You always did, didn't you? Like I see through yours, too. I'm concerned for you.'

He pats my arm, his wrinkled claw of a hand on my skin. 'Not because of that psychopath you married. I don't believe for a moment that he'll harm you. Especially not once you've finalised your will. But I'm worried that you'll slip down again. Like you did after David.'

'I won't.' I don't meet his eye.

*　*　*

Bobby begrudgingly lets us change his pyjamas and tend to him so that I can dispatch Pauline to the shops. She seems glad of the break, and I see her furtively lighting a cigarette as she walks up the path. Emma holds Bobby over to one side of the bed as I slide the flannel gently across the fragile xylophone of his ribcage. The effort of being moved wipes him out and his eyelids close reluctantly.

I know he's been enjoying having Emma and me here. He always did thrive on drama.

I spend an hour doing the things that I've been avoiding for the past few days. Looking at my multiple WhatsApp notifications, emailing Katrina, and checking through the avalanche of emails. Messages from suppliers, PR stuff, dull invites to uninspiring new restaurants. I don't see Emma in the doorway.

'Are you ready?' She's holding up one of the recording devices.

* * *

My house looks alien. As if it's been tinted a different hue. Turned into something darker and uglier. The afternoon light reflects on the windows and they stare at me like unseeing eyes. I've messaged Adam and told him that I'm still needed with Bobby but that we'll talk tomorrow. By tomorrow, there'll be nothing to talk about. No negotiations. He'll be trapped and I'll be liberated.

He claims he's not at home today but his record on telling the truth is sketchy. Emma and I stand on the street, a few houses down. She has her back to my house. I'm angled to check for any signs of occupancy. We wait ten minutes, my legs weak, my hands trembling.

'You can do this. I'm watching. I'll call your phone if I see him coming down the street and you can run out of the back door.' Emma steps back into the shade of a London plane tree.

The house smells alien. There's an empty pizza box on the side and Adam has discarded a pair of shoes and a jacket on the floor by the kitchen sofa. Both items that I bought for him. There's a row of empty beer bottles on the countertop. His usual forensic tidiness is slipping. He's unravelling.

I feel like I'm in some tawdry spy thriller. The recording devices weigh down the pockets of my jacket.

The first one is easy. I plant it behind the cookbook stand in the kitchen. Adam won't see that one. He lets me make all the food or he orders takeaways. The sitting room smells of a perfume that I don't recognise. Something cheap and musky. Adam and Becky must be being careless. I glance at my sofas and feel queasy, a brief thought of them copulating here whilst I was away entering my head like a twisted tableau. I prop the second device up on the mantelpiece, behind a stack of embossed invitations to various weddings and parties that will be a bore to attend.

I should have known that he was in the bedroom before I opened the door. My nose should have picked up his signature lemony scent. The ridiculously priced one that I buy for him from Mayfair.

'I thought you were out?' I force myself to breathe. Adam pushes himself up the bed, stretching his torso and lifting his arms in a performative yawn. Twisting his body to the light for maximum effect. His toned skin glows, contrasting against the white sheets.

'Sorry, darling. I fell asleep.' He pushes the sheets down to his waist. 'Welcome back. I missed you.'

I force myself to think. Eyeing the door behind me, calculating how fast he could move, whether I could escape if he launched himself at me.

'You still haven't told me about Rome. How was it.'

'Hot and busy. I'm exhausted.' He makes eye contact and I know that he knows I'm lying. His lip curls into a smirk. The lamp by his head looks tempting. I could happily abandon all my propriety, my years of restraint, to feel the ecstasy of smashing it into his smug face.

'You must be tired. Don't bother to tell me your *stories* about Rome yet. Why not climb in and keep me company?' He pushes the sheet further down to the top of his groin.

'I'm in rather a hurry, actually. I need to sort some things at the restaurant. I've been away too long, and it doesn't run itself.'

'Shame.' He steps out of the bed, stretching again. I avoid looking, hating the very fact that he exists. He steps towards me, and I jolt backwards.

He sneers. 'What's wrong, Celeste? I'm just going to the bathroom.'

* * *

Emma looks grey. She might be better than she was but she's hardly in rude health. I stride past her, hissing at her to follow me in five minutes. Once we're back at Bobby's house, I tell her what happened. How I placed the final device behind Adam's bedside lamp while he was in the bathroom and then fled.

Emma takes a laboured breath and says she'll make the call now. She sits on the edge of the sofa, insisting that I leave the room. Her cheeks flood with blood at the shame of what she's about to do. I suppose it would be rather bizarre for me to sit and listen to her discussing how to kill me with my husband.

I look at the clock as she enters the kitchen, surprised that only minutes have passed. I unclench my fists.

'Well?'

'He fell for it. Every word. He lapped it up.'

'But did he say anything incriminating for the recording?'

She walks across and takes my hand. 'He said that he wants me to kill you. He said when. He said how. We've got him now.'

Chapter Forty-Seven

Celeste

I apply enough make-up to disguise my weariness without making me look like a clown. Foundation and lipstick bleed into the creases now if I'm not careful. My restaurant 'uniform' of vintage Chanel feels like it's from another life. I'm dressed as the Celeste the staff and diners will expect to see. This retro chic disguise.

I tell myself that I can't hide forever. That I'll be fine to go out tonight. We have the recording now. We're almost there. Emma is going to go and pick up the device shortly. Adam has told her that he's going for a meal with an old friend tonight so she should be fine. No doubt he really means a night with Becky in a cheap hotel.

My body already feels lighter, like I've offloaded a burden. My mind less fragmented. Things are going to get better. I'll be free from Adam's tyranny. The thought of Bobby jolts me back.

I take a deep breath and step into the darkened street. It's good to feel the night air on my skin. I need the release of being away from Bobby for a while, from the inevitability of death. The last carer has been for the night and checked on him. He looks no worse today, but certainly no better. Emma's family are out at a party. It's her stepfather's mother's birthday. She'll be back and asleep on the sofa before they all return. Keeping up the pretence that she's been too ill to leave the house.

London has always been my refuge, my comfort – much like Paris was when I was a child. The move to the English countryside in my teenage years was a disquieting time. Being carted there like baggage when Adele married Bobby's father. All that empty space and lack of people to run to for help, the claustrophobia due to the lack of public transport options that left me stranded. There's comfort in London's neon-lit streets that mask out the stars and illuminate the oppressive night sky. I prefer the security of comprehensive mobile phone reception and shops that open twenty-four hours a day, the proximity of people. I'll take the brutality of humanity over the barbarism of the natural world.

I exit the train at London Bridge and cross the concourse towards the Tube. My heels beat out a staccato rhythm. It's hard to resist the urge to look round at each set of footsteps behind me. My hand clutches the rail with unusual ferocity as the escalator takes me down towards the platform. It's almost deserted, just a man standing too close to the platform edge and a woman clutching her arms across her chest. I stay back, pressed against the tiles, scanning the platform. I wonder if Bobby is right. If I am close to losing it. The fragile veneer that protects me from the darkness eroding away again in the wake of another failed marriage. A group of women gush out from the escalator, staggering on their too-high heels, their voices loudened by after-work drinks. I look away.

There's another restaurant opening just off Piccadilly that good manners dictate that I must attend. That and the fact that Katrina has hinted again that my publisher is about to drop me if I don't get back to work and regain my public profile. It's neck-achingly dull as I stand, tensed and ready for all the semi-strangers who I must talk to. Mentally prepping comments to volley into the air. Neutral-faced food tastings and benign nods as I look over their too familiar menus. The day-bright flashes of cameras like migraines in my vision. It's tedious but reassuring to be back in public, however jarring the night.

It's late when I reach the warm glow of Loisirs, the familiar Art Deco lettering spelling out the name that I chose in gold. The restaurant is dominated by off-duty City workers tonight. Collars now loosened around the men's chafed throats. Their younger spouses or partners smiling back at them with polished perfection. The women constrained in business suits and heels or squeezed into impractical evening dresses. Hiding their hunger as they pick at salads, dutifully watching the men slice into their blood-rare steaks.

Simone is at the desk as I walk in, looking exactly as formidable as I like her to look in a bias-cut dress. Surrounded by angular glass vases crammed with cut dahlias that are the colour of fresh wounds.

'Ah, Celeste. You look as magnificent as ever.' This is a kind lie. She mimes kisses on both of my cheeks. 'He is here, already. I sat him at your table. We've chosen the wine for him, naturally. I know that your husband is a hopeless sommelier.'

'My husband . . . ?'

I somehow keep my voice even but familiar jolts of panic run down my legs and arms, making me feel limp and unsteady. I repeat in my head that I'll have the recording soon. I'm safe.

I have two choices here. Flee and humiliate myself in this place where my image and standing is firmly established. Or I face him again. I choose fight over flight.

I swallow hard and lift my head. Smiling, I nod and walk across the restaurant towards him.

Chapter Forty-Eight

Celeste

The room suits Adam's bone structure. He's in a pool of light cast from a glass pendant that illuminates this most private corner of the floor. They've seated him at my usual table at the back of the restaurant. The one that's always reserved for last-minute visiting glitterati who want to sit away from curious glances, or for me, when I make an appearance. The time when I was here every night is past and my appearances are more sporadic, more of an event now. It's hard to continue to parade yourself in front of strangers when there's a voice at home constantly telling you how flawed you are.

How did Adam know I was going to be here? Has he been tracking me somehow? Is that how he knew I wasn't in Rome?

I try to bat my fears away. I'm sure that Adam does know I was lying about Rome. I could see it in his eyes earlier today. In his sarcastic emphasis on certain words. But he can't have known what I was really up to these past few days, that I was plotting with Emma, about the plan, or he wouldn't have spoken to Emma on the phone so candidly.

I wonder if he's been calling the restaurant to see when I'm here. Or if I left the invitation for the opening somewhere in the house. He'd guess that I'd come here afterwards. I rack my brain as to how he'd know my movements.

The truth occurs to me. He could easily have found my electronic diary. I remember that I left the laptop open in the study. A cold dew of sweat forms between my shoulder blades. My stomach lurches and I feel the urge to vomit. He knows my schedule for today, for tomorrow. For every work event pending. He can be everywhere that I am. And he'll have seen the email chain between Katrina and me. He'll know for certain that I cancelled the Rome trip. That I've had solicitor's appointments.

His lips are stained red from the wine. He stands up when I walk towards him, the smile disingenuous. I'm compelled to let him kiss my cheek, to sit down across the table from him. I can get this over within a few minutes, save myself from humiliation in front of the staff. They would hate me making a scene as much as I would hate myself for it.

'Why are you here?' I wait till the waiter has left before I begin speaking, soft-voiced. 'I wasn't expecting you and we spoke earlier.'

'Celeste. I know that you know about everything. I've made the most appalling mistake. I want to explain myself. I knew you wouldn't hear me out at home so I thought we could talk here. It's private enough.' Our table is shielded from the other diners by a pillar and the noise of numerous conversations is cushioning us. He reaches for my hand, but I withdraw it from the table, just in time. His fingers rest on the linen cloth. He's clever. He has me at my most compliant. I'd never make a scene here. I have my reputation to uphold.

'I know that you know that I've slipped up again and I'm sorry. It was pure folly. Just a silly infatuation that went too far. She didn't mean a thing to me. It's always been you, Celeste. Just you.'

'What absolute bollocks, Adam.' I rarely swear. Even now I can't summon up the words I really want. The foulest of invectives should be spewing from me. I should be reaching across and spitting into his face. Scraping my nails down his cheeks till blood runs. But my practised composure is too ingrained.

He pulls the solemn face of contrition that I know so well. Sorrowful eyes, a slight bite of his lower lip in consternation. There's something tawdry about his performance tonight. End of the pier rather than West End. He's frayed at the edges, a thin sheen of sweat coating his forehead. The skin around his eyes is streaked with narrow lines. I don't recognise this Adam. We've been through this before – the maudlin confessions and the acts of penitence – but he's always maintained his composure before. I can see that he's started unravelling. I breathe steadily, effortfully, and keep my gaze fixed upon him.

One of the newer waiting staff arrives and puts down two plates.

'I ordered for you to save time. I know you always love grouse when it's in season.'

The grouse carcass sits in the middle of the plate. Its legs pointed upwards in a facsimile of painful death. The oil shining on the bird's puckered skin. Adam slices into his, revealing the blood-soaked flesh.

I push the plate away. Adam starts to eat and I sit, helpless. The fear of indignity stopping me from walking away.

'The thing is, Celeste, I'm happy to leave our marriage if that's what you want, but I need what I'm owed.'

'What you're owed? What the fuck do you mean?' I have no trouble finding the right word this time.

'I don't want much, Celeste. Just half of everything. I don't think that's too much to ask for, is it? You have had a lot from me over the years, after all.' He rests his elbows on the table and frames his face with his hands.

'Well, given that you knew where I was going to be tonight, I'm guessing that you also know that I've seen my solicitor and drawn up divorce papers. You're out of the will. You'll get exactly what you're owed. Nothing at all.' Anyone looking at us would think we were just having a polite middle-class conversation about the latest performance at the Royal Opera House or a weekend in the South of France. Our faces are masks.

Adam lifts his elbows from the table and his hand darts across, grabbing my wrist. I feel the bones of his fingers crushing my hand.

'There's one way out of this marriage whereby you aren't hurt. And that's by paying me off.'

Adam pulls back as Marco appears, gliding across, charming and unruffled as ever. He's the best maître d' that we've had at Loisirs. It may sound dreadful of me, but I always prefer to have the most handsome men, like Marco, as front of house. Beauty has currency in business. I stand on shaking legs and do the expected air kissing, whilst he ushers me back into my seat, chiding me for bothering to even acknowledge him. It's a game we always play.

'Marco! The grouse looked perfect but I ate too much up in Piccadilly. I couldn't manage a bite. We won't be having pudding either, I'm afraid. Adam just had a text message, and he has to go. It's this poor friend of his from drama school. Her career's on the skids after being in some awful soap. I've told him to go to her and try to sort her out. She's quite sick, isn't she, Adam? Mentally I mean. Terribly disturbed.' I pause and sip my water.

I turn to Adam and smile, lowering my head and looking up at him.

'Now, run along, darling. Becky's need is greater than mine and I'm sure that I've got lots of dull things here to occupy myself with after my lovely little holiday.'

I pass the rest of the wine bottle back to Marco for him to decant for the staff for the end of their shift. 'I'll see you later.' There's little that Adam can do now but get up to leave.

Marco retreats. Discreet as ever.

Adam moves his face towards mine, his face set, dark eyes narrowing. I recoil. His hand cups the back of my head and he kisses my cheek. I freeze, even though my instincts scream at me to push him away.

He whispers in my ear.

'Fuck you, Celeste. I don't want your money anymore, you twisted old bitch. I'm just going to make you suffer. Watch your back.'

I feel a flutter of panic about the recording device.

He knows too much. He and Becky may even have worked out that I was with Emma.

I'm wondering what he actually said on the phone to her today. How he phrased it. Whether it will have any power.

Adam can slide out of any mess. And he'd sacrifice anything or anyone to keep himself untarnished.

Chapter Forty-Nine

Celeste

Before I can leave, there's the established steady trickle of greetings and I adopt my practised expression. I manage not to tremble when I hold the pen to sign off the new menus with Francois. All the time fighting to push away the images that are simmering in my head. Pictures of Adam and Becky in hotel rooms, of Adam and Emma in my bed, of the parade of previous women. Thoughts of Bobby's stertorous breaths. Of Emma in my dressing room with the knife.

Marco comes to wave me off at the door, touching my arm lightly and wishing me well. I refuse Marco's offer to call me a cab and wave him back inside Loisirs.

I scout for a taxi. They usually crawl around these streets like beetles but there's none tonight. After a few seconds one swings by but before it reaches me, a man in a tuxedo and a woman who can barely stand step in front of it. The taxi swerves across to them and the man bundles the drunk woman into the back.

The road looks empty. I contemplate going back in but decide against it. Thinking that fresh air will help. I refuse to be afraid. What threat is Adam on a populated London street, anyway?

But the walk back to London Bridge station doesn't clear my head like it usually does. I should have guessed it wouldn't. It's that leery time of night when London is emptying out its day visitors. Wine-soaked City workers stumbling from the bars. Back to the outer boroughs, their suits crumpled, their shoes replaced by trainers, incongruously garish with their muted workwear. Tourists wearily trudging back to hotels, theatregoers heading primly back to the suburbs. The hordes of homeless people are settling down for the night in doorways on piles of old cardboard, heaped with blankets.

There must have been some kind of sports match tonight. There's that tribal feeling in the air of people who've gathered and are either victorious or defeated. It's hard to gauge which. Either way, the air is caustic with threat. A group of men in nylon shirts are blocking my path on Southwark Bridge, staggering drunkenly. The noise is overwhelming as they jostle each other, falling and pushing as they walk towards me. Open cans of drink slopping onto the pavement, the alcohol rarely reaching their mouths as they roar and yell. I try to step into the cycle lane to pass but they spill over, knocking me into the road, almost pushing me into the path of an oncoming car.

'Watch your step, love.' A red-faced man grabs me by both my arms and pulls me back onto the pavement. I instinctively push back at him, my arms flailing at his soft torso.

'Calm the fuck down, will you, love? I'm helping you. I'm hardly after a feel of your saggy tits.' The beery-breathed mouth looms into my face. I push through them and like some extraordinary dance end up back against the parapet of the bridge, the Thames churning below me, the man still holding my arms.

'I was trying to help. You can't help women like you though, can you? Fucked-up ideas about men. You bitches think we're all rapists.'

There's laughing and more jostling as I straighten my clothes, adopting a passive stance and looking down at my shoes as I push forward along the bridge. The final straggler, a sweaty boy with red cheeks, lags back slightly as his pack runs on, chanting again.

'I'm sorry, miss. He don't mean it. No disrespect, OK?' My seemingly great age has spared me from them. He must see a woman in her forties as nearer his mother's age, his grandmother's age even, than his own.

Their chants recede as they race over the bridge, shouting challenges to each other about who can run the fastest, like overgrown children. The rest of the bridge is empty apart from the reassuring sight of a young couple holding hands, heading towards me. I lean against the parapet and take a breath. A police boat races under the bridge, overtaking a Thames Clipper, devoid of passengers. I breathe in the toxic city air that my lungs are accustomed to, untroubled by the exhaust fumes from the occasional car that rushes by on the road behind me.

I turn around ready to continue, ignoring the footsteps approaching behind me, expecting a pink-faced jogger clad in Lycra to pass me by. The hand grips into my shoulder and pulls me around. I hear my gasp.

Adam's face is red, sweat soaking the roots of his hair. His handsome face made ugly by rage. He pitches closer towards me and I try to step back but there's nothing but the water below me and the cast iron of the bridge against my back. My skin is electric. My limbs rigid.

His face pushes towards mine and he opens his mouth to speak but closes it again. For a moment I think that he's about to kiss me. My mouth opens slightly, but not in shock, more in expectation, an imprinted response.

'Adam, please. Stop it.' My speech is broken as I try to take in air and speak at the same time. He ignores me, his face hard, cruel even. I think to the recordings and regain my composure. 'You don't want to hurt me. I know exactly what you've done, and I have evidence.'

He slackens his grip. 'Oh, you mean when I plotted your murder on the phone this afternoon with your pathetic little accomplice?'

'I . . .' His face is set in a sneer.

'You two really aren't as clever as you think, are you?' He rams his hand into his pocket and pulls out one of the recording devices. 'Do you mean this evidence? I saw you leave it in the bedroom. I was watching you through the keyhole when I went to the bathroom. You really need to up your game if you want to be a criminal. Some people aren't cut out for it.'

I don't look as he throws it over my shoulder, and it arcs off the bridge. There's no sound as it hits the water behind me.

I close my eyes for a second. Waiting for it to begin. Yielding to my coming death. I have no other choice. I can't fight him. There's no one here to help me.

He rams me against the side of the bridge. I try to scream but nothing comes out. I'm holding my breath. My lungs, my voice rendered useless. There's no one near enough to gesture to. One of those lulls that you get at this time of night where pedestrians seem to come in pulses. The young couple are now in the distance and the only other people are on the other side of the bridge, eyes trained only on the pavement or on each other. There's an occasional car speeding past. Drivers who would think nothing of a couple standing here. City lights, the Shard lit up in the background. Tower Bridge behind me.

His hands encircle my throat, and the view starts to fade.

Chapter Fifty

Emma

After Celeste left, I waited. When enough time had passed to be sure that Adam would be out, I rang him.

'Emma! How are you feeling?' His voice grates me now that I know that all this has just been play-acting.

'I'm still pretty weak. I've just woken up. I know you're busy tonight but I just wanted to hear your voice.'

'That's sweet. And likewise.'

'Where are you? It sounds busy.' I can hear traffic in the background.

'I'm just walking along the Thames. I'm on my way to meet my friend for dinner.'

It's safe. I can go to the house.

* * *

The device is gone when I arrive. The bedroom is carnage; the lamp by the bed smashed, the bedside table knocked over. There's a hole in one of the panels of the bathroom door, like someone has punched it. A maniac finally surrendering to monumental rage.

I crawl around on the carpet, knowing that it's futile. Knowing that Adam must have found the device. That he'll be on his way to find Celeste.

I run down the stairs, almost falling as I go, righting myself on the banister. The lounge is in disarray. The contents of the mantelpiece thrown on the floor as if Adam has swept his hand along and jettisoned everything away. The second recording device has gone too.

I reach for my phone to warn her. There's two per cent left on the battery. I've forgotten to charge it. I've been so busy avoiding Becky that my routine has become broken. My fingers are numb and uncoordinated, like they belong to someone else, as I navigate to Celeste's number and wait.

My phone dies just as her voicemail kicks in.

Guessing that Celeste must be at her restaurant by now, I use the house phone to call for a taxi, hoping that there'll be enough in my account to cover it. I stand by the door, trying to catch my breath. Waiting what feels like hours for the cab to arrive. I keep thinking of Celeste, of what a saviour she's been for me. I won't let her down now.

The driver isn't a talker, thankfully. He sings softly to himself when a song he likes comes on the radio. I quell my urge to scream at him to go faster. To break every speed limit. To tell him that a woman's life is at stake. One of Celeste's kitchen knives digs into my side. Stashed in my jacket, sitting awkwardly in my inside pocket, poking my ribs. A potentially useless weapon for someone like me. Someone who might falter, trip, disassociate again. Already a proven failure.

* * *

Loisirs is the kind of place that I wouldn't dream of going to. Even if I could afford the prices, I'd only resent the cost, tallying up in my head what this could buy for Ava and me. Imagining how many outfits we could get from the shopping centre in Lewisham. The softly lit window with the half curtain in olive green reminds me of films about Paris. I run up and peer through the glass. Scanning the room for Celeste. There's no sign of her.

The knife weighs down my jacket on one side. A thin, pointless garment that barely keeps out the night air. I stand for a second, a foolish figure on a hopeless mission. It's only as I scan the area that I see Celeste. Her distinctive dress sense standing out amidst the crowd of people near the entrance to the bridge.

I start to run over when I feel a hand clamped roughly over my mouth, a presence propelling me into the shadows as I'm dragged into a doorway opposite.

'Don't make a noise.' The lemon fragrance fills my nose, my body momentarily gives in to the reflex and relaxes back against his. I don't struggle, just nod assent.

'You really fucked this up, Emma, didn't you?' He twists me round to face him and slams my back against the wall.

I prise my tongue from where it's stuck on the dried-up bed of my mouth. I need to stall for time. Celeste is the primary target. I gamble on the fact that there'd be no point killing me.

'Why did you do it, Adam? We had something, didn't we? We were good together.' Saying these honeyed lies makes my stomach contract. 'I thought you loved me.'

'There was never an us.' His face is a sneer of revulsion. I feel his saliva hit my skin as he hisses the words, and my head turns away. His hand clasps the back of my skull, yanking me back around to face him.

'You're pathetic. You know that. When I've killed her then you'll be next.'

I see his head turn, gauging where Celeste is. She's within running distance. He could easily catch her.

'There's no point to this now, Adam. She's changed her will already. You won't get anything.'

He steps backwards, releasing me. His fist clenches into a hard ball as he turns and pulls back his arm, as if about to punch me. His breathing quickens. He arches his spine, examining me. His lip curling. Face crimson. His words hiss into my face.

'Do you think you're anything special? Anything more than a pitiful little cripple? You're nothing.' He pushes me to the ground, and I don't resist. Letting him think that I'm weak still. That I'm not having one of my better days.

'Fuck the pair of you.' He scrutinises me briefly, like a scientist pondering on exactly what species something is.

Then he's gone, walking across the road towards the bridge and Celeste. Merging into a crowd of football supporters as they jostle him playfully, high-fiving him as he makes his way through.

I push myself up, my hands scraping against rough brick. Waves of nausea hit me. I catch my breath and feel for the knife.

Anger pulses in my chest, forming a hard knot. Adam feels etched on my retinas. That deranged, sneering mouth mocking me. The face of a violent deceiver who's now running towards the woman who saved me. Celeste, who has treated me with more kindness and empathy than my own family.

I can't let him near her.

My fingers lock around the knife, the handle moulding

to my flesh as my grip tightens. The rage has morphed into a steady focus. Something powerful and unstoppable.

My legs are surprisingly strong, my stride measured but wide as I make it across to them. Adam has Celeste pinned against the bridge. Her back jammed against the balustrade. His hands around her neck. With a final push of energy I make it to them, lifting my arm high and striking his back, the knife scraping against bone at first, his head twisting violently towards me.

His face is a pitiful tableau of shock and I hit again. The knife scraping, piercing his flesh, hitting vital organs. Exactly like he taught me. I go for the rib space where his heart is. I watch him fall to his knees, blood pumping out, air hissing as the life seeps out of him.

The relief I feel is palpable. I've done it now. It's almost complete.

I hadn't told Celeste yet about this gift that I was planning to give her. That I was always going to kill Adam. How else could I repay her kindness? It's the only way I'd ever keep her safe from him. I just didn't expect to have to do it so soon.

I've learned a valuable lesson with Adam and Celeste. There are more things than territory that are worth killing for. Sometimes you have to kill to protect the people who you care about.

Chapter Fifty-One

Celeste

The noise is a sound that I haven't heard before or since. A horrifying noise that I hope never to hear again. Metal scraping against bone. The knife hits his back, causing him to gasp in pain, contorting his face as his neck twists round, straining the ligaments of his throat. Then he turns and it slices through the skin of his chest, into his soft flesh, blood spraying out. His hands drop to his sides, and he keels over, landing on the pavement between me and Emma.

The relief is momentary before panic sets in.

'What have you done? Oh *God*. You stabbed him!'

'He was going to kill you. He was going to push you into the Thames.' She's still breathless from running. A faint patina of sweat on her face, blood on her hands. Her eyes are bright.

'I aimed for the heart and lungs, just like he showed me when I was going to stab you.'

Adam lies before me in a pool of blood. I drop down and my stockings snag on the pavement as I look up at Emma. I jolt my head around as a woman cruises by in a car, windows down, the sounds of her shouting the lyrics to a song ring out as she drives by without stopping.

'I went to the house and the devices were gone. I knew he was angry because he'd smashed stuff in the bedroom. Punched a hole in the door. I tried to call you but then my phone died, so I had to rush here to make sure you were safe, and I saw him . . .' Her speech is urgent and garbled. She drops down to her knees too and we flank Adam on the pavement. 'I was scared.'

'What the hell are we going to do now? Someone must have seen you.'

My head flicks around. There's still no one coming on our side of the bridge. A couple of around my age pass by on the other side of the road, the noise of their conversation, their laughter, seems impossibly normal. I push forward, my instinct is to run to them, to scream across for them to help me. Tell them that someone has stabbed my husband and we need help. To just scream.

The urge to get myself as far away from Emma, away from the blood seeping from Adam, is overpowering. I want to run and run until my legs can't carry me anymore.

I dare to look down. Adam is half on his side. He's grey, a hideous pallor in stark contrast to the dark pavement. The knife is sticking out of the left side of his chest.

Emma's voice is slower, calmer now. 'Take the knife and conceal it under your jacket. You need to throw it in the river. Pretend that you're being sick over the side with the shock. Then drop the knife over the edge. Do it now.'

Her words are commanding. I don't question her. This is the only thing to do. Emma and I are linked now. The act that she's committed reflects back onto me too. I won't be seen as blameless here when everything comes out. And how could I leave her alone with this? With what's essentially my mess.

302

Two women runners pass by on the opposite side of the bridge, shouting a conversation, seemingly oblivious to us.

I shield him from the view of eyes or cameras with my back and I grasp the handle. It yields, coming out of his flesh with surprising ease. There's a faint sucking noise. His flesh gurgles as I stash the knife under my jacket. I'm quick as I wipe the handle on the side of my suit, removing our fingerprints, and I bend over the parapet, pretending to vomit into the water. Stepping back, I wipe my mouth with a handkerchief, just after I've tossed the knife, the Thames absorbing the weapon. I dip back down towards Adam. His blood is flowing faster now, gushing from his side in a torrent, and forming a puddle that looks black in the dim light. Lumps of it congeal like pieces of offal.

My focus fades in and out and I inhale sharply to try to ground myself. A jogger dressed in black passes right by us on the pavement. His hood is up, headphones trailing. He barely even glances down at the three of us, probably immune to the sights and sounds of London at night, filling in the blanks and assuming one of us had too much to drink and stumbled.

'Celeste, I have to go now, before someone comes. Call an ambulance. I'll see you at Bobby's when you get back from the hospital. OK?' A car passes by and I see the driver, a young woman staring ahead at the road. A white van follows, the driver barely glancing at us. Just another normal London night; a man lying drunk on the pavement whilst two women assist him.

I scan the bridge. 'There'll be cameras. There's always cameras. We've been seen, haven't we?'

'There are no cameras here. I looked.' She gestures and I see that there are people coming along the bridge from both directions. 'I can't go now, though. It's too late.'

You're never alone for long in this city. A couple, my age or so, are approaching us from the left whilst three men are nearing us from my right.

'Call 999 now and stay standing. I'm just a passer-by, OK?' Emma's tone is firm. As if she's instructing a child. 'You've never met me before. I'm an ex-nurse who wanted to help. I came across you here with Adam and passed a man in black with his hood up running across the bridge and towards the South Bank. Neither of us got a look at his face. OK? I'll see you back at Bobby's later. We'll be fine.'

My hand reaches for my aching throat where Adam just had his hands. I fumble in my bag and pull out a Hermès scarf, knotting it quickly around my neck to cover the redness where he'll have left an imprint.

The front of Emma's clothes are soaked in blood – just as they would be if she had tried to examine him, to revive him. My jacket is punctuated by circles of black where blood has leaked into the green fabric. His face looked achingly pretty in the few seconds it takes him to die. He's a colourless form in the neon light. Ghastly and subhuman.

Emma's hand darts into Adam's pocket and she takes out the burner phone, shoving it into her bag. People start running to us. She grips my hand and then releases it. I rush to the side of the bridge and this time I actually do vomit. The contents of my stomach spill into the Thames. We wait for the emergency services to come as camera-phone lights flash. People crowd around us, voices echoing in the night.

Chapter Fifty-Two

Celeste

Police stations are hideous places. I had no first-hand knowledge of them prior to tonight. It's all chipped paint and careworn furniture. No amount of TV crime drama could prepare you for the odour. The lobby smells of sweat and vodka as an elderly man lurches about, supporting himself on the counter. At first glance, he's immaculately dressed in a fitted waistcoat and sombre trousers, but his face is etched with dirt and his fingernails are black half-moons at the end of cigarette-stained digits. He's spewing out profanities with a cut-glass accent.

The police officer leads me straight through to a back room, leaving Emma behind in the chaos of the reception area. People look up and stare at me as we pass through into the inner sanctum. I'm not sure if they're recognising me from TV or just staring at what a state I'm in. My blouse is stuck to my breasts with Adam's blood, my skirt clinging to my thighs. There's a ladder in the knee of my left stocking.

When I go to the bathrooms, I see that there's blood

smeared across my cheek. A lock of my hair hanging down over my forehead, the ends tinged with red where I pushed it back. I can still feel Adam's hands on my throat.

The police officer has taken my clothes as evidence and given me a sweatsuit in thick grey cotton. Another first. I never wear sportswear. It's an incongruous look on me. I unclip my hair so that it hangs down, covering at least part of my neck. The skin on my throat is red but not noticeable yet. It'll be an abstract painting of blues and yellows tomorrow.

I wash the blood from my hands and face as best as I can with cheap soap and cold water and reapply make-up with a tremulous hand. A young woman at the next sink asks me for a cigarette and when I decline settles on asking for money. I don't have that either. She swears at me and a spray of her spit showers my face.

I fill in forms. Give a vague description of an assailant who wasn't there, the jogger who won't be found. Adam was pronounced dead at the scene, hoisted into the back of the ambulance on a stretcher. They left with no sirens blazing, no need to rush to save the unsalvageable in a pointless festival of light and noise. The incessant camera phone flashes added to the neon glare of night-time London. People are ghouls. They couldn't resist flocking around at the perimeter of the police tape, snapping photos of this poor newly widowed woman doused in her husband's blood.

* * *

It's late when I finally get back to Bobby's house.

'She actually did that. She saved you. I'd like to say that this is incredible but it's really not, is it?' Bobby reaches across for a tissue to dab at his yellowing eyes. 'We kind of knew that she had it in her, didn't we?'

'I don't know. No, actually, I didn't think that she did have it in her if I'm honest.' I'm sticky from the partly washed-off soap at the police station. The remaining smears of Adam's blood. I haven't showered yet. I rushed in to see Bobby, to grasp on to some semblance of comfort amidst all of this chaos. The sweat suit is on the floor of the room and I've pulled on a silk dressing gown. I don't know whether to just throw the awful thing away or if I'm meant to wash it and take it back to the police station.

'I could have lost you.' Bobby strokes my arm. I'm lying on my back on the bed, exhaustion flooding me.

Bobby looks even more unwell tonight. His breathing is more pronounced, more evident somehow. His ribcage visible as he labours with each breath, wincing occasionally. I offer him morphine syrup, but he declines, flapping a hand at me as if I've suggested a gin and tonic that he isn't quite in the mood for.

'Well, he's dead now. You're safe from him.' He looks directly at me. 'You didn't help to kill him, by the way. If there was so much blood pumping out, then it sounds like he was already dying from the knife wound. Nothing could have helped. Taking the knife out would have just sped it up a little. From where I'm lying now, that doesn't seem like such a terrible thing for a person.' He squeezes my hand.

'But, Bobby, Emma was carrying a knife with her. And she instantly clocked that there were no CCTV cameras on the bridge.'

Bobby mutters something else.

'What's that?' I move back to his side.

'Who gives a shit about what Emma intended to do. She looked out for you. Who else but me has ever done that?

307

We have to look after her, Celeste. Protect her. This isn't her fault any more than it's yours.'

His voice is almost a whisper now. 'And don't ask her about the cameras. Or the knife. Who cares? You're both safe now. Have a shower and then go down and wait up for her. She'll be exhausted and in need of some nurture. I think you can manage that.'

* * *

Emma doesn't get back from the police station till two in the morning. By which time, my phone has rung so often that I've had to mute it. The first journalist rang barely an hour after I got home. Doubtless one of the camera-phone-toting onlookers has called the press. Honeyed words of faux sympathy masked the writer's desperation for salacious nonsense to print. She wanted high drama, celebrity widow rending her clothes in anguish. She got my usual go-to protective mechanism of polite but haughty and came away with little more than a few generic words before I disconnected the call. It'll be all over the newspapers by tomorrow morning, regardless. I'm sure it's online already. Thankfully, they shouldn't be able to find me here.

When Emma walks into the room her face is worn, shadowy under the eyes, her tone flat. Her black top is hanging oddly on her body. It takes me a moment to realise why. Her clothes are hardened with Adam's dried blood. Her hands looks scrubbed clean but the cuticles and nails are stained. There's a smear on her neck.

'It was fine. Honestly. I was only so long because things kicked off at the police station. Some really posh old bloke punched a woman in the face, so there was a lot of commotion. To be fair, she'd called him some pretty nasty

308

stuff. She was at that point of drunkenness where you just give way, so I don't think she felt much, anyway. She just went down.'

I try not to look at the residue of Adam. To focus on her eyes and ignore the traces of blood. She sips at the decaffeinated coffee that I've made for us both. I should have given up the pretence that we'll sleep at all tonight and gone for full caffeine. It would taste better.

'I was just there to fill in forms. They weren't that interested, really. It's not like I could add anything new to your description of the attacker. I was just a boring formality to them.'

'Well, let's keep it that way. I don't know how you're so calm. We shouldn't be this calm, should we? What if they get suspicious when this illusionary mugger doesn't show up on any nearby CCTV?' My mind starts to spiral.

'He was going to kill you, Celeste. You know that, don't you? We just did what we had to.'

'I don't know. I just don't know. I'm sorry that you got sucked in by him. But you – you actually killed him.'

'We're not meant to apologise anymore. You said that in Whitstable. Remember?' She drains the last of her mug of coffee and looks at me in a childlike way.

'Can I go for a wash before I go home? Bobby's shower is so much nicer.'

* * *

I genuinely don't sleep at all this time. I just sit, staring at the TV with gritty eyes. By six in the morning the BBC London news has reports of a murder on Southwark Bridge. An unnamed thirty-four-year-old killed in a knife attack, a suspected robbery. The usual thing about police appealing for information.

It's a certainty that Adam will be named later, along with me. My phone is left on mute on the side in Bobby's kitchen and I resist looking at it. The shower pricks my skin and I wash and wash. Bobby has left some Aesop body lotion on the side, so I smother myself in it. I have this sense that regardless of how much I wash, my skin will have that taint, the smell that you get when you pass the butchers' stalls at Smithfield Market. Stale blood and offal. I dress carefully, ready to face the day. A fresh scarf around my neck. I have an appointment at the police station again this morning.

Once it's a reasonable hour, I face the phone and make the necessary calls. Katrina is unsurprisingly unruffled by the news. She's nauseatingly sympathetic as she tells me she'll deal with it all. I suspect she's gleeful underneath her pretence of worried friend. After my recent failures with the promotion work and the threats of being dropped, she'll see this as just the boost that my career needs. She'll already be looking for a positive spin on this for the publisher, finding an angle that will increase book sales.

Adele is calm and practical too. She's been widowed twice and divorced twice more, so losing husbands is her metier. She counsels me on my appearance: how to dress and what she feels is the appropriate make-up style for the newly bereaved. I ignore her suggestion that being widowed will bring some men to my door and that I should embrace the opportunity with relish.

Chapter Fifty-Three

Emma

The police station was fascinating. A lot like a hospital with its chaos amid rituals and order. The green paint on the walls reminded me of the first ward I worked on as a student nurse.

In spite of the cacophony, I sat with a pervasive calm about me. My hands surprisingly steady. My knees not trembling. I occupied myself whilst I waited by scrubbing my hands in the bathroom, watching the water turn reddish brown.

Real blood doesn't look like it does on television. Becky had a storyline in *Castle Street* where her boyfriend was stabbed in the market by a rival gang member. 'Tania' looked up at the sky, wailing in pain as she cradled his dying body before the end music kicked in and the credits started rolling.

Adam's exsanguination was nothing like that. Nowhere near as sanitised. His blood flowed in nauseating gobbets, clotting as it hit the pavement. Forming clumps. His face sinking in on itself, yellowing under the streetlight.

The shower at Bobby's is merciful. My top crinkles as

311

I pull it over my head. Pulling at my skin where Adam is bonded to me. The remains of his blood cling to my thighs as I pull the soaked trousers away. The shower hits me, and I wash until the water runs clear. Taking a nail brush to my fingers and scrubbing again until they smart. I stop and look. They're clean now. No traces of blood.

I can stop. I'm not Lady Macbeth.

Celeste comes out of Bobby's room as I leave the bathroom.

'I just wanted to say thank you.' There's a stiff formality about her manner. Like she's the old Celeste who I thought was the reality.

'For what?'

'For saving my life. Adam was going to kill me.' She moves forward and grips me in a tight hug. All traces of aloofness gone. 'You saved me, Emma.'

Celeste didn't need to thank me. I did what I had to do.

We're almost safe. But not quite.

There's one last thing to deal with.

I go back home.

Chapter Fifty-Four

Becky

I'm back in the living graveyard for the elderly and irritating. Another long and tedious night shift with these dullards. My mind is fragmented tonight. I sit in the staffroom on my break and the nurse has to ask if I'm OK twice because I keep drifting off into my thoughts and not answering her.

This nursing home would never have been somewhere that I'd have chosen to work but it was there. An easy shoo-in via Ann, to keep her and Dad off my back whilst I waited for the moment to relaunch my acting career and become rich again. That moment didn't arrive, though, and I've become a fixture in this grey-bricked monument to death and suffering.

Naturally, I have methods of making my time here more manageable. You didn't think that I stopped manipulating people after *Castle Street*, did you?

An obnoxious staff nurse was gone within a week when they discovered a stash of benzodiazepines in her locker after an anonymous tip-off. They were easy to snatch from that open trolley. The handyman who was a little too liberal with his hands left after his wife had an anonymous letter and found a text message exchange on his phone between him and Brenda, the lead care assistant. Whiny Brenda was deposed too but that took time. A slow drip of hints whispered into the ears of the most impressionable of the residents. Once their belongings started to disappear, they all pointed to her.

My phone sits dead in my pocket. I've messaged Adam five times now with no reply. He messaged me yesterday afternoon to say that he had something to deal with and that he'd be in touch later. Nothing since. It's not like him to go quiet on me.

He worries me. He shouldn't act alone. Without my steering we'll never get the life we want. And I have a plan. I know exactly how to make Emma do precisely what we want her to. I know the thing that's most important to her and exactly how to use it.

* * *

I can't resist walking past Adam's house on my way home. Correction, Celeste's house. It was never his. I don't believe now that it ever will be. His car is there, that silly little MG. It's smattered with dead leaves, which is strange as Adam would usually have fastidiously cleared them off by now. I'm standing by a tree at the end of the road. The foliage is all dropping, opening up the street, leaving it stark and angular, knobbly branches jutting into the grey sky.

Celeste shoots out of the house, before I have time to move. She's toting her basket over the crook of her arm. I can't help but notice that she's wearing the same Liberty scarf that Adam gave me. The same one that Emma has in one of her drawers, too. It's tied to one side, above a trench coat, complementing the orangey-red of her lipstick. It suits her better than it would have done me. She stops and looks at me, making eye contact. I turn and start to walk away but she shouts to me.

'Becky, come back.'

Well, I wasn't expecting this. So, Celeste knows who I am. I don't know whether to mutter, 'Oh, shit,' or stop and congratulate her on her deduction skills.

'Oh, come on. It's a bit late to pretend you don't know me. I've known about you for months. You're not the first. Just one in a long line.' She puts her basket down by the gate and walks towards me. 'You're probably the first one who's tried to kill me, though, I'll give you that much. You have a definite distinction there.' Her voice is too loud on the street.

'I don't know what you're talking about.'

'I thought you were an actor, Becky? Albeit not a particularly good one, I suspect. What was it you had your five minutes of fame in, a tacky soap?' She maintains eye contact, her lips twisted into a sneer. 'I know about you and Adam, Becky. I told you that I know. What part of that are you not understanding?' Her face is ashen behind cunningly applied blusher. She looks older, her face drawn. Her words are emphatic, but I can see her hand shaking before she puts it firmly into her coat pocket.

'There's no point in you hanging around here. You won't find Adam. Don't you read the newspapers?'

'What the fuck are you talking about? Where's Adam?'

'Well, he was lying dead on the pavement last time I heard, but I imagine they've got him in the morgue now. He was murdered last night.'

I scramble for words but find none.

'By the way, I'd rather you stayed away from the funeral.

I think it would be distasteful for you to come.' She scoops down and picks up her basket again. 'Goodbye, Becky. And please keep away from my house.' She walks slowly down the street, picking over the tree roots that have erupted through the tarmac of the pavement.

I stand there for a long time, willing my legs to move. My body and mind are split. The pavement beckons me. I long to give in and fall down here, screaming with rage. To lie in the street like Emma after one her attacks. It takes all the power that I can dredge up just to stay upright.

I tell myself that this can't be true. There's no way this is true.

My phone pings. I'm sure it's Adam, and that twisted bitch was lying to me to get under my skin.

But the message is from Ann. I know it'll have taken her five minutes to tap out the paltry text, her fat red fingers picking out the buttons, her tongue between her teeth.

'*Emma not feeling good. In bed. Can U pick up Ava later?*'

The screen on my phone shatters as I hurl it to the pavement.

Chapter Fifty-Five

Celeste

We've been under siege since the early hours. I've made a plea for privacy and respect from the press but that isn't going to happen. They found me at Bobby's quickly enough. The media making the link with my famous stepbrother and guessing within hours that I might be here. They're camped out on the street, taking up all the parking spaces, ready to snap photos of me when I leave the house.

I've told Emma to stay away. We debriefed here last night but it's best for us if she stays away now. She'll be safe at her mother's house. Becky wouldn't dare touch her there, surely.

Bobby's been sleeping all day. There's no one to speak to, just me and my thoughts. Pauline came and we washed Bobby but other than that it's just been us. I've spent so much time alone that you'd think I'd be used to it by now, but this feels like an incarceration. Like I've evaded death only to sit and wait for the only man I've ever really loved to die.

My childhood was bleak till Bobby came along. There

were seemingly endless days spent in our apartment in Paris after my father walked out. When my mother would be shut in her room for weeks on end. Always in the act of lifting either a cigarette or a glass to her mouth. The mouth that was still immaculately daubed in lipstick, a kimono spread decorously around her bone-thin legs.

My role was to be unobtrusive. Which was hard for a five-year-old. I'd return home every day to the voiceless apartment, that elegant replica of a style magazine interior with its sharp edges and gloss.

Periodically, Adele would decide that life was worth living, even when she was going through the deepest of humiliations. Or she'd find a new man to briefly validate her beauty. During such times, she'd be there waiting for me when I got in from school, immaculately dressed, a mother again. Holding up her rouged and powdered cheek for me to kiss, as if I'd imagined the preceding weeks in a feverish dream.

Then the next husband arrived and with him, Bobby. My beloved stepbrother.

*　*　*

Pauline said kind words when I told her what had happened, which made me cry. She was helping me to wash Bobby this morning and I had to walk out of the room for a minute to compose myself. It helps me, I suppose, to look like the grieving widow, but really I was only touched by having her comfort me. I don't have many people who do. Bobby isn't able to speak at all today. Well, not with any coherence. He drifts in and out of consciousness, breathing in an on/off pattern. He still grips my hand but his eyes are glassy and gelatinous. The rapid change terrifies me. He was so alert

318

last night when I came back from the police station. I know what this must mean.

There's already been a picture of Emma and me online from the tawdrier end of the press. They've wasted no time. Someone has sold them a crystal-clear smartphone photo of us. Taking photos at the scene of a tragedy, rather than helping out – I think it must now be people's instinct before calling the emergency services. In the picture, I'm standing on the pavement on Southwark Bridge with one bloodstained hand at the side of my face. My blouse is spattered with deep crimson spray, my suit crumpled. My face cruelly clear and in focus. Emma is hugging me, concern written across her brow.

The picture filled me with panic at first. We've already been seen together. Seen by Pauline, by people in Whitstable. Maybe people have seen Emma with Adam, too. I reassure myself that nobody would jump to the bizarre conclusion that I had anything to do with Adam's death. There's a small chance that someone might associate me with Emma from before, then they'll surely think that the press got it wrong. Like they frequently do. That they mislabelled Emma as a bystander when she was actually a friend who had the misfortune to be with us when Adam was stabbed.

The press story is that Emma's this brave woman who stepped in to comfort me. The valiant former nurse. There are riffs upon the theme of the kindness of strangers but it's all bluff. The point of the piece is to titillate. To say look at this celebrity brought down by tragedy. Roll up and see the incredible middle-aged woman breaking apart. See the glamour dissolve in front of your very eyes. She's just like the rest of us, not immune to trauma.

* * *

'We just need to try not to panic. You're safe there.' I'm ringing Emma from the burner phone that was Adam's. She wiped it clean, but it still has a faint taint of bleach where she washed the blood away.

'I'll be watching Becky like a hawk. I'm still feigning illness but Peter saw my picture in the paper so I had to tell them that I had a burst of energy, which happens, and that I'd taken the night bus and walked along the Thames because I couldn't sleep. Becky hasn't mentioned it yet. But she will.'

'Becky can't do anything bad to you there, can she? Surely she wouldn't harm you under your mother and stepfather's nose. And if she did, she'd know that I'd know it was her. She isn't that stupid, is she?'

'I don't know. I honestly don't know.'

I feel tired suddenly, fantasising about lying on the bed next to Bobby and not having to get up for days and days. 'We'll stay in touch, and I'll help you, but we must lie low for now.'

'Will we be OK?' There's a note of childlike desperation in her voice that surprises me. I'm becoming used to Emma taking control. Maybe it's my turn to be strong for us now.

'Yes. We will both be absolutely fine.'

'If you need help with Bobby, shout me. I can sneak in.'

I fob her off. It would be good to see her, but we can't risk it.

I go and sit by Bobby's bed, listening to the rattle of phlegm on his tired lungs, trying to ignore the irregular, gasping breaths. Earlier, I sneaked out through the back route and went to fetch more clothes from my house. The cool void of the rooms was oppressive. I threw clothes into my bag without my usual careful folding. My cotton gloves damp with sweat from my palms.

I saw Becky on my way out and I couldn't resist. I taunted her like a child teasing a dog that she knew might bite. Only suddenly Becky looked more like a beaten puppy.

*   *   *

Three days have passed since Adam died and the press have drifted away, leaving me and Bobby here in this mausoleum. I don't believe in retribution but if I did then tonight was mine. Bobby didn't go peacefully, as I'd hoped he would. He was never going to do that. His last hours were a mess of thrashing and confusion. He found some supernatural strength to try and fight the final part. He always was the last one to leave a party.

Thankfully the district nurse arrived quickly and gave him a sedative. I watched as a needle pierced his perfect flesh. It kicked in quickly and his eyelids drooped closed. He loosened the grip that left bruises on my wrist and slid his hand into mine. Fading away hours later in a series of long jagged breaths with a faint smile on his face. The two of us alone in a calm and beautiful place. His sanctuary. His creation.

I shouted to the nurse and she came back in and helped me to attend to his body. The end of an era.

*   *   *

I message Emma and tell her about Bobby and she responds with soothing words.

Emma messages to check on me again the next day. I'm glad to hear from her. The other messages I've had feel distant and remote. Emma's means the most. She was there near the end, after all. And she delighted Bobby.

It's odd not having her around. Our time together was so intense that it's cemented a bond.

'*Hope you are as OK as you can be. I can come if needed.*' I know she means that. I'd love to have her here but it's too risky if we were seen.

I message back: '*No need. Stay where you are. It's safer that way. Are you OK there?*'

She replies: '*Can't bear to look at Becky. But am OK.*'

Then another message the following day: '*Shout if you need me. Worried about you.*'

I message back: '*Thank you. You're so kind. But don't worry. I'm thinking about you and awful Becky.*'

'*She won't do anything. But she won't get away with this.*'

Then: '*She knows that I know what she did. I'm sure of it.*'

Today she sent the most calming series of texts. Pitched exactly right. I cried when I read them. Then, when I asked if Becky was behaving: '*I don't think that I can let her go unpunished.*'

How could I not offer to help?

I owe her my life, don't I?

I answer back.

Part Three

Chapter Fifty-Six

Emma

Autumn 2022

'You're awake!' Ava manages to make this sound both gleeful and accusatory. She's in that pre-adolescent state of fluctuating between truculent teenager and child.

She sets down the coffee mug next to my bed then moves to the corner of the room, her back to me. 'Granny showed me your picture in *The Sun*. What did it look like?' she asks.

'What did what look like?'

'The man. Did you see him die?' Ava tidies the bookshelf with measured actions, speaking over her shoulder. When I answer she turns to me, eyes hungry.

'I was worried more about the woman on the bridge. I could see that the man wasn't going to get better. I was a nurse once, remember?'

She walks to my bedside and hugs me so tightly that it takes my breath. Exhausted, I lie back. I'm not exaggerating my illness now. Since I killed Adam fatigue has melted into my flesh. I'm struggling to think or speak. I've been welded to the bed or sofa, trying to avoid Peter by feigning sleep. Attempting to second-guess Becky through a muddied thought process. Wanting to reassure Ava that I'm OK. All of which I have zero energy for.

I don't know if this is the FND or just a natural reaction. That's the thing when you're ill. You forget what's a 'normal' reaction and what's sickness. And it's not like there's a page on Google that'll tell me how I should feel after killing a man.

Later, when I summon enough strength, I check the burner phone again. Pulling it out from under Ava's bookcase. I don't trust Becky not to search my bags. I don't trust her at all. I try to go back to sleep but the wood pigeons are making too much noise. There's another message from Celeste on the burner. I long to see her in person and check how she's coping. I have a vested interest in her keeping it all contained. Bobby dying will have unmoored her. She may be falling apart, becoming unwise and unhinged. Grief is a terrible thing.

When a crow dies, several of them will fly down and parade around the corpse on the ground. Vast numbers sometimes. The crow even looks like a mourner with its shiny black plumage and its hunched posture. Nature's own Victorian undertaker. There are theories that they're grieving – but there's another theory too. That maybe the crows are just looking, learning about death, applying their cool analytical minds to it. Which is sensible.

I succumb to sleep and it's only when I feel Becky's hand on my arm that I wake again. She's been no different over the past few days, just as attentive and helpful as always. Letting me use her bed whilst she's at work so that I can rest, sending my daughter up to me with coffee and plates of supermarket biscuits. I see in her eyes that she knows that I know about everything she's done. And she knows that I understand what her role was.

This performance pains her. As much as it pains me. We both know this. We're practically sisters, after all.

I wonder if her head contains the thoughts that run through mine. The notion of my hand in the small of her back, pushing her down the stairs. The satisfying smack as her head cracks on the hard floor. The kitchen knife sliding between her ribs and the gratifying rasp of air that would hiss out. Does she wake from recurring dreams, as I do, with thoughts of smashing a body inch by inch, bones breaking under flailing fists? I suspect that she does. That I'm the victim in her fantasies, as she is in mine.

It's not hard to keep myself out of her way with this hibernation. I hide in sleep, luxuriating in my twisted dreams. This need for inactivity is genuine, physical. The fatigue is victorious. My body can rest now, everything allowed to shut down.

'How are you doing?' She sits on the side of her bed and her cool hand strokes my back. I manage somehow not to recoil, to not pin myself against the wall or grab her invading hand and snap her fingers back till they fracture.

'I'm OK.' My tone is flat.

'Emma, I haven't asked this yet since you came back, but why did you stay at your friend's last week? I was worried about you.' I'll give Becky credit. She hasn't lost her acting skills.

'It wasn't anything big. Just what I already told Mum. I was staying with my friend Lauren to give me a break from Peter. She has a spare room.' I keep my eyes closed, her weight on the bed an unbearable presence. She knows that I'm lying. Much like I know that her questions are disingenuous.

She strokes my cheek and I hold my body as still as I can. 'I wish I could help more. I'm so sorry you're going through all this.'

'Are you?' I stare straight into her eyes. She breaks eye contact first.

'Of course I am. I just want to try and get you better.'

'Becky, I'm not going to get better. We both know that.'

She's quiet for a few minutes. I close my eyes again, hoping that she'll just leave.

'I know. Sorry. I didn't mean to say it like that.' She pauses for a moment. 'Emma, why were you on Southwark Bridge that night?'

'Just bad timing. Like I told your dad. I couldn't sleep and I felt stronger. I needed air. So, I got the night bus down to walk near the Thames.' I sit myself up more on the bed and lock eyes with her. 'I can't get it out of my mind. The thing on the bridge. It was pretty awful. That poor woman.'

'I know. The poor woman.' She echoes me but her voice lacks conviction.

'Worse than that, though. The man. I don't ever want to see anything like that again. His face was horrific. He had such a beautiful face. You could see the pain and fear as he died. All that blood. So much blood.'

She jumps up and walks out of the room, her expression set and immobile. I do something I haven't done in days: I smile.

* * *

There are some birds who lay precisely two eggs. They hatch the chicks, and the birds begin to grow up together. Then

328

the battle begins. There's only room for one of them; the parents can't tend to them both. They always knew how it would end. The dominant one kills the other, so that there's just one chick remaining. A fierce tussle and a push and it watches as the loser falls from the nest and breaks apart upon the ground.

There's a name for when someone kills their own sister. It's called sororicide.

Chapter Fifty-Seven

Becky

Emma knows everything. We're both just playing this silly little game around each other. Seeing who can play their part the best. You don't grow up with someone without being able to read them.

Not that she's making it difficult.

Fortunately, she's not difficult to avoid, even in this cramped hellhole. She's asleep so much and when she's awake she's either snapping at Dad or trailing off on the bus to her new friend's house.

I put on my coat and go out. Anything to clear my head. I'm turning into Emma, roaming the neighbourhood like a lost soul. I'm trying to stay as focused as I can but it's impossible. I'm so far from where I should be. So far from the teenage girl who was destined for stardom. It's not like it used to be where soap stars were killed off and then ended up in panto in Prestatyn. I could have been big. Look at Suranne Jones and Sarah Lancashire. Hell, even Margot Robbie started off in *Neighbours*. That should have been me. A glittering A-lister.

My husband Harry and I let money run through our fingers like it was water. Feathering our Hampstead flat with furniture and clothes. Like a pair of magpies collecting our spoils. Travelling first class, posing at airports for the photographers who we'd tipped off. Five-star hotels. Top restaurants. Until Harry decided he liked his fresh new co-star more than me. And the *Castle Street* producers decided that I was too much trouble. And I came crawling back here.

I'm so wrapped up in thoughts that I don't see Celeste coming until she's right in front of me. She's dressed like a Hitchcock heroine. An ageing Hitchcock heroine who needs a glow-up.

'Becky. I need to talk to you.'

'You do?' I'm caught in the shock of the moment. There are no sharp retorts on my lips.

'Come with me. We could have coffee.' She tries to smile but it's clearly fake.

I'm intrigued by her bravado. I walk beside her up the street and into her house.

'Go through. You know where *my* kitchen is, don't you?' I let the dig slide.

'I'm tired, Celeste. I don't need your coffee. What do you want?' My tone is exactly the right shade of pointed. I haven't even bothered to take off my coat. I don't intend for this to take long.

'OK. That's fine. I want to talk to you about Emma.'

'And what do you have to do with Emma, Celeste?' I feign a naïve look. I've still got it. Acting never leaves you. 'I don't know what my stepsister has to do with this.'

'I don't think we need to pretend anymore, do we?'

'You tell me.'

'I want to appeal to your better nature. I want an

331

assurance that Emma is safe. There's no point hurting me anymore, is there? Adam's dead so you wouldn't get any of my money. But I'm worried about you getting revenge on Emma.'

'Revenge for what exactly?' I want to laugh. If this woman knew what I'm planning she'd be running from me, screaming.

'If you want me to get to the point, then I will. I'm willing to offer you some money to leave Emma alone.'

I wait for her to say what she's tendering. I know what I want. What I *will* get. I've revised my expectations. My plans are toned down and modest now. I don't expect to get all of Celeste's money. I just want her stepbrother's house. I've looked on Zoopla. It'd be worth at least 1.5 million pounds.

'Five thousand pounds and a promise that this is all over.' She sounds like she's offering me the world. Patronising bitch.

I don't bother to look at her. I turn on my heel and walk out. The door slams behind me.

* * *

I'm going to need to take drastic measures.

I have another plan.

Ava.

Chapter Fifty-Eight

Celeste

Bobby has an alarming amount of stuff to clear. I've already spent days sorting my own house so that there isn't a trace of Adam. Not a cufflink, a coat, a shoe. Now it's time to address Bobby's stuff, which is a more daunting task. Death brings so much work. Administration and tidying. Having two funerals to arrange is a joyless process. The dates hang over me like twin ghouls.

The police talk about 'releasing' Adam's body to me. As if it's something to be freed. I just need these funerals to be over. To move on with my life.

No doubt, there'll be clusters of press photographers loitering like carrion birds wherever I turn. My phone has rung endlessly. I've already turned down an interview on *Lorraine* and one in some tacky magazine. Katrina is firing off obsequious emails. Apparently, the sales of my last three cookbooks have risen astronomically. I'm back in the bestseller list. Tragedy spurs people to act. It seems that they'll buy my book as an act of respect and sympathy or maybe just through prurience. *Roll up, roll up and see this tragic woman.*

It's strange but I feel that Emma is the only person who understands what I'm going through. I would like her to come with me to Adam's funeral, for support, but that will be out of the question, obviously. Bad form to have the person who killed the victim at his funeral.

I wish I knew what to do about Becky. My idea of paying her off hasn't worked. Maybe I should have offered more. I thought that five thousand pounds would be a lot to her but I miscalculated. It's not like I have piles of cash lying around, anyway. My money is tied up in property. Adam made sure that he depleted my savings.

I'm thinking, but the solutions are all so drastic with so much cost for me.

* * *

'Which room shall we start with?' Pauline is wearing a pair of old jeans and has a scarf tied around her frazzled hair.

'How about we start upstairs and then work our way down?'

She smiles tentatively and grabs an armful of empty boxes.

'I might have to leave you to it towards the end of the day. I have to go to a meeting with my agent. My new book is about to launch.' I have a sudden thought. 'Would you like me to bring you a copy back?'

'That's very kind, Mrs Dupont, but no thanks. I don't cook things like that. My kids wouldn't touch it.'

I can't help but laugh and she joins in. Pauline has been absolutely amazing. She's sacrificed a few days of leave from her care assistant job to help me clear the house, although I am paying her well above the going rate.

'OK. Well, if you see anything of Bobby's that you might like then let me know. And call me Celeste, by the way.'

'Oh, I couldn't take anything. That wouldn't be right.' She stands awkwardly. When I see her looking at an art deco figurine later on, I offer it to her and she's quick to wrap it up in layers of newspaper and put it in her bag. I hope she enjoys it.

* * *

I don't miss Adam at all. I ache for Bobby, of course. His loss is like a wound. But the other person I'm missing is Emma. The intensity of the time we spent together in Kent has wedded her to me. I need to see her.

There's things we need to discuss.

Chapter Fifty-Nine

Becky

Sea birds fly below us. Their bodies shine white as they swoop in and out along the cliffs, the sea below a rocky mass. I walk back, pulling my phone out.

'Stand a bit further back.' Ava turns around and steps gingerly towards the cliff edge. Looking down. She grips her arms around her abdomen. 'You're fine there. You won't fall.' I hold up my phone, starting the recording. 'No point taking the photo if you're not near the edge. That's the fun of it. Makes you look brave. Emma will love this.'

'But I'm not brave, am I? It's frightening. And there's a sign saying it's not safe.' Ava's eyes are wide and she's clutching her skinny arms across her chest. Perfect.

'Can we go back? It looks like it'll rain. And I'm scared now. I don't like it here.'

'You can move when I say that you can.'

I finish the recording.

She walks ahead of me. I wait until we're back at the caravan park before I send the video to Emma's phone.

'*I have Ava. Tell Celeste that we need to talk again.*'

There's no response and the WhatsApp message remains unread. I keep checking for the blue tick. The caravan smells of fried food and desperation. A fucking caravan. This tin box with its symphony of beige 1980s interior design. I borrowed it from Denise. She's trying to suck up to me, so she was more than happy to hand over the keys when I asked. I suspect she's after having Christmas off when I do the next rota. It's laughable that anyone would settle for this dump for a weekend away.

'I don't like it here. Beachy Head wasn't nice.' Ava's voice is as whiny as ever.

'It's a cliff. By the sea. There's nothing frightening about that if you watch your step.'

'I want to go home. Mummy's not well and I want to be there for her. And you're being weird again.'

'She's fine. And you don't need to be there. She should be looking after you, anyway.'

She glares at me. 'She tries.'

'Ava, I've brought you on a free holiday. Try and have fun. It's nice here.' She looks up at the scratched plastic window of the caravan and the rain that's now pelting down. The sound of water hitting the roof is deafening. 'Just go and watch TV or read a book. You're shredding my last nerve.'

'I want to go home.' She looks towards the caravan door.

'Soon but not yet.' She sits in the corner seat and sighs, picking up her book.

'*I want more than the shitty amount Celeste offered. Ava is on the edge. One push.*'

The message with the video is showing up as read now and my phones start ringing. I reject three calls from Emma. She leaves a rant-filled voicemail, which I delete.

'*Play nice. I've got your child here. She needs to be kept safe.*'

'*What do you want?*' I picture her face typing this and I want to laugh.

'*Just her brother's house. I know you can make her give it to me.*'

'*I'm calling the police now.*'

My fingers type out the next message with ease. There's something almost fun about this final bit. '*If you go to the police then I'll tell them that you and Celeste know each other. You'll both be locked up when they look more closely into what happened to Adam.*'

Then I send: '*Show me proof that she's willing to pay. Then I'll let Ava go.*'

'*I'll sort it. Leave Ava. Please,*' she replies.

'*I won't stop. You or Ava won't be safe till I get what I want.*'

Chapter Sixty

Emma

The video and messages leave me shaking. My phone drops to the floor. Ava looks terrible. Her eyes are unfamiliar, widened with terror. Her usual spirit diminished as that monster forces her to stand at the edge of a cliff. This isn't an idle threat.

Sinking to my knees, I'm full of self-reproach. I've done this to us. Becky and Adam may have set me up, but my stupidity and desire has wreaked the worst possible consequences. The endangerment of my child.

The police aren't an option here. If Becky tells them that the story me and Celeste told them was a lie, then things will unravel. They'll soon start to dig deeper. They might realise that the mysterious hooded man was an invention and that I'm responsible.

That way Ava would definitely be away from me. I'd be locked up.

I do the only thing I can and plead with Celeste. She soothes me like a mother offering a warm embrace. She's going to pay Becky off, and I can have my daughter back.

What else can we do?

Chapter Sixty-One

Celeste

Loisirs is noisy, a low buzz, punctuated by laughter, metal on porcelain and the tinkling of glass. Marco greeted me warmly, touching my arm with his hand and offering condolences. I'm fully armoured in a 1960s Chanel suit and light make-up. My hair freshly styled this morning in Chelsea. Poised in front of all the eyes that are trained on me. Posture rigid, my face benign.

'Sweetie. I've literally cried for you every day.' My old friend Anna shows no emotion as she sits down but then she can't. Her face bears few marks of humanity. I don't know who her surgeon is but she would benefit from a new one. Her age has long been a secret and she never admits to anyone that we were at boarding school together. The comparison with my haggard skin would give it all away.

I don't know why she cares so much about her appearance. There are worse things about ageing, like the sense of irrelevance, becoming invisible. I'm jaded and worn, loaded with ennui at having seen so much.

'It's OK. I'm doing fine, honestly.' She reaches across and

takes my hand with her own and I try to hide my flinching. Her flesh gripping mine feels heavy and unwelcome.

'What will be your next move? I was wondering if you'd like to come with me and Demetrius to Greece. We're going to Hydra next week to close the villa for the winter. The air would do you good. It'll be pashmina weather but you can still sit out in the evenings and there'll be wine. Speaking of which, what are we drinking?'

At the end of the meal, I weave my way through to the bathroom, smiling and nodding to people as I go. I don't get the burner phone out till I'm in the cubicle. Despite the insistent buzzing in my bag, there's no way that I could have pulled that out at the table without raising eyebrows. Well, not Anna's eyebrows, of course. They can't be raised.

'She's got her. Becky's taken her and she's going to kill her. She will. She'll do it. I know she will.' Emma's words are running into each other, and I have trouble working out what she's saying.

'Slow down a minute. Whatever this is we can sort it.'

'Becky's taken Ava. She's sent me a video as a threat. Ava on a cliff. Like she's going to push her off. She says she'll hurt her. She's asking for Bobby's house.'

'She wouldn't do that, would she? And I don't even own his house yet. He's only just bloody died, for God's sake.' There's a damning silence. 'OK. Let me think. What if we make her an interim offer of twice the money I already said I'd give and we'll tell her I will sign over the house.'

'I don't think that will stop her. She has Ava, Celeste.'

'Tell her to come back now and I'll meet her at your house and negotiate. I can arrange to get legal documentation agreeing to sign the house over when it officially becomes mine.' I try to think fast. 'I'll go to the bank now and take some money out. We can send a photograph of it to her straight away and tell her that an initial ten thousand is waiting for her if she comes straight back.'

'OK.' There's a new edge to Emma's voice and I don't like it. It sounds like defeat.

'We can sort this. And I'm going to get you and Ava out of there. I have plans for you both.' There's a parental firmness to my voice. 'You can stay in Whitstable indefinitely.'

I have to sort this for Emma.

Hopefully this will be the end of our troubles.

Chapter Sixty-Two

Becky

My head feels eroded by the drive back from Beachy Head with that sulky child beside me. Dad's battered old van is joyless to drive.

The end is in sight.

Celeste will lose Bobby's house but's that's no hardship for her. How many houses does that woman need? She's arranging to have legal paperwork drawn up promising ownership to me. Emma will have a bedroom she can sleep in again. She can hide out from my dad and she'll be free of me. It's a happy ending for us both.

When we arrive back I occupy myself looking at property on Rightmove while we wait in Dad's van. Ava sits quietly beside me. She knows better than to speak. I'm thinking that I'll sell my new London house and buy a place in Brighton. It's handy to get to London from there. I'm going to start going to auditions again. I'll start small but I can work my way up to something. I'm talented. This time, I'll win.

Celeste rings. She'll meet me in ten minutes at my house

to hand over the cash. I drive the van round and park outside.

I go up without Ava. Emma isn't in the kitchen or lounge. I check my room and she's not there either. Thank God I don't have to see her miserable face. It would kill my mood.

Celeste will be here soon. I drag myself to the settee, pull my feet up and sit, letting the sound of a programme about some tedious couple looking at houses in the Cotswolds wash over me. The TV echoes in the rare emptiness of the house.

The doorbell rings and I let her in. I'm watchful. She may still pull a trick out of the bag. Maybe she'll try to record me. I'll be mindful of what I say. My muscles tighten and my mind snaps awake.

'Hello, Becky.' She's wearing a Chanel suit in pale pink, flaunting her wealth at me. In her hands is a cake tin.

'You brought me a gift?' I sneer. I don't want food. I want the money and the documentation from the solicitor about the house.

'I'm tired of this. I just want to draw a line under it all. I think that we can be civilised. Do you have a cafetiere? I brought coffee with me.'

'There's instant coffee there if you want it. Knock yourself out.' She walks into the kitchen and starts looking through the cupboards. I don't care about her seeing the chipped plates and cheap tableware. This won't be my life for much longer. 'Let's get on with this. I want the cash and the documents.'

'Hang on. Let's sit first. We can be good-mannered. I need to talk about the procedure with the house and go through the boring paperwork.' She has a chic little Gucci briefcase with her, which she opens on the sofa cushion. There's a sheaf of papers in there. She pulls out a thick brown envelope. 'And the cash is here.'

I open the envelope and see the stack of notes. This is a good start.

'Here. Try this. It's from my last cookbook. It's a French recipe for a Gateau au Citron.'

The arrogance of this woman. She's baked a recipe from her own pathetic book. She takes a piece herself and forks a small amount into her mouth.

'The icing is a bit too sharp for me. I think I went overboard on the citrus.' She pushes the icing into a neat line on the plate. 'Lemons are so evocative of Adam. Don't you think?' I ignore her remark.

'It's very . . . gracious of you to make this. Especially when you've lost so spectacularly.' I enjoy the drip of sarcasm on my tongue, savouring each word. Letting my mouth form the sardonic grin that I so often suppress. As if I'd be impressed by her feeble little housewife routine.

The cake is actually delicious. Lemon cake has always been my absolute favourite. I hadn't realised how hungry I was. All I've eaten all day is a limp ham sandwich in the roadside café while I waited for Celeste to get back from the solicitors.

I carry on eating. I look up and Celeste's eyes are studying me, like I'm some kind of art exhibit. She looks away. I resist the urge to scream at her, to just leave the fucking papers and the money and get out of my sight.

She starts fiddling with the little case and rifling through the papers, donning a little pair of glasses. She gets up and walks to the kitchen counter, placing her half-eaten cake on the worktop. 'One second, Becky. I just need to fetch something.'

I try to speak but my mouth feels limp and useless. I'm so tired. The relief that this is almost over floods through me, and I just want to lie back and sleep. Rest in the glory of my future self.

Celeste stands at the bottom of the stairs and shouts for Emma. There's a noise above and I hear footsteps walking across Dad and Ann's bedroom. She must have been hiding in there. The weirdo.

Emma's posture is forceful today. The broken slump of her frame replaced by a confident walk.

'Have you given her the money? Where's Ava?'

Her words rush out. I try to speak but only a strange noise comes out. A strangled rasp. Emma turns her head towards me. Her expression changes. I go to sit myself forward, but my arms are jellied. My vision clouding.

'Celeste. What have you done?' Emma's tone is frantic. 'And where's Ava? I need to find Ava.'

I know exactly what Celeste has done.

Chapter Sixty-Three

Celeste

Have you noticed how rage fluctuates? If you're fortunate enough, the wave of anger will hit its peak when you need it most. Propelling you to finally leave a bad marriage, to tell that selfish friend that you really can't listen to another word from their mouth. Face your potential blackmailer perhaps. And stop them once and for all.

Becky is sliding down the sofa, her body in an absurd position, legs splaying and her torso half off the cushions. Her greying skin is beaded with sweat. Her breathing erratic. Emma walks towards me and clasps my hand, fingers intertwining with mine. I feel her breath on my cheek.

'You did this for *me and Ava?*' I look over and the colour has drained from Becky's face. She's the shade of stale cream. The rattling wheeze has almost stopped. The room is quiet. I don't look at Emma but I feel her eyes upon me.

'But she had Ava. Now we don't know where she is.' She looks from me to Becky. Her head moving frantically.

'She's fine. She's in the back of that white van outside. I called to her and she knows you're coming.'

I'd been waiting for Becky to arrive. I'm pathologically punctual. I was lurking on the corner of the street. She parked the van and I saw her open the back doors and shout something inside. As I arrived at the house, I sneaked round the side that was shielded from view and banged on the metal. Ava banged back. I told her I was a friend of her mummy and that she just needed to wait for a little while longer and we'd come and let her out. She sounded surprisingly chipper. She has her mother's strength.

'Just hold on a second. We need to do something quickly first.' Her body is straining towards the door.

'Do what, Celeste? What did you do to Becky?' Her eyes are wild with panic. I speak in an even tone.

'Remember the sleeping pills that Adam put in the drawer to make it look more convincing when I died? I kept them.' I gesture to a cake tin on the worktop. 'I made a lemon cake. The citrus disguised the taste of the pills.'

She glances at the half-eaten slice on my plate. 'Celeste, did you eat it too? Are you okay?'

'No. The pills are in the icing. I didn't eat that.'

A gurgling sound emanates from the sofa.

'We had to do this, Emma, or it would never have stopped. Circles and circles of violence going on and on. We're safe now.' I tell her what I need her to do.

She walks over to Becky and takes her phone from the bag beside her, taking her hand and using her still-warm finger to unlock it. She starts typing.

'Done.' Emma types Becky's final WhatsApp message of desperation, which she sent before she killed herself. The message that she didn't see in time because she was asleep upstairs. Her family will buy it. She sleeps a lot in the day, after all.

She grabs the van keys and races out to retrieve her daughter.

I have a vague urge to cry. But what choice did I have but to protect Emma and her daughter? This strange woman who came into my life to end it, but ended up saving me. I've paid her back now.

I stand, keeping my eyes averted from the sofa. Time is meaningless. People talk about things slowing down in a crisis. About time stopping. This doesn't happen. Instead, my brain whirs. From the photos of Adam with Becky, to finding Emma in the bedroom, through to this scene of horror. The images merge into one. I can't think anymore. There's nothing but me and this dead monster in the room.

I wrap the remaining cake in foil and put it into my basket, along with the burner phones. I'll dispose of them later.

I walk down to look for Emma and Ava.

I hope she'll accept these gifts with good grace.

Chapter Sixty-Four

Emma

I've got Ava back. I had to restrain myself. Fight the urges to take her in my arms and squeeze and squeeze her. Not letting her away from my side ever again. She starts crying when she sees me.

'Mummy, why was Becky such a bitch? She's been so mean to me again. She left me in the back of Peter's van!' I don't tell her off for using a bad word. I stroke her hair and wait for her to stop crying, repeating over and over that everything will be all right.

She looks up and spots Celeste hovering nearby. She stares at her.

'You're the woman from the bridge.'

'Gosh. Well spotted. Me and your mum bumped into each other again and it turns out that we're almost neighbours.'

Ava spends a few more seconds taking Celeste in. 'And you're friends now?'

I reassure Ava, telling her that Becky isn't well and that I need her to go with Celeste for a short time while a doctor sees Becky. Celeste is soothing but assertive, putting her at ease. Talking to her like she's a small adult, which Ava appreciates.

They walk away and I go back in to Becky.

When I eventually have to tell Ava that Becky killed herself, she'll accept the sequence of events. I'll ask her not to tell anyone about Becky's odd behaviour towards her. She'll stay quiet if I tell her it would upset people.

When it comes to explaining to Peter and Mum, I'll tell them that I came downstairs alone. That I found Becky lifeless and then called the ambulance. They're away. He's surprised her for her birthday and has taken her on a Warner Hotels mini break on the Isle of Wight. I'm dreading making the call to Mum to tell her there's been a terrible tragedy. They were both besotted with Becky.

I'll say that Ava was upstairs when it happened but I called my friend who took her for me while I dealt with things. They won't question the timeline and they'll think I mean Lauren. They won't ask Ava about it, either. It's not like they really engage with her, is it?

I'll show them the ominous text that Becky sent to me, saying that she couldn't take living in poverty anymore. I'll tell them that Becky had confided in me that she was feeling depressed and like she couldn't go on like this but had sworn me to secrecy. That I wasn't overly worried because she'd promised me that she was making an appointment to see the GP. I'll no doubt have to say this in the coroner's court too.

*   *   *

Peter and Mum are on their way back. He sounded broken on the phone. I almost felt pity for him. The ambulance has taken Becky away, her phone bagged up and taken by the

351

police along with the empty strips of pills that Celeste left by her side. The coroner informed.

I strip the sheets on Becky's bed, my bed for now, and throw them in the washer. There's nothing left but an empty bed and a wardrobe full of chain-store clothes to show for her endeavours.

I call Celeste and she brings Ava back. They both seem in good spirits. They've made biscuits together. They're delicious. I tell Ava an age-appropriate version of the story that Becky has taken her own life.

We'll talk again later. For now, there's a TV programme on with Chris Packham. We watch the birds.

'Ava, I'm sorry that I've not been much of a mum lately. It's been tough with me being ill.' The sound of my forced swallow emanates in my ears. 'And I'm sorry that I wasn't there to protect you from Becky being horrible.'

'It's OK.' She smiles, but only with her mouth.

'I've got something really big to ask you. I don't need you to answer straight away. It's just something to think about. I've been offered a place for us to live. By the seaside.'

This is the final part of Celeste's plan. It's a generous offer – how could I refuse? She wants me to have the house and Ava and I need it. There's logic here.

She doesn't speak. I continue. 'It's a little town called Whitstable. Do you think you'd like that?'

'Can we look at it online later?'

'Of course.' We sit quietly for a while.

'Can we take Sparrow if we go?'

* * *

I told Celeste a bird story one day when we were in Whitstable. I think about that now, as I sit here. Some cultures take dead bodies up to mountaintops and leave them there on stone altars. The body is left to decompose or to be ripped apart by carrion birds or vultures, before they bury the picked-clean bones. It has a name: excarnation. It's all about returning to nature.

I'd like to see Becky's body left out in the open air. Adam's too. Not as an act of faith or environmental reckoning but as an example to others, a humiliation. Like when they put the heads of criminals on spikes for all to see in the Middle Ages. This monumental failure left out as a lesson to others who might consider trying to wrong other people. People they deem weaker than them.

Becky had to go. It was the only way this would ever end. With half of the players lying dead on the stage. The other half of the cast victorious.

Celeste and I are now bonded for life. It's mutually assured destruction – we both have the power to destroy each other. But we wouldn't do that. Not after everything we've been through.

Part Four

Chapter Sixty-Five

Celeste

March 2023

I've broken so many rules. Those unwritten societal norms that women like me live by. The requirements of being a strong, independent woman. The conventions of being a boss. The etiquette of bereavement.

I'm in a new relationship already. It's with Marco, the maître d' from Loisirs. I had no idea that he was even attracted to me, hadn't even considered his physicality. We just always did this dance around each other in the restaurant. This flirtatious game that I thought was only a polite ritual on his part.

It started with a few unguarded words, a brief yet embarrassing tearful moment and our barriers came down. We ended up going on a date. It feels so odd to say that word at my age. At our age. Marco's a year older than me. It was an old-fashioned evening, a meal in a poorly lit restaurant in Soho and a theatre trip. His hand respectfully moving towards mine during the second act, our fingers lightly linking.

Marco has left Loisirs but Margate isn't far and we see each other often. I've given him and his brother some pointers about their little seaside restaurant. It has a way to go yet. I haven't found a new maître d' who's anywhere near as good as Marco. I considered selling up. Leaving this house and my restaurant and moving to North London. Getting away from this house with its Adam-shaped stain in the fabric of the place. I won't go, though. This area is my territory, mine and Bobby's. Adam is not driving me out of my home. I don't think about him often. About what we did to him and Becky. We just did what we had to.

*   *   *

Ripley is asleep in his basket. He doesn't seem to have noticed that Adam's gone. He wags his tail and follows me with pleading eyes, always looking for food. We're growing to tolerate each other.

I go up to my bedroom and lounge back on the bed. It's that glorious time of the afternoon when I'm full after a plate of sugary tinned spaghetti, cheap supermarket butter oozing through the lurid sauce. An illicit nap is the most delicious thing of all on a day like today. There's a breeze blowing the curtains, sharp March air inching in. I don't get up to close it, just pull the blanket a little higher.

I lie back and listen to the birdsong. Such a beautiful sound. I should listen to it more often.

Chapter Sixty-Six

Emma

March 2023

I'm not better. The resolution of my illness was never going to be part of my story. I still have hope that one day I might be functional. Not better but functional. That would be enough.

I can live inside this body. I'm still in pain and I still have sensory losses, patches of absence on my body. The ghost sensations that haunt my skin. Days of crippling fatigue still envelop me. I follow their ebb and flow.

'Mummy, what time are we leaving?' Ava is pacing the kitchen, checking off her inventory of what we need to take with us, Sparrow stalking her heels.

'Soon. Just let me get everything together and then we can go.' She smiles at me, this unfamiliar child of mine. I've missed so much of her growing up, but what choice did I have? I had to keep her safe. Sacrifices must be made in life – but it turns out that we both missed out.

But she's the same child who I held at my breast. The diffident pre-adolescent is fading again now. She's more awake somehow, happier, and so am I. She's doing well here. She likes her new school and there's a palpable change to us both. I feel safe with her, and I can see that she feels safe with me.

London and my recent past feel like a dark memory, a nightmare that lasted for months. I'm calmer here, even with the constant sound of the waves beating at the stones on the beach. I've stopped going back to the city to see Dr Bronson. Partly by my own choice – it's too far to travel. Partly because he thinks we've done all that we can. He referred me on and I'm now on a waiting list for mindfulness-based cognitive behavioural therapy. The idea is appealing. No talking about the past with a therapist. There's far too much that I have to be careful not to say. It might make a difference, it might not. I try to be optimistic but I'm also a realist.

There's a support group that I used to go to online for people with functional neurological disorder. I'm not posting on there at the moment. I'm wary who I chat with now, hesitant over the keyboard. I don't want to attract more chaos with strangers.

I still read other people's posts, though. It's comforting to know that these people are still there. That there are people like me. People from ordinary backgrounds who've been interrupted like I have.

They're almost like me, but I don't suppose that any of them have killed anyone.

* * *

'Mummy, are you ready yet?'

'Almost. I just need to quickly put some make-up on.

360

Give me five minutes.' I don't wear much, I never have, just a dab of mascara and a pale lipstick. Bobby's bathroom is bright, welcoming me with its warm glow where the sun infiltrates the room.

We've made this house our own. We haven't added much. We couldn't afford to do that, but we've spilled over into the place. It still feels like one of Bobby's stage sets but the play is a different one now. Ava collected pink shells. No other colour, just pink. She loaded them into jam jars and filled the window ledges. She's moving on to bits of glass now. Weathered pieces of blue or green glass that wash in from the sea, grazed rough by the tides. My bird books are neatly lined up on the coffee table, a picture of Daddy propped up on the dresser. Between us we stay on top of the housework, cook each other simple meals.

Sparrow likes it here. She stalks along the seafront path, glaring at tourists. She's devoted to Ava and the feeling is mutual. They curl up on the bed together and Sparrow trails her around the house.

Mum visits fortnightly. She's renewed. Younger and lighter. Peter is gone. His business has folded along with their marriage. He had to find a new target for his growing rage, someone to take his grief out on, and with just my mother there, it was her. She was less tolerant than when it was directed at me.

Peter is sleeping on his mother's sofa in her one-bedroomed flat. Not even a room to call his own.

Mum's about to move, abandoning the old house for a flat. She's swapped with a family with two daughters. They're similar ages to what me and Becky were when we met. One is thirteen, the other is six. I hope that they get on with each other.

Lauren is coming down here to see us next week.

She's still single, swearing off men for the time being. Still as glamorous. Her vision is back now, and she's had no relapses, thanks to the new MS therapy she's on. She has had to stop working as a beautician due to the numbness in her hand, although she remains hopeful that she can find something else to do. She tells me that she's too high-maintenance to be on benefits for long. That she'll never be a 'supermarket own brand' kind of woman. I'm hoping that she's joking when she says that she might start an OnlyFans account for people who get off on neurological disorders.

'Have you packed the crisps, Mummy? I don't just want sandwiches on their own. That's too boring. And don't forget Grandad's binoculars. I don't think there's much point going without them.' I fished out Dad's old pair from the garage before we left London. We take it in turns looking at the marshland birds. There's a nature reserve we can get to by bus when I'm having a better day.

'Yes, and yes. You drive a hard bargain.'

'Are we going then? I looked online and there's been some new sightings. I've stuck Post-it notes in the book of the ones to look for.'

The space and light here takes my breath away. There's a whole breadth of view that just doesn't exist in London. I like to think that the sea and I tolerate each other's presence. There are new birds to see as well. A whole fresh set to get used to, stories to learn about them. They're different from the savage urban creatures of London. I found a book about marine birds in a charity shop, so we can name them, check them off in a notebook with a biro.

'Will there be enough sandwiches for all of us?'

'Yes! My goodness. You're a nag these days.' I smile at her to show that I'm teasing.

'Someone has to keep you in order. I don't want Auntie

Celeste to come and be hungry. Will she stay all weekend this time?'

'She will. I've fished out the picnic basket and a rug, but I might be being optimistic with the weather.' It's a bright March day. The kind that tricks you into believing that spring has finally come, only for there to be hailstones and harsh winds the next minute.

'I'm sure that Auntie Celeste will bring something nice for us to eat, too. She usually does. She'll have filled that basket of hers with cakes and biscuits, I suspect.'

* * *

My favourite bird lately is the sandpiper. They're tiny, hopping about in the marshland on improbable legs. They sometimes have same-sex pairings, with two women helping each other to raise the chicks. Sometimes a single parent too. A bird who sits on the nest day and night, hopping off briefly during the warmest part of the day to forage for food.

'Do you ever miss Becky?' Ava pretends to be busy, straightening the books on the shelf. She always does this when she has something difficult to say.

'Of course I do. She was my stepsister.' I don't lie to Ava often. Only when absolutely necessary.

'I know that what happened was sad but I don't miss her. She wasn't nice to me.' She takes a break from her repetitive inventory of the things we're taking. 'And I have you back now. I like being with you better. I'm old enough now to know what to do if you're ill.'

I move to the sink and fill the water bottles from the tap.

'We can both look after each other now, can't we?'

She smiles at me, the sweetest sight.

363

Children can be so astute, can't they? I don't think about Becky often. To the rest of the world, she's just someone who's consigned to the annals of pop culture history. A scant Wikipedia entry, an ex-soap-star with an occasional mention on Reddit discussion boards.

I didn't even go to the funeral. I was having an off day and I wanted to conserve my energy. She was always telling me to rest when I wanted to spend time with my daughter, so I'm sure she'd have understood.

I certainly don't ever think about Adam. He's a distasteful footnote in my history now. As if he never existed.

The biggest irony of all is that Adam's original plan was somewhat fulfilled. There was a swapping of murders. It worked out well.

Evil exists – I know that. But that's not me. I'm just a woman who responded to my circumstances. A product of grief, deception and bullying. A trapped bird who had to fight for safe territory for my little family. For somewhere we could grow and try to mend ourselves. I hope that I don't have to kill again. I'm watching Marco. Making sure that he treats Celeste how she should be treated.

I really do think that Ava and I can be happy here.

There's a light tap at the door and I hear Celeste's glorious voice as Ava lets her in.

Epilogue

Pauline

March 2023

I never became attached to a patient before. They told me not to when I first started, so I've always tried to stick by that. They're all different, of course, but they're all the same too. Young, old, rich, poor. They're just another ill person who needs care and I'm the carer with thirty minutes to do about an hour's worth of work in.

Bobby was different, though. For one thing, he made me howl with laughter and few patients do that.

Bobby was unique. People sometimes ask you questions, vague stuff like 'have you got kids?' Their eyes glazed when you answer, but that wasn't his style. He made me sit down every day. He'd have me perched on the side of the bed and ask me all kinds of weird stuff. I was a bit freaked out to start with but then I started to kind of like it.

I even went to his funeral, although I just crept in at the back and left as the service ended. To say I was underdressed is an understatement. It was like some West End party for a show, and I didn't exactly fit in.

Celeste told me to take something from Bobby's house and I did. It felt wrong at first but she insisted and so I took an ornament. Just a little figurine of a woman with her head flexed upwards and her arm in the air. It was one of Bobby's favourites. I put it in pride of place on the mantelpiece but Dave wasn't keen. Said it didn't suit the room. He tends to make the decisions on everything. I wrapped it up and put it away.

I was watching *Flog It!* last night and there was a similar one on there, went for £300. So, I decided today that I'd have a look at it again. Maybe sell it. What's the point in having something nice that's worth money when it's in a box? Especially with the bills how they are. I can imagine Bobby laughing with me about it. Shouting at me to get the bloody thing out and try and get as much for it as possible. Have a weekend away at the coast with the money or he'd come and haunt me. So, I've unwrapped it to look at the base and double-check that it's definitely like the one on the programme. I fetch an old paper of Dave's to wrap it back up a bit more for the journey to the antique shop.

I don't read the papers often or watch the news. So much sadness in the world. It just depresses me. That's why I hadn't seen this article before. There's a picture of a soap actress on the front page of an old *Daily Mail*. It's about the death of Becky Whitehouse. I remember her from when she played Tania in *Castle Street*. She was a nasty piece of work. Tania, I mean.

I never actually met Becky. I don't know what she was like, but I often pop into a tatty little café for a coffee and a bacon sandwich mid-morning. I used to see her there sometimes with Adam, that perfect-looking husband of Celeste's who was stabbed to death up in town. The one with the dead eyes. They'd be hunched over a table whispering to each other.

My blood ran cold when I read that Becky had died too. The article didn't state the cause, so I looked up the inquest online. There's a photo of her at some awards thing. Dressed up in garishly expensive clothes that only made her look cheaper if you ask me.

Further down the page was a photo of Becky's ex-husband. The gay one who does all those big films. And then there was a photo of her family outside the coroner's court. A burly man who looked like he'd been crying, with a bland woman by his side. And Emma. Her stepsister, apparently.

I looked up Celeste's husband too. It looks like they still haven't found out who killed him. I did read the papers the day after *he* died. I wanted to know what had happened so I wouldn't say the wrong thing. I remember the stuff they wrote about Emma and Celeste and thinking at the time that the papers must have got that wrong. They said that they met for the first time on the bridge. That Emma was a passing ex-nurse running to help. I didn't suspect that there was something odd going on. I thought it was just a mistake.

But something really isn't right here. Why would they pretend they were strangers? Why lie? Celeste pushed Emma out of the way, into the lounge that day when he was upstairs. Why was she hiding from him? And if he was also knocking off her stepsister behind Celeste's back . . .

It's makes me wonder what they're hiding.

I feel a bit sick about it all but I don't want to be involved really. I decided that I was going to ask my husband, Dave, see what he thinks. I know exactly what he'll say, though. Him being a police sergeant. He's going to make me talk to the investigating officer, isn't he?

I don't want to get them into trouble and have to go through a lot of fuss. I've grown to like Celeste, and that funny girl with the bad leg was really kind.

It might all be nothing. I'll think about it for a few days.

Author Note

Fiction has always been my source of comfort and distraction. Heartbreak, bereavement, work issues? I turn to novels to find solace and answers. Mental health problems, stress, the horrors of ageing? I dive into a good book and escape. The voices of other people and the sharing of their experiences, places and situations soothe me and make me feel connected, less alone somehow.

In 2020 (just before the pandemic hit) I was diagnosed with multiple sclerosis, which halted and upended me. I'm still processing this and learning how to manage my life. There was an initial period where I listened to Lana Del Rey's saddest song on a loop, hugged my dog and talked it over with my partner and friends. Then I turned to fiction for connection, searching for representations of chronic illness. There are some shining examples but there are also a lot of tired tropes out there.

For example, the sickly-sweet ill woman who has no personality or purpose. Or the unwell person who in a shocking twist is revealed to be a fraud. And then there's the inevitability that there can't be stasis and that the ill character must either get better or die at the end of the story.

I've been a crime fiction fan since I was an adolescent and have always loved how crime stories can keep you gripped, show extremes of human emotion, and can also illustrate and illuminate aspects of life and society. People say to write a book that you'd like to read. So, it was logical that I'd draft a crime novel, choosing to feature my viewpoint which is coloured by chronic illness. I also chose to try to upend the tired tropes.

I was a nurse before I became more unwell, and this also inspired me. Lots of things haunt me but there are two extraordinary incidents from the early Nineties, when I was a student nurse, that stand out. The first was when I went to a new ward and noted that there was a young woman having a seizure on the floor. Seizures are alarming but not unexpected in a hospital. What was unexpected was that the staff were stepping around her, ignoring what was happening. I was told that under no circumstances was I to acknowledge 'what she was doing' as she had a 'hysterical illness' and was 'just faking it'. The consensus plan between the medics and nurses was that depriving her of attention might cure her.

On another placement I encountered a woman who'd collapsed in public and had a weakness down one side of her body. She was extensively tested but nothing was spotted on her scans. However, she was unable to walk, and we gladly helped her to perform her daily activities and pushed her round in a wheelchair. Until a few days later when her symptoms entirely resolved, and it was decided that she was either 'hysterical' or 'a fraud'. The staff opinions about and the treatment of her weren't entirely favourable from that moment on.

I'm not passing judgement on the staff involved, tempting though it is. I'm definitely not judging the patients.

Everything has a context, and I was only a peripheral player here so I can't unpick this.

A few years later I developed issues of my own that would lead me to be judged harshly at times. Strange sensations plagued my left-hand side. It was like a ghostly presence was tightly gripping my hand and foot. Invisible spiders crawled across my face, and I felt like I was being poked with sharp needles in my leg. My tongue was numb, and I was crippled by fatigue. The sort of fatigue that felt like I was boneless and with no muscles.

I saw a neurologist who mooted the alarming idea that I could have multiple sclerosis and sent me for an MRI scan and a raft of blood tests. The results were all negative and my symptoms were attributed to stress. I readily accepted that my mind had made my body behave in strange ways. I *was* experiencing high anxiety. I'd left a long, abusive relationship and my life was in turmoil. The answer was logical, and I felt embarrassed to have wasted people's time.

The symptoms resolved but not for long. The numbness and fatigue would come and go at regular intervals, bringing with them persistent nausea, stumbling and clumsiness. Even an episode of temporary blindness in one eye that lasted for two months. I was seen by a raft of different consultants, re-scanned repeatedly and continually told that there was nothing organically wrong with me. My GP at the time even told me that they should name a 'special little syndrome' after me. People in my family and social circle began to voice their opinion that my illness was 'all in my head'. I didn't have a case to argue against this and tried to carry on, hiding my symptoms where I could.

It took nineteen years before I was finally diagnosed with MS after a relapse that numbed my left side from my toes to my rib cage. It now seems that there may have been evolving damage and inflammation in my brain and spine all along but that that the swelling may have gone down before I had the previous scans, which were often done many months after attacks. It's impossible to know for sure.

I felt oddly relieved at the diagnosis. That I finally had a label for what was wrong. A badge of honour that might finally stop people judging me. According to medical research, my case is rare. Most people with a diagnosis of functional neurological disorder aren't found to have underlying organic changes such as MS. Although the symptoms can be similar or worse than a raft of other neurological conditions.

In 2016 I saw an excellent play about a woman with FND called 'Still Ill' by the Kandinsky Theatre Company. It didn't quite bring about a lightbulb moment, but it did make me reconsider my own past and things that I'd seen in my nursing practice. All of these strands came together over time and influenced my writing.

I don't have functional neurological disorder and probably never did. I'm unsure if the two patients who I encountered did either. But I decided to channel my experiences of having an undiagnosed neurological disorder into this book. My intention isn't to speak for everyone with this condition or to sensationalise it. Emma isn't FND. She's a fictional representation of a person who has some of the many FND symptoms. Nor am I saying that people with FND are murderous and prone to becoming unhinged. That's definitely not the case. Emma is a fictional extrapolation of what might happen if someone is pushed to their limits by multiple negative factors.

Who knows what Emma's future might be? But for the purposes of this book, I wanted a fictional representation of chronic illness where the protagonist isn't saccharine.

371

Someone who doesn't get better or die. And who's definitely not faking it. She's certainly not doing that and never was.

FND is a real and distressing condition. I'm sure that there are people who have functional neurological disorder or medically unexplained symptoms who have exemplary treatment, but the statistics are bleak, and the negative labelling is sadly still a thing.

Useful Links:

https://www.fndaction.org.uk/
https://fndhope.org/about-fnd-hope/fnd-hope-uk/
https://www.nhsinform.scot/illnesses-and-conditions/brain-nerves-and-spinal-cord/functional-neurological-disorder/
https://mstrust.org.uk
https://www.mssociety.org.uk

Acknowledgements

Thanking people seems such an easy task but the reality is that so many people have helped with this novel that it would be a long and tedious list to read. I also run the risk of missing people out and causing huge offence. It might also be embarrassingly gushing and that's so not me.

I'm therefore extending a huge umbrella thank you to everyone who has helped and supported me. You've all done so much, and I appreciate it.

I must give a special mention to my agent Hannah Schofield of LBA and my editors Rachel Hart and Raphaella Demetris at Avon, as well as Helena Newton and Rachel Rowlands, who have all shaped the novel in ways that I couldn't have imagined without their insanely talented and on point input. I also have to mention my fellow writers Callie Kazumi and F. Q. Yeoh who were kind enough to read early, ugly drafts of the novels and offer incisive views.

I was selected as an awardee on the London Writers Award, and this was invaluable in improving my confidence, knowledge and skills. Spread the Word is a fantastic organisation that has launched many writers' careers. Long may they continue.

My partner, Paul Roberts, has been unwavering in his tolerance of being ignored when I disappear for hours into the spare bedroom and bang away on the keyboard. Paul is the partner who I have always wanted and needed. My diva poodle Frida has been less tolerant but will always be an inspiration.

Special thanks to Philippa who was an early reader despite being severely unwell at the time. Your insight regarding FND was much appreciated.

To all the other amazing people who have helped me, I am truly grateful to all of you.

Book Club Questions

Please note that the following book club questions contain spoilers – so proceed with caution!

1) All three narrators of *Sick to Death* could be seen as being unlikeable/unsympathetic in different ways. How much did you empathise with each of them?

2) Modern medicine looks at the care of chronic illness in a holistic way, rather than concentrating on physical factors alone. How much do you think the social and psychological aspects of her circumstances and of being chronically ill have affected Emma?

3) How important is the sense of place in the story? Do you think things might have been different if the story was set in a different city?

4) Emma had unfounded accusations of 'hysteria' levelled at her in the past. How much do you think her gender, class and age played a part in this?

5) In fiction, it's common to see certain tropes associated with characters with a chronic illness. Typically, characters only have two outcomes: they either get better or die. Emma states that this was never going to be part of her story. Is this something you have noticed in the

representation of chronic illness in fiction, and how do you think *Sick to Death* differs in that regard?
6) What do you think the future holds for Emma and Celeste?